ifabbri publishing, 225 Montgomery Street, Newburgh, New York 12550

Printed in the United States of America
First Printing February 2005

Library of Congress Cataloging-in-Publication Data

Smith, Peter
        Instructions from Seville / Peter Smith
        ISBN 0-9762491-0-3
        LCCN: 2004113894

To the two too frank Franks.

Author's Note

In 1506 Pope Julius II made the bold decision to demolish the ancient basiclica of St. Peter, the church that had marked the tomb of the martyr since the reign of the Emperor Constantine, and build a new one. Subsequent history has generally, but not unanimously, celebrated the outcome. At the time, however, the move pounded a wedge into the heart of contentious Rome. The aristrocacy took it as an affront: inauthentic and extravagant. The old Basilica was theirs. Its destruction would mark the end of their pre-eminence. For the architect, Donato Bramante, it was the opportunity to cap his long and distinguished career with a great masterpiece. Europe's merchant banking families, the Chigi's, the Fugger's, the Medici's and others, whose accounts intertwined in a vast and far-reaching network of enterprises, must have rubbed their hands in glee, anticipating the profits they would make supplying both the building materials and the financing for what was, by any measure, an enormous undertaking.

During that first decade of the 1500's many notables of the High Renaissance, names familiar to us all, passed through Rome. They were not spending their days posing on pedestals. Michaelangelo was there, hard at work on the design for Pope Julius' tomb. He had recently installed his famous *Pieta* in the old Basilica. The elderly Leonardo da Vinci was trying to sell paintings. Niccolo Machiavelli, a diligent emissary from Florence, passed through regularly. Ludovico Ariosto would have offered readings from his work in progress, *Orlando Furioso*, adventures of the chivalric world that was ending; just as members of the Roman Academy were looking backward to the classics, among them Vitruvius, to find a suitable artistic and intellctual framework for the future. An intense young Martin Luther, on a pilgrimage to St. Peter's, would later proclaim that the Eternal City was an entrance to Hell.

The initiative to take down the old Church may well have been Spain's. Her power was on the rise. Wealth from her new American colonies was pouring in. And, the fleshpot at the center of western Christendom was antithetical to the austere form of Catholicism that she enforced at home. Smashing down the old images and building Rome anew may well have been part of her strategy to dominate the Church. A strategy, albeit, far more subtle and refined than those she was unleashing in her new colonies abroad.

Peter Smith

"The freedom of states has been preserved by the cunning of architects."

Vitruvius

Instructions from Seville

Part I

The New St. Peter's

1

The Presentation of the New St. Peter's

Rome 1506

Someone in the audience coughed politely. Donato Bramante looked up. They were getting restless. But the light was not yet right. There was another cough, a more insistent one this time. Bring your presentation to an end, it said. Wind it up. The eminent architect bowed slightly and steepled his rough hands in a respectful gesture that begged the august assembly to indulge him for just a while longer.

The Princes of the Church, splendidly robed in scarlet, were gathered in the crumbling apse of Saint Peter's ancient basilica. They had already indulged Bramante for hours. They had listened to him as he patiently and methodically explained his radical design for their new church. They had granted the great architect their full attention as, one sheet after another, he unfurled his carefully rendered plans and meticulous perspective drawings.

But after all those hours Bramante was still not sure where things stood. What did they think of it? Did they like it? Did they hate it? Bramante could not tell. Their faces revealed almost nothing. They were like an impervious wall. Even when his immense and elaborate model—a masterpiece in its own right, crafted down to the smallest detail to represent what the new building would look like—was wheeled out, their faces were blank.

Concealing his frustration, Bramante, short and burly, stepped back and bowed again. In his plain brown cloak he looked like a thrush lost in a yard of bright red roosters. Appearing modest and deferential before his powerful hosts and patrons was important. At 62 years of age the renowned architect had made many presentations. Experience had made him sensitive to an audience's mood. This one was now restless and impatient. He had not yet won them over and his time was running out.

Bramante glanced upward. The light coming through the high clerestory windows was fading. The lower part of the nave was cast in shadow. It was almost time, but not quite. They will have to indulge me a bit longer, he thought. He had not quite finished showing them the new church that he fervently hoped he would live to see replace this one, this ancient place, that for more than a thousand years had enshrined the tomb of the martyred Saint Peter. You will have to wait just a little while longer, thought Bramante, I am not finished with you. But he simply bowed and retreated into the shadows behind his model.

The model was as large as a small chapel. Its curving walls, cupped vaults, classical cornices and arcades towered over him. Its voluptuous, sensuous volumes—modeled in elm and walnut and polished to a soft luster—soared twenty feet above the floor and culminated finally and gloriously in a ribbed dome surmounted by a cupola. The entire construction rested on a circular base sixteen feet in diameter and dominated the space in front of the altar.

Pope Julius II and his attendant Cardinals had been presented with a vision that was radically different. They were surrounded by ample proof of that. Where this old basilica was long with five rows of narrow aisles, Bramante proposed to replace it with a church that would be "X" shaped in plan. Both arms of the "X" would be equal in length. It was not a Latin cross. This alone was a radical departure. And there was more. A high dome, reminiscent of the Pantheon and Florence's Duomo, but more buoyant, seemingly weightless, would rise above the center of the "X" to mark Saint Peter's resting place. The concept was almost pagan. Where the old basilica was dark, earthbound and heavy in feeling, a band of windows under Bramante's great dome would flood the new church with light. Where this tired old basilica was a jumbled warren of chapels and reliquaries—a testament to a thousand years of accretions, and patchwork repairs, Bramante's new design, clear and unambiguous, would adhere to an ordered geometry of circles within squares and squares within circles. It was right there in front of them. Each arm of the cross-shaped plan ended in a vaulted semicircular apse. Four smaller domes, miniatures of the dominant central one filled the four squares between the arms of the cross and were equally light-filled and buoyant. To complete the composition four tall towers would mark the corners of the square plan. There it was. It was extraordinary. The Princes of the Church should have been astonished.

Alone in the shadows Bramante heard another cough, deliberately rude this time. Above him a pigeon rustled and flapped in the rafters. Even the birds were getting restless. Well, they would have to wait, too. Timing now was critical. What came next depended on the light. There had to be enough light to see the model, but there could not be too much. Bramante was determined to seduce these stone-faced Princes, and for that the light would have to be dim and soft.

Bramante looked up at the darkening windows. He needed a few more minutes. Behind him, the great wooden doors at the end of the nave were straining. It was almost Vespers. Throngs of restless pilgrims were milling in the square, massing on the steps and under the old portico. They were pressing against the doors eager to enter the sanctuary. Soon the ushers would throw back the bolts and the hordes would come rushing in. Bramante's work had to be finished before that. He could afford no distractions. Bramante leaned forward and pressed his broad, ruddy face against one of the model's small windows. *"Siamo pronti?"* he whispered hoarsely, peering inside. Are we ready?

Two young apprentices, crouching within, whispered back from the dark, *"Si, si, Maestro."* They were eager. They were ready. *"Tutt' a posto,"* Everything was in place.

Bramante put his ear to the model. He heard a flint strike. The apprentices—invisible as ghosts in their gray smocks—were working hastily, lighting lanterns and positioning them carefully behind cornices and columns inside the model. They set other lanterns like footlights into recesses in the model's floor. Bramante straightened his shoulders and breathed deeply. The nave was almost dark, as warm yellow light began to flicker through the model's windows. Light from the high cupola washed the dome in honeyed amber. This was how the new Saint Peter's would appear on an evening such as this. It was coming to life.

When he was satisfied with the effect, Bramante relaxed and walked behind the model to the other side.

In the audience someone cleared his throat. Bramante tensed. By now they should have been completely won over. He balled his hands into fists. Seeing his glorious design illuminated like this should have stunned them into rapt silence. He pressed the heels of his calloused, ink-stained hands to his eyes. For months he and his crew had worked night and day on this presentation. Its acceptance was crucial. It was the culmination of his life's work and it was not reaching them. Bramante heard the impatient rustle of stiff silk and the soft shuffle of expensive slippers on the worn stone pavement. His stomach churned. Behind him in the dank old basilica's long darkening nave priests scurried about preparing for the evening service. The great doors to the square were straining. The voices of the throng outside grew louder. Time was up.

Bramante hesitated in the shadows and looked upward. He raked his fingers through his unruly fringe of gray hair. The enormous black eyes of Christ Pantocrator, wide open, stared down at him from high in the apse with an expression that might have been amazement or shock. It might also have been anger. It was most certainly not indifference. Bramante refused to panic. He squeezed his eyes shut and made the sign of the cross. "I begged you, I prayed, for the vision to do your work," he whispered. "How can I be failing?"

His design was so clear, so perfect. How could the men of the Church not appreciate that? Their restrained response was at best respectful. But they must not be seeing his plan. If they were, their enthusiasm would be unbridled. They would be on their feet cheering. What had gone wrong?

"After all these years am I losing my touch? Why am I not reaching them? If I say 'A,' they hear 'B.' If I show them 'X' they see 'Y.' Every single thing I show them, either by magic or subterfuge, is being misconstrued. It is as if—deliberately and confoundingly—everything I say is being falsely translated into a foreign tongue."

Bramante breathed deeply, trying to slow his racing heart. Now was not the time to lose confidence. It was too late for that. Inside the model one of his apprentices dropped quietly through a trap door to take his position under the base. Like an athlete getting ready for an event or like a man about to be judged, Bramante exhaled slowly. He pressed a cracked thumbnail to his lips and murmured, *"Prego Signore."* Please, Dear God.

Weary and frustrated, the architect lingered in the shadows watching his audience. He had one more card to play, and not much time to play it. I should be grateful, he thought. At least they aren't hooting or catcalling—not yet anyway. They just sat there, stone-faced, against the shimmering golden backdrop of all the heavenly witnesses they presumed to represent on earth: the Holy Apostles, humble Saints and generous Angels, the Lamb of Christ, the Tree of Life, all rendered more than a thousand years before in tiny mosaic fragments of colored stone and glass. Bramante studied his patrons' world-weary faces, trying to discern what it was they were thinking. Some of the older clerics were slumped down in the folds of their robes, trying to hide. Others were craning their necks, albeit discreetly, curious to see how their colleagues were reacting. The tightly clenched jaws of some, it saddened him to see, betrayed suppressed rage.

Bramante picked anxiously at a hangnail. Had they not heard a word? Had they not understood? Had they seen nothing? He had made the argument for his design as clearly as he knew how. He had presented its logic. He had shown them its geometry, clearly and forthrightly. He had explained its sources. His confident voice had filled the nave for hours with noble references from scripture and the classics. He had firmly planted the intellectual and philosophical roots of his grand scheme in the rich soil of history. He showed them, he proved to them, that his design was the inevitable culmination of all human civilization up to that very moment. Or so he thought.

These were learned men, not fools. They must have understood. Bramante's face burned. They are judging me . . . they are judging my work, God's work, he thought—not for what it is—but for petty political reasons.

This was not supposed to happen. Where was the Pope? The Pope had a job to do. Bramante frantically sought out the face of his benefactor, Pope Julius II, among the restless princes. When he found him, his heart sank. Julius, luminescent in white satin, was asleep. His pink face, resting in his fluffy white beard, looked like a newborn baby dozing in soft fleece. Bramante's scalp prickled. He pressed a hand to his mouth. Never had he felt so alone, so abandoned. True, the Holy Father was an old man. And, yes, it was true, he had been attentive for many long hours, but still it was Julius, the Pope, who had commissioned this work. It was the Pope's pet project. The Pope above all others was supposed to show enthusiasm for it. He was to have rallied the Cardinals' support. Was it not Pope Julius, after all, who had declared the old basilica's structure unsound? Was it not this Pope who, time and again, whenever a great chunk of the old roof came crashing to the ground, would proclaim that it was a message from on high, that God Almighty himself was demanding that the old basilica be demolished and one more worthy of his greatness be built?

Bramante's mouth filled with the bitter taste of words unspoken. He tasted the sour bile of questions unsatisfactorily answered and the dead ashes of answers to questions that he had never asked, because he knew they would not be welcome. Could repairs be made to the old Basilica that would allow it to sustain the ravages of another thou-

sand years? Bramante had no doubt that they could. He even suspected that the Pope's excuses for advocating its destruction were false.
He suspected the Pope of paying to sabotage the old structure. The
truth? Bramante did not know the truth and he did not care. These
were not his concerns. He was offered the opportunity to design the
most extraordinary church that Rome, and in his own candid opinion, the world would ever see, and he had seized it. Here, right now,
in this long darkening nave, with the throngs pounding the doors,
was Bramante's chance to cap a long and distinguished career with a
building that he was certain was destined to become a profound, eternal symbol, that would in time surpass the Hagia Sofia in
Constantinople, all the great cathedrals of France, the Duomo in Florence and perhaps even the Parthenon itself. Pope Julius was thrilled
when he saw Bramante's first sketches. He was captivated by the design and endorsed it on the spot, as Bramante knew he would.

What had gone wrong? Pope Julius' enthusiasm was without res-
ervation. So committed was he to the plan that he had promised
Bramante the reward of plenary absolution, forgiveness for every sin
he knowingly or unknowingly may have committed during his entire
life, once his design was approved and construction begun. That was
no small thing. Plenary absolution meant a guarantee of life everlasting. Bramante was counting on that, not because he had led a particularly sinful life, but 62 years was a long time. Who knew what unconfessed debris might be lurking in the dark to trip him up at the last
minute?

"I did my part," Bramante muttered angrily to himself as he glared
at the Pope, seeing in the old man's sleeping face his own absolution
slipping away. Why had the Pope failed to do his?

It was being whispered on the streets and in the taverns that Pope
Julius was a megalomaniac; that he wanted to rebuild Rome to glorify
himself, like a conquering Caesar. In some quarters of the city the
Pope's easy willingness to sweep away Rome's past was taken as a
personal offense.

Bramante had heard it all and was unmoved. If he had learned anything over the span of his life it was not to give a damn about his

patrons' motivations. Motivations made no difference. Whatever they were, his job was always the same. It was to use his gifts and his skills on their behalf. He was working for the Pope. If the Pope decided that the old basilica would come down, so it would. If the Pope decreed that it was time to make a powerful symbolic gesture by stating emphatically that Rome and the Papacy had to be clearly and unambiguously the center of Christian Europe, Bramante would make it happen.

Motivations. Politics. Intrigue. Bramante cared about none of that. Of course his design would bolster his patron's image. That's what it was for. But that was not all it was for. Above all, the new church would be to the glory of God. It would be a gift from Bramante to God, a fitting finale to his life's work.

"I am doing my part," Bramante said again under his breath. He placed a hand tenderly on the model, reassured by its satiny warmth. Inside his two apprentices tensely awaited their next cue. Bramante set his jaw. Enough. It was time for Pope Julius to wake up.

Bramante stepped briskly back into view and snapped his fingers. At once the huge illuminated model behind him began to turn very, very slowly, like a planet emerging from the dark. This part of the presentation had been planned with great care. Bramante and the crew had rehearsed it over and over again until it was absolutely perfect. He turned and faced his audience confidently, almost defiantly, and watched as warm lamplight spilled from the great model and passed slowly and hypnotically across the great men's faces.

There was not a sound, not a cough, nor any restless shuffling. Light and shadow and the model's slow rotation had caught the austere Princes of the Church off guard. Bramante had their full attention now. They were spellbound. The slow, slow rotation had made them uncertain for just an instant whether it was the model turning, or if, instead, it were they—aloft, floating in the dusk, drawn out of themselves and their surroundings—woozily moving around it; seduced, enticed and consumed—Bramante hoped—by a desire stronger than their prejudices, to want his plan to become real. From beneath, Bramante heard the quiet rumble of turning gears. As he watched the great model turning, the irony of deploying mystery and wonder to convey the clear rationality of the plan entered his mind. He suppressed it.

Bramante abruptly turned his back to his audience, and with the vigor of a young man clapped his hands once, loudly. The sound reverberated like thunder through the nave. The Pope's eyes snapped open. The turntable stopped. A second later, with another huge boom, the model burst open. The audience gasped as the two young apprentices deftly swung one of its quadrants aside. The huge model was constructed like a Chinese puzzle. Bramante clapped again. Another loud bang shook the ancient basilica. Another segment was moved aside to reveal the model's interior.

The clear and elegant geometry of the model's surface belied the richness that was to be seen within. The Pope and the Cardinals stared in amazement. The footlights cast warm shadows across the model's interior, highlighting its rich detail, enhancing every dentil, every rib, every arch and keystone. The new church's curved and vaulted spaces were painted in gilt and enamel to represent the colors and luster of the precious materials that would actually be used. The magnificent model shimmered in the soft light. The underside of the great dome was ribbed in gold. The panels between the ribs were painted to suggest a heaven of soft clouds and ascending angels. The four smaller domes were likewise painted, suggesting lavish frescoes. The floor was patterned to represent inlaid marble. Tiny, jewel-like figurines of saints and martyrs inhabited miniature chapels and niches.

Bramante turned to his audience with an almost fierce insistence that they be swept off their feet by the elegant, luxurious, cloudlike, endlessly unfolding promise of eternity that he was offering them. If they were not with him now they never would be. His burning eyes went from face to face. To his disappointment he saw that he had still not persuaded everyone. Those men from aristocratic Roman families coldly resisted what they saw.

One of them, an arrogant Roman, jumped to his feet and shouted, "For the price of this model alone the sinking foundations and battle-weary walls of our beloved old basilica could be repaired." There was a low rumble of agreement.

It was Donato Bramante's turn to show no emotion.

The angry Cardinal went further, shouting and catcalling that the Church was already picking them clean, exacting payment, extorting tribute that was unjust and unwarranted to fight its battles with the Emperor, and with the King of France. And don't forget, he hastened to sneer, what it costs to support this lavish court. He railed that the price of doing business in Rome was a never ending and escalating process of payoffs; and that these grandiose plans—and here he waived a long hand dismissively at Bramante's model—would only make matters worse for them. Rome, he reminded them, already had a great and venerated church—this one right here; and it was his ancestors who had built it. "We and our ancestors paid for this church with our fortunes!" he proclaimed, "with our sweat, and we defended it with our blood! Our people," he shouted, "have kept it standing for more than a thousand years. The very idea that you," he thrust his arm at the Pope, "and your lackey architect here, would so much as consider razing it is an affront we will not endure."

Drained, Bramante retreated behind his model. He would not fight. He had no more to show, no more tricks up his sleeve. Relieved that the presentation was over he was, nonetheless, ruffled and dissatisfied. He had said what he had to say. He had shown them everything he had. Alone in the darkness he shrugged and asked himself, "What more could I have done?" The raving cardinal was only one voice. Were there enough other votes out there to support his scheme? How many were against him? He didn't know. Generally, these Princes of the Church were so guarded, so accustomed to being observed, that each facial expression, each gesture, was made with a studied serenity. Most of the time nothing that they thought, unless it was time for the thought to be made known, was obvious; which made the Roman Cardinal's sudden outburst all the more shocking. He wouldn't have dared it unless he knew he had support. It meant that there was a contingent ready to take an opposing stand. But what, Bramante asked himself again, what more could I have done?

His two young apprentices were waiting for him behind the model.

Their eyes were bright and expectant, eager to know if they had ful-filled the maestro's expectations.

When he saw them Bramante boomed, "You were perfect!" with an enthusiasm he did not feel. The two boys had indeed performed perfectly, and with an exaggerated flourish Bramante bowed his thanks to them. Piero, the younger one, a country boy, stood rigidly at at-tention and blushed. Small for his fifteen years, and rosy-cheeked, he looked more like a child than a young man. Antonio at eighteen was a full head taller than Piero, and wore the cool demeanor of an urban sophisticate. With an affected flourish Antonio returned Bramante's courtly bow.

Because the boys had performed flawlessly, Bramante considered inviting them to accompany him for the next part of his presentation, but on reflection thought better of it. There was opposition to his design. That was made all too clear. He did not want his boys to wit-ness any doubt, or hear any criticism. He needed their unswerving loyalty and devotion. "Put everything back together and then come and rescue me from my adoring public," he said with a rueful snort, and tossed each of them a silver coin, "Then we'll go out and have some fun."

Young Piero stared wide-eyed at the coin in his hand as Bramante disappeared into the crowd that was now streaming into the Church.

"Let's wrap it up," said Antonio, irritably, tugging the younger boy's sleeve, "We still have work to do." They had to close the model and lock it in place.

Piero nodded like a sleepwalker, grateful to be told what to do. Four nights without sleep, working around the clock on the presen-tation, was taking its toll. He could barely hold his head up. Back home in Bracciano he went to bed early and rose before dawn. Here in Rome talented young apprentices were expected to work round the clock if they wanted to succeed, and Piero most certainly wanted to succeed.

"Wake up," said Antonio tugging at him again, "Don't fall asleep on me now. I'm going underneath to pull out the bolts. When I give the signal rotate the sections back together."

Piero nodded and climbed back up onto the model's base to wait for the cue. He felt light-headed. Vespers. He sat back and let the hum of male voices floating in all directions from the church's cavernous depths, wash over him. He sighed deeply, succumbing to the soothing chant.

"East!" Antonio shouted. With the presentation finished there was no need to whisper. Startled, Piero jumped up, grabbed the eastern apse and pulled. It closed with the solid click of a finely made cabinet door. He sat back down and waited for the next cue. Through the model's small windows Piero watched as the tide of pilgrims washed into the nave. They had come from far and wide to make the round of the holy shrines that were packed into the old Basilica's every nook and crevice, and to see first hand Bramante's glorious vision for the new Church that was being talked about in the streets of Rome and throughout the countryside.

"West!" shouted Antonio. Piero jumped. There was a metallic clank as a bolt dropped, and Piero pulled the next section back into place.

"Center!" called Antonio. Piero bent over and hurriedly cranked the wooden gear that brought both halves of the tall central drum together, enclosing him inside. There he sank to his knees, barely able to stand. Spent, he lay down and stared up into the model's high dome. His eyes felt grainy. Music and the sound of voices collected and reverberated all around him. "I am the first person to attend Vespers here in the new church," he whispered. Squinting, he saw his still wet scumble of paint become real frescoes that told the story of St. Peter's life: his travels, his founding of the Church, his crucifixion and burial. He dreamed of being high in the dome and actually painting those frescoes. The music rolled over him like warm surf.

Antonio crawled up through the trap door and rapped the base loudly, "We're finished. Let's go. Let's get out of here."

Piero whispered drowsily, "It's so beautiful," looking up into the dome, stifling a yawn.

"Yeah, I know but it's hot as Hell in here, too, and I've smelled enough glue and varnish to hold me for awhile." Antonio was tired and irritable. He had been through these marathon presentations before. It was not new to him. He was hungry.

Piero sat up slowly and rubbed his face. He pulled off his cap and shook his head of black curly hair trying to wake up. He crawled to a tiny window and yawned, "Look at this," he whispered. Antonio crawled over. Just outside, inches away, faces were studying the model: bankers, clerics, penitents, amazed faces, smiling faces, angry scowling ones, faces stunned by the daring design. Knowing he could not be seen crouching in the dark, Piero stuck out his tongue, feeling giddy, wanting to do something idiotic and outrageous.

Not in the mood, Antonio said, "Come on. Let's go," as more and more people pressed up against the model. Antonio removed his cap and smoothed his sandy hair making himself ready to be seen in public. The curious mob neither interested nor surprised him. He was a Roman. He'd seen it before. Piero thought that Antonio's fashionable haircut resembled either an upside down bucket or a broom.

"I don't want to leave yet," said Piero, his hazel eyes half closed, "Just look at this." He was transfixed by the spectacle, the color, the mob, the faces making faces. "I want to watch for a while." Piero yawned again and made himself more comfortable.

Antonio dropped through the trap door. Piero didn't budge. Antonio reached up and tried to pull him down. "Enough," he said, and then with a knowing laugh added, "Let's go and rescue Bramante from his adoring public."

Piero put a finger to his lips and pointed out the little window. "Can't we stay here and watch?" he whispered.

❧

2

Rome

A smiling Bramante nodded and waved as he meandered at leisure among the hundreds of worshippers and oglers shuffling across the worn stone pavement. He knew many of these people. Rome was a small town. Well aware of the importance of post-presentation politics, the architect was on a mission. He watched and listened. He was curious. He hoped everyone was talking about his design. He knew what the Cardinals felt about it. Now he needed to know what the public thought. He strolled over to a group of people, some in rags others in fur robes and silk gowns, standing in front of St. Veronica's Chapel. The chapel enshrined the shawl used by St. Veronica, a matron of Jerusalem, to wipe Jesus' face on his way to Calvary. A fistful of coins clanked into the collection box. Bramante stopped and waited to see the imprint left by Christ's face on the cloth. The drape concealing it snapped open and then quickly snapped shut. Some around him fell to their knees and wept. Others blinked, annoyed, insulted by the brief teasing glimpse, not sure what they had seen, but not daring to complain. Was it really the face of Christ?

Bramante dumped a fistful of coins into the box and stared at the gap in the drapes, forcing himself to not blink. The drape snapped open again and then quickly snapped shut. The pilgrims shuffled on. Behind him the sound of a wooden bench being dragged across the floor echoed through the dim stone forest of soot-smudged columns. Will my new church make them fall to their knees and weep, he wondered.

Just then Rafaello Cardinal Riario grabbed hold of him and spun him around, "You have outdone yourself, Bramante," he announced clasping him by his shoulders and shaking him just a little, the way one does a small boy who has performed well. "I am duly impressed." Bramante hoped he meant it, but something in Riario's tone raised doubt. Riario was of medium build with a fleshy face and large ears. His alert eyes darted every which way, constantly searching, not wanting to miss anything, avoiding Bramante's.

Squirming out of the man's grasp the architect clasped his hands to his chest, and said, "You are too kind, Excellency." Bramante well knew that Riario would only really be impressed if backing the new design were to his political advantage. He sincerely hoped it was. The Cardinal was one person whose endorsement Bramante counted on. He and the Cardinal had known each other for many years. The Cardinal's mother was a Sforza, the Milanese family that launched Bramante's career many years before. He had been working for them and the Riarios now for what seemed like an eternity, most recently on the design of the Cardinal's own grand palace. He had attended their weddings, funerals and christenings. He thought of himself as one of the family, and took their patronage for granted. They thought of him simply as Theirs.

"The design is brilliant. I am sure." Riario said, looking around, deciding with whom he would talk next.

Bramante, quite sure of its brilliance, grunted appreciation and tried to sound more pleased than he was. He wanted the Cardinal's undivided attention. He had the impression that, like a dog, Riario was able to aim his big ears at will to pick up distant conversations.

Looking over Bramante's shoulder Cardinal Riario said, "It is an honor to share you with the Pope and God Himself, if I may be so bold as to include myself in such august company," trying his dead hand at humor. "I don't suppose you will have time for my modest little domestic project now?" He cocked his head to one side, teasingly, and raised a heavy eyebrow. His 'modest little domestic project' was a palazzo he had commissioned Bramante to design years earlier. Even by Roman standards it would be enormous, occupying an entire city block.

Bramante said affably, "I will always have time for your wonderful project. It is so very close to my heart." He had been working on the design for decades, and felt that it was a complete waste of time, that it would never be built. Riario—out of the blue—would pressure him to prepare drawings and then for no apparent reason lose interest, and ask him to stop work. It was no closer to being built now than ten years ago. Riario's habit was, after much discussion, to finally agree to proceed with a design, only to abruptly and for no apparent reason, change his mind. A year later he would reappear with a completely different set of demands. It was infuriating. The project had languished. Bramante had nothing but yellowing stacks of paper to show for all his work.

"We seem to have resolved the problem of that dead saint," said Riario breezily, looking around, implying that nothing would stop him from going forward now.

Bramante was about to ask how the problem of that dead saint had been resolved, but decided not to. He neither cared nor needed to know whether or not old Pope Damasus' resting place would be disturbed. "Is that so?" the architect said, arranging his tired face in an expression he hoped conveyed pleasure if not outright enthusiasm.

"Yes, yes indeed. Aside from the mortifying cost of your plan, there shouldn't be anything now to prevent us from proceeding right along," he said cuffing Bramante's shoulder.

"That delights me," Bramante said. Over Cardinal Riario's shoulder he saw the first section of the model being carefully rotated back into position. Near it a crowd was gathering at the entrance to St. Peter's tomb. If people were all hot and bothered about Riario's new palace churning up consecrated ground—well, he shuddered to think what an uproar digging up St. Peter would cause.

"We will summon you when we are ready to proceed," the Cardinal said.

Pressing his palms to his chest Bramante bowed as Riario turned away. Slowly he moved his hands down the front of his cloak as if to wipe them clean. A group of priests brushed by daintily lifting their hems to avoid him—black against dark in the cavernous space.

Bramante turned and squared his shoulders. The church had filled with people. The ancient Basilica's forest of heavy, dark columns framed what looked to him like an endless series of transparent cubes. Thick, misshapen tapers in heavy iron chandeliers cast a dim yellow glow. The old Basilica reminded him of a three-dimensional game board where every amber cube was occupied by a different clique.

Roman society was aggressively on display. The city's *illuminati* swirled around laughing raucously, shoving each other, arguing and posing just as they would in a public square. In stark contrast, the pilgrims, penitents and worshippers shuffled quietly around the shadowy side aisles dumping coins into tin collection boxes, lighting candles and whispering prayers.

Pushed and pulled by the crowd, Bramante felt part of a formal dance that at times almost lifted him off his feet, moving him first in one direction and then in another. Like dancers everyone nodded, bowed, turned and moved away, brushing past each other, engaged with another, but at the same time aloof and apart. They reminded him of mannequins, posing but real, and he knew well that their energy, their fire, their passions, hatreds and distrusts were there submerged behind their frozen doll-like faces.

Bramante allowed himself to be drawn into the dance, moving first in one direction and then in another, watching and listening. He waved and bowed, smiled and nodded, turned and stepped aside, letting people pass, enjoying the buzz his design was causing. "Wonderful" someone said seeing him. "Extraordinary," said another, smiling through unmoving lips. Perhaps all was not lost, he hoped. Art and politics were tricky. Public opinion could yet turn the tables in his favor.

The crowd forced people together in unlikely pairings. Bramante was surprised to see old Count Prospero Colonna engaged in an animated discussion with a known ally of the Orsini family. Normally, these men either hissed openly at each other or kept their distance. The Colonna and the Orsini clans had been on opposing sides of every important issue for as long as anyone could remember. When the Colonna allied themselves with the Emperor against the Pope, the Orsini would inevitably pledge their forces to the Pope. If the Orsini went to war on the side of Venice, the Colonna would aid their opponent. Their feud was centuries old. Curious to hear what they were saying, Bramante pushed his way toward them.

The old Count, stooped over and bow-legged like a chimpanzee, was hanging on his nephew Ottavio's arm, gesturing wildly, his eyes bugging out of his head. Spittle foamed at the corners of his mouth. Now and then he thrust a claw like-hand in the direction of the model. Bramante shrank back. Faint praise was disheartening enough, barefaced hostility—well, I don't need that, he thought, trying to slip past them unnoticed. He failed. Ottavio, the nephew, spotted him. If looks could kill, I'm dead, thought Bramante. He knew that, as a class, all these Roman snobs resented the razing of the Old Basilica, and frankly, he was tired of hearing it; tired of listening to them trace their lineages to the dawn of civilization and fed up with their constant boasting about how their families built this church with their own sweat and blood. Big deal. Aside from their fancy names, most of them didn't have a pot to piss in. You can't keep everyone happy, he thought. "*Beh*," he muttered pushing his way by them.

A group of pre-occupied bishops dressed in black and sashed in purple shoved Bramante against a red porphyry column. "Sentimentalist," he huffed under his breath, looking back at Ottavio Colonna. The young man, still watching him, looked like a large stinging insect in his tightly fitting carapace of black leather armor.

Bramante slapped the cold chipped stone and looked away. The old church was a mess: black columns, red ones, bright white ones, fat and thin ones, capitals of every description chipped, broken, too big for the columns they sat on, or too ridiculously small. They supposedly came from the Emperor Nero's circus. That's what people said. In promising contrast to this dingy scavenger's pile, his elegant model rose above the throng, clear and logical, exquisite in its mathematical perfection; its every curving surface, window, door, detail and ornament in perfect harmony. Above it from the dilapidated center of the apse, Christ's penetrating stare caught him. Sighing, the tired architect said out loud, "You demand too much of me," his words swallowed by the thrum of other voices. He wanted to hide his face from that stare, but knew that no matter where he went those eyes would find him. "When is what I have given you enough?" He felt the heat of bodies pressing against him and pushed himself away from the column, back onto the game board.

A flock of earnest penitents vacated one square as a colorful flock of merchants filled it, talking loudly and gesturing flamboyantly. Moving around them Bramante acknowledged the ferret faced Niccolo Machiavelli, an emissary from Florence speaking with a stranger. He thought he heard him describe his design as a "clever strategy." But, perhaps he had misunderstood.

Bramante was not surprised to see the young sculptor, Michelangelo Buonarotti and a companion, hovering near the French Chapel. He had never liked Buonarotti, thought he was too full of himself. Like a fox intent on his prey Bramante made his way through the crowd eager to share the cool reception the cardinals had shown him with a fellow artist. "Buonarotti! Buonarotti! Buonarotti!" he called out. "It never fails. I always find you here in the very same place! Do you ever leave?" He threw his head back and barked a laugh at his own joke. The sculptor's Lamentation of Christ, The Pieta, was perched on a ledge above him. "I hope this tired old building can hold that thing up," he taunted, waving at it dismissively. It was a gift from the French King to atone for sacking Rome eleven years before in 1495. At every large gathering the sculptor, with affected nonchalance, positioned himself strategically at its feet daring passersby not to pay him a compliment. "Michelangelo, *Angelino, Angeletto, Angelissimino*," Bramante teased. He could not find enough ways to diminish his name, "We would hate to see you crushed under the weight of your own work."

"Shall I say something flattering in return?" asked the sculptor scowling.

"Don't say anything, nothing at all," the architect answered with a practiced smile, "A compliment from you would be like a condemnation." He was on the gleeful brink of seizing the chance to tell the smug young artist that he had a squiggly black pubic hair on his cheek, just under his left eye, when a large figure wedged itself between them.

"Bramante! Bram-ANTE! BRAMANTE!" the huge man sang his name right into his face, "It is stupENdous! You are a GEnius!" Agostino Chigi, Rome's pre-eminent banker, impossibly fat, looking upholstered in layer upon layer of colorful embroidered cloth raised his great arms to Heaven and bellowed the architect's praise for all to hear.

Bramante, small and drab in comparison, waved off the effusive flattery with a gesture of practiced modesty. This was more like it, he thought.

"NO!" Chigi dropped his ham like hands onto Bramante's shoulders with a thud and leaned forward. "It is a MARVEL! AMAZING beyond mere words to describe," he sang. Bramante struggled to keep his legs from buckling under the banker's weight. "Donatello, Donino," the big man cooed and gurgled like a pigeon. Could he make the architect's name more endearing? "I am SPEECHless," he wheezed as if truly out of both words and breath." Behind his back Bramante heard the ostentatious laugh Michelangelo was having at his expense. "It is a Vision of Heaven to be sure," Chigi inhaled and lifted his mighty arms, spreading them wide once again as if to embrace Bramante's stately model, which at that very moment was being locked in place at the foot of the nave.

"Thank you, thank you, Signore," said Bramante regaining his balance. He knew that he ought to feel embarrassed by the effusive praise, but he did not.

The banker then asked abruptly, "How many tons of lead do you estimate it will take to cover that roof?" his lilting tone gone, suggesting to Bramante that their two visions of heaven might not be quite the same. With a tremolo that anticipated the thrill of hearing a high number the banker then asked, "And gold? The inside of the dome is gilt isn't it? How many hectares do you think that might be? Take notes," he wheezed, snapping sausage like fingers over the horizon of his shoulder at his almost equally enormous son, before lumbering toward the model, his splayed thighs scraping.

Bramante fell in behind them glad to have the two large men clear a path through the pressing crowd, feeling like the runt in a parade of festooned and caparisoned elephants. "I will, of course be needing vast quantities of everything," he called out, "carnelian, beryl, onyx, porphyry for the inlays." Just then young Chigi stopped short. Bramante fell flat against his soft, upholstered flank. Trying in a dignified way to regain his balance without touching the young man's massive rear end Bramante heard the elder Chigi sigh, "Father Ximenez," his honeyed baritone having returned. Smoothing his cloak, the architect saw the senior Chigi, with considerable exertion, drop to one knee, his mouth pursed reflexively in search of a ring to kiss.

Ignoring the slumped banker the tall gaunt priest extended his ropy hands to Bramante. "A powerful vision," he said in a heavy Spanish accent. Ximenez' lined and weathered skin had the wind-beaten texture of old canvas. He was accompanied by four priests dressed simply in black. They stood in formation behind him like a protective palisade. All wore heavy wooden crosses. A sixth member of the contingent, a monk with a pink face and soft hands stood apart studying the model intently, jotting notes and making sketches in a notebook.

Pleased by the compliment, the architect took the priest's icy fingers in his own warm hands. "Your satisfaction is my reward," he said fumbling for an appropriate form of address. Ximenez' plain black cassock bore no identifying mark of rank, making him look like a simple parish priest. Judging from Chigi's fawning and the attention shown by his entourage Bramante suspected that this was not the case.

Ximenez' eyes bore into Bramante's. They were like polished black stones. A fine scar puckered the left side of his mouth and extended up his cheek. Bramante thought he looked more like a soldier than a pastor. "There has never been a greater need than now for something like this," he said, referring casually to the model.

"Something like this," Bramante heard himself repeat too quickly, insulted that the singularity of his design was not obvious to the man. 'Something like this,' indeed. He immediately regretted showing his annoyance, but his design was not something 'like' anything and nothing else could be 'like' it. His plan was inevitable, pre-ordained. He tried to release himself from the man's grip.

"I am a simple country priest," Ximenez said tightening his grasp and smiling on the right side of his face. "Forgive me. I have no sophistication in matters concerning art and design. I meant no offense."

To repair his wounded dignity Bramante proclaimed, "Your country has always been sophisticated and forward-looking in such matters." It was a blunt reminder to this bumpkin that the Spanish Court of Aragon and Castile, Ferdinand and Isabella themselves, had commissioned him to design the splendid and now celebrated little church on the Janiculum Hill that marked the site of St. Peter's crucifixion. Bramante wasn't just a little nobody designing any old "something." Satisfied that he had put Ximenez in his place, he decided to show no further pique. If the Spaniard had deliberately meant to insult him he wouldn't give him the satisfaction of letting him know that he had succeeded. He was relieved when the priest gently released his grip.

"But the time is now. Don't you agree?" Ximenez insisted. "Look at this place," he said making a sweeping gesture as if unsheathing a saber. "Just look at this." Waves of chanting, ringing bells, mumbled prayers, weeping and the howl of uproarious laughter rolled over them. The priest's black eyes began to quiver. Disgust and scorn transformed his face into a grimace of pure hatred. "This isn't a church," he spit the words out. "It is a Turkish bazaar," spreading the fingers of his outstretched hand as if to condemn everything he saw. "This is a pagan gathering, a carnival. Just look," he hissed, "the venerated mother Church of Rome has been reduced to this: a down-at-the-heels harlot shaking her ass on a back street." He turned suddenly back to Bramante, glaring.

Bramante, stunned by the priest's vehemence, resisted the temptation to look for comfort in the face high in the apse.

"Maestro!" someone shouted.

Bramante turned, grateful for the diversion, and was relieved to see Antonio and Piero pushing their way toward him.

"Aha!" he barked his little laugh. "You have come to rescue me from my adoring public," he said poking Piero in the belly and making him jump. "You go on ahead. I'll catch up," and he shooed them away.

&

3

La Taverna nel Teatro di Pompeo

Breathing hard, beyond exhaustion, Piero fell against the tavern wall. His springy black hair was damp with sweat. He and Antonio had run most of the long way from the Vatican to the *Campo dei Fiori*, slowing to walk only long enough to gather the strength to run again. "I'm really awake," he said gulping for air. The street was dark.

"Yeah," Antonio said between breaths, his chest heaving. He leaned forward, hands on his knees. "Me, too," and coughed at the pavement.

Piero turned and slumped against the wall feeling the cool, prickly stucco through his smock.

Antonio stood up and straightened his shoulders. He smoothed his hair down with both hands and took a long, deep drink of air. "Ready?" he asked.

Piero nodded like a puppy. He was ready. Leaning against the wall he shut his eyes and felt his body sinking as if in a dream, breathing more easily. Lightheaded, exhilarated and relieved, he was thrilled to be working on the most ambitious, the most fantastic project the world had ever seen. He was relieved that he had not screwed up. Nothing he built had fallen off the model. He hadn't coughed or sneezed or tripped. He hadn't turned the great contraption to the right when it was supposed to go left, and he didn't set it on fire in front of the holy Princes of the Church while he was moving the lanterns around. Everything he was supposed to do he had done perfectly. Was he ready? Of course he was.

Pompey's Tavern was the watering hole for Rome's left bank neighborhoods. After work everyone from the St. Eustachio and Campus Martius districts gathered here to eat and drink, socialize, gossip and plot. Piero and Antonio came whenever they had a night off. Work had kept them away for weeks and they were eager to see their buddies. They had a lot to tell them.

Waiting impatiently for Antonio to finish preening, Piero's mind raced back to his first few weeks in Rome. They had been awful. As Bramante's youngest and newest apprentice he was given all the worst jobs: mopping the floor, trimming sheets of paper, mixing smelly rabbits foot glue, pulverizing charcoal for ink: pure drudgery. And because he looked like a kid everyone treated him like one. He was a runt and that made him the grunt. But that sorry state of affairs, he proudly reported in a letter to his parents, had not lasted. One afternoon, out of the blue, Antonio flew into a rage of frustration trying to decipher Bramante's hastily scribbled notes; cursing, throwing pens, anything he could get his hands on across the room, yelling and jumping up and down. The other apprentices dropped what they were doing and rushed over to calm him down before hurriedly putting the studio back in order. If Antonio had been caught pitching a tantrum he would have been dismissed on the spot.

When Bramante returned, the painters were back at their easels, the model makers were hard at work and Piero was at Antonio's drawing table translating the Maestro's annotated sheet of scribbles, dots and erasures into a coherent drawing. There would be no more swabbing floors or stirring glue pots for Piero. Bramante paired him with Antonio and the boy quickly showed promise as a draughtsman and painter. Above all, Bramante liked the careful way Piero approached his work. "You are a problem solver," he told him the day he assigned him to the presentation for the new St. Peter's. I might still be a runt, thought Piero, but I'm not a grunt anymore. Now I am a runt with a future.

A smile flicked across his face. He pulled his tired shoulders from the wall and proudly held up his head. A rush of excitement warmed him. He could barely contain himself. Just wait until the guys inside hear about how we did, he thought.

Antonio thrust his chin up and was setting his eyelids in that half-mast way, trying to appear sophisticated and coolly indifferent to all the heads he knew would turn when he made his entrance. It was a big story and it was theirs to tell. Antonio took a last deep breath and with a cocked eyebrow asked, "how's my hair?"

Piero nodded affirmatively. It was as good as it was going to be for hair that hadn't been washed in two weeks.

"Let's go," said Antonio and kicked open the heavy plank door to announce their arrival. He stood aside and let Piero march in first like a conquering hero, his little chest puffed out, before slouching in behind him casually checking his fingernails.

The place was dark and smoky. Sides of meat and game birds roasted over a pit fire in the middle of the largest hall. Other than the hiss of fat dripping on the fire there was very little sound. Piero squinted through the blue haze. Antonio blinked and then blinked again. Long walnut tables that smelled of wine and bread, and which were usually crowded with men talking and eating were empty. Antonio's slouch stiffened. Piero's puffed chest caved.

"Are we dreaming? Is this a bad dream?" piped Piero, looking into the empty tavern. He dug his nails into his palms to wake himself in case it was.

Antonio didn't answer. Steam rose from his sweaty smock and he blinked again hoping their audience would magically appear from wherever they were hiding. Finally, his face hot with embarrassment, he said, "*Merda.*" Shit.

"What do you mean, shit?" demanded Piero. "Where is everybody?" Clenching his fists he resisted the impulse to stamp his feet. As soon as the words were out of his mouth he knew. Everyone was at St. Peter's looking at the model, their model. "*Merda,*" he said. "Shit." His ears burned with disappointment. How stupid could he be?

"We're not going to take home any gold medals for this little maneuver," said Antonio, his eyelids coolly repositioning themselves, slouching again.

"You're supposed to be the smart one," whined Piero and punched Antonio in the arm, not hard, but not a light tap either.

Antonio punched him back, "What about you, you little prick," he growled rubbing his arm, "You're supposed to be the budding genius," and he kicked Piero in the seat of his pants, propelling him a couple of steps forward. "Don't worry. They'll show up. They can't stay there all night," he said walking past him into the gloomy tavern. "Anyway, I'm starved. Let's get some food."

Piero, angry with himself for not foreseeing this, followed him. There wasn't much choice.

"We can tell everybody about it later," said Antonio offhandedly.

Pompey's Tavern, officially named *La Taverna nella Grotta del Teatro di Pompeo* was, as the name made clear, built into the collapsed underbelly of the Emperor Pompey's Theater. 1300 years before it provided Rome's citizens with a rich diet of comedy and tragedy. More of the latter was the young apprentices' mood as they made their way through the smoke and gloom looking for anyone, anyone at all to tell their story to. A boy cranked a spitted goat over the cooking fire. A serving girl wiped out a big copper bowl with sand and a gray rag.

The place owed its popularity to its location. It was far enough away from the Vatican to permit relatively uninhibited discussion, and nearby the new neighborhoods of Florentine, Spanish, French and northern European business people, who were settling in the Campo Marzio District. Social, business and political clubs all met here. Each one, long ago, having claimed its bit of turf inside the ruin's grotto-like vaulted chambers. Its worn brick walls were hung with emblems, colorful banners, coats of arms, prizes won at tournaments and races, any and all trinkets and souvenirs that held the slightest symbolic or sentimental significance.

Piero and Antonio moved like swimmers through the smoky air. They ducked under a massive brick arch. Before them were more arches. File after file of them seemed to diminish in size, until the last one vanished out of sight around the ruined theater's curvature. They made their way to the alcove reserved for the august members of the Roman Academy. There a broad brick staircase, wide enough for ten people to pass abreast, ascended steeply and ended abruptly at a blank wall. A lone poet struggled, pushing a table to the opposite wall for a stage.

"Tonight's the night they're having that reading from what's-his-name," said Antonio in a tone that made it clear he didn't plan to stick around for that magical event.

"Should be interesting," said Piero, meaning it.

Antonio rolled his eyes.

The Academicians sought inspiration among the elephantine staircases and ramps that once brought people by the tens of thousands to the original versions of the plays and histories they took pride in copying. Professor Laetus, their tutor, dressed in a toga, his bald head gleaming through an oak leaf garland, sat hunched in a corner practicing his lines.

Above them a mezzanine of smaller vaulted rooms overlooked the main floor. Up there Rome's young gentry met to gamble, gossip, conspire and scheme while keeping an eye on everything that happened below. It had aptly been nicknamed "The Hornet's Nest." If avoided, it was generally benign, when disturbed, watch out. Cautiously Piero looked up. To his relief the "Hornet's Nest" was empty, a peaceful night sky was all he saw through a broad open archway.

Members of the neighborhood Sporting Club huddled around a table talking, eating, repairing and polishing their bridles and tack. Deep within the grotto a band was rehearsing. The flatulent sound of a horn bounced off the hard brick walls. Piero laughed. A few men played at cards in another shadowy recess. In Pompey's Tavern everyone had his place. Pompey's regulars were not shy about asserting their territorial rights. When foreigners and pilgrims came in from out of town they were quickly, and often physically, shown where they were welcome and where they most definitely were not. It was a place where anyone, or almost anyone, at any time of the day or night, could count on finding at least a few kindred souls with whom to argue, eat, drink, gossip and plot. Unfortunately, for Piero and Antonio tonight was not one of them.

Crestfallen and resigned to each other's company they settled themselves at the table reserved for apprentices and artisans. Their eyes burned from the smoke and the long days and nights of work without sleep. Antonio reached for a loaf of bread, tore off a chunk and stuffed it in his mouth before passing the loaf to Piero. Chewing slowly they stared blankly into space. The bread was old and sour and made Piero think of the straw in the quail cages back home. He stifled a yawn. In their gray work smocks, vapor rising from their hair, they looked like the ghosts they were, immaterial, gray against gray in the shadowy tavern, the invisible beings who had animated the great model of the new St. Peter's. Antonio pulled a heavy flagon across the table and poured out two beakers. Absently Piero took a long swallow. The rough wine warmed and relaxed him. A glowing log hissed and flared in the cooking trough before rolling to one side.

Piero broke the silence, "Wasn't it fantastic?" he asked reverently through a mouthful, meaning the presentation.

Antonio, elbows on the table, hypnotized by the fire and the rhythmic turning of the iron spit, didn't answer.

"It's really going to happen, isn't it?" Piero persisted. A quiver of excitement brushed the nape of his neck. "We're really going to get to build it, aren't we?" The wine made him want to talk.

Antonio, through a mouthful, said, "Yeah, sure we are." He was confident. "Bramante knows how to strum those old goats," and washed his words down with a gulp of wine.

They stared into the embers. The muted sound of the band struck up again, and again the horn hit a flatulent false note. Piero laughed.

Antonio took a gulp and coolly asked, "By the way, did you hear the Pope fart?"

Piero, taken by surprise, laughed again, trying not to spray crumbs across the table. "I thought it was you," he cried.

"You would have been the first to know if it was me. Christ, it was stuffy in there," said Antonio deadpan, referring to the air quality inside the model. He chewed slowly, watching Piero press his lips together trying not to laugh. Antonio loved making people laugh when they didn't want to and Piero, a born laugher, erupted, predictably, into ripples of uncontrollable laughter.

"You're lucky it wasn't me," said Antonio still showing no expression. "With those lanterns burning, the model would have exploded."

Piero snorted, red faced, and waved for him to stop, pointing frantically to his full cheeks, imploring him with a violent shaking of his head not to say another word. Tears streamed down his cheeks. "Stop. Don't make me laugh anymore," he pleaded, laughing harder, barely moving his mouth.

Antonio looked straight ahead. Then, as Piero regained control, he wrinkled his nose as if at a bad smell.

With a squeal suggesting bread had gotten stuck up the back of his nose Piero, choked and begged for mercy, "Stop. My stomach hurts!" His face was numb. His cheeks were puffed out and sore. He tried to drop his face into a serious pose and swallow, but he couldn't. The corners of his mouth wouldn't stay down. They kept jumping up. It wasn't that funny, he knew but, nonetheless, he couldn't stop laughing. Exhaustion and wine were spinning him out of control. He threw a piece of bread at Antonio missing him and gasped for air, "When I heard it I thought, 'Dear Jesus, don't make me laugh now.' The boss'll kill me." The words came out as a muffled squawk.

Gazing into the distance, his eyes half closed Antonio said, "He wouldn't have had the chance . . . an explosion like that . . ." He paused to take a small, genteel sip from his beaker. ". . . would have wiped him out and half the College of Cardinals with him." He painted a picture in the air with both hands, "Splinters everywhere. Can you see it? All of them, lanced to death by pieces of expensive inlaid shrapnel."

Piero threw his head back, laughing and choking, crumbs showering his smock.

Antonio, pleased with himself, smiled contentedly into the smoky gray gloom.

Wiping his tear-stained face Piero reached for more wine as his spasms of uncontrolled hilarity gradually subsided. He poured. The fire hissed. Coming off his laughing jag he felt suddenly overwhelmed by homesickness. "I wish my father were here," he said quietly. He drank, letting the wine swirl around in his mouth. It was warm. His eyes brimmed. "He'd be proud of me today." He missed his family. Bracciano, Piero's home village, was two days ride north. His father managed a large estate there. The Duke of Bracciano made a point of identifying children among his workers who showed promise. An eager student who learned quickly, Piero had been singled out early. At age ten he was helping his father make patterns for tools. At twelve he learned to operate the dams, sluices, and water wheels that distributed water into the estate's irrigation canals. He was smart, a credit to his family. For the Duke, the boy's potential was capital to be as carefully nurtured, cultivated and managed, as his fields, vineyards, fisheries and herds. Staring ahead into the embers Piero murmured, "We're lucky to be here."

Antonio folded his arms on the table and cradled his head. "We are."

"Are you asleep?" he whispered, looking at Antonio.

"I'm just resting my eyes," Antonio said. A hank of his fashionably cut hair lay in a puddle of spilled wine and wicked it up like a paintbrush.

"The Duke hopes I'll be another Leonardo," said Piero quietly. "He told me."

"A little Leonardo of his very own," said Antonio mocking him.

Defensively Piero said, "Maybe I will be."

"Maybe you will," mumbled Antonio, sorry for making fun.

Piero, his eyes heavy, said no more, mindful of how fragile was the luck that brought him here. Astride the threshold between wakefulness and sleep, he tried to remember what he expected Rome would be. He tried in his mind to reel himself back those few months and look innocently forward again, but he could not. The short time he had spent in the City made everything before recede into a vague background. Woozy, he rested his face in his hands. They smelled of candle wax, varnish, paint and bread. He remembered as a boy being told stories of Rome, and he tried to recall the old images of victorious legions passing through triumphal arches. He tried to envision Roman throngs climbing to their seats in the theater that was once right here, just over his head, but he could not. That Rome was not the Rome he knew. He tried to recapture the pictures his father had painted in words. He strained to imagine reclining on a sunny hillside while Saints Peter and Paul preached the gospel to pagan Romans, but it was no good. He couldn't do it. This Rome, the city he knew, was brown, not white, not brilliant and shining, but dusty, a construction site, noisy and chaotic, ruined and rundown.

Piero's eyes fluttered, glassy, reflecting the fire's red and orange embers. The Duke had mussed up his curly hair the day he told him he was going to work for the great Bramante. He told him he had high hopes for him. His father beamed. His mother had looked stricken, but she smiled. Remembering that morning made tears spill down his face. He licked them away, warm and salty, from his upper lip. "That Piero was not me," he said, glad that Antonio had fallen asleep, as his eyes closed.

4

La Taverna nel Teatro di Pompeo

The heavy door from the street banged. A scene of cardinals, a marching Roman legion, his mother waving goodbye, the model of the new St. Peter's, overlapping images, irrational and unrelated like reflections on a pane of breaking glass disintegrated slowly. Torn from sleep, Piero opened his eyes. People were walking up and down a wall. Slowly and with great care he unstuck his face from the table. Cool air skimmed across the stone floor and swirled around his legs. Sparks from the cooking fire swirled upward. He felt dizzy. The noise was thunderous: plates banging, people talking and laughing, joking just like any other night at Pompey's. He buried his face in his hands and rubbed his eyes to wake up.

"You slept through my entire performance," said Professor Laetus, pointedly from across the table. His arms were folded across his chest. He was still dressed in a toga. An oak leaf garland was centered on his high forehead making him look like an annoyed porpoise trying to jump through a tiny hoop. "I was brilliant, too." His mouth was pursed more in disapproval than disappointment. "I'm not getting any younger, you know. You might not get another chance."

"It sounds like your audience was more manageable than mine," said Donato Bramante. He was sitting beside Laetus and reached for the wine flagon.

At the sound of their voices Piero bolted up. Antonio, oblivious, slept on, his head resting on the table. An immense horse fly grazed on crumbs stuck in his hair.

Bramante sniffed the wine and recoiled. "You boys have been drinking this swill?" he asked, looking at Piero, and pushed the beaker away in disgust. He snapped his fingers to catch the attention of a serving girl. She ignored him.

"They were captivated," said Professor Laetus, speaking of his audience. "You could have heard a pin drop. Cicero himself could not have done a better job of defending the Republic than I did tonight," referring to the subject of his reading.

Bramante snapped his fingers again and waved for the girl, "Enchanted my ass. They were all asleep. Not just these two," he said pointing at his two apprentices. He turned impatiently and banged his beaker on the table to get the girl's attention. "Besides, didn't the Republic collapse in spite of all his words?" he asked over his shoulder.

"Yes, it did, but you're wrong. My audience was enchanted. And what would you know, anyway. You weren't even here." The professor pressed his lips together before saying, "You didn't even have the courtesy to show up."

"Listen, I was trying to salvage my own project." Losing hope of ever catching the girl's eye, Bramante turned back to the table and poured himself a small amount of the brownish fluid. He brought the beaker cautiously to his mouth. Tasting it he shuddered. "Well," Bramante proclaimed patting his lips to reassure himself that they had not dissolved, "how shall I describe it? Low tide, perhaps with depressing notes of hoof parings, wet wool and mold?"

"They gave you a hard time did they?" asked the Professor without sympathy, realizing no apology would be forthcoming.

Bramante, wagging his head from side to side said, "Let me put it this way. It was the worst response I have ever received to the best work I have ever done in my entire life," and banged the beaker on the table.

Antonio moaned at the sound and rolled his head to one side. A sticky eye blink showed him where he was. He sat up straight. The fly, sated, flew off.

"I have even been given a new nickname," said Bramante.

"*Il Ruinante!*" crowed Professor Laetus with gusto.

"So you've heard it."

"*Il Ruinante*, Yes, the wrecking ball!" the Professor hooted, " I don't know why you're surprised. I'm not."

"You're never surprised," said Bramante. He was about to tell his two apprentices that they looked like perfect examples of the art of taxidermy when a mass of sable-trimmed brocade glided into view behind them.

"I was hoping to find you here," said Chigi, the Younger, in a mellifluous voice that made Bramante wonder if both Chigi's took singing lessons. "I want to say again how impressed my father and I are with your design." Bramante moved to rise. "No. No. Don't get up! Please. Have you met Fra Juan?" he asked presenting the pink faced monk Bramante had seen at St Peter's. He had been with Father Ximenez' entourage.

"I have not yet had the pleasure," said Bramante extending his hand. "I saw you at the presentation. You were busy making sketches."

"Yes, yes, that was me."

"Do you have interest in architecture?"

"Oh, indeed I do," said the monk, apologetically, "Unfortunately, I never had any talent."

"Ah," said Bramante, "that's too bad, but not to worry. There is enough talent at this table for everyone." Then, winking broadly, he continued to say, "Although you would never know it to look at them," indicating his two apprentices across the table. Piero looked down sheepishly. Antonio pretended not to have heard.

You.g Chigi's nostrils quivered at the sour wine and the stale bread littering the table. With a pained look on his large face he asked, "May we join you?"

"Of course. Certainly. Please," said Professor Laetus enthusiastically." The more the merrier!"

Turning to the kitchen Chigi sang out, "Girl!" and raised his heavy bedraped arms. Like a conductor leading a vigorous allegro he then waved broadly and energetically, pumping the air, tossing his head and swirling around. Immediately, as if shot from a cannon, two churls sprang from the scullery, wiped the table clean and spread a crisp white linen cloth.

Bramante sat back and shook his head in disbelief. Tablecloths at Pompey's, since when? A squadron of breathless serving girls burst suddenly through the steam and smoke, bearing platters of fragrantly seasoned meats and, to his relief, several corked, not open, flagons of wine. Enjoying the musical tinkle of crystal goblets Bramante looked absently into space as if seeking someone who might explain why it was that he was invisible and Chigi was not.

Piero thought he had fallen asleep again and was dreaming. Antonio's appetite returned with an audible rumble.

Curious, Bramante turned to see what Professor Laetus was making of this miracle of the loaves and fishes, but the professor had cornered Fra Juan, and was preparing him for a reprise of his reading. Clearing his throat and in his most stentorian tones the professor launched into the finale of Cicero's tirade against Marc Antony:

> "*After the honors I have been awarded, Senators, after the deeds that I have done, death actually seems to me desirable. Two things only I pray for. One, that in dying I may leave the Roman people free—the immortal gods could grant me no greater gift. My other prayer is this: that no man's fortunes may fail to correspond with his services to our country!*"

When he came to the end, Professor Laetus raised his face heavenward and shut his eyes tightly. No one made a sound. With a flourish, he then dropped his chin to his chest. The wreath flopped to the table.

"Bravo! Bravo!" crooned Young Chigi as the Professor retrieved his garland from a platter of chicken legs.

Bramante looked across the table at his two apprentices, crossed his eyes, and applauded softly.

"Yes!" said Brother Juan nodding his pink face enthusiastically, "Yes!

Yes! How splendid! And how true." He looked up and down the table, delighted, "So many wonderful things today."

"Indeed!" boomed Chigi. After a moment he asked, "Tell me professor were you able to get to St. Peter's to see Bramante's grand design?"

"Oh yes, Oh yes, *I* wouldn't have missed *it* for the world," said the Professor in a harsh tone, rebuking Bramante and his two apprentices again for missing his recitation, "but I slipped out early so I could be back here in time for my own performance." He picked a piece of chicken skin out of his wreath and placed the garland carefully on his head.

Piero and Antonio fidgeted waiting to be invited to eat.

"Eat! Eat, boys!" boomed Chigi, spreading his arms wide. "And what did you think of it, Professor?"

"Aaaaah, the new St. Peter's, " he said as if savoring the sight of a beautiful woman. "It is a delight, and I mean that sincerely, Bramante," Professor Laetus said patting the architect's sleeve. "Truly. It stirred me deeply. It reminded me of the description of the New Jerusalem in the Revelation of St. John from the new testament."

"And the City lieth four square! Its length as great as its breadth . . . !" Bramante began reciting the passage, imitating the Professor's loud stage voice.

"Exactly," said the Professor talking over him even more loudly, "that's the one. Brilliant. I could see it. I thought, my God he has captured it right down to the Twelve Gates.

Bramante smiled, pleased that the Professor had appreciated one of his sources.

"I marveled at the order, the symmetry, the clarity, the perfection of the proportions of each part of your composition, Bramante. Looking at it I knew that I was seeing the work of a master who had reached the pinnacle of his creative power." He smiled warmly at the architect before looking at the others. He had their attention. Chigi nodded in agreement. Fra Juan was clearly enchanted by the Professor's words. "I thought," he continued, "that Rome could be in no better hands than Bramante's." He sighed contentedly before taking a sip of wine. A master of the pregnant pause, he held their attention for a long thoughtful silence before saying, "But then . . ."

Bramante's shoulders fell. Smacking the table he said, "I knew there would have to be a 'but then,' sooner or later. Couldn't it be later, Laetus?" Looking sharply at the old professor, " I've had a rough day."

"But then . . . ," sighed Professor Laetus adjusting himself on the bench, "I am of two minds about this amazing scheme, maybe I should say I am of several minds."

Chigi, eager to hear what Professor Laetus had to say, pulled himself as close to the table as his girth would allow, "Most of us poor souls are lucky to be of but one mind, some of us even less than that," he giggled flapping his fat hands at himself.

The Professor raised his garland and patting himself on his high glistening forehead said, "Yes, yes, this is my gift from God." His students, he knew, joked behind his back that the reason his forehead was so high was because he had two brains, one stacked on top of the other. "But," looking pointedly at Antonio to let the young man know that he was well aware of the source of their little joke, he said, "it's a burden, too, being a man of many minds. Let me tell you what I think. Let me share a little of my ambivalence"

Bramante scowled darkly.

Professor Laetus reached calmly for his glass. They would hear what he had to say. He wet his lips, "My mind feels benumbed by what I saw this evening. When I arrived, the basilica was packed and noisy. I, and I suspect much of Rome, was there to see what Bramante and the Pope have in store for us. I had to fight my way through that throng of smelly foreigners. Everyone was talking. It sounded like wind roaring through the church." He cleared his throat, "I hope you don't mind my rambling on like this. I saw the model at the end of the nave, the high dome warm and glowing. What a wonderful sight." He paused to drink. "I hesitate to say anything at all." He stopped. "My thoughts are not yet formed." All but Bramante looked at him expectantly. He resumed, " I feel as if a jumble of elbows inside me is jostling to make room for all sorts of ideas that are not in agreement. Each wants to force itself to the foreground to make itself known." He chuckled as if to himself, " Of course the wine may be contributing to my confusion," he said looking at the bottle. With the exception of Bramante the men laughed politely as the old professor raised his glass and with a sly wink, drank.

"On the one hand," he mused, "I rejoice, truly rejoice, at the thought of this beautiful building being built. That it will grace Rome like an exquisite jewel I have no doubt at all. When I saw it, well . . . It seemed almost as if the hand of the ancients, or had I better say God Himself," he corrected, nodding apologetically to Fra Juan, "had reached through the ether of time to animate my friend, Bramante here, and you boys, too," he said across the table, "to create this magnificent thing. But then one of those sharp little elbows inside me pushes that thought aside to make way for a troubling question: How can I rejoice at this when it means the loss of our ancient church?"

Bramante grumbled and shifted in his seat.

"Yes, yes" the Professor went on laconically, "maybe it's just an old man's sentimentality, as simple as that. And I can accept that if that's all it is, but there are more elbows pushing and bumping around and I know I will not be able to sleep for the mental turmoil they are causing me. Why now? I ask myself. Why does it have to happen now? I do want to see this apparition of yours become reality," he said turning to the architect, "of course I do, but I don't want it to happen at the cost of so much of Rome's glorious history."

"You have to take a position, Laetus," grumbled Bramante shaking his head. "You have to. You can't be wishy-washy about this. You can't make an omelet without breaking eggs. You either want to see Rome gloriously reborn, or you want to wallow in the muck and mire, chaos and confusion of things as they are!"

The professor sighed and laid his wreath on the table, letting a hole of silence open around them, walled by the background clatter of dishes and other voices. "The City has been leveled, burned," he finally said, "Entire blocks of buildings are being destroyed. Every day more is lost. I see Rome today as even more devastated than it was after Charles V finished with us twelve years ago. How is what you propose different from that?"

"It *is* different, and you know it!" Bramante snapped, banging the table.

Ignoring the outburst the Professor calmly said, "Oh yes, yes, of course it *is* different. I know that." His question had been for affect. "There are no gibbets set up out there in the Campo dei Fiori. The blood on the streets washed away long ago. Our girls are not being ripped from our houses and raped by French soldiers. The Jews are back in business instead of being hanged and left for the crows and the dogs. Yes, yes, I know it's not the same, and yet I feel a loss now just as great as I did then. I weep. There is not much of our old Rome left. Do we now have to lose our great old basilica, our old and dear friend, too?"

Piero reddened and looked as if he had been slapped. Antonio chewed slowly. Young Chigi froze, a drumstick halted an inch from his mouth. An empty smile hung across Fra Juan's face like a line of damp laundry. His jaws set, Bramante shook his head violently, no, no, no. His project had taken on a life of it's own. It was out of his hands, beyond his control. It spoke for itself saying things he didn't intend.

When no one answered, the Professor took a drink and then calmly resumed, "And now another of those elbows jostles to make room for an even more cynical thought." He jabbed his elbows from side to side to dramatize his point and leaned toward young Chigi." Move aside, you sentimental old man, a voice says. Get smart. Building this church is just about money." Chigi froze again like a fish caught staring up from the water into the glare of a torch when suddenly, like a wounded actor, Professor Laetus clutched his side and cried, "Aah!" in theatrical agony. "I feel another jab," he whispered, "another voice struggles to make itself heard. No, it says hoarsely, 'This is about Power.'" The professor stopped and wiped his glistening brow with a forefinger before saying, "Then a soft breathless voice inside my head, a little girl's voice, says, 'No, No. It's about God's love.'" He said it in a light, mocking way, making it plain that he thought it was not, and smiled Fra Juan's own numb smile back at him.

Professor Laetus then fell silent and looked directly into the eyes of each man in turn. Chigi shifted his weight and looked away. Deep in his sleeves Fra Juan dug his fingernails into his palms. Antonio and Piero sat completely still. Bramante, seething, was about to say something when Professor Laetus raised a hand to silence him, "I fear that it signals conflict to come, this grand scheme of yours. A battle." He spoke with force before saying more softly, "I hesitate to use that word because it conjures images of violence, of people hacking at each other with broadswords and battleaxes. That's not what I foresee, not at all. I mean to say that I see your project becoming a rallying point for a battle to claim what I can only describe as a territory of the mind." Shrugging as if to dismiss his own remark, "I say that, but I don't really know what I mean." He blotted his brow with the sleeve of his toga. "I suppose," he went on replacing the garland, "that all I can say for certain is that there will be more to this grand, seductive plan than meets the eye."

Bramante exploded, "That's very elegant, Laetus, but all you are telling us is that you are confused! You want to see the rebirth of Rome. Look at you. You sit here masquerading as a Roman senator. You revive the classics. You posture and preen, but the fact is, you want everything to stay the same. You want to experience the glory that was Rome, but you don't want to give up the Rome you fondly call home. All you are really telling us is that you don't want to give up the back streets where you first got laid or the dumpy hole you lived in when you were a student. You're a selfish old man, Laetus. You want the glory that was Rome without having to sacrifice your little memories. Well, for Christ's sake, you can't have both!"

Fra Juan turned bright pink and crossed himself.

"It's my two brains," said the professor, coolly, playing to Piero and Antonio, who dared not laugh. "Each wants what it wants."

"Oh stop. You may think your view is clear. It is not. Your position is weak." Bramante looked him straight in the eye. " You have to make a choice. Take a stand. Look around you. Can't you imagine a better world than this one?"

"I can envision a worse one, too." He winked, teasing the boys. " And I will likely be facing either it or a far better one than even you are offering me soon enough. I am 82 years old, after all. Indulge me."

"Don't blow me off with your clever jokes," said Bramante. "You'll bury us all."

Laetus slid his glass away and looked straight ahead. "You are my friend Bramante, and I admire you greatly, but we disagree." In a deliberate, measured way he then said, "You are wrong. I don't have to make a choice or, as you say, take a stand. I don't have to because I don't accept the alternatives you present. Why is it either the new Church or the old? Because you say so? Because your *patron* says so? You have your rules Bramante. And for you that is marvelous. You can barricade yourself inside your fortress of formulas, equations, theories and principles. The rest of us live in a messier world than that. You may do what you do with utmost grace and skill. You may hit every note perfectly. But in the larger context—in the world we all inhabit—I regret to say that you may be entirely out of tune. Because you have followed your rules and laws you have convinced yourself that everything you do is absolutely right. You have elevated the tools of your trade to something akin to Holy Writ. You may believe that your formulae, your principles, your learning, are gospel, but in truth they are merely your tools. Not to be crass, my friend, but would it be so different if the boys and girls for sale in the *Largo Argentina* were to expound a gospel based on their wigs, perfumes, dyes and unguents?"

"And now he's calling me a whore!" bellowed Bramante like a wounded ox, stunned.

"If the shoe fits," Laetus remarked sliding the glass back to himself . "But you overreact, my friend. My concern is authenticity. You're concern is merely style. I am talking about history. You are creating theater. Your vision, however well intended, however beautiful, is merely an intellectual contrivance. I don't think you can build a foundation for the glorious future you expound on the soft ground of your superficial images once you have eradicated all that has meaning. Call it nostalgia if you will."

"It's late," said Bramante abruptly. There was no point in pursuing the discussion. It was indeed late, too late perhaps. His two apprentices were no longer comatose. Piero's face laid bare for all to see the collapse of his fragile acceptance that everything Bramante did was absolute. Perfect. For that Bramante would never forgive Laetus. Tossing the boy a coin would not mend the damage the old man had done. He could fight back, skewer Laetus as he had done countless times before, get the better of him, win his argument and still lose. Checkmate. This game was over.

"You really should have come to my reading," said Professor Laetus smiling at them all. "I was splendid."

The door to the street banged open. A gust of cool air sent ashes flying. A troop of young barons in black strode across the main room. Taking the stairs to the mezzanine two at a time the hornets swarmed back to their nest. Piero looked up. Ottavio Colonna, a day's dark growth on his lantern jaw, glared down at them. Behind him, through the wide arch, a single silver cloud drifted across the dark evening sky.

5

Via dei Banchi Nuovi

Young Chigi lumbered along the dark Via dei Banchi Nuovi under a thin moon, relieved to see lights shining in the second floor salon. Everyone was still there.

The banks that gave the street its name stood proudly, shoulder to shoulder at the head of the Ponte St. Angelo, or at its foot, depending on one's point of view. The bridge was one of only two in the city that spanned the Tiber. It connected the Borgo, the precinct between the river and the Vatican, with the rest of the world, the nexus between the sacred and the everyday. The Tiber's deep sludge flowed underneath like a thick moat. The bankers positioned their establishments on the worldly side of the river facing the bridge for quite practical reasons. They would be the last stop on the way into the Vatican and the first stop on the way out. On the way in you needed cash. On the way out you did, too.

The street was pitch dark. Young Chigi hurried as best he could, eager to get home to join the game.

Making his way carefully down the dark street, Young Chigi tried to organize the information he was bringing home to his father. As far as he was concerned the evening had been a complete waste of time, and he was not sure that he had anything useful to tell him. The conversation at the tavern was a jumble, two old men needling each other; the professor running on about authenticity and theater; Bramante, haughty and defensive. And that old Fra Juan, he sat like a lump, barely said anything, just nodding his head like a simpleton. Why his father insisted that he invite the old monk to join them was a puzzle. Down the street, the lighted window wasn't far off. And as for those two kids: they might as well not have been there at all; bumps on a log.

Something scurried along the ground. Young Chigi quickly stepped aside to avoid it. The Tiber's rats were black and big as dogs. "Uggh," he shuddered and stumbled forward. His knee struck something sharp. "*Merda,*" he said, shit, and reached out to keep from falling. He leaned against a wall to regain his balance. The street was strewn with rubble: bricks, stones, chunks of plaster and lumber. A maze of small old houses stacked and wedged between and on top of one another, blue, pink, yellow and tan, was being razed to make room for a merchant's grand new palazzo. "Why can't these clods keep the street clear," he muttered, angrily, meaning the construction crew. A sharp pain shot through his leg. "*Merda,*" he said again, shifting his weight. This new palazzo, like his own family's, would be completely different from the old houses. Chigi straightened up and put all his weight on one foot. His father would not be pleased to learn the street was blocked. Leaning on the wall he reached out with his injured leg probing gingerly for a clear path. There was more debris. Or would his father care, he asked himself. He was financing this and many of the other projects in the district, acting as banker and brokering the building materials. 'It's making us money,' his father would say, 'stop whining.'

Proceeding cautiously, young Chigi slid his feet along the ground to avoid stumbling again. The pain subsided. In broad daylight the new palazzi, banking houses most of them, were as opaque as they were now in the dark. There were never women shelling peas and gossiping on their doorsteps every morning as there were in front of the old houses. There were no doorsteps. No windows opened into little rooms revealing tables and chairs, beds and playing children as there used to be. Windowless at ground level, the new buildings' plain walls were like masks that hid everything behind them. The fat young man let the wall guide him toward the light.

When he finally arrived, he rapped the heavy bronze knocker three times. "*Ecco mi,*" It's me, he announced, The sound echoed along the narrow street. The solid, flat door, large enough for carriages and mounted horses to pass, was covered in sheets of studded metal. Palazzo Chigi was typical of the new establishments that were springing up like mushrooms throughout the district. More than simply the august banker's residence and office, the edifice served as the administrative center for his many and far flung businesses. There were accounting rooms, file rooms, secretaries' offices, a vault, a mail room, a translator's office, public rooms for receptions and entertainment, a chapel, a school and a library. On the ground floor there was a stable for horses and a place for carriages. Servants lived in the attic. Barracks near the stalls housed their small private armed guard who protected their persons and their interests. The palazzo Chigi was like the capital of a miniature nation. Waiting for the guard to let him in young Chigi flexed his knee. It would be sore tomorrow.

The party was in full swing when the big young man dropped his massive cloak onto the outstretched arms of a footman. A fountain bubbled in the courtyard. Laughter filtered from the second floor as he stiffly ascended the broad staircase. He was not too late. Ebony and mother of pearl clicked softly on the richly patterned silk table cloth as he waddled in to join his father and their associates in the *salotto*, the card room. He loved the monthly banker's meetings.

Rome's bankers had formed a sort of club, and it was the elder Chigi's turn to host their meeting. The mountainous man sat facing Cardinal Riario. To assure their success merchant families delegated a percentage of their offspring to careers in the Church. Maximillian Fugger, the austere scion of the German banking house sat between them. The thin lipped, gray eyed man controlled almost every business transaction north of the Alps. The sharp tongued Roman financier, Guido Spannochi, sat opposite him, completing the foursome. Their many businesses interlocked.

They fixed prices. They held monopolies on rare products and jealously guarded their sources and trading partners. They lent short-term money against such risky ventures as future shiploads of plunder from Spain's new colonies, and the coming year's crops. They joined or opposed one another as circumstances dictated. Together they exercised considerable influence over the economies of all the European states, and because of that were as powerful, in some cases more powerful, than many. These four were a force neither princes, nor kings, nor the Church itself willingly crossed. All, without exception, were interrelated by blood, marriage or business alliances. Private loans to nephews, cousins, partners and spouses were made and traded, often surreptitiously, tightening the bonds of obligation among them.

Enjoying a relaxed round of dominos and gossip, they did not look up when the younger Chigi entered the room exaggerating his limp. Friendly business rivals during the good times they all endeavored, if not to outdo, at least to match, one another's hospitality, making pleasure of business. It was plain to see that Chigi's hospitality had not disappointed them. Their faces were flushed and their eyes bright from an indulgent evening of rich food and good wine.

The elder Chigi glanced briefly at his son slowly orbiting the table. Looking back to the game he said, "Father Ximenez stopped me at the unveiling. He seemed curious to know the general reaction to the design for the new St. Peter's." A tile clicked. Sharing information was as indispensable to the merchant bankers' success, as was making profitable deals, fixing prices, establishing interest rates, and creating monopolies. Withholding information, of course, had its place, too.

Intently studying the pattern of dots, Cardinal Riario said flatly, "It's brilliant, I'm sure. I was there for the presentation, too."

Fugger with a fast click, "It's bold, very bold, and if you ask me they made a very sound decision."

"Exactly," remarked Spannocchi, the oldest of the group, 'This is good business. Julius is no fool," his hand sliding ivory across silk.

"Not like Borgia you mean?" asked Chigi in his honeyed tone, fishing for information, not looking up from his move. He was referring to Pope Alexander V, a Borgia, a Spaniard, and Pope Julius II's predecessor.

"I guess I do," answered Spannocchi, "But in his defense, Borgia didn't start out as a fool. I always thought he was a fool who was made not born. He was given a lot of encouragement." The men all smiled at that. "No, seriously," he went on, "at the end I had the feeling that it was the support, the unlimited financial support, that really undid him. All the money seemed to transport him and the entire Borgia clan into a realm of unreality."

"To another realm indeed! I wonder which one!" chimed Chigi, innocently.

The men laughed uneasily. The rise and fall of the house of Borgia was still fresh. They could laugh about it now, but it was not so funny at the time. Spannochi had been the late Pope's private banker and, therefore, a partner of sorts in his heart stopping rise and fall.

Spannocchi, laughing, "They were either scaring the shit out of you or making you laugh. Do you remember that famous Carnevale a few years before he died? Alexander, so fat, so ugly, so desperate for anonymity, but wanting so badly to win the prize for best costume, do you remember, he decided to conceal himself by going disguised as two people? Playing to the Roman Academy, who were the judges, he decided to go as the dual Gods: Castor and Pollux. The Academicians were delighted, but when word got out it raised the hackles of those Spanish purists. I can still see it. His entrance was enormous. His costume, two costumes really, was very clever. He really looked like two people. The impression left on the crowd, though, was not that of the paired gods, but rather of two large, not especially attractive women. To make matters worse, everyone thought that the women were those renowned Ostranophagus twins. Do you remember them?" He moved a tile. "I think they may still be around. They came to Rome as girls, or maybe not exactly as girls, but they certainly came to be thought of as girls." He took a sip of wine. "They did a brisk business among that indolent form of life that hovers around the edges of the Holy See." He caught himself, and raised an eyebrow at Riario who was concentrating on his next move. " I was there that night. In spite of the two masks and the clever design of the costume, it was the shoes that gave him away."

When the laughing stopped Chigi remarked, "Seriously, though, you stayed with Borgia through all of it, Spannochi. Loyalty in this business is rare. Present company excluded, of course. Weren't you ever afraid of being taken down with him? Didn't you ever want to jump ship? Cut your losses?

Spannochi, smiling, tilted his head thoughtfully to one side before saying, "I was a little afraid, but only a little. Between us, since it's all ancient history now, I can tell you." He sat back, "when things started to get rocky, an emissary from the Spanish legation and the Court of Castile stepped in and promised to guarantee any loss I might incur. I thought it was nuts and I asked for some proof of their good will. They responded by paying off half the Pope's outstanding debt within a week–in gold."

Riario, clicking a tile, said, " That's only half, so you did cut your losses."

Spannochi, waved off the Cardinal's remark, "No, let me finish. I was also given a share of the booty coming in from Spain's new conquests. I had that commitment on paper."

Chigi, surprised, said with admiration, "No wonder you stuck with them!"

"And the income is still coming in," said Spannocchi.

Riario shook his head in admiration, "And all along I thought you had brass balls! No one's ever offered me a sweetheart deal like that."

"Nor me," said Chigi,

They all laughed again, a different kind of laugh, at once begrudging, admiring and envious. Chigi exchanged a look with his son that told the fat young man to keep his mouth shut.

Spannochi then said, "You've been very quiet Fugger, what would you have done?"

Fugger answered, "With a guarantee like that why would I say no? Papal loans don't usually come secured."

"That's for sure," said Riario raising his glass.

They all drank, as Fugger continued, "No, you gamble on the choice of Heaven or Hell. Heaven and your money back if you go along. Hell on earth if you don't!"

The wine had warmed them all up. Their spirits were high.

Spannochi feeling expansive said, "And another thing: during all that time, guarantees and all, I spread the risk among my friends." Spreading his arms in a mock embrace of them all, the old man blew each of them a kiss.

They threw their heads back and roared like the lions they were, slapping the table and scattering the tiles.

Nearly choking, but not really amused Riario said, "You mean *we* were all funding him without knowing it?

"You and almost everyone else. The Jews were even helping to fund it through small short term notes that kept my cash flowing."

Raising his goblet, Chigi rose unsteadily to his feet and in his warm baritone sang, "Here's to you, Spannochi. I don't know of another banker in Italy who could have pulled that off and kept it a secret." Chigi now knew how to do his deal, what to expect and how to up the ante. He knew that Spain had interceded before, which meant that Spannochi could have absolutely no part in this. Clearly Ximenez must never know that he, Chigi, knew about Spannocchi's deal.

Spannochi in a more thoughtful reflective tone said, "You know, back then it seemed to me that all that money was meant to finance a Spanish takeover of the Church. And I didn't care one way or another." The others nodded having subscribed to the same theory themselves. "But after the beast became uncontrollable, I thought they would cut him off, stop the money and get rid of him. They didn't. They did just the opposite. They gave him more. It was the money that fueled his craziness and his son's, too. Cesare is completely nuts, not to be believed. And the daughter, well I don't have to tell you. The Spanish stoked the fire that consumed their very own Pope with money. The money drove the entire Papal court into a state of frenzied excess. It became a game to see who could be more obscene. I have to say I subscribed to it myself. When I think back . . . I am almost ashamed to have been part of it."

"Almost ashamed" said Fugger, coolly, and they all roared again.

☙

6

The Villa Colona

Pointed stars spiraled wildly in an ink dark sky. His eyes strained to see. His heart pounded. Lightning flashed, outlining distant hills in silver. He blinked. It was dark again, darker than before. The stars one by one winked on, spun slowly and then winked out. A warm sour-smelling mist surrounded him, sickening him. Something cold and dry brushed his leg. The fog was suffocating. He tried to run, but his legs would not move. He held his breath and covered his nose. There was another flash. He watched in stark terror as fiery red veins leapt upward inflating a billowing luminescent cloud that quivered for a moment between buoyancy and collapse, then shrank slowly and disappeared behind the hills. Blackness. A single star arced and then, sighing, fell to earth. Silence. The stars blinked on again and then blinked out. A heavy mass, cold and wet, slammed against his groin from below and dropped him, breathless, to one knee. A gust of hot breath whispered wordlessly into his face. He struck out hard, first with his right arm, then with his left, and then fell forward on all fours. Silence. He then heard the low thud of hooves and the creak of chains and wagon wheels. A cluster of incandescent, blood-shot, spheres bloomed, hissing and sizzling, into the night sky silhouetting an enormous wooden tortoise coming toward him like a domed mountain through the fog. Behind it the sky exploded in clouds of light then went dark. Blinded, he heard it approaching, lumbering, dragging itself, scraping the ground. He tried to cry out, but his mouth was filled with sour earth. He smelled horses. He smelled the tortoise, musty and cold. Threads like spider webs slithered silkily across his face. He smelled shit and heard the snorting of an immense beast pissing heavily on dry ground. Tongues of flame licked at him. Swords of lightning stabbed his guts. Black snakes slipped over his legs like rivulets of dry water. Demons, their spines in flames, reached up and then sank back into the earth blowing sulfurous curses at him and laughing.

Dripping with sweat he bolted awake. Crouching in his rumpled bedclothes, his fists clenched, Count Colonna flailed in torment. "This City is maybe not so eternal after all," he half mumbled, half growled. Behind his high walls he knelt trembling, pressing his eyes to stop the onslaught of images, trying to soothe his fear, quiet his thumping heart. His piles were killing him and his bed stank. He breathed deeply. Shivering, he was unable to move.

"I am a Roman," came the words from far back in his throat. "I am a Roman before I am a Catholic." The words forced themselves from his lips Pressing his fists more deeply into his eyes he felt fear and shame, grief and horror. "What is anathema, anyway? Can Hell be worse than this, night after night?" Cool, damp air scented with pine, laurel and musky earth filled his lungs calming him. Dawn. Thank God. Light would wash away the horrors of the night. "The Old Basilica is my church. We built it," he rasped, "Goddamn it!"

The sky darkened. Horses whinnied and stamped. Spinning stars burst upward in crazy spirals. He smelled the horses, smelled the tortoise, musty and bitter, heard the chains creaking and the stamping of feet. Terror clenched and shook his heart. His body contracted into a tight ball. Silence and blackness. A whisper and a sudden breath in his ear.

"AAAAHH!" he shrieked.

The gentle kiss of his 14 year old granddaughter, Alessandra, woke him. "Nonno, Nonnino, wake up, wake up. I heard you yelling, I thought someone was attacking you!" She shook him gently.

"A TROJAN HORSE!" he croaked, barely able to get the words out, gagging on phlegm.

"Calm down," the child said and perched lightly behind him on the rumpled bed. She wrapped her arms around him. "Poor Nonno." She rested her chin on his shoulder. His hair was damp with sweat.

" The monster was made of wood," he said hoarsely, staring wide-eyed, terrified at the still vivid specter. "It was a city in the shape of a tortoise with domes and pinnacles and lanterns. It was immense. It grunted and snorted and blew flaming clots of snot in all directions. When it suddenly burst open the sky caught fire. Everything turned red. Soldiers spilled out running every which way. I tried to get away. I tried to cry out but my mouth was filled with dirt and it crushed me down like a bug."

"Shhh. Calm yourself. It was just a nightmare. Calm yourself. Try not to think about it." The small, frail girl got up, gathered her nightdress and climbed onto a chair. Pulling open the windows she said. "Look, the sky is becoming light."

"My angel," he said looking at her pale sad face. "My little angel," he said again. He wanted to hold her close the way he did when she was a tiny child. "Thank you, my sweet baby, thank you." His eyes brimmed.

"Come Nonno, look."

Across the valley the day's first golden light stippled the pines on the Janiculum Hill. Fog and chimney smoke rose from the City between. Swallows, darting and swooping, chased away the demons of the night.

&

7

The Church of Santa Maria in Monserrato

Fra Juan sat against the bare wall behind and to the left of Ximenez, noting every word in a tight, tiny script. They were in the priest's sparsely furnished study. Ximenez, head of the delegation from the Spanish Holy Office, austerely dressed in black, asked the fat banker sitting across the dark table, " What is the general consensus, Chigi? I don't mean to put you on the spot, but we in the Church, of course, are all very enthusiastic about Bramante's scheme for St. Peter's. What are people saying? Everyone has seen it by now."

"Everyone in Rome has seen it," sang the elder Chigi, Chigi the Magnificent, as he was permitted to be called, the honor bought and amply paid for. "The design is a marvel. The model itself is a dazzling work of art. As you know, we Romans are hard to impress and even we can't stop talking about it. It's the most extraordinary undertaking the church has made in a thousand years. And, no, you're not putting me on the spot at all. I don't think the reaction is anything you hadn't expected." Smiling, " The troglodytes are opposed to the demolition of the Old Basilica, but we who are not buried in the past see the practical necessity for a new church. The old one's falling apart at the seams." Practical necessity was, truth be told, of little interest to Chigi. Mark ups and fees for handling the transshipments of building materials on the other hand, and the interest and fees for financing the huge project held far more allure. His mind clicked like an abacus.

"How are the intellectuals reacting to it?" asked Ximenez studying every square yard of the portly, ostentatiously dressed man, wordlessly judging him, thinking 'we Romans' indeed. He knew that Chigi was neither a Roman nor hard to impress. He was a lucky bumpkin from Siena.

"Well, according to a cousin of mine, the academics are divided. Those in favor, the literary types, feel a measure of satisfaction knowing that the design is based on principles set down by Vitruvius. You know, the architect to Augustus Caesar. His *Ten Books* are the classical reference, therefore, in their view, an irreproachable basis on which to design the new church, the next best thing to finding a source in the Bible," regretting immediately his poor choice of words, "for architecture, that is."

"Mmmm. And the opposition? What are they saying?"

"There are troglodytes among the literati, too!" Chigi groaned, spreading his heavily draped arms

"Meaning?"

"I'm no intellectual, you understand, and I'm not sure, given my own favorable disposition toward the plan," he mopped his big florid face, "that I can present their point of view clearly. Opponents of the new church, and of the idea of what we call the New Rome in general, take issue with the destruction of the old church and the ancient sites. The old basilica, they say, is a building that itself dates to antiquity. Where is the sense, they ask, in replacing it with a new church that, although built according to rules laid down in antiquity, is still new?" He shrugged. "That is it in a nutshell," and he flapped his pastry puff hands. "Professor Laetus charged into Bramante about that the very night of the presentation at Pompey's." Fra Juan, eyes down, took down every word verbatim. Outside the dull drone of construction noises: clanking iron on stone, clattering carts rumbling over cobblestones, raspy voices barking orders, filled the silence that followed Chigi's last remark. All around blocks had been cleared to make room for new buildings. Construction was ceaseless. New streets were slicing through the maze of the old quarter.

Ximenez, elbows on the table, pressed his lips to his steepled fingers. After a thoughtful moment he said, "There are bound to be malcontents who would oppose change of any sort. We hope that as we proceed people will come around."

Chigi, smiling warmly, lifted a conspiratorial eyebrow and said, "Build it and not only will they come, but they'll come around?"

Ximenez, with a dismissive wave of his hand said, "Exactly. Now on a practical level: are you comfortable managing the financing for this project? It's an enormous undertaking that neither you nor I are likely to live long enough to see completed.

"Let's hope that we will! Anyway, business has a life of it's own and continues in spite of us," he smiled. "As for comfort, I have never doubted the ability of the Church to meet its obligations, if that is what you mean." He shifted his weight to prepare Ximenez for a little bit of resistance. "This, however, on top of all the capital projects the Church has already committed itself to . . . You'll understand if I request some time to think it over. It will require a creative approach.

"And the utmost discretion," snapped Ximenez, standing to signal the end of the meeting.

&

8

Lake Bracciano

The hornets were swarming.

A scouring south wind blew through the camp straining their tents and rousing them. Dust spiraled, leaping along the ground like ghostly dervishes. Racing air fanned their cooking fires, blowing white smoke. Beyond the encampment a chapel bell boomed, its frenzied clanging amplified by the wind, then faded suddenly, drawn away. Branches clattered. Grit scraped. The beaten earth darkened and brightened under the fast moving sky. In the distance the lake's surface quivered like the silver skin of a great fish.

Count Colonna awoke to the roaring wind and the clanging bell. His tent strained against the wind. He tasted lemons, lavender and sage in the rough air. He panicked, remembering where he was and then lay back and breathed deeply. He had slept well for the first time in months. He felt like a soldier again. Wincing, he rose stiffly onto one elbow. Pain shot through his shoulder. He opened the tent flap. The gritty wind blasted his face. He was here to make peace. Peace. The word, the idea itself, grated.

He looked out. Dozens of tents were arranged in two files like an armed camp. Peace. It looked more like war.

He was not the first one up. Ottavio, his nephew sulked near the cooking fire. Sleeping on the ground, his old uncle snoring raggedly in his ear, was not his idea of a night out. Across the way their host, Giordano Orsini, Duke of Bracciano, thin and weathered, smoke swirling around him, sat staring into the dying coals of his fire. Outside their tents the others waited in silent groups of two and three.

Ottavio moved to help his uncle. Withering him with a fierce glare the old Count said gruffly, "I'm fine. Stay where you are," refusing Orsini the satisfaction of watching him dragged out of his tent like an old dog.

Orsini looked away. Seeing his rival crippled and in pain would have once been satisfying. The time for such gloating was past now. He stood. Acknowledging no one, Orsini walked the length of the camp. He stopped at the last tent and turned back. Facing the camp, standing ramrod straight, he made it clear, without a word, that it was time to start.

They had come from southern Tuscany, Umbria, Latium, Abruzzo and Rome. Traveling by night in small parties of two and three to avoid being seen, fording streams and following narrow mountain roads in darkness, pitching camp and sleeping during the day was not their custom. Unaccompanied by servants or guards, plainly dressed, displaying no colors or crests, they had arrived the previous evening, exhausted and inconvenienced, expecting to find accommodation suitable to their station at Orsini's castle overlooking the lake. Instead, intercepted on the road by the Duke's guard,   the representatives of central Italy's most illustrious families were brought to this remote place, more an armed camp or a bandit's lair than the setting for a convocation of titled barons.

Colonna rose stiffly, as Ottavio stood by, ready to assist. A pale sun barely brightened the morning as the men, hesitating, followed Orsini to a compound of rude stone buildings beyond the camp. There, between a three-story house and a small chapel that faced each other across an overgrown courtyard, a broad open shed had been swept out. Inside, tables of rough- hewn planks were arranged in a large square. Dust and dry manure mixed with the smell of hay. Orsini went in and took a place on one side. Count Colonna followed, limping noticeably and stood at the table across from him. Hesitantly the others gathered around. Outside, chestnut trees tossed from side to side like rag mops, brushing and scraping, their leaves rattling in the dry wind. Orsini looked calmly at each man, sizing them up. In a reedy voice he said simply, "I am grateful that you have come."

The men were more wary than offended by Orsini's cool appraisal. They were on their guard, prepared for subterfuge, or an ambush, possibly mayhem. None had reason to trust the others. No reason, certainly, to trust either Orsini or Colonna, who stood facing one another monumentally across the table. Their two families had been feuding for generations. Their ancestors, their fathers and they themselves had schemed and connived for centuries to control the Papal State. They had debased each other's names. They had devoted their lives to lying, cheating and betraying one another for political advantage by forging expedient alliances with all the families represented at the table, adopting political positions and adhering to them fanatically for only as long as was necessary to accomplish their material purposes. All present were aware of the history and the potential for danger. Anything could happen, and yet they had come.

Orsini, sounding worn said, "You are the only people on the face of God's earth to whom I may confess," as a violent gust scraped a branch across the yard.

Count Colonna felt his nephew Ottavio tense.

"I will not lick my wounds or whine about what has befallen me," Orsini said evenly.

Count Colonna, uncomfortable standing, shifted his weight. Orsini had been excommunicated. Seeing his adversary shaken by the Pope's decree surprised him. Colonna himself had come to view Papal retribution as part of life's natural ebb and flow, like spring floods or lightning: inevitable, it happened every now and then. That was the risk. Everyone knew full well, too, that such decrees were capricious and reversible. When you paid the Pope his price for forgiveness and confessed your wrongdoing, it was over. The decree would be lifted and you would resume doing business as before. Simple. But this affair between the Pope and Orsini was different. Orsini had been caught advising an enemy on matters damaging to the Pope's strategic interests, and this time not just the Duke, but every member of his family, man, woman and child of them, were condemned to eternal damnation; they and all their descendants after them sentenced to Hell everlasting because of his treachery. Colonna shrugged it off when he first heard the news, as merely a particularly expensive indulgence that would have to be paid, and was amused by Orsini's embarrassment. On reflection he saw it as a warning. If the Orsini's, who Colonna always viewed as Papal toadies, could be so disrespected what was in store for him? On further reflection he wondered if it all wasn't a ruse. He would find out. Looking into Orsini's almost colorless gray eyes, seeing his rival's genuine distress, Colonna felt sympathy, and even found himself grudgingly envying Orsini his naive belief that such a piffling thing as a Papal condemnation still mattered.

His head high Orsini glared at them. In a deep rasp he growled, "But I do mean to tell you, gentlemen, that excommunication and eternal damnation by that fucking madman mean nothing to me!"

Leaning forward he then pounded the table with both fists, *"Excommunication!? Can Hell be worse than being humiliated by the Ladies of the Church who are selling our Italy to the highest bidder?!"* He pounded the table again, and then, his anger building, he banged it again and again and again.

Ottavio leaned forward suddenly and shouted, *"NO!"* and banged the table in his turn.

Their reticence vanished as if sucked out of the shed by the roaring wind. One by one the men pressed forward and shouted, "NO!" pounding their fists on the table like a drumbeat, "NO ... NO ... NO!"

Orsini lowered his head. His scarred hands, balled into fists, were shaking. The drum beat persisted, "NO ... NO ... NO ... !" its volume and cadence building. He looked across at Colonna.

When the pounding and the chanting gradually subsided and there was no sound but the wind Colonna leaned forward and growled, "NO!," his eyes flashing, stunning them. Throwing his head back he then roared "NO!" again, like a lion, and pounded the table with his gnarled fist.

The pounding resumed, "NO ... NO ... NO ... !" measured at first then rising to a thundering crescendo.

Orsini raised a hand. When they were silent he said, "Good." And then with a fierce expression, "It is time for us to do something about it!" Shouts of approval greeted his words. The pounding resumed. Raising his hand he called out gruffly, "But first, we have work to do. Who is our enemy!"

"The Pope!" Ottavio cried out.

Flatly Orsini said, "Perhaps," and motioned for them to sit down. Eager now to participate, aware of each other's heat, their eyes were bright. "Before we name our enemy, as you suggest, Colonna, we need to know ourselves, who we are. We are friends and enemies. We share the same blood and soil. Most of us, however, have never met face to face. To start, I propose we go around the table and introduce ourselves." Not waiting for concurrence he commanded, "Annibaldi, if you would, please begin."

Count Colonna leaned over and whispered gruffly to Ottavio, "When it comes to us you do the honors—keep it short."

Annibaldi, feverish, rose to formally and at length, thank the Duke for his leadership and hospitality. He commended his courage, the nobility and greatness of his family and shared his dismay at the Pope's disrespect. He then proceeded to enumerate the holdings, offices, accomplishments, virtue, and titles of his own patrimony, resurrecting, lest anyone dare forget, the long forgotten, possibly imaginary, ancestor who was a close associate of St. Thomas Aquinas. Next a representative of the Buoncompagni family, jumped to his feet, offering similar salutations, thanks and compliments before reciting at excruciating length his family's contributions to the fields of science and mathematics. The Caetani followed similarly.

When his turn came Ottavio rose. "I am Ottavio Colonna," he said simply. "This is my esteemed uncle, Count Prospero," and sat back down.

"Good," whispered the old Count, satisfied.

The Conti spoke next. After them the endlessly feuding Corsi and Crescenzi families were shocked to find themselves sitting side by side, realizing it only when Corsi rose to speak. Representatives of the Frangipani, Paparveschi, Ruspoli, and Savelli clans, each in their turn stood and announced themselves. Some had seen better days, having little now to show for their pedigrees besides their haughty bearing and cultivated accents. In all they numbered more than thirty.

"A proud and noble assembly," Orsini said after the last introduction, "I am comforted, as I am sure you are to hear our glorious histories and greatness recounted all at once and under one roof. We all know who we are and from where we come," he said, pulling his shoulders back and looking at each one, "but we are not here to proclaim our past glory. Our future is at risk." Colonna nodded gravely, agreeing, as did others. "And why is that?" Orsini asked. "Why is our future at risk?—I will tell you. You shout 'The Pope!' You shout his name and bang the table." He looked sharply at Ottavio. "I say no. No, the Pope has his way because we have forsaken our strengths. We have become weak. We have forgotten that we are a family; that we are Romans," he rapped the table for emphasis. "I am as guilty of this as anyone, perhaps more," he said in deference to Colonna. "We are here to speak frankly for once," The older men bristled at the insult, but staged no umbrage.

Colonna shifted from side to side on the hard bench, impatient to get to the point, "So, what you are saying is, let's cut the posing and the formal crap and get down to business. Am I right?" They tapped their iron rings on the table confirming that he was. "Let's move it. I'm not getting any younger."

Orsini forced a cool smile. " Now, I want to go around the table again. This time I ask each of you to state your reason for coming here. If you had no reason, you would not have come. We need to know where we stand. Who will be first?"

Sighing and with a quick little shrug Crescenzi stood, "Why hold back? Let me be the first one to speak. You know us. For generations my family was at the center of political activity within the highest circles of the Church. We managed nominations for cardinalships and for the Papal throne itself. Everyone remembers the fierce election of 1492 that brought that Spaniard, Borgia, to St. Peter's throne as Pope Alexander VI. After that we were swept aside." Faltering he said, "I had misgivings about coming to this meeting. I still have. For all I know you may be poisoning my well while I am sitting here talking to you." He laughed, a little whinny, to show that he was not serious. When no one reacted he rushed on, "I'm not sure that anything useful will come out of this but what the Hell. The world is changing. We are losing ground." He looked into the rafters searching for words. "Alliances among us have always been temporary. Who knows, this meeting may amount to nothing more than a brief re-union, but I hope we can accomplish something useful."

Orsini asked, "What do you hope to accomplish that would be useful?"

"I see a shift in power to foreigners," said Crescenzi. "Specifically, I would like to see that power shift back to Italians, to us."

Colonna looked skeptical and snorted derisively.

"All right," said Crescenzi, "we're being frank, aren't we? Then, I would like to see power come back to me, me and my family,"

"That's more like it," cackled the old Count getting a few laughs, "Good for you."

Balthasar Boncompagni stood up and began to lecture, "Bear in mind," he intoned, "that, unlike almost every other country, here in the Papal State the Church is not only our spiritual center, but also our governing body. It bears reminding that the Emperor Constantine, more than one thousand years ago gave these lands to the Church and established that relationship." The scholarly Balthasar warming to the rich sound of his own voice continued, "It bears reminding, because we often overlook the fact that we do not have our own King or a government separate from the Church. Our esteemed colleague, Crescenzi, just described a significant shift: the Church is controlled by foreigners. Now foreigners, and by foreigners I mean 'not us,' may be motivated to take control of the Church for any number of reasons. Spain, for example, may want to reform the moral authority of the Church more to her liking. France may want to prevent her from doing that. The Emperor in Germany, we know, wants to consolidate his influence once and for all. But regardless of their individual reasons the outcome for us will be the same." Lulled and put off by his pedantry the men were not prepared for his conclusion. "As the Church becomes more international, more dominated by foreigners, we become dominated by an occupying, foreign power. We, the traditional backbone of the Papal State, risk becoming a sort of colony on our own lands. You asked why I came here. I'm here because I don't want that to happen."

There was a rumble around the table as his words sank in. Ottavio reddened in anger. Under the table Count Colonna dug his fingers into his nephew's thigh to keep him quiet.

Umberto Annibaldi, whose family also had been thoroughly intertwined with the Church, was recognized, "That's very provocative: a colony on our own lands. That's what you said, Buoncompagni, but come now –really. That's absurd. This is the center of Western Christendom. There are no invading armies holding swords over our heads. We are not naked savages to be brought out of the wilderness in shackles to the true faith."

Boncompagni replied, "There has been a great shift in wealth in Europe. Spain's conquest of the New World has brought her riches beyond belief. That wealth, I believe is enabling her to, quite simply, buy the Church and, I will say it again, colonize Italy."

"And, if you follow Boncompagni's logic, we are part of the package Spain thinks she's buying!" snapped Count Colonna.

Orsini was about to silence him, but after a quick assessment changed his mind. Colonna was an old crank, a cantankerous throwback, crusty, reactionary and nostalgic for the soldier's life, all noise and bluster, but he represented a generation of *condottieri* that was held in great affection.

"I have a dream, a nightmare that comes back night after night, ever since I saw the model for the new St. Peter's. I think I am in Hell. You all know me. I know that some of you think I'm an old cracked pot, and maybe you're right, but let me tell you; in that dream I see the new church as a Trojan Horse, a Roman siege machine built like a monstrous tortoise." His eyes widened seeing the beastly contraption bearing down on him. "Just like you said, Annibaldi. The foreigners are buying the Church and using it to invade us. I wake up and the nightmare is still with me. Now, I'm listening to you and I think, this is not just something that might happen. It's not just a bad dream. It *is* happening. In the dream I am afraid that it is over, that we had, that I have, been overtaken; that it is too late; that we are defeated." The wind scraped a tumble of dry weeds against the chapel door across the yard. A thin cat scurried for shelter.

Orsini asked, " Colonna, do you truly think it's too late to do anything?"

The old man shrugged and grunted before saying plainly, "I don't know."

Orsini looked around and slammed the table, "Is it too late?! Is it?!"

Count Paparveschi's hand shot up. Short of breath he jumped to his feet and said frantically, "OK, for once in my life let me tell the truth. So help me God, for me it virtually *is* over. I'm practically broke. We live like paupers on our own estates, and now I'm told that I am supposed to pitch in and pay my share for a new Church. I was going to try to do something even if it meant going deeper into debt, but now—I see what everyone is saying–we might as well be paying for our own hangman. And if I am not mistaken we are the ones who paid for the church that's still standing there. The last time I was there it looked fine to me. It wasn't in any worse shape than my house." He took a quick gulp of air," I'm paying for the Church's wars, we all are, which unless I am missing something, have not helped me one bit. My house is falling down around me. I feel like a servant, shackled to the Church, obligated to it. I have no doubt about why you, Orsini, took the action you did when you sided with France. Was it France? Or was it Venice?" He shook his head, manically, "What difference does it make? You made the best deal you could. I understand that. But, me, I'm sinking. We're planters not soldiers. My family hasn't fielded a force of men in over a hundred years. I'm trapped." Stumbling over his words, "I'll be honest," he panted, touching his chest, his heart thumping, "being here scares me to death. The reason I went into hock in the first place was to pay the Church to protect myself from all of you."

Bernardo Ruspoli broke in, talking angrily over Paparveschi, "My family has taken sides, too," he shouted, "We all have. We've been with the Pope against the Emperor, and we've been with the Emperor against the Pope, but in truth the choice never meant anything. Our interests were always selfish. One of us, my father or one of my uncles, sticks a wet finger in the air to see which way the wind is blowing and then tries to buy time choosing the most favorable breeze. My reason for being here is selfish, too. I want to survive. I want my family, our way of life and our name to survive. I don't want to be the last of my line. I don't want our noble history to be erased on my watch. I am not interested in being a minor nobody in a Spanish or German or French province. That is not acceptable!"

Orsini attempted to regain control, "Colonna, you said that the new church was like a Trojan Horse." Looking around the table he asked, " Does anyone else see it that way?" his gray eyes searching.

Paparveschi, faster and more shrilly, " That's what I was trying to say. I think he's right. It will destroy our old Church, the one our ancestors built and defended and worshipped in. This new building doesn't represent us at all. You could say that it's proof that the Pope is marching over us. Colonna, your description of it as the Trojan Horse is right. Our traditions no longer seem relevant. For me, for us, because I mean my family and me," he gasped for air, " the ability to participate as a person of standing is no longer possible. I see these fancy new palaces going up, and it's a world that's beyond me. Again, I confess that part of the reason I'm dead broke is because we were sucked into trying to keep up with all the changes going on around us. My daughters needed the latest fashions. My wife needed to hire the latest architect to do the most up to date things to our villa. We had to have portraits of our children done by the newest and most fashionable painters. I can't tell you what a fool I have been . . ."

Orsini raised a hand, embarrassed for and by him, "Paparveschi. We have all been fools."

Obsessed, Paparveschi rushed on, ". . . I began to doubt my own judgment. I wanted to put a stop to the extravagance. I said to myself, is this a trick? Am I being duped? Is this whirlwind of change meant to ruin me? Or am I just a failure? Have I mismanaged my wealth? Am I in this fix because of my own stupidity? I truly don't know. But I can tell you that the turning point for me was the day I heard my wife and me talking. I know, I know, it sounds strange, but it felt as if I were outside my own body. I heard our conversation as a stranger would, listening at the door. I heard us describing the kind of marriage we wanted for our youngest girl. We were talking about her the way we would talk about a goat or a cow. We were talking about a suitable marriage for her, sure, but at the heart of it we were describing her attributes and her shortcomings and trying to find a way to peddle her for the best price we could get. It was as if we were about to march her up to the auction block and bid her off. I am disgraced to make this confession, but it's true. I was treating my own child like a farm animal that was for sale. I was ready to pimp her, trade our name, to the highest bidder to pay off some of my debts. You called the new Church a Trojan Horse," His voice braking, "It is . . . It is . . . It represents an enemy that has killed me and my family as surely as if we were mowed down by an invading army."

Aware of Ottavio's building rage at Paparveschi's show of fear and defeat Colonna dug his claw like fingers deeper into his thigh, "Just stay put," he growled.

Young Savelli cut in, "We are being treated like fools!"

Boncompagni, dropping his pose yelled out, "Colonna's right! It's time to wake up. Our power, our prestige, our property and wealth have been steadily eroded for a long time now. Their plan to demolish the church is the last straw. It is so blatant, so bald; they know we are weak. It shows they are ready to finish us off."

"That's because we are fools!" growled Colonna, releasing his grip and slamming both hands on the table. He was thinking of his granddaughter, Alessandra, while Paparveschi was talking. "God damn it! When did this happen? When did it happen that the Church and the shopkeepers took control? To be people of standing we have to spend ourselves into penury. For what? To show that we are equal to these bankers, these money lenders? My goddamned wife nags me to death." He waved as if to ward off protests. "No. No. Don't get me wrong. She's the love of my life. Don't laugh." Someone laughed. "In her day she was the most beautiful girl in Rome. But now she's making me crazy. Last month she says to me," in a mocking singsong falsetto he whined, "'We should have a portrait painted of Alessandra. She's our little granddaughter.' I looked at her. '*Beh*,' I said 'What for?'," his voice cracking again in falsetto, "Because,' she says, 'Caterina Fugger had a portrait done of her daughter.' '*Va fa'n'goul* Caterina Fugger and her daughter,' I said! 'But there are young painters around who are still cheap, not like Leonardo,' she says back to me. '*Va fa'n'goul*, Leonardo,' I said! All this crap because Leonardo painted a portrait of that stupid looking Giacondo girl, the one he carries around with him all the time." He spat thickly into the dust. "Even her husband wouldn't buy it. Give me a break," he railed, "Since when do they call the tune?" and coughing, spat again.

"Don't hold back, *Segno!*" laughed Ruspoli, tapping the table.

Boncompagni in his plummy voice announced, "There is a horrible logic to it when you stop and think, "These people, these merchant-bankers, lend us the money to buy the goods they sell us at a hefty profit, earning the interest on the credit they extend to us. Change is in their interest. Every change in fashion forces us, who are, frankly, like sheep and go along with it, to buy in, pay for the goods and buy their latest confabulations on credit? We are weakened and they are strengthened by our susceptibility to frivolity."

Crescenzi, calmly, "It's a strategy that has worked for a longer time than you may realize. Speaking from the inside. My family, you may or may not know, was in the inner circle that engineered the election of church officials. Their primary strategy was to keep the titled families, us, feuding with one another to divert us from what was being engineered. The Church has been a master of divide and dominate for a long time. They have a genius for being able to encourage the temporary alliances that give the appearance of legitimacy to their political dealings. You could say that this is just the latest in a long line of diversions that, perhaps is so obvious that it can no longer be concealed. Keeping court life ever changing and expensive is part of the strategy."

"It's a conspiracy to ruin us!" Ottavio shouted jumping to his feet. Branches scraped against the side of the shed. Side conversations erupted around the table. The hornets were buzzing. All were talking at the same time, yelling in each other's faces, their words colliding. "They keep upping the ante!"…"A conspiracy?"…"Conspiracy or not, if it functions like one what's the difference?"…"It is destroying us!"…"Why has it worked? We need to know so we can resist."…"We must fight back!" Ottavio was gesturing, waving, smacking the table, pumping the air with his clenched fists …"I feel obligated to go along, so that my family can hold its head up. I can't have my wife and my daughters looking like fools or bumpkins."…"Those bastards!"…"Our ancient City is being leveled to build a new one. Our sacred hills are being carved away."… Wind swelled the shed like a deep breath. "Common pricks!"…"We are reduced to running a few steps behind the coach, pathetically trying to keep up."… "And we're losing ground."…NO! … NO! … NO! …

The drumbeat resumed . . . "And then feeling like fools for it!" Pounding they yelled; roared what was, at the same time, beneath and beyond words, a battle cry, an eruption of pent rage, humiliation, fury and refusal . . . "NO . . . NO . . . NO . . . !" Savelli shouted to Crescenzi, "If I follow your line of thinking, Crescenzi, if I accept that what you say is true, and I am not sure I do, then I am forced to ask, if the enmity among us was fabricated as a diversion, what else was?"

Colonna sagged. Orsini looked at him with the patient eyes of a hawk.

Boncompagni shouted to be heard above the ranting. Scouring grit blew through the shed. "I know what you are saying, Colonna, the last straw for me was when Riario hired Bramante to design yet another one of those obscene palazzi." He snorted, "I could care less about the palace *per se*," and waved as if shooing away a fly. "I am not an envious man" he stressed, "not at all. What stunned me was the disinternment of Saint Damasus' remains, the fact that they would violate consecrated ground to make way for a palace. A palace." He reared up very high, "I was deeply shaken by that. I still am."

Butting in, Crescenzi tried to calm him with a scholarly explanation, "But of course, there was never any certainty that Damasus was really buried there. Some accounts have his grave out at S. Agata. Others locate it somewhere out along the Via Ardeatina. No one really knows. I don't think you should be concerned."

"That's not the point," Buoncompagni said imperiously, like an orator shouting a proclamation, "The site was associated with him and his life and works. We believed it to be his resting place and venerated it as such. That is what is important."

Ottavio, enraged leaned in, "We are being erased, made to disappear, just as Rome herself is being leveled and rebuilt! We are being ripped from our soil and thrown down to bake and die in the sun. You're pimping your daughters for money. We are selling our titles. We are marrying our girls off to these common swine!"

Count Colonna shifted uncomfortably on the bench and bellowed loudly enough for everyone to hear, "My wife is looking for a good match for Ottavio here. A good match, face it, means a girl with money." Ottavio turned on his uncle furiously and scowled. "He'll wind up with some

soggy little cunt from Genoa, the daughter of some newly minted merchant, so we can enjoy her money to pay off the debts we owe to Chigi.
That fat slob."

"Her money!? Your money!!" someone yelled out.

Colonna snapped back, "Those fucks!" Still worked up about the
portrait, "And did I tell you? Wait! Wait! You have to hear this! My wife
actually went to that painter's studio. Even after I yelled at her. He showed
her his new pictures. Get this. One has the Pope witnessing the miracle of
a bleeding Eucharist 200 years ago. I know Julius isn't a kid any more, but
come on, 200 years ago? And then she said there was another one showing the Pope expelling Syrian invaders from the Temple in Jerusalem. When
did he do that? A million years ago? She said it was beautiful. What's this,
I said, The Pope as this, the Pope as that. It's not enough for him just to be
the Pope any more he's got to control all of history now, too? The artist
told my wife that all the people in the pictures were the Pope's friends.
He told her they all kicked in hefty sums to be "immortalized" at these
great moments in history.

"Now he's selling history!" someone called out.

"He'll sell anything!" came the response.

"I said to her, the next thing your going to tell me is that he's working
on a picture of the Pope as Jesus, Mary and Joseph, all three of them at the
same time. *Porca Miseria!* I can see it now. The holy family, all three of
them, with long white beards."

The men threw their heads back and laughed, pounding the table.
Orsini remarked coolly, "It sounds to me as if the New St. Peter's is not
the only Trojan Horse."

Ignoring Orsini's mild attempt to refocus the discussion Count
Colonna continued, " I had to see for myself," He repositioned himself,
elbows on the table. A shutter slammed against the wall across the yard.
"I went to the chapel the artist is working on. You know me. I just barged
in to see what he was doing." He took a deep rattling breath, "I nearly
died. He's painting over all the old frescoes: The Signorelli's, the
Perugino's, the della Francesca's. If I'm not mistaken we paid a hefty sum
for them." He looked around the table. No one contradicted him. "Remember how they made us pony up for all that artwork?" The older men

nodded. The younger men waited. "Well," he leaned in closer, "It's not there any more. They're gone . . . Do you want to know what's there instead?" He looked across into Orsini's cool gray eyes, "I'll tell you what's there: pictures of naked bodies swimming around in the air, swirling and tumbling all over the place. They all look like wrestlers. The ones that aren't naked are dressed like rich bankers in clothes that I can't afford to buy." He grabbed his cloak and showed them a worn patch near his elbow. "And the women he has floating around up there on the walls, get this, they're all blonde. Yeah, blonde, sure," he grabbed his crotch, "What the fuck is going on?" Ottavio crossed his ankles. "And he showed that stuff to my wife, the blondes, the naked wrestlers tumbling around. In what? I guess it was supposed to be Heaven? Heaven for who? It's created Hell for me. My wife saw that shit. I've been married for 48 years and now I'm ashamed to take my clothes off in front of her."

Orsini got up, and walked away from the table. Colonna stopped ranting and pulled Ottavio back to his seat. With his back to them Orsini looked out into the dry glare and waited for them to calm down. A plainly dressed servant, clutching a mail pouch, was crossing the courtyard. Leaning into the wind, he tried to bow before hurrying out of sight. Orsini turned to the table, "We set out to describe our enemy," he said raising his reedy voice above the sighing wind, " You talk about paintings, buildings, fancy clothes. Is that it? Is that all?"

Count Colonna wanted to hit him. "Those are the weapons, the arsenal," he growled. He was stiff from sitting for so long and irritable. "They are aimed at all of us," angry at having been drawn out to state the obvious. He stood up and stretched. "I don't know about you, but I for one could use a piss," and limped out into the turbulent glare, tugging at the seat of his pants. " Let's take a break."

Ottavio followed his uncle, glad to feel the wind beat his face.

&

9

"What now?" Ottavio whispered to Count Colonna, his uncle, as they reentered the shed. The wind had died leaving a calm bright afternoon. Outside servants were striking the mess tent and clearing away the remains of lunch. The old Count avoided looking at Orsini who had already taken his place. Overhead a lazy fly buzzed loudly in the rafters. "What now?" Ottavio repeated. The old Count thumped his nephew's shoulder fondly, but didn't answer. Goat bells clanked beyond the wall. Whispered conversations ended as the men took their places. "It's like being served a poison dessert. You can't stop eating it and you know it's killing you," Paparveschi, was talking, muttering, but not to anyone, as he came back in. "It's extortion. Either you go along or . . ."

"Or what?"

Ottavio didn't see who asked. Nearby, water splashed noisily into a channel that fed the lake. Unable to endure the silence Ottavio looked around and demanded, "Now what?" His uncle moved away from him and sat down. It was merely a matter of time before the hornets would start stinging one another. Ottavio was supposed to keep his mouth shut and listen. Orsini sat calmly watching the servants clean up. Ottavio raised his voice, "Where do we go from here? This morning we banged the table and made wise cracks . . . Now what?" Devising every small way to not respond, the men ignored him: examining their fingernails, brushing away the buzzing fly, glancing at the floor for things they had not dropped. " What is this? No one has anything to say?"

"Cretin," someone said under his breath, not meaning to be heard.

Ottavio lunged across the table, "What then?!" the first sting. "You have something to say?! Say it! Why are we here? Do we fight or not?" With unexpected speed his uncle reached out and yanked him back. "This is bullshit!" Ottavio cried, red-faced, throwing off the old man's grip. "Let's go." He grabbed the old Count by the arm and hauled him to his feet. "Let's get out of here."

The Count turned to him, his face transformed by rage. Thrusting one foot behind he shoved Ottavio back. When he began to fall the old man grabbed Ottavio's arm and reflexively spun him around. Ottavio hit the floor face first, the old Count's boot rammed into his spine. "We stay," Colonna growled. "You don't give the orders."

Squirming Ottavio shouted, "This calls for war!" His uncle's boot pressed down harder. "We're losing everything and you all just sit here! Was I the only one paying attention this morning? This calls for war!" Count Colonna's fierce expression did not concede to Orsini that his nephew was now fair game, nor did it admit that Ottavio was an idiot. It neither requested that the young man be excused, nor did it apologize.

"You think this calls for war," Orsini said blandly. "On whom would you declare it? This morning, Colonna, you talked about an invading Trojan tortoise." He chuckled. "Shall we field an army to march into St. Peter's and hack that extravagant model into splinters? Won't that teach everyone a lesson? You complained about the high cost of living, about drowning in debt. What shall we do . . . ? Deploy a force to butcher the bankers? That can be done, as you well know. You talked about frescoes," shaking his head in amazement and disgust, " . . . frescoes showing naked, perfect bodies that offended your sensibilities, and made you feel ashamed of your droopy old ass. Aah. I know. Why don't we arm an infantry with buckets of paint, then? Colonna, you said these things were our enemy's arsenal. Bramante's work force is more than two thousand strong. Shall we capture their bricks?

Colonna released Ottavio, who scrambled to his feet, humiliated, slapping dust from his knees. To his uncle's relief he did not stomp out but retreated to his place at the table wiping his nose. The old Count sat down heavily, spent from the physical exertion.

"We could defile the art and look like fools." Orsini made a point of not looking at anyone, speaking as if to himself, "Or perhaps we should ambush the Pope and hold him for ransom." The temperature in the shed rose. Sensing it Orsini laughed, "You like that one."

"Who would pay to have him released?" grumbled Colonna.

"No one I suspect. Not the French. No, I doubt it. They'd install a Pope of their own . . . wouldn't be the first time. The Emperor? He would do the same. And then what? We'd be stuck with an old Pope nobody wants."

"We'd have to kill him." It was Ottavio, venomous.

"Making us what? Do I have to tell you? Pope killers, murderers ripe for attack by all those who calculated the odds and chose not to pay the ransom; all those who would not hesitate to feign outrage as an excuse to wipe us out and claim our lands. No, Ottavio, war, I think, is not so simple, nor is murder.

"Is this leading anywhere?" Count Colonna slumped forward, his elbows spread wide, embarrassed more for, than by Ottavio.

"It is." Orsini said curtly, "I think rather, that our circumstances require us to declare peace."

Colonna blinked in disbelief.

"Peace?—How is that different from surrender?" It was Ottavio, challenging and smug.

"Surrender?"

"You're proposing we send up a white flag."

"I proposed nothing of the sort."

"You said . . ."

"I said that I think our circumstances require us to declare peace."

Ottavio reddened and began to respond, but finally, to his uncle's relief said nothing.

"You are jumping to conclusions, Ottavio. The peace I suggest would be among ourselves." Someone tapped his ring lightly on the table, hear, hear, in support. Orsini turned to them. Opposite, Colonna hunched forward, his gnarled fingers spread wide on the rough boards, and looked hard into the pale gray eyes of the man he had never met on the battlefield. In a long life of mutual conflict the essential symmetry of the two of them facing each other, their fair weather allies arrayed around them, as now, had never once occurred. It had taken humiliation and puny necessity to draw them from the shadowy patterns of their ancient enmity. He regretted that he would never see their two armies at dawn, like chessmen, blocked in exquisite formation on a misty green field; he regretted never having engaged in honorable, ordered combat with Orsini, a deep regret surging from the realization that truce, or peace, or whatever this would lead to, marked the end of them. Orsini had realized it first. So be it. But having needed to come here, being left no choice other than the concession that joining forces for their mutual defense was the only functional alternative meant, without saying so, defeat. Sagging, sore from the exertion of subduing Ottavio, who sat there sullen and smudged with dust and manure; furious at having had to do so, as if to prove in front of everyone that the young man's instincts, developed and encouraged, as his own had been, were now obsolete. The lazy fly buzzed near his ear. He slapped at it. Overhead a pigeon flapped dust. Colonna clenched his left hand into a fist. Without a word he tapped his iron ring on the boards twice, lightly: hear, hear. Hesitantly the others followed suit, tapping their rings, submitting, each in his own way and for his own reasons to the need for unity, if not peace. The sun baked courtyard was now empty and still.

"Let's look at our situation." Colonna finally said, after a long silence. "How will this peace, as you call it, be viewed from outside?"

"That will be up to us." It was Orsini.

"The Pope will see it as surrender." muttered Ottavio, resentful, seeming to have shrunk in his black leather cuirass.

Looking at Ottavio as if at an idiot, Orsini said, "Think it through. The Pope has Spain pressing from the south. The Emperor threatens to cross the Alps and invade us from the north at any time. Then there are the French. Their last incursion, I daresay, should still be fresh in his imagination. It is in mine." His brother had died, imprisoned in the bowels of the Castel St. Angelo for conspiring with the enemy. "The Turks are out there somewhere in the wilderness." He waved vaguely at the blanched, dusty courtyard. "And we are here in his lap. Our history of fighting with each other, which suited past administrations according to you, Ruspoli, doesn't serve him now. United we offer him two advantages: the first would be as a united force to put in the field against either or all of his foreign adversaries, if he has to. The second would give him a docile, unified Papal State to turn over to whichever one he may be forced to accommodate, or to the highest bidder, as you said this morning, Boncompagni. Our peace gives him the option of thinking of us either as troops or as chattel. That's how the Pope will see it."

"This is insane! You want us to dig our own graves! You are truly mad! This "peace" of yours is just a sorry excuse for total capitulation. You are leading us to slaughter. It's a trap to deliver us to the Pope in exchange for lifting your excommunication!" Stinging again, Ottavio looked to his uncle for support.

Count Colonna, fed up, slammed the table, "Shut up and listen! We are talking about the way others will see it. Think!" and turned away from him to say, "This morning, Paparveschi, you described our situation in terms of a battle, a battle lost." He spoke gruffly. "I say yes, let's treat our situation as a battle; not one that is lost, but one we can win." A vegetal stink rose from the men, excitement at the prospect of combat mixed with fear. Tasting war's long absent, sweet bitterness coat his tongue Colonna said, "Let's assess the field." He planted his arms on the table, a general working through a plan, "Hasn't the Pope gotten himself into a squeeze play? The excommunication of your family, Orsini, was a feeble attempt to get at us. By "us" I mean all of us sitting here." They were paying attention. "He wants us all out of his hair. He figures we will shrink back in fear of having the same thing happen to us. And face it. It could happen. To engage in battle with him we all have to be ready to face damnation and risk bringing our families down with us."

"I think we all know that now," someone said gravely.

Colonna barked, "If anyone does not accept that possibility, now is the time to leave." It was an offer, not a dare.

No one moved.

"You are all willing to take that risk?" He asked it not as a challenge, but as a simple question. He asked it as much of himself as of them. Without a word each nodded his assent.

Ottavio, petulant, " We're giving the Church all the cards. As soon as he finds out about this, the Pope will claim it as a victory."

Orsini ignored him, focusing his pale gray eyes elsewhere and said, "We have to present it differently." As if from a faraway place he said, "I say we simply present him with our truce. We offer him nothing but the fact that we have made peace among ourselves. We can dignify it and call it a *Pax Romanum*, a Roman Peace." Smiling he said, "Something portentous sounding that he can use in a decree. Let's see how he responds."

Ottavio, flustered, "I don't follow you. What are you saying?"

"Do I need to repeat the litany of humiliation and degradation we all gave vent to this morning?" The statement was like a soft wind on cooling embers. "Look at it from Julius' point of view." He was thinking aloud more than answering Ottavio. "If I were Pope . . ." Colonna snorted, amused, thinking of himself as Pope. "I would be frightened. I would wonder if the game was up. I would wonder if they are plotting to assassinate me? Have they joined forces with my enemies? Will they offer the French safe passage through their lands, march on Rome and destroy me? I would wonder where I went wrong. I would wonder how I could have misjudged us. He will see, immediately that the Church's strategy of keeping us at each other's throats like crabs in a barrel is over."

"What if he forms another alliance with Spain or Venice and comes after us?"

"He can't afford war any more than we can. The Church's fortunes are committed to his grand public works. That is his arsenal, remember? Besides, he will have no idea of the depth or shallowness of our strength or support. No, he won't take the chance. He will suspect that our Roman Peace is more extensive than it is." He opened his eyes wide, " I say, *Let's offer him our Peace and then give him Hell!*"

It was like a puff of oxygen. The embers ignited. As one, they banged their iron rings raggedly on the planks: once, twice, then again and again in a wild frenzy. Ottavio, looked around, confused. Orsini raised a hand.

Colonna cackling, amused, enjoying the possibilities, feeling like a soldier again, echoed Orsini, "The Pope will like this *Pax Romanum*. He has to keep things quiet on the home front. But we must never proclaim loyalty to him. That would cause havoc among our other allies. We can't have that." He threw his head back and roared hilariously at the new possibilities their truce presented. "He will have to beg for that." This will be *our Pax Romanum*, for us, not for the mother Church or for the Papal State, not for Spain, not for the Venetians or the Emperor or the French, but for us, for Romans!"

The tapping started up again, randomly at first before building to a rhythmic drum beat. They pounded their fists , shouted and laughed; thumping iron, reverberating wood and voices, colliding, barely intelligible. "We'll all be condemned to Hell one way or the other," someone yelled. Order descended into chaos. Colonna and Orsini let the hornets buzz, and sting. "It buys us time!" . . . "Having us feuding with one another no longer is a viable strategy for the Church" . . . "It doesn't work for them anymore" . . . "The feuds and vendettas are not working for us" . . . "You heard him. We wouldn't be in this miserable fix if it had." . . . "Maybe it did work, but now it's time for something else." . . . "How do you mean it worked?! We sided with the emperor. We aided Spain and the King of Naples. Then we allied ourselves once again with the Pope. All we did was squander our resources" . . . "Without our knowing it, for all the wrong reasons it worked." . . . "It didn't work" . . . "But we kept them on their toes!" . . . "You're dreaming!" As the afternoon wore on their mood improved. Their anger, after flashing to the boiling point, slowed to a steady simmer.

"Alright, so accepting the Peace buys us time. What then?" asked Annibaldi.

Orsini looked at him.

"The best strategy for a victory is to not have to fight," said Boncompagni.

"It's worked for them."

"It's cheaper than fielding an army. That's for sure."

"What fuels the fire of their subtle invasion?"

"Money," said someone without hesitation.

"Yes, the ability to spend unlimited amounts of money."

"So?"

"We have to stop the flow of money to the Church."

"How can we do that?"

"Let's explore it." Orsini rapped the table and called them back to order, "Annibaldi, what were you saying?"

"I was about to say that we can certainly stop contributing our own money to the Church by reducing our contributions. Don't buy any new offices. Nowadays they cost more than they bring home, anyway, as a practical matter."

Savelli spoke up, "We can also freeze our support by not underwriting any new works of art or building. Do not commission a new chapel. Do not, I stress, do not, commission those portraits of your granddaughter," wagging a finger at Count Colonna and laughing.

"Don't worry," Colonna said coughing rheumatically and slapping the table.

Boncompagni," But do we control enough to make a difference?"

Colonna struggled with what he was about to say, "Hold on. How about this? We present our *Pax Romanum*, so called, as a humble defeat, a surrender." Surrender–it was not the word the men wanted to hear, nor was "humble." Ottavio stiffened and turned beet red. Colonna said, "Calm down. We're not going to ride in waving a white flag. Just bear with me. What I am saying is, we have to make it clear, without coming out and saying so, that we have come to this truce because we can't afford the cost of conflict; our coffers are drained. We said so. We know so," He struggled to say, "Alright, we cry poverty. We state economic necessity as the reason for coming to terms." He stopped and coughed. Wheezing he said, "No one will be surprised when our contributions start to dry up," He coughed again, choking on the truth, " when we don't buy indulgences or offices. That's the capitulation. If he endorses the Roman peace he can't press for money, too. He can't have it both ways. He's not stupid. He'll realize that he can't squeeze blood from a stone."

"Which is not far from the truth for some of us." It was Paparveschi.

Colonna ignored him. "We have to keep the Pope wary. Crying poverty will make him less inclined to suspect a plot. We want to give every appearance of weakness, of defeat. That is important. The impression that our truce is fragile should be encouraged, so that they treat us with caution and deference. He has to believe that the Peace among us is fragile."

Orsini from across the table, "He will any way. He knows us."

Boncompagni, ever the mathematician, "Do we actually control enough to make a difference? Can anything we do hurt the Church?"

Colonna, " Control? You mean our contributions, or what? As far as control goes, think about it. What do we already control? Make a list. Watch. It amounts to a lot."

"What do you mean? Some of us control nothing. Zip. Zed. Some of us are in hock to these pigs up to our eyeballs. They're the ones in control," whined Paparveschi.

Colonna plowed ahead, "Look at all we control. I'll spell it out for you. Think for a minute. Your roofs may be leaking," to Paparveschi, " but you still own the land, the fields, the forests, the orchards, the vineyards. If we cooperate we can control the price of every basic commodity in central Italy. Between our holdings," looking at Orsini, "you and I even control all the fresh water flowing into Rome. Your water from Lake Bracciano and Martignano here serves the Borgo and the Vatican. Our water from the Aniene and the Alban Hills serves the rest of the City. I don't know about yours, but our water is controlled by three little valves; one at the outflow of each lake and one at the diversion of the River Aniene."

Orsini, keenly interested, tapped his ring, hear, hear, "Let's ask ourselves: What can we do that no one else can do?" He pointed to Savelli.

"What Colonna says is true. Together we control the land and the water and the food. We can manipulate prices by creating artificial shortages."

"Which we should be prepared to do!"

"Starve your enemy and feed your friends!"

"We have to be careful not to appear as brutal and lacking in concern for the people as the Pope has been and as his invading cronies have been. We are Italians after all. We want our people to be loyal to us when the time comes. We have to strike a careful balance."

"We can create an artificial drought by closing or reducing the water from all the lakes: Bracciano, Matignano and Albano. Slowly, ever so slowly, drip by drip."

"And the droughts and the higher prices that follow have to be attributed to others . . . outsiders. The bankers!"

"There'll be an uproar if we jack up prices."

"Cutting off the water isn't so subtle. They'll notice."

"But I need to get my stuff to market. I need the quick income to pay my bills."

"You're thinking the old way. Remember, we will be at peace. We will not be competing with each other any more. We will be cooperating." Colonna coughed again and said, "We will be rigging prices to make more money. Every *solido* more we can make is one less our adversary has to spend screwing us."

"I get it. I get it," said Ottavio gravely but unconvincingly.

"But my interest payments to the bankers won't stop. It's easy for you, because you've got some cushion. I'm on the balls of my ass," squawked Paparveschi.

Growing tired, listing sideways, but with vehemence Colonna shouted, "Those cocksuckers want an apple they'll have to pay plenty for it. They want olives. They want figs, meat. They'll pay! Either that or go hungry. *Godammit!*"

Boncompagni returned to Paparveschi's concern, "What about the debt to the bankers? That's a real problem for some of us. If we don't solve it we have no solidarity. If we can't all act on this together it won't work at all."

"If we cry poverty as our reason for the truce, no one will be surprised when our borrowing goes down."

"But I need cash, now!"

Savelli shouted over the rest of them, "Then we form our own bank and pay off the debt to Chigi, Fugger, the Sansovini, the Medici, all of those blood suckers. We have to do it ourselves.

"How?"

"Maybe we'll have to make some short term loans from the Jews, relieve the debt to the others and . . ."

"I don't know about that, but relieving the debt to the bankers can cause the church a lot of problems," said Boncompagni, thoughtfully, looking to Crescenzi for corroboration, excited by the idea. "The merchant bankers are financing the Church's big plans. They're advancing the money for this great New Rome, the new and better version, better than the real thing itself, to hear them talk. If we pay off our debts the bankers won't have that money to turn around and lend to the Church. Cutting out the bankers would close down their revolving fund. If we can short circuit their flow of cash we can do some damage."

The idea was catching on.

"Money," Colonna, liking what he heard shook his head, yes, "we'll buy our way out to buy our way back in."

"Let's form our own bank for internal balances only, and create credit accounts for those of us who need it."

"It must be done carefully and discreetly to not draw attention."

"But we need seed money for a bank. Where does that come from? You can't keep borrowing from the Jews and expect them to keep their mouths shut. They'll figure it out and raise the rates. It will be the same as it is now."

"How about stealing it?" cackled Colonna at his own joke. "Seriously, I have an idea, you young guys," he said with a broad wink, "I'd like to encourage each and every one of you to go out and bring home the bacon. Seduce a rich bitch and bring her money back to the family. Never mind the comment I made about those soggy cunts from Genoa." He threw his head back and, coughing, laughed wildly.

"Jesus Christ," said Paparveschi, cringing, " I can see it now. One quadrant on my family crest will show a soggy cunt."

"If you're lucky, maybe more than one!"

"*Porca Madonna*! I like it! I like it a lot!" Colonna hooted and slapped the table. "I hear you have your eye on that what's her name?" he elbowed and snuggled up against Ottavio.

"Sabina Chigi," someone yelled out for him.

"She's got great tits, too!" another one shouted as Ottavio seemed to shrink further.

Descending to the occasion, the old Count, phlegm rattling, said, "She can shove her tits up her ass for all I care. Just bring home the bacon. This is business," and thumped Ottavio encouragingly. "There's something useful you can do for us."

Rapping the table to rescue the conversation, Orsini said, "To summarize our battle plan...," which he proceeded at length to do, weaving into it the plight of the Argonauts, cast away onto uncharted seas in which bankers became a windless expanse of baking ocean, the Pope a Cyclops and Bramante a Siren. Concluding he said with confidence, "We will prevail. We will reclaim our own lands on our own terms. We will reclaim the dignity of our names, our noble histories and our way of life. By the time he finished, red Mars had punctured the clear sky above the chapel. The sinking sun spread wide purple shadows across the courtyard, and highlighted the chestnut tree's dusty, saw-toothed leaves in dull gold. The stone house glowed deep orange.

Pale, fragrant smoke from their dying campfires fires rose into a black sky stippled with stars as the men spoke quietly in small groups. Count Colonna led Ottavio patiently through a reprise of the day's discussions. The younger man feared that the peace would not hold, that it was a trap. Looking into the glowing embers his uncle said, "Julius will accept our Peace and praise it. He needs it, remember? But he won't believe it and he won't trust it."

"Do you trust it?"

"If we can maintain the appearance of the Peace among ourselves, that will be enough. You can be sure that our friends hunched there over their own fires are, at this very moment, evaluating everything we discussed and are already seeking ways to refine it, shall we say, to their own personal advantage. The appearance of peace will in itself be enough to keep the Pope on guard and on his best behavior. He has to be afraid of our truce on its face, but he also has to be afraid of it falling apart."

"But, what if it doesn't work?" asked the Ottavio.

The old Count sighed and spat into the fire, "Well, if our opponents don't know that we are at war with them, how can we lose?" When Ottavio offered no sign of comprehension he said, "Let me put it another way, even if we lose, if they don't know we have lost then they have not won.

And . . . ," he paused offering his nephew the opportunity to complete his logical thought. When he didn't he said, "And if they don't know they've won, then we have not lost." The old count yawned and rubbed his face. It was late and he was tired.

Ottavio staring into the fire said, "You never told me who the enemy was."

Part II

The Wilderness

10

Roma

7 March 1508

To My Dear Family,

Before I tell you about the most amazing day let me apologize for
the long silence. Maestro Bramante, as I have mentioned before,
keeps me very busy. I don't get much time to myself, and when I do
I am so worn out I just want to sleep. All of us—apprentices,
workmen, everybody—get up before dawn; which is alright, I am
used to that and don't mind. First we go to mass and then we work
all day with short breaks for breakfast and lunch. We don't finish
until late in the evening. By then I have barely enough strength left
to eat supper and crawl into my bunk. I don't mean to complain,
and I don't want you worrying about me. I am well and I would not
trade my life here for anything in the world. I learn something new
every day. Some days I spend outside making sure the workers are
following the plans, but mostly I work in the studio. Before the big
push to get ready for the ground breaking I was spending every day

painting backgrounds for portraits. Somebody else fills in the
people. I am not very good at drawing figures yet. But God willing,
I know that some day I will bring honor to our family, and make the
Duke proud. It won't be soon, I fear, but it will happen. You'll see.

Last week the first stone was laid for the foundation of the new
St Peter's. To get ready we all were forced to work long days with
no time off for more than a month. A thousand laborers worked in
shifts around the clock knocking down all the buildings that were
built up against the old basilica. Torches and bonfires were kept
burning through the night so the men could see. The noise was
horrendous, what with all the banging and chipping, and all the
falling masonry. When the old buildings came crashing to the
ground teams of horses pulling sledges hauled the rubble away.
When they were finally down and the site was cleared Bramante
thought the hard part was over and he had a big feast for all his
workers, but then the digging started, and the work got even
harder. The men really couldn't dig. They keep hitting caved in
brick walls. Each shovel full turned up something else. They kept
finding chunks of old columns and pieces of old statues. There
were layers of pavements inlaid with pictures of wild animals and
sea monsters. They found snake nests and rats in the hollow spaces,
and dry, rotten timbers full of bugs. There were human bones, too:
skulls and leg bones, little fingers. Every shovel full brings
something else to light. It was like watching an exhumation. At
times it was awful, but it was fascinating, too. All the debris has to
be removed so the foundation for the new building will rest on
solid rock. Otherwise it will fall down.

Whenever an interesting architectural fragment turns up, like an
entire column, or a capital or column base my job is to get the
workmen to carefully lift it out of the wreckage. Then I measure it
and make a sketch of it for the file. One of the last pieces I recorded
was a sculptural frieze in marble showing a battle scene. Bramante
was not so interested in the sculpture, but was very insistent that I
record all the angles and sizes of the molding surrounding it. After

I did that, Bramante had a laborer smash it and cart the pieces to the limekiln.

Signore Bramante gets crazier by the day. He thinks we will never get through all that stuff, and he pushes everyone to work harder and faster. He is like a madman. To make matters worse the Pope comes by every day and yells at him to hurry up and put on more men. He does this in front of all of us. Bramante yells back "But there are already two thousand men at work." After the Holy Father leaves Bramante yells at us. The week before the groundbreaking he was in a rage. The Pope had stormed off and Bramante shouted after him, "I can work as fast as you can pay!" The Holy Father must have heard him, but he pretended not to. Then Bramante laced into us to speed up and not be so lazy. It's insane. We all work like dogs,but no matter how much we do, it's never enough.

A few days ago Bramante sent a crew up to bash a hole in the old basilica's roof. When they did, a huge section came crashing down. I was down in the excavation when it happened. It sounded like thunder. When I looked up a huge cloud was billowing up through a great gaping hole in the roof. Bramante said later that he was sick and tired of people talking about repairing the old building. Enough was enough, he said. I went inside to see what it was like. A mountain of timbers, roof tiles and plaster rose from the floor under the hole. Dust particles hung in the air swirling slowly, covering everything in a fine powder. When I looked around; well, I have to tell you, it isn't really inside anymore. It's more like outside. The bare sky throws harsh daylight across the walls, and across the floors. Light reaches deep into the side chapels. Without the roof the nave looks like a common street lined with market stalls. For some reason I felt embarrassed and a little queasy seeing it that way—raw, naked and ordinary. I am sorry you never got to see the old church.

But enough about work, that's not what I wanted to tell you. We got today off. My friend, Antonio, and I decided that if the weather was good we would spend the day outside the City walls.

After awhile, you know, Rome presses in on you; all the work, the noise, the confusion - not like home. Don't get me wrong, I love being here, but I needed to escape. I needed to breathe fresh air. I wanted to see the wilderness and not see walls.

Before I forget, one more thing. Babbo, you will be pleased to know that one of my jobs was to rig up the limekiln on the construction site. Bramante figured out that if we broke up the marble slabs we hit when were digging, and burned them—and the columns and the broken sculpture, too—we could make lime. Then the debris wouldn't have to be hauled away. It would save time and give him a free supply of mortar for the new building. I designed a kiln like the one you built for the Duke, only bigger with more ovens, seven of them, underneath the chamber. The set up is very long and requires a lot of charcoal to keep it going, but it really cooks. I wish you could see it. You would be proud of me. Bramante is happy with it. It produces enough lime for him to use on all his other projects, even more than he needs and he sells the surplus for a good price. By the end of the workday I am as black as a moor from showing the men how to stoke the kiln and keep a steady heat.

But getting back to today. We got up before dawn. The sky was clear and we skipped mass. While it was still dark we headed to the Tiber, but instead of going across at the St. Angelo Bridge, the way we always do, we stayed on this side of the river and went through the Porto S. Spirito. Just outside the gate it's still almost like countryside. Almost. You have to squint and pretend. It's not like at home. We couldn't see very much in the dark, but I could hear the river running by to our left, and smell it. There were people camped along the bank. Pilgrims Antonio said, coming to St. Peter's. Well, they're in for a big surprise. When we hurried across the river downstream at the Tiber Island the bells were tolling 6:00. I wanted to cover as much ground as we could before the sun came up. I wanted to run until I was outside the City walls. That's how eager I was to get out of the City. Bats were flying, beating their wings overhead, black against the pale brightening sky. Swallows were swooping from rookeries on the Palatine Hill, clouds of them spiraling up into the air. It was so beautiful. Water from last night's rain dripped from the trees, and the air smelled washed.

Before I forget. I started to tell you about yesterday's big celebration; when the first stone was set for the new church. We all got the morning off - sort of. We still had to be there, only in our best clothes. There was no digging, no clanking no dragging sledges. The kiln was banked, not hot enough to make smoke. It was calm and quiet when the Pope, at the head of a procession of Cardinals, and all the rest, came out a side door from the Old Basilica and went to the edge of the excavation to bless the first huge block being moved into position. Behind them you could see the smashed in roof of the old church. It was all show. The block was placed there the day before, but Bramante, in his everyday work clothes, not all dressed up, made it look as if he had been there all night. He made a big show of yelling at a few laborers and kicking a mule and then adjusting the tension on the pulleys and rigging as if he was setting it himself, right then and there.

Up on the rim of the excavation the Pope celebrated Mass. He sounded angry. It was a hurry-up-and-get-back-to-work kind of mass, not thankful or grateful, more like a command or even a threat. People looked at each other surprised by his tone. And then, you have to picture this: the Pope has his arms up in the air almost shaking his fists at God. At least that's the way it looked to me, when all of a sudden the ground beneath him starts to give way. I blinked my eyes and the next thing I know he's sliding down into the hole. Down at the bottom Bramante must have heard the rocks sliding, because he looks up and panics. I nearly soiled myself. There's the Pope sliding down the embankment. The cardinals are all scampering back to get away from the edge. All by himself the old Pope had to scramble up the collapsing side of the hole. I don't know what happened to his crosier, but his miter rolled halfway down the slope before it stopped short, upside down, and filled up with dirt and rocks. When he clawed his way up onto solid ground he turned around, looking even angrier than before and grabbed a shovel that was on the ground. In a rage he dug up a big clod of dirt and threw it, and the shovel, like a lightning bolt, at Bramante down at the bottom. For a minute it looked like it was going to turn into a funeral. I fell to my knees and crossed myself more for fear of laughing than anything else.

But that's enough about work, I really want to tell you about my day off while it's still fresh in my mind. Where was I? I remember. Antonio and I were between the Palatine Hill and the Circus Maximus, still in the City. The Tiber was behind us and we were making good progress. It was cool and dark. I was running along behind Antonio, very excited as I said, feeling free, when suddenly he stopped. I ran right into him, and both of us went sprawling. I jumped up, immediately on guard expecting the worst. I didn't know why he just stopped like that. Professor Laetus told us to be careful, because brigands, who would just as soon slit your throat for a few solidi, as look at you are lurking everywhere. I crouched down ready to fight for my life, when Antonio got up and said, "I'm starving, let's get something to eat." I was relieved, but at the same time, as I said, I really wanted to break out of Rome. I had this picture of myself bursting through the City gates into the wilderness, free for a few hours to wander through the fields and forests among the wild beasts. Antonio wanted food, but I was hungry for Eden, and protested, saying we could stop for something later. I won't bore you with his whining and complaining, but to make a long story short, he won. I gave up and once more fell in place behind him. He turned onto a muddy trace. "It's a short cut," he called out to me, that went around the Palatine to a place he knew where the nuns make a good breakfast real cheap. At one point I stumbled and fell flat on my face. I was a mess, mud spattered and soaked to the skin. I was wearing my good holiday clothes, too, because the Professor told us to look presentable. The safest way to travel, he said, is to join a group of respectable people, because there is safety in numbers. That's what he said. With mud encrusted legs there was no way any respectable people were going to let me join their party. Things were taking a rather bad turn. In this state we would be going out into the wilderness on our own.

After what I think were a few wrong turns, that Antonio refused to admit, we wound up on a narrow street that curved up from the big amphitheater. We followed a long high wall for a while, when suddenly Antonio stopped short and yanked on a rope hanging through a weathered wooden door the same color as the wall. A loud bell clanked. Chickens started cackling and scratching around. A rooster screeched, and I heard goats. Almost immediately, as if she had been waiting right behind the door, the tiniest little nun I ever saw peeked out. Her face was completely hidden by her wimple. We dumped a few coins in her hand and she let us in. She pointed for us to wait at a small table against the wall while she went to get us some food. She didn't say one word. While we waited I jumped up and down trying to shake the mud off. Then I stretched my legs out hoping they would dry. I was soaked through and so cold my teeth were chattering.

Across from where we were sitting the top edge of a high curved wall caught the sun's first orange light. Antonio said it was an old round church built out of old columns and stones from ancient Roman buildings. He said that the church and the grounds around it were supposed to be a representation of the New Jerusalem, the way it was described in the Apocalypse. It was interesting, but to me, right then freezing to death, it was just another wall.

The tiny nun came back with hot milk and bread and honey. While we ate, the edge between orange light and blue shadow moved slowly down and around the church's tall drum-like shape. It was supposed to be the New Jerusalem. We were helping build the New Rome. Antonio was right, it was interesting and I wanted to see the inside.

We finished our food and went looking for the sister to let us into the Church. It was very quiet. No chickens. No bells, just the sweet voices of women singing behind the wall. We tried the church door. It was locked. Something heavy thudded onto the wet ground. I didn't see what. We walked around the building, looking for another door, but a high wall intersected the round church and blocked our way. We were in the shade and it was cold. We followed the wall away from the round church to a gate, but it only led us into an orchard of small bare trees. We went across the orchard through another gate, but it dead ended in a laundry yard. I felt lost in a maze. I couldn't see the tall drum shaped church anymore. I was becoming desperate. I wanted so much to escape Rome and here were lost in Jerusalem, soaking wet.

A branch cracked. I turned. Antonio was climbing a tree. He waved for me to follow, and then jumped over to the top of the wall. I scrambled after him. We dropped from the wall into a wet grassy field. Another shortcut, I asked. I was angry now. My rear end was soaked. I looked like a bum.

I was about to start railing when Antonio with an "I told you so" look on his face pointed down the hill. A straggly file of people cast long shadows in the early light on the road below.

"The Old Appian Way," he said proudly, "What did I tell you?"

What could I say? I didn't know whether it was or wasn't, so I trotted along after him like a lost dog, and was relieved to see a high gate tower through the pines. Finally, I was going to get out of the city. I don't mean to make Rome seem like a prison, but in a way it is. It's is all over you. It never leaves you alone. The walls press in. Its oldness is always up close. I can't escape it even in my sleep It fills my mind and lives inside me like a burrowing worm.

We pushed our way along the Appian Way against a current of people streaming through the St. Sebastian Gate. People, donkey carts, horses snorting and slipping, pressed around me. I stumbled once on the wet cobble stones and feared being trampled. When I got up I didn't see of Antonio. Disoriented, I wasn't sure where I was. The crowd was shoving every which way. I looked up and saw that I was half way through the gate, but I was not sure which way led in and which way led out. I froze. It was a madhouse. I didn't

know which way to go, and just kept turning around and around
looking for Antonio when an arm yanked me into a dark recess
"Where do you think you are you going?" It was Antonio with a
guard I recognized from somewhere, the tavern maybe. They
pulled me into a small dim cubicle in the gate tower's base.
Antonio had persuaded the guard to sneak us up to the top of the
rampart for a peak. We had to be quick, he said, and pushed us up a
dark twisting stair. Narrow slits in the wall helped us see. Tripping,
I followed them up feeling entombed in the tight space, eager to
reach the top. At last, I would see the wilderness beyond the walls.

By the time we got to the top and the stair opened onto the
rampart I was short of breath. I stood back for a moment before
venturing out and closed my eyes against the bright light. I wanted
to savor my first sight of the wilderness. When I opened my eyes
and looked down I was shocked. I can't begin to tell you how I felt.
Disappointed, I guess, a little stupid even. I had a picture in my
mind of a biblical wilderness, a bleak and barren landscape, pure
and severe, a desert beyond the city walls the way I imagined it
from the stories you used to read to us when we were little, Babbo,
about Moses in the wilderness where God was waiting. I am
embarrassed to admit that deep in my heart I thought that outside
the walls day would turn to night, that the damp moldy air I
breathe would turn dry and clean and that I would hear wild beasts
howling free, that God would be there. But instead I opened my
eyes to see a sprawling encampment that looked like garbage
washed against the wall by a tide. There it was. The sun was up by
then and it was just the world, the same old world. I felt cheated. I
wished I had stayed in bed, that the day had not moved beyond
dawn. I wanted to run backward to when I still believed there was a
wilderness out there.

The guard poked his head through the door and told us to hurry
up. Antonio was looking out, all excited. "Isn't this fantastic?" he
said, "What luck to run into this guy." He pointed out the Alban
Hills to the south and said that, way up top was where Cicero
lived, and that there were deep lakes up in the forest there where

during the full moon Venus used to sing. An aqueduct reached
across the plain and vanished into the hills. "It still carries water
into the City," Antonio said excitedly. The guard was getting
nervous and hissed for us to hurry. We scrambled back into the
stair tower and tumbled down after him as fast as we could. He
pushed us out into the mob that was pressing through the gate.
"They're all going to St. Peter," the guard said.

"They're going to hear the Pope say mass and to see the model
we made," Antonio called back to him, laughing, as the crowd
swallowed us and shoved us into the ramshackle camp. I felt sick
and a little weak. Soldiers pushed through roughing people up,
checking them out. There were food stalls and souvenir stalls
covered in coarse black wool. There were people hawking. The
place stank of unwashed bodies and old food. Pilgrims, hundreds,
maybe thousands of them, were coming up the Appian Way from
the south, jostling to get near the stalls. They were from Greece,
from Asia, from Egypt and Jerusalem. They were dark people from
the south, people from the real wilderness. They crushed toward
the gate, pushing and shoving, elbowing and yelling at each other.
Burned by the sun and unwashed, they looked wild. Old sweat
etched dry streams through the dust on their faces. Their dirty
cloaks were festooned with badges, ribbons, bows, thorny little
branches tied with twine into little wreaths, and crosses, crosses of
all sizes made of every imaginable thing. I'd seen people like them
in the Basilica muttering to themselves and fingering their
keepsakes. Three legged pilgrims, men, women, young and old
leaning on rude staffs hung back fearfully at the edge of the milling
crowd. We fit right in, covered in caked mud, pilgrims ourselves.
There wasn't much chance of being kidnapped by "brigands"
looking the way we did.

Out of nowhere a dark man in a striped robe suddenly appeared
between Antonio and me. "Where are you going, young pilgrims?"
he asked. We ignored him and tried to move away, but he persisted.
The mob pressed against us and we couldn't pull away. "We're just
looking around," I said lamely.

"Beat it," said Antonio.

"You don't need to be rude," the man said. His accent was Spanish I think, "You appear lost. I just offer my help."

We tried to shake him off by ignoring him, making out he wasn't there, but he kept insisting that he would be happy to help us. Would you like something to drink? Are you hungry? Would you like something to eat? The man took us each by an elbow. He was not going away and food, as you well know, is a magic word. We stopped resisting.

"My cousin has a stall further along. Over there," he said and steered us through the pressing throng. I held my head as high as I could, and fought my way through, trying not to breathe. It smelled like a goat pen. There were people squatting on the ground gnawing away at a roasted chicken and spitting the bones on the ground. Others were crowded around a huge caldron, buying bowls of soup that smelled like tallow. A big shinbone stuck out of the pot. Mercifully our guide steered us by them. When we finally came to his cousin's food stall he pushed us forward and introduced us. "These are friends of mine, Jared. I am taking them out to the catacombs. Make us a nice picnic." Jared, the cousin, nodded without smiling, or saying anything. I started to protest; we hadn't agreed to do anything, when a shaggy man burst from the crowd, yelling and saying that the bread he just bought was moldy. The man was huge and filthy. Jared, the shopkeeper, looked at him in a tired way and told him he was mistaken, that the bread he sold was fresh.

"Look at this," shouted the man, thrusting forth a hard lump of moldy, blue-gray bread in his gnarled hand, "What, do you take me for an idiot?" He looked crazy. His eyes were bugging out and his face was red. He had that wild look that old Ermano had when the priest said he'd been overcome by St. Anthony's Fire.

"You didn't buy that from me, Pilgrim. I saw you take that filthy piece of crap out of your cloak, you conniving thief. You can wear all the crosses you want," Jared said, pointing at all the stuff pinned to the man's cloak, " It won't make anything out of you. My bread is fresh." And it was true. The bread on his table was fresh, still warm from the oven, and smelled wonderful. But the pilgrim persisted. "You filthy Jew, are you calling me a liar?"

"You are a liar. You know it and God knows it. You can wear all the badges you want. It won't make an honest man of you. I think you spent all your money on those trinkets to pin to your cloak to advertise your piety, and now you don't have anything left for food." Jared handed the crazy pilgrim a piece of fresh bread and said, "Here, take this as a gift from a Jew." The Pilgrim snatched the bread, spat at Jared, and vanished back into the crowd.

"I'm sorry," I said. Antonio looked at me like I was crazy. The shopkeeper, Jared, smiled faintly.

Our guide said, " Why should you be sorry? You are not him and he is not you."

I felt something rub against my leg and looked down. A small boy in a skullcap was scavenging discarded chicken bones off the ground and collecting them in a basket.

While Jared packed the food our guide introduced himself. His name is Levi. Antonio and I finally stopped resisting; we did want to go to the catacombs, after all. That was the main part of our plan. Levi knew how to get there. We didn't. Levi knew where to find food. We didn't, and he seemed OK, not a "brigand", to use the professor's word.

The next stall sold religious souvenirs. The hawker announced that they were true relics. A sunburned woman knelt on the ground praying, weeping and kissing a small cross that she held to her lips with both hands. There were folded stacks of black cloth that the hawker claimed were exact replicas of St. Veronica's veil. To me they looked just like the rough wool used to shade the stall from the sun. I hope, Mother, you won't mind that I didn't buy you one. There were crowns of thorns piled up

on one side of the counter. Front and center was an array of
what looked like ivory crosses. A sign said that they were true
relics made from the bones of sainted martyrs. Each was tagged
with the story of the saint it came from. They were charming.
Levi saw me admiring them. "I have a cousin who deals in relics
even more beautiful than these," he whispered, leaning close.
"Don't buy anything here. My cousin will give you a good
price." There was a rustling behind the stall. The little boy in the
skullcap was dumping his basketful of chicken bones into a large
box that was covered by one of Veronica's veils. A huge
shinbone that looked like the one in the soup pot was sticking
out of it. A hoof, too. I don't know what came over me, but I
just started to laugh and couldn't stop. Antonio looked at me
like I was crazy, but when he saw what the kid was doing he
broke up, too. You know, once I get started it's hard for me to
stop laughing. The man named Levi just looked up at the sky
and shrugged.

We headed out along the Appian Way against the human
current flowing into Rome. By then the sun was high and the
road was packed with people. Their noisy jostling had
completely dashed my hopes. People were slipping and
stumbling on the hot black paving stones. Up ahead, what
looked like an ornate carriage was moving slowly. It blocked the
old road, forcing people to trip and stumble around it. Levi saw
it, too, and I think sensed my flagging enthusiasm, because he
said that if we didn't mind leaving the Appian Way he knew a
path across the countryside to some catacombs carved into an
ancient quarry. "It is well off the beaten path, very beautiful," he
said, making it sound almost like the wilderness I was longing
for. My childish visions flooded back and for a fleeting moment
my enthusiasm returned.

So we left the Appian Way and followed a grassy trace along a
low, stone fence. Away from the commotion of the pilgrimage
route the countryside was beautiful, and I was reminded, again, of
home. Insects buzzed in a lazy way. Little chameleons scurried in

and out of the wall. To the right of the path hard dry vines growing in gray soil showed signs of new growth. Higher up the slope olive trees were edged in silver against the blue sky. On the left new wheat was sprouting in soil the color of charcoal. I breathed deeply and felt, at last, that I had escaped Rome.

We stopped after awhile and shared the picnic. Levi asked what we did and we told him, rather too proudly now that I think about it, that we worked for the Master Builder, Donato Bramante. Levi had heard of him, of course, everyone has, and knew about the great plans for the new church. He lives in the Jew's Ghetto near the Tiber Island and goes out on Sundays to guide pilgrims and guys like Antonio and me out to the ancient places. The priests can't do it on the Sabbath. He told us that his family came from Spain, where all the Jews were forced to leave some years back. He said that if they hadn't left they would have been killed. He told us that his father packed the family up and came to Rome when he, Levi, was only ten years old. I asked him what Spain was like. He said he didn't remember.

When we finished lunch we started walking again. Before long the stone wall made an abrupt right angled turn, but the path continued straight ahead, descending steeply between two round hills. The cultivated fields and vineyards ended, and we found ourselves hemmed in on both sides by scrubby woods. Levi was walking ahead of us. It was mid afternoon by then and hot. The path turned to the left, and I lost sight of Levi. Ahead the path appeared to end at a small copse. Antonio ran forward. I followed. It was very still. There was no sign of Levi. We approached the stand of trees cautiously and saw that the path made another sharp turn, this time to the right. We followed it. In the distance we were relieved to see Levi standing completely still. He motioned for us to stop and put a finger to his lips. Suddenly Levi shouted. We stopped. At once thousands of meadow birds lifted out of the dry grass, beating the air in a frenzy, casting a swirling shadow. Levi laughed as his shout echoed back to us. He clapped his hands delighted, and waved for us to catch up to him. When we did we found ourselves surrounded by the scarred walls of an old quarry.

A bare bleached escarpment, that looked as if the earth's flesh had been flayed back to reveal bare bone, enclosed us on three sides. It was impossibly still. There was no breeze, no sound. Levi gestured for us to follow as he disappeared again, this time into a narrow opening in the quarry wall.

It was cool inside and dark. When my eyes adjusted to the darkness I saw that we were in a tall, peaked chamber, like an immense crack. It was wide at the bottom and narrowed to a fissure high above our heads. The floor was dusty and dry. The rock overhead was smoke blackened. I tripped over the tumbled remains of a rough wall. "People once lived here," Levi said. We followed him deeper into the cave. When I looked back I was no longer able to see the entrance. Water dripped. I smelled candle wax. Levi snapped his fingers, loud in the silence. A small lamp in the palm of his hand highlighted his high cheekbones and arched brows. He pointed to a narrow flight of rock cut steps that led up to a ledge. We followed him up hugging the wall and then walked carefully in single file along the rock shelf for quite a way. I focused my eyes on the flickering light and kept my shoulder against the wall to keep from falling off the edge.

Levi stopped suddenly and turned to face us. He snapped his fingers again and raised his lamp to show us a narrow passage that branched off on our right. He then lit a candle for each of us and gestured for us to go in. The gallery was barely wide enough for one person. Tiers of niches honeycombed the walls on both sides. There were bundles of bones in some, and dry shreds of rotted cloth. Other niches were sealed up with clay tiles or stone slabs. Inscriptions, some of them quite long, were scratched into the soft rock above each one. There were crosses, and scratchy little drawings, too. In one gallery the graves were marked with stars of David.

My candle went out. I panicked. I couldn't see anything. "Come this way," I heard Antonio whisper. I followed his voice into another narrow passage. Levi re-lighted my candle with his and we moved on. More passages branched off the one we were in, all lined from floor to ceiling with more cubicles. We came to a dead end and found ourselves in a square room with rock cut benches on three sides. In the middle of the chamber was a square block, a table or an altar, also cut from the rock.

Levi put his lamp on the altar and sat down. Simple drawings and inscriptions completely covered the walls and ceiling.

"There are stars of David on some of the graves," I told him. "In one gallery Jews are buried with Christians."

"Everyone was a Jew once," said Levi. I was shocked, but tried to hide it.

Writing covered every bit of the wall from floor to ceiling. It was in Greek and you could see by the different styles that the inscriptions were written by different people. Some were big. Some small. Others were fancy. Some were rude. Some of the inscriptions were tightly written. Others, low on the wall, seemed to have been written by little children. Levi snapped his fingers and raised his lamp. I looked up to the ceiling and was startled to see Jesus' roughly drawn face looking down, as if he had been watching us and listening to us the whole time. Around his face was an inscription interwoven with little pictures of birds, animals, vines, flowers and the sun. It was in Latin. Antonio read it aloud, translating for us:

> The arrangement of the names of Christ is manifold:
> Lord because he is Spirit; Word because He is God; Son
> because He is the begotten Son of the Father; Ma,
> because He was born of the Virgin; Priest, because He
> offered Himself as a sacrifice; Shepard, because He is a
> guardian; Worm, because He rose again; Mountain,
> because He is strong; Way, because there is a straight
> path through Him to life; Lamb, because he suffered;
> Corner Stone because instruction is his; Teacher,
> because He demonstrates how to live; Sun because he is
> the illuminator; Truth, because he is from the Father;

Life because He is the Creator; Bread, because He is
flesh; Samaritan, because He is the merciful protector;
Christ, because he is anointed; Jesus, because He is a
mediator; Vine, because we are redeemed by His blood;
Lion because He is King; Rock because He is firm;
Flower because He is the chosen one; Prophet, because
He has revealed what is to come.

I don't know what came over me. I didn't understand what it
meant. I fell to my knees. My fingers dug into the floor's cool dust
as Antonio recited the words. I blinked my eyes. The light from
his lamps flickering across the ceiling animated the words. The
vine seemed to be growing, searching for light. The little birds
looked as if they were about to raise their voices and sing. How
long I knelt in the dust I don't know. It may have been only a
moment. It may have been an hour. The next thing I knew I was
sitting on my haunches with my face in my hands saying, thank
you, thank you, thank you, over and over again. I felt all the
people whose hands had once scratched the pictures and the words
into the rock right there with me.

I felt groggy and sat still for a while. Antonio and Levi were
speaking as if nothing unusual had happened."The words of a
saint," said Levi. You have saints packed in the walls all over the
place here Thick as thieves," he laughed. Our candles were running
low. I have to remember to ask Professor Laetus to explain the
inscription.

Levi got up and left the chamber. We ambled after him back
through the maze of galleries, into the main cave and back along
the ledge. When we reached the bottom step, daylight coming
through the narrow opening thrust a blinding gash of white light
across the floor. We emerged like mice, squinting and blinking,
into the quarry. Outside Levi was talking to some people. My
blood ran cold, thinking that they were brigands and that we were
trapped. We had hardly enough money to haggle with Levi for
lunch and his tour, and I remembered the professor's warning: it

was worse if you didn't have any money, he said, it would make the thieves angry, rabid like fierce dogs, he said, and they would kill you just like that, and he snapped his fingers. Levi waved for us to go on ahead, that he would catch up. What a relief. The people were just sightseers like us with their own guide, a brown man in a flowing white robe.

Before leaving the quarry Antonio and I stopped for one last look. One rock face was cast in rose-colored shade. The cave entrance and the sightseers were washed in rich amber light. Levi passed a small leather pouch to the man in white. Antonio said that it looked like a scene Buonarotti had just plastered over. It did, too. The late afternoon light transformed the bleached scene of earlier in the day to one rich with yellow and orange. I breathed in the fragrance of the earth and was thrilled. This was the wilderness. I can't tell you how happy it made me.

Levi caught up to us just as the top of the City wall appeared beyond a rolling swell of shaggy grass. I stopped, reluctant to go further, not ready to rejoin the mob on the road. Antonio said, "Here's a riddle for you: What enormous beast has no teeth and 20,000 legs?" I shuddered at the thought, unable to imagine, and shrugged. "The queue of pilgrims along the Via Appia!" he said, delighted at having stumped me. A beast, indeed, I smelled it before I saw it, still pushing itself through the Porta San Sebastiano. There were even more people now than there were earlier in the day, shoving, yelling. Some stood weeping. Others were wandering around dazed. It was like watching a swarm of flies around a drying wound. The sight disgusted me. God forgive me for saying it, for even thinking it.

After a little haggling we settled up with Levi, and headed back into town.

In spite of our many detours, it was a wonderful and exhilarating day, and I wanted to share it with you.

I must close now. I am truly exhausted and have to be up early for work tomorrow.

Again, I offer my apologies for the long silence. You must know that I miss you all terribly.

Your devoted son,

Piero

11

The Quarry

Dodging and darting against the surging crowd Levi made his way out along the Appian Way, turning off onto a barely discernable trace further along than the one he had travelled earlier in the day with Piero and Antonio. He then backtracked through fields and orchards to the path that went down into the quarry. It was dusk. The scarred rock face was completely in shadow when he arrived. He walked quickly to the cave opening, but instead of going in he turned left, following the base of the cliff into a narrow close. He stopped there, his back flattened against the cut, and looked around. When he was sure that no one had followed him, he ducked down behind a large stone block. He listened. There was no sound. Crouching he moved swiftly and silently to a dense thicket a few yards ahead.

Here he stopped again, alert to any unusual sound, his heart beating steadily. Satisfied that he was alone, he dropped to the ground. Crawling on his belly he slipped into a low opening, a crack where the escarpment met the ground, barely high enough to squeeze through. His chin was pressed into the dirt. The rough rock, weightless but in its way menacing, scraped his shoulders and the back of his head. He made his way forward like a salamander for several long minutes until he no longer felt the rock scraping against him and stood up. He lit his lamp and followed the narrow void deep into the earth.

A steep flight of steps, similar to those in the other cave, brought him to a ledge where the limestone bedrock met the layer of soft volcanic tufa. Levi moved quickly along the ledge and entered another maze of burial galleries, turning right, then left and then right again, arriving finally in a small chamber, roughly hewn from the soft rock. The room was bathed in warm lamplight. There were no paintings, no inscriptions. It appeared to have never been finished. The cubicles lining the gallery that lead up to it were empty. The man in the white robe stood as Levi entered, and they embraced in formal greeting.

"Djem, my friend," said Levi, seating himself at the hewn stone block, " How's the tourist trade?"

Djem smiled, " Not bad. You know, every little bit helps." In the warm light his eyes and face were the color of honey. A leather pouch was sitting on the floor. He moved it aside and sat down across from Levi, "How goes it with you?"

"The same," Levi said with a suggestion of humor, or perhaps mischief, in his voice, "an honest day's pay for an honest day's work," Levi drew a small cloth sack from a fold in his robe and placed it on the stone block between them. "The guards are always peering through those slits at the top of the city wall, but they are so stupid, I almost have to jump up and down to make them notice me, to prove to them that I am engaged in an obvious form of employment. I wouldn't want them to get suspicious."

"No you most certainly would not," said Djem, seriously, " nor would I."

Levi shook his head, his brows raised in amazement, "And then, after I practically point myself out to them, I have to go and make a pretense of being horrified and offended by those dolts when they ask for a cut. They are truly imbeciles."

"Come now," said Djem, his voice as honeyed as his skin, "We wouldn't be legitimate businessmen in their eyes if we didn't protest. The pay-off is part of the price we have to pay, and face it, it's a small price, too, to keep them looking where we want them to. We really shouldn't complain, Levi. On the whole business is good. The pilgrims keep coming. They need to be fed. They beg to be fooled and, as good businessmen, it is our duty to fulfill their expectations with all the fake relics and votive trinkets they will buy. Were the guys you took out today interesting?"

"I guess so. They are part of Bramante, the architect's, army of artisans working on the new church. They're apprentices, nice enough guys, full of enthusiasm. They told me the city is crawling with pilgrims, and that the old basilica is already coming down. They told me that parts of the roof have already been smashed in. It didn't surprise me to hear it. It's the same chaotic mob scene at every gate into Rome, and everyone's got money to spend. Word of the new church is spreading fast. People are coming from everywhere. That new building is already creating work for us, and construction has hardly begun. Those two guys said that, so far, it's just a hole in the ground. Construction is going to go on for years to come, and people want to see the old Basilica before it's completely gone."

"I have never seen it," said Djem, knowing that he never would, either the one coming down or the one going up.

"Nor have I," said Levi as if he didn't care. Alien, apart, Rome existed for them as the world of air and sun existed for fishes in a shadowy stream, a roiling surface of light and color dancing alluringly above. "Business will be very good for us, but can you imagine how it will swell the coffers of the church?"

"I cannot. I cannot even begin to think in sums that big. I am satisfied thinking about what it will do for us."

"May God bless them all."

"May they be blessed with what they deserve."

Levi and Djem spoke in a soft argot, an alloy of Spanish, Hebrew and Arabic, fused over the centuries by their ancestors, businessmen in the Jewish and Arab quarters of Cadiz, Granada and Seville. Their two families had done business together in that region of Spain for several generations.

Almost twenty years before, after the fall of Granada in 1489, the political climate in Spain got hot for Muslims and Jews, and Djem's father joined the Islamic migration out of Spain. After an unsuccessful attempt to settle in the Maghreb, the north coast of Africa, the family had come to Italy where they joined a community of Turkish exiles living under house arrest outside the walls of Rome. Their stronghold was the ruined Circus of Maxentius out along the Appia Antica near the mausoleum of Cecilia Metulla.

Levi's family left Spain in 1492 just as the Inquisition was kicking into high gear. Spain offered Jews the alternative of either converting to Christianity or leaving Spain. Levi's father had no interest in either choice, and made a counter offer to King Ferdinand of 30,000 ducats in exchange for his family to stay in Spain as Jews. Ferdinand's initial response, if rumor and family legend were to be believed, was favorable and enthusiastic. However, Fra Torquemada, the Grand Inquisitor, Purifier of the Faith, got wind of the pending deal and riding a swell of high indignation, again according to rumor, pointed a black gloved hand at the king before the entire court and likened him to Judas Iscariot for stooping to even consider such a base exchange. Ferdinand backed off, quenching his penury with embarrassed righteousness, leaving Levi's family with no choice but to leave Spain. The story told in their household, embellished as time wore away truth's finer points, was that they owed their present prosperity to Judas Iscariot, not once, but twice. That 30,000 ducats, his father delighted in telling him, became the foundation of the family's many small enterprises. Rome had turned out, after all, to be relatively hospitable. And relative hospitality was as good as things ever were and would ever be.

Comfortable with each other, Levi and Djem enjoyed their shared history of exile, their status as refugees, alien but at the same time modestly successful in this place of excess, and the immediate present. Little in between the old stories and this moment was shared. Neither had ever socialized with the other's family, nor had they ever visited each other's homes to break bread. Neither spoke of wives or children, or hopes for them or dreams. This was business. They settled down to work.

"Djem, my father said that if Seville had been as much fun for the Christians as Rome is he would have converted in a minute."

Djem laughed, "Remind your father that my family actually did become Christians." He reached for the leather pouch at his feet and opened it, "They threw us out anyway." He withdrew a sheaf of papers.

"You must not have been very convincing as Christians," Levi said. They had shared this little joke before.

"My father thought that it was enough just to say you were a Christian," Djem said, spreading out the papers and weighing the corners with small stones, "In his view that was all the Christians did."

"But, think, if he had succeeded and had really fooled them, we would have missed this wonderful opportunity to do business together." Levi opened the sack and spilled the coins onto the altar, scooping them together in a neat pile.

Djem grinned, "for my part I'm glad they are such stiffs, and I'm glad my father was such a bad actor."

Their two families had arrived in Rome at about the same time. Levi's became part of the Jewish community near the Tiber Island. The community of exiles was small. Word traveled fast. Before long they became reacquainted, and forged—once again—the alliance that had long served their families so well in Spain. Their formula for success was simple. Invest in small but sound enterprises. Lend money wisely and in small amounts. Stay out of politics, because, no matter what, as an outsider, you would never have any influence. Perfect a facade of ignorance and modesty, but know as much about everything as you possibly could. Never give anyone reason to fear you. You might know everything about everything, but it could mean your death if others were to know that you did. Never display your wealth; that was for Christians to do. In the final analysis money was only there to save your skin when the going got rough. That was history's lesson. When a scapegoat was needed you would likely be it. The purpose of money was to buy and maintain your freedom and that of your family.

The strategy was the reverse of that observed by the princes they did business with. Their stock in trade was fear. Yours, their families never stopped reminding them, was to be afraid, to show respect, to grovel when necessary. You would never receive respect in their eyes, but you would be necessary to them and because of that you would be permitted to keep your head connected to your body.

Levi and Djem were their families' bankers, and this hidden catacomb was their bank. They always met here alone and in secret. They did not observe a regular schedule. Coded notes were exchanged between their fathers. The two old men, themselves, never met. They had not seen each other in 16 years and were resigned never to meet again. They advised and instructed the two younger men who carried out the business arrangements. Only the four of them knew of this meeting place.

Levi took his lamp and left the chamber. He made two right turns through the burial galleries and stopped at an empty cubicle. He knelt and, reaching in, brushed aside several handfuls of small bones. He scooped away bits of loose rock exposing the back wall. With a metal blade he pried away a heavy flat stone. Behind it was another small compartment from which he removed a book and brought it back to the sepulchre.

Djem was at the table studying the sheaf of documents when Levi sat down and opened the book. It was a ledger, which contained the records of all their transactions. The two men leaned over the book to review and evaluate the details of each small loan: a metal-smith had paid off the final installment on his small loan and now requested another to purchase material; a tailor wanted to expand his business to meet increased demand. There would be a gap between his production and the profit, he had explained, and he needed a short-term loan equal to the amount of two week's pay for an additional tailor. A weaver found his demand increasing for yellow cloth. He and a tinter wanted to join forces to make an advance purchase on enough yellow dye to guarantee their supply for the next month. The requests were modest and reasonable. Djem and Levi knew the artisans who asked for the loans. Dependable, hardworking people their requests were routinely approved.

Djem, a Muslim, could not charge interest to his fellow Muslims. Instead, he received a fee for each transaction. Levi, not so restricted, charged Djem interest on the short-term money he loaned him. Djem ran calculations on the abacus, dictating the sums to Levi who entered them in the ledger. They interrupted the monotonous litany of names and figures with chatter about the various people with whom they did business, gossip mostly, and small talk, comfortable conversation in the warm lamplight.

"Chigi, they call him 'The Magnificent' now, by the way," said Levi, "summoned my father for a meeting." By "Magnificent" he was referring to His Eminence, the Pope, having recently granted, presumably for a sizable sum, the right to add that embellishment to the banker's name. "He wants to borrow some money from us - short term." Djem continued working the abacus, interested, as Levi went on to say, "We thought it odd. The big bankers usually borrow from each other. Chigi, Fugger, Medici; they all borrow on accounts with each other all the time. They never come to us. Why would he? But I shouldn't say never. Every now and again one of them asks for a small quick loan, but that's rare."

"It seems odd to me, too, said Djem, the abacus clicking softly, "Does your father have any idea as to why?"

"He thought perhaps it was personal, something Chigi didn't want the other bankers to know about, but who knows. It's a puzzle. My father always suspected that the few times they came to us before was to cover gambling losses, things like that. Maybe it's that. Maybe that fat son of his, but who knows?" Levi said glancing at the ledger.

"The son has a gambling habit?" Djem asked.

"No, no. I don't know. I didn't mean to suggest anything. I was just throwing out a possible reason. It might be gambling, but who knows. It might just be that the great man wants to buy something for a girlfriend and doesn't want anyone to get wind of it. It's probably nothing. But he's asking to borrow a large sum of money."

Djem raised an eager eyebrow, "How much?"

"He asked for 40,000 ducats. Said he'd pay it back in a month."

Djem stopped working the abacus and put it down, surprised by the amount, "That is a lot of money."

"It certainly is, but he's good for it," said Levi. "And we can charge him 1% for the month: fast easy money. What do you think?"

Djem frowned and shook his head slowly, "I'm not sure. Let's think about it. You're right: it would be easy money, and sure his credit's good, but do we want to appear that flush? These big guys are accustomed to extending and receiving credit, paying each other back in a casual way with paper once or twice a year. We're not in that league. We're a small cash operation." He gestured at the modest pile of coins between them. "If they were late in paying us back they could sink us, and all the small businesses that depend on us, too. No. Let's not be too accommodating. I think 40,000 is perhaps too "Magnificent" a sum for us to lend to one person. Here's what I think. We don't want to hold paper and we don't want to tie up that much hard cash. Your father should go back and tell him he doesn't have that kind of cash. Offer him half what he asked for: 20,000. The worst that can happen is that he won't borrow from us. With silver getting scarce lately it's a seller's market for money and there's no shortage of customers."

With a broad smile Levi said, "It's always a seller's market for money in Rome these days.

"You know, have your father whimper and whine a little. Have him say something like, as much as we'd like to help you out with the full amount we just can't. We don't have that kind of money."

"My father plays that role very well," said Levi. "He can be truly nauseating. Your plan makes sense. I will suggest it."

With the Chigi loan resolved Djem changed the subject, "Speaking of great men, he laughed derisively, "I had a visit from young Ottavio Colonna a few days ago. He rode out to pay a call.

Levi shuddered in disgust, "Great man indeed; guys like him chill my blood. Whenever I see him or any of his cronies I try to make myself invisible and shrink out of sight. None of those guys even knows I exist."

"So much the better."

"What was the occasion for the visit?"

"We have recently received a shipment of horses from Turkey. One animal in particular is absolutely spectacular, a real champion, a two year old with a red mane. Old Count Colonna, you know, loves his horses, and out of respect I always give him the chance to see them before they go on the block. Colonna is our landlord after all.

"So what happened?"

"Ottavio came out alone all pumped up and sneering, treating me like a lower form of life."

"What else is new? Did he buy anything?"

"Yes, I am pleased to say, he did. After seeing the horse he went back to talk to his uncle, the old Count, and returned the very next day. After dickering back and forth I sold him the horse for 10,000 ducats. He drove a hard bargain, but we didn't do badly. Everyone's happy. Ottavio has already named the horse Testarossa, The Redhead, and comes out every day to watch it train. Part of the deal is that we agreed to keep the horse in our stable and train it until the races. He wants it to be a surprise and make a killing. I have the cash, in gold, to put in the vault," Djem said and patted the heavy leather pouch sitting on the floor beside him.

12

Ottavio Colonna, encased in padded black leather, pressed his thighs into the charger's sides and dug in his heels urging the great horse forward through the surging crowd. "Out of my way!" he shouted, "Move!" Like a paper boat in a strong current the horse drifted sideways to the incoming stream of visitors and pilgrims. Tempest struggled to maintain his footing. Ottavio standing in the stirrups, tried vainly to steady him as the shoving mob forced them broadside back through the Saint Sebastian Gate. Furious, impatient to get through, Ottavio reined Tempest in hard. The great black horse reared up tossing his mane and snorting. The crowd parted, backing away to avoid being crushed when the full weight of the animal's front hooves came cracking onto the pavement. Ottavio reared Tempest up again and spun him around. Digging in he thrust the charger through the crowd pressing through the gate, shouting and swinging his crop to clear the path. Building speed he raced the great black horse out along the Appian Way at a thundering gallop, scattering people onto the verge. Like rows of dominoes men and women fell to the ground, burdened under the weight of their belongings, shouting curses and dodging to avoid being run down.

Two miles out Ottavio left the Appian Way and turned onto a dirt trail, which after a few hundred yards, rounded a low hill. The harsh sounds of people, carts, animals and traffic faded away. He reined Tempest to a slow walk and leaned forward to stroke the great stallion's damp neck. Both were breathing hard, their hearts pounding. Ottavio sat back and wiped the sweat from his face.

All about him, as if strewn there by an enormous hand, were ruins of an enormous scale: high brick vaults, crumbling, coffered chambers; corners of walls built of brick set in a diamond pattern. Eroded and cracked cylindrical shapes. Scraggly trees gripped the ancient masonry with their gnarled roots, squeezing the brick back into friable clay. There were tilted arches, fallen columns: bare husks of a world that appeared to have been built by a race of giants.

Ottavio filled his lungs with the cool smell of earth and wet clay, calming himself, struggling to accept his uncle's instructions. The ancient litter strewn about, reminded him of Saint Peter's, bashed to bits, almost wrecked now, open to the elements. At mass yesterday leaves, and wind driven rain washed across the old basilica's ancient pavements, seeping into the tomb of the saint. Ottavio wanted to cry out. Enraged, he felt, without being able to put it in words, that the last living connection between the heroes who built these fallen monuments and himself was being severed. He felt the desecration of the church as an assault upon his own person as surely as he would a physical blow. By night from his bedroom the sky across Rome glowed an infernal red, lit up by that wrecking ball of an architect, Bramante, the Ruinante's, bonfires. This was war. No one else seemed to realize it. Everyone made him feel foolish for even thinking it. His uncle said, "Think!" But think what? He could not think. He was trained to respond. What now with thinking? But the old Count, his uncle, was a clever old dog and Ottavio trusted him. But what if he was wrong? It would be all over for them, as it was for old Orsini, the Duke of Bracciano. What if it was too late? Ottavio pictured himself similarly gray and translucent, a walking ghost, fading gradually and inevitably from the light, retreating from the world of flesh and blood while still alive.

The image frightened and enraged him.

Ottavio reined Tempest gently to a halt. In the silence he closed his eyes and breathed slowly and deeply, again, and again, instructing his pulse to slow, feeling a slow throbbing force rise from the earth through the great horse, into the soles of his feet and through his legs, upward through his entire body. Tempest quivered and sighed at one with the earth and his rider.

Willing himself to be calm Ottavio picked his way slowly through the fallen monuments. He stopped again and tried to savor the morning. He admired the orchards and fields that extended in every direction as far as he could see. It all belonged to his family. In the distance the terraced slopes of the Alban Hills, the ancestral seat of the Counts of Tusculum, his ancestors, stood outlined against the clear morning sky. He was part of everything he saw. He set his jaw and proceeded slowly toward the Circus of Maxentius.

At the first sound of human activity Ottavio sat up straight in the saddle, lowered his shoulders and held his head high. Tempest, sensed his master's posture, and changed his own bearing. As one, horse and rider readied themselves to make a proud entrance through the time ravaged western gate of the Moors' settlement.

The ancient Circus was a long narrow race course defined by worn rocky embankments. Scoured for a thousand years by wind and rain, melting into the earth, picked at bit by bit for its bricks and stones, the old structure was now but the barest skeleton of Emperor Maxentius' splendid hippodrome. All that remained were a few broken sections of spectator's seating and the heavy brick vaults that supported them. A stone partition, worn and crumbling, divided the 450 long meter track down its length. Rome leased the vast ruin and the land surrounding it from Count Colonna for use as a detention camp. Exiled Spanish Moors and captured Ottoman Turks were confined there and had, over time, transformed its arched and vaulted spaces into apartments, workshops and stables. It was like a beehive. Every cell was occupied. Loosely guarded and unsupervised the settlement enjoyed a measure of prosperity. The residents produced metal work and coarse woven textiles and were part of an extensive network that provided the Italians with horses and other merchandise from the Levant. The settlement had become an integral part of the regional economy. Its small industries enhanced the material well being of everyday Roman life and complemented rather than threatened the business and trade networks of central Italy's powerful merchants.

As Ottavio approached he looked through the gate to the empty track hoping to catch a glimpse of Testarossa. Gone to seed long ago, the track was now more a grass gash in the earth than a race track. Facing away from the track, and out of sight, the rug weavers, the metal-smiths, the dyers, the wood turners, the leather workers, the spinners, and the embroiderers, all huddled over their work like birds in a gargantuan dovecote. Red, orange and yellow skeins of brightly dyed wool, drying in the sun across wooden racks, cast a reddish gold light on the ground in front of the tinters' stall. At the far end of the track, through the Eastern gate, were paddocks for horses, sheep and goats. On the north side of the vast structure, occupying high vaulted chambers, were a madrasa—a religious school—and the mosque. The harem was built into the uppermost tier opposite the main gate. None of this activity was visible to Ottavio. Visitors were only admitted to the track. He had never been invited to the private quarters, nor was he curious to know what was there. Ottavio had only one thing on his mind as he approached the gate. His heart beat faster. The magnificent Testarossa had become an obsession. He had thought of little else since he saw the beautiful creature for the first time.

That day, as today, he approached the crumbling gateway planning to promenade in a wide circle. He did this to allow Djem, his host, sufficient time to compose a proper greeting. That day, as today, he heard the sounds of work: metal being hammered and the hiss of forged iron being dipped, white hot, into cold water, somewhere out of sight. Adjusting his posture, straightening in the saddle, he passed through the gateway. White steam rose from behind an upper tier. He surveyed the length of the monumental stone partition that ran down the center of the empty racecourse, making the distance from end to end appear much longer than it actually was.

Ottavio passed the halfway mark of his promenade and stopped, surprised and disconcerted, as he was every time he came here, to find himself face to face with the Djem, who seemed to materialize, magically, as if from thin air. He looked into the Moor's handsome, brown face and tried to connect him with stories he had heard. There was a Turk named Djem, a brother of the Sultan, who was once a minor legend in Roman society. His colorful presence was much sought after at banquets. The late Borgia Pope bandied him around like a pet monkey, going so far as to even have him taste his food for him to make sure that it wasn't poisoned. Ottavio wondered if this was that Djem. Had he been there at Borgia's last supper?

They exchanged formal greetings and compliments before dismounting. A groom led their horses away. Djem ushered Ottavio to what had once been the imperial box. A sheer white canopy, fluttering lightly, had been set up to shade them. A boy stepped forward, and from an enchased brass ewer, poured three cups of sweetened mint tea. Ottavio, seeing the third glass, looked questioningly at Djem, who smiled and set the third glass out into the sun. Immediately it was set upon by a swarm of bees. Djem gestured and said in his warm baritone, "for the uninvited guests." The bees completely covered the third glass scrambling over one another and buzzing furiously, their wings making a sound like frying, fighting for a taste of honey, drowning each other in the hot liquid but ignoring the other two glasses. The boy set a plate of sweet cakes on the low table between them and retreated. Ottavio looked at the empty racecourse and waited for his Testarossa to appear.

When Djem had whistled that first day four horses had appeared from behind the center partition at the far end of the track; each mounted by a rider in a white tunic. Two were chestnut, one was black, and the forth was jet black with a flaming red-orange mane. Djem and Ottavio watched them slowly parade the length of the course before disappearing behind the partition.

Seeing the black horse with the red mane for the first time had taken Ottavio's breath away. She was truly the most beautiful horse he had ever seen. Watching her move lightly down the course he hardly breathed. Confident and proud, bandying her youth, she moved as if she were floating. Her coat glistened and rippled in the bright sunlight. She was desire. She tossed her shocking red mane. Ottavio's tongue lay dry and leaden in his mouth. When the four horses disappeared behind the center wall Ottavio Colonna felt as if abandoned by a lover.

Djem, seemed to have read his mind and said," We have nicknamed her "Testarossa", the Redhead.

Djem had whistled again and the horses reappeared at the far end of the track; this time proceeding toward them at a trot. Again, Testarossa seemed to barely touch the earth. Her head high, she tossed her red mane.

Ottavio had watched closely, studying Testarossa's every move, trying not to show his excitement. He asked a question about one of the chestnut mares, but his eyes did not leave the Redhead. His mouth was dry. He cleared his throat. He tried not to reveal his desire. He had to have her, but he had to negotiate a good price.

The four horses once again disappeared behind the barrier. Ottavio waited. Djem sat beside him silently. The breeze rustled the canopy. The bees buzzed furiously in the hot tea. Ottavio became anxious. Where was she? He turned to Djem about to vent his impatience when from behind the barrier he heard the thunder of hooves. His pulse quickened. The four racers burst suddenly into view at far end of the track. Running at full speed they flew past the imperial box making the canopy snap and flutter in their wind. Testarossa led by two lengths.

Ottavio was stunned. His hands were cold as ice. It had taken a moment for him to realize that Djem was speaking. With his palms pressed apologetically to his chest he said, "I'm afraid that's all I have to show you." He clapped for more tea.

Ottavio had raced back to Rome that day to tell his uncle about Testarossa. He knocked and barged into the old Count's study without waiting for a response . He related every detail of the meeting with Djem. The old man listened intently, hearing the words, sensing his nephew's brimming enthusiasm and his desire to own the red-maned horse.

The old Count stared out the window for a long moment before saying, "I know you want this horse for yourself." He looked away and then asked, " Is it fast?"

"She's beautiful."

"Is it fast?" the Count snapped.

"Yes," Ottavio answered.

"You want this horse badly." Ottavio had looked at the floor. "If it's fast and as spectacular to look at as you say, it will have greater value to us than as just another trophy for your stable."

Ottavio felt as if he had been punched, but struggled to conceal his disappointment. The first sight of Testarossa racing, flying down the track toward him, her red mane like a flame in the wind, possessed him, "She is everything I've said." His voice cracked.

Count Colonna said harshly, "Not owning it will be better for us."

Ottavio was crushed. His eyes stung. He felt his color rise. Knowing that his uncle had seen his disappointment made him feel angry and ashamed.

"This is an opportunity to settle some debts. The Moor has to give us a good price," the Count said.

Ottavio tried not to appear confused. In one breath his uncle told him they could not own the horse. In the next breath he talked about buying it. "What are you thinking?" asked Ottavio quietly.

"I'm thinking of our outstanding account with Chigi," He paused for a second before spitting out, "The Magnificent!" He snorted and looked away. "In the spirit of the strategy we developed at the Council in Bracciano we have to get rid of that debt. And the sooner the better." He shifted in his seat. "Now, this is what I think, and I want your frank opinion. I know for a fact that Chigi likes to make a big splash. He wants to become a bigger somebody in Rome than he already is. He's a trader, a merchant. He's made a pile of money, but he wants more than that. He wants more than wealth. He wants to be a great man. He wants to be one of us," He said it with a dismissive sneer. "Like all these newly rich he wants a pedigree. He wants respect." The old Count laughed without mirth, "Word is that he's bought a piece of property on the right bank of the Tiber, beyond the Porta Santo Spirito, and has already started to plan a monumental villa for himself there. His vanity knows no bounds. We need to be financially independent of him. I don't want him riding any higher on our backs."

Ottavio nodded solemnly. "I understand. We said that we are at war and that freeing ourselves from the bankers was essential to our strategy. If you want to play on Chigi's weakness for showy display then, honestly,

I can't imagine him not wanting to own this horse." He wanted to weep.

The Count listened to Ottavio describe Chigi in terms that he himself, up until that very moment, would have used to describe Ottavio; and was proud of him for appreciating their opponent's point of vulnerability and for overcoming that same weakness in himself. "You can always buy another horse," he said gruffly, "but we have to seize the opportunity that presents itself. The horse is fast, you say."

"Like the wind."

"I trust your judgment. Completely." Count Colonna compressed his lips and looked sharply at Ottavio, "Buy the horse. Drive a hard bargain with Djem. Tell him it's not for us, that it's going to be a gift for an ally of mine, and that you are under strict instructions from me to not overspend. Don't be shy with him. You know his technique. He'll evade and try to slip out of making a firm price. He'll offer you another cup of tea. He'll charm you to death. He'll ask you what you think the animal is worth and when you tell him..."

"He'll make that clicking sound with his tongue and look up at the sky."

"Exactly. Play it his way for a while but then be right in his face. Make your best offer. If he rejects it, just tell him that's as high as you can go and leave. Now, your offering price should not be so low as to insult him. Be sure of that. We want the horse. It may not come to that, but if it does I know he'll come back to negotiate some more. He doesn't want to offend us. We must not pay Djem more for this Testarossa of yours than 10,000 ducats. That's considerably more than we have ever paid him for a horse before. He won't be insulted."

"We will then offer the horse to Chigi in a private deal in exchange for all of our notes, which in total amount to 20,000 ducats, give or take, plus cash, another 20,000. So, here it is," He laid out the arithmetic to make it completely clear, "We buy this Redhead for 10, sell it to Chigi for 40. Out of the 40 he relieves 20 netting us 10. We can lend that 10 to the Pax Romanum Fund to help get some of our allies out of hock."

Ottavio nodded, following the arithmetic.

"If this Redhead is all you say Chigi will want it on looks alone, just as much as you do," He thrust a claw like hand forward and poked Ottavio in the belly, "We'll be 10,000 ahead and out from under our debt to him."

"He will want Testarossa. I have no doubt."

"And then if the horse is as fast as you say, we suggest that it be kept a secret. He'll like the idea of showing up on race day with a winner, surprising everybody. I know him. He'll want to hear all the oohs and aahs. That has to be part of the deal. I will insist on that. Only he and you and I will know about it."

"How can we keep it a secret?"

"You will bring the horse here by night. We will invite Chigi to see it. Tell Djem that I insist on seeing it here - that I can't take the time to go out to his place. He won't object. We have made purchases that way before. When Chigi buys it and we have the money bring the horse back to Djem, pay him and do not bring the horse back into Rome until race day.

"What about Djem?"

"As far as Djem is concerned the horse is ours. Tell him you want to surprise everyone on race day. Keep it out at there with him. Train it out there yourself. Make that part of the deal. Go out there every day. On race day when this Testarossa makes its appearance we'll make another killing." The old man cackled and slapped a ropy hand on the arm of his chair.

Ottavio passed through the gate into the hippodrome as he had each day since his uncle made their deal, eager to see Testarossa, furious that she belonged to that fat pig of a leech, Chigi. The track was empty.

Djem, in a white robe, astride a dappled Arabian, watched the affected entrance of the young Italian from a shaded recess just inside the portal. His amber eyes studied Ottavio's haughty expression, the raised chin and the horse's stiff, parade gait. He admired how much better the horse was than the rider. Djem quietly emerged into the sunlight when Ottavio passed through the gate, and fell silently into place several paces behind him. He then stopped, turned and waited.

Halfway through his promenade Ottavio found himself face to face with Djem. The two men bowed. Ottavio dismounted and sullenly tossed Tempest's reins to a groom. Djem clapped his hands. Testarossa appeared at the far end of the track. Ottavio's heart lifted when he saw her red mane toss lightly. He whistled. Testarossa recognized him and reared. She ran to him, light as a feather, seeming barely to touch the earth. Ottavio caught her bridle and drew her close. The beautiful horse lowered her head. Ottavio kissed her before swinging himself up into the saddle.

"I will join you for refreshments in an hour," Djem said pointing to the fluttering white canopy .

"I'll call if I need you," said Ottavio trotting away to begin his workout.

Djem withdrew through the gate at the far end of the track. He stopped to water his dappled gray at a broad stone basin. Before going into the paddock he turned to watch Ottavio and Testarossa turning the post at the far end of the track. He admired how closely the color of the horse's mane matched the red coloring of another black mare grazing at the far end of the paddock.

13

Santa Maria in Monserrato

Ximenez sat back. His right arm shot forward. " Don't disgust me with your piety." He spat the words across the table like a clot of venom. A scar hiked the corner of his mouth, making him look like a hooked fish. Shaking with rage the gaunt priest glared coldly at Fra Juan through splayed fingers. Everything he had worked for was tottering on the brink of collapse. The incessant noise from a construction zone outside: hammering, the spine curling squeal of un-oiled iron wheels, men shouting orders, others cursing back, rattled the windows and made it impossible to think. A pulley snapped crashing tons of brick to the ground. Ximenez jumped to his feet, and opened his mouth as if to roar, but caught himself and sat back down to deal with this new affront from within his own ranks.

"Father Ximenez," said Fra Juan, stunned, making an attempt to soothe him, "What are you saying? I was merely expressing concern." The timid monk rested his hands on the stack of papers before him to steady their trembling.

"I am saying," hissed Ximenez, leaning forward, his black eyes quivering in their sockets, "that we have a job to do. Have you forgotten?" His eyebrows shot up repeating the question. "Our mission is to rid the Church of corruption. To do so we must destroy this befouled city's primary symbol and build it anew. It is our sacred obligation to purify Rome. Period. Not complicated. Not a subject for philosophical discourse."

The men were assembled in the small office at the new Spanish Church of Santa Maria on Via Monserrato. Raucous construction noises from outside filled the room. Ximenez had wanted to escape the City for the calmer setting on the Janiculum Hill. It was quiet there and Chigi would not be able to find him so easily. Up there he would have had time to think, to put together another plan to find the money, to stall; but he had waited here, pointlessly as it turned out, for the courier's pouch to arrive.

Shocked, Fra Juan persisted, saying quietly, " But this is a moral question, not a philosophical one, Ximenez." He withdrew his soft hands from the papers and folded them in his lap. The four other men in the room, dressed in plain black cassocks watched the exchange with apprehension.

Ximenez said, "There is much at stake. We either succeed or we fail." The purpose of their meeting was to review the latest missive from Seville. A battered leather mail pouch lay empty on the floor against the wall where Ximenez had thrown it. It had contained no gold, not even a letter of credit.

Fra Juan, outwardly calm, rearranged the sheaf of papers set on the table before him, neatly aligning the edges. "Perhaps it is a sign. Perhaps God is telling us to stop." His voice was barely audible.

"We cannot stop!" Ximenez shrieked. "We have our instructions!" He thrust his chin at the pile of papers in front of Fra Juan. "You just read them, my brother, most elegantly. The instructions are clear. God wills us to persist. We need not doubt his will. We need cash. We cannot do what we need to do with Seville's paper and fancy words alone." He opened his mouth wide and slowly emphasized each syllable of each word again as if speaking to a deaf child. "We - need - cash. There - is - no - cash." He cast an eye at the empty pouch. "What do they have to say about that?" He swept a long bony hand across the table scattering Fra Juan's carefully stacked papers across the room.

The old monk shrank back blushing pink, and then, terrified, fell to the floor and began rummaging through the papers. He held up a letter. "It says here that the fleet from the Indies has been detained for reasons unknown and that our allotment for the St Peter's project will be forthcoming at the earliest possible date."

"But they don't say when."

Fra Juan opened his mouth to speak, but made no sound. He shook his head no and looked downward. The other four remained silent. The construction noise outside increased in volume around them.

"There is no letter of credit? You are certain?"

"There is none." Fra Juan attempted another sound.

"You said?"

"It must be God's will that we stop," Fra Juan blurted, locking eyes with Ximenez.

Ximenez looked away and folded his arms tightly across his chest digging his fingers into his ribs to restrain himself from inflicting physical violence. "How do I convince them? How do I make them understand?" he moaned plaintively. He delivered his question to a place high on the wall behind Fra Juan, a spot where, perhaps, God might be perched, and from where He might even offer an answer. He returned his attention to Fra Juan and sighed, "Forgive my anger. I don't mean to dismiss you or your moral concerns, but I am so repelled by the corruption that surrounds us that I am brought to the limit of my patience." He lowered his eyes. How, he wondered could the old monk, Juan, have the effrontery to question his moral authority? Any of the other four he could understand. They were barely weaned from the nuns. They were no cause for concern. Ultimately they would do what they were told to do. They were soldiers. They didn't ask questions. If they had any thoughts or any doubts about their work, or anything at all, for that matter, they kept them to themselves.

"Our mission is so simple. We have agreed, have we not, to devote ourselves to ridding the Church and this Holy City of Evil. That is our mission everywhere: to rid the world of heresy and paganism.

"You say those words together. Do you mean to suggest that the College of Cardinals be put on the rack or that the methods we use to enlighten the heathens in the wilderness of the Indies be employed here in Rome, brother Ximenez?"

With mute fascination the other men watched old Brother Juan cross into dangerous territory.

Ximenez sighed and hung his head. Clenching his fists he took a shallow breath. "Of course, I do not mean to imply that Rome is inhabited by savage heathens, nor am I suggesting that the Church hierarchy is infiltrated by heretics," but he said it in a way, stretching the words, to not totally discourage the possibility.

"You are speaking about the Pope, Ximenez, the Infallible Vicar of Christ and the Curia, remember?" admonished Fra Juan.

Ximenez eyeballs began to quake in their sockets, "You need not remind me, Brother," he whispered, spraying a fine mist of saliva, like a snake.

"My apologies, then. With all due respect, perhaps I do not understand." The monk's face changed from pink to a blotch-work of red and white.

Looking up again to the place high on the wall Ximenez explained, "Our point," He used the administrative plural to put Juan back where he belonged, "is that it is Our mission to save the Church from corruption, from the influence of scholars, from the arrogant nobility who are more pagan than Christian, from heresies that squirt from the very earth we occupy here in Rome.

"Like we saved Borgia, you mean?" Juan asked, regretting the remark almost before he said it. He was referring to the notorious late Pope Alexander VI, a wealthy Spaniard, who ascended to the papacy sixteen years ago in 1492.

"That was a tasteless reference and I resent your inference."

Juan stared him down, "I meant to infer nothing. You spoke of evil erupting from the very earth beneath us." He said and nodded his head deliberately at the door leading to the church. Alexander was buried under the floor of the nave, not twenty paces from where they sat. " I was reminded. That's all." Placing a Borgia at the helm was intended to expedite Spain's mission to propagate its version of the Faith in Rome.

Ximenez looked down and tried to compose an expression of pain and remorse while he grasped for a way to dissemble. He didn't have time for this. There was work to do, ground to be regained. Chigi was after him for money. He didn't have it. The fat pig of a banker was whining and puling and wringing his hands about their deal, but Seville had not come up with the cash to keep the work going on their single most important project. For all he knew that hog and his bloated son were waddling down the street this very minute to rap on his door. He was grateful, at least, that some of the old basilica had come down, but most of it was still there. The pagan temple was still there! If the money didn't show up and Chigi cut off the Pope's line of credit that goddamned Bramante would completely abandon the site. He was desperate. Half of Bramante's crew had already been taken away from the Church, and were working on Cardinal Riario's new palace practically next door. He didn't have time now to contend with a suddenly renegade old windbag lecturing him about morality. From outside the chink, chink, chinking of masons chipping stone penetrated the space around him, offending him like a child's sing song taunt. Chink-kachink. Chink-kachink. Chink-kachink. Riario's palace was going up and St. Peter's was not coming down. His heart shook in his chest. His vision was blurred by rage.

"That was a strategy, too, as I recall?" Fra Juan parried, mistaking Ximenez' silence for acquiescence, mistakenly feeling he had gained the upper hand.

The Spanish Court of Ferdinand and Isabella had engineered, and paid for the election of Borgia to the throne of St. Peter as part of their house cleaning. They had recently expelled the Moors from Spain. The Jews had been invited to leave at about the same time. The houses of Aragon and Castile were bestowing Christianity on their newly encountered heathen charges out there across the globe. Controlling the papacy would obviously enhance Spain's mission to propagate the Faith.

Ximenez answered calmly, "Yes, it was a strategy, and if it gives you any satisfaction, I admit it had its problems." He wanted to shriek, to jump up and grab the pink monk by the neck, thrust his long fingers at him and turn him to dust. What was he whining about? Spain's colonies were paying off. Wealth poured in from the Indies, from Eldorado. It's our job! Don't you see? He wanted yell into Juan's fat, pink, stupid face.

It's our job to use this gift from God to buy control of the Church. We are succeeding. We got Borgia elected. We won the throne of St. Peter for this work. We have Pope Julius now. We cannot afford to lose him. It is all working for us. We have to spend what it takes to redirect Rome away from its pagan roots. Do I have to explain yet again, he wanted to roar, that it is the mission of the Inquisition, our job, to add Rome to its list of colonies, and manage her in a way that will make Greater Spain the only countervailing force in Europe to the Holy Roman Emperor in Germany. When we succeed everyone else will have to succumb, The French, those idiot English, the Emperor himself, because then there will be but one path to salvation, and it will be through us. The final solution, the amalgamation of Spain and the Church will rid the world of heretics, as it did those suicidal Catharists, Manicheans, academic humanists, and any and all revisionist, re-interpreters of the True Faith. Have you forgotten all this? He wanted to bellow it in the monk's face. He wanted to draw a sword and hack out the man's tongue. But he did not. Choosing instead, with considerable effort to appear calm, he said simply, "and I regret those problems more deeply than I can say."

"Now, now, Ximenez, don't be so modest. No, in fact I would say that you succeeded too well!" Fra Juan responded with uncharacteristic harshness.

Ximenez, smoldered, but appeared outwardly chastened by the monk's rebuke. The other four men remained frozen in place. The many and terrifying variations on the story were well known to them. Borgia had taken to the Papacy like a bear to honey. Vast sums of money and the prospect of unlimited earthly power propelled his court into a frenzy of conspicuous social competition. At first dismayed, Ximenez and his superiors in Seville soon convinced themselves that the Pope's zeal and flair was a sign from God, and let the situation unfurl treating it as an opportunity to create a papal court that would be the envy and desire of the entire world. They went with the flow.

When Ximenez offered no response Fra Juan plowed ahead. "Are we repeating past mistakes? In light of recent history I think we are entitled to present that challenge without being ridiculed - for our piety."

"Meaning?" asked Ximenez, looking away from him.

"Meaning that spending your way to your objective may be as unpredictable and unsound now as it was sixteen years ago with Borgia." Ximenez listened as Fra Juan reminded them of the fortune they spent creating Borgia's Papal Court. The monk pointedly asked, "was it appropriate for Spanish ascetics to manage luxury and excess for our own austere purposes? Had we not counted on the relish with which Alexander took to his role? Need we be reminded of the circuses, the grand and elaborate jubilees, the carnivals, the weddings, for, you will recall there were a few, for his daughter Lucrezia, celebrations that would have made Cleopatra's triumphal entry into Rome pale by comparison." Borgia had turned the Papal court into a nonstop pagan orgy. "Yes," Fra Juan said, not giving Ximenez the opening to lecture him again, " I understood then and I understand now. Our objective was to distract the Italians from their scheming and intriguing, too worldly, ways. They were to be brought back to the Church, purified and then made whole, baited by the luxury, beauty and wonder of court life. But we overplayed our hand, Ximenez. Rather than an object of envy, dignity and respect Borgia presented something to disgust and shame almost everyone. Don't deny it. The Italians came to resent him. Everyone saw Borgia not as a new and exalted Vicar of Christ but as a vulgarian. He lived openly in the Vatican with his acknowledged children, Juan, Cesare, and Lucrezia, and with his mistresses, Giulia and Vannozza, two of them! The Romans referred to it as 'the Zoo'!"

Ximenez' head was spinning, but he looked abashedly downward.

Juan, unable to stop, rushed on to remind them that the French were revolted as well. King Charles marched on Rome and sacked the City. Buildings were burned. Jews were strung up in the Campo dei Fiori. The daughters of noble Romans were torn from their palaces and raped, while the Pope ran squealing like a fat sow across the rooftops of the Borgo to take refuge in the Castel St. Angelo. His pink hands painted the vividly remembered scenes in the air as he spoke.

Spare me the history lesson, Ximenez groaned inwardly, posing his face in thoughtful attention to Juan's remarks, "I take your point, but this is different. We have learned from those painful experiences, and We thank you for reminding Us. Our intentions, as you well know, were pure." He paused for a moment to reflect. "Perhaps We were guilty of being naïve, unworldly."

"But the results are what they were." Juan, shot back, his voice rising. "These experiments...these methods. Are we guilty of abandoning our own faith by harnessing forces that we do not understand? Back then we enlisted most of the seven deadly sins to do God's work. Envy. Greed. Gluttony. Sloth. And all the rest. What does that make us? Whose instrument? I still pray for forgiveness for those transgressions." He clasped his pudgy hands together, "Are we throwing a match into the stable to rid it of flies? What does Christ say to do? I think we must pray together," His voice began to waver overwhelmed by his passion and his fear. His confidence abandoned him and he dropped to his knees.

The others sat as if turned to stone not knowing what to do.

Ximenez tightened every muscle in his body. Looking at each of them, his face remained outwardly calm. Where, he wondered, is the teamwork of yesteryear?

"I am afraid," whimpered one of the young priests, and dropped to the floor. His chin fell against his chest and he began to pray.

Mumbling, imploring God, Fra Juan looked up to his own spot on the wall, "It may not be so easy to end this. Are we once again harnessing evil to correct evil? We must ask ourselves that. Are we exceeding our authority by becoming involved in secular matters? Was that the lesson we should have learned from the Borgia affair? The end was not good." Outside the dull thudding of workman's hammers stopped suddenly. No one said a word or moved. Ximenez' stabbed the monk with a black look. Juan shrank back, "I only mean that..."

"Never mind," Ximenez cut him off, and recomposed his face into an expression of vacant piety, " The secular and the spiritual are one. There is but one way, one truth, and it is through Christ. Do you not agree?"

"I do not disagree. But I am reminded of the violence. What if there is violence again?"

"The sheep who refuse to return to the fold will be trampled by the herd, but we shall have saved the herd. It is our task to show the way to Christ." Ximenez saw that his argument was having little affect on Fra Juan. "Your suggestion, then?" he asked after a prolonged pause.

Fra Juan shifted uncomfortably. His advantage punctured by the challenge, Juan said nothing.

Ximenez spoke to his spot on the wall, "I must lead them through these hard hours, and raise them above their fears. That is what they are begging me to do, isn't it? They are, each and all, good men, men committed to the mission entrusted to them. I must delve deeply into my own soul to find the strength to lead them out of their fear and make them understand."

Juan murmured, "The end was not good."

Ximenez knew very well the images consuming Fra Juan. It was barely five years since the Borgia Pope's son, Juan of Gandia, was found floating face down in the Tiber, gutted like a fish, his pale entrails streaming behind him in the brown water. It was payback for the lurid excesses of the Holy Father. That's what everyone said.

"Let us pray to the Blessed Virgin," intoned Ximenez, and he slowly lowered himself to the floor.

The others followed his example and knelt.

"Holy Mother of God, we ask you to re-direct our spirits away from fear and doubt so that we may do your work," he implored in a flat monotone. "Help us to help others to see the true light of the true faith. Give us the strength and guidance to not waiver. Make us one in our devotion to your work. Make us pure. Make us worthy of your holy grace. Give us the sight to see clearly that which is truly evil. Give us the sight to recognize that it is Satan who is driving a wedge between us. Give us the sight to see that Satan is afraid, and that because he is afraid he is trying to make us afraid and weak by reminding us of these fearful things. Let us not forget that the Devil tries to corrupt us through self doubt, through doubt of God's true intentions and message and Word.

"*Hail Mary, full of Grace....*" They chanted together.

The calming prayer began to soothe their doubt and chase away the images invading their minds. The fearful stories began to evaporate like shreds of lifting fog. Their thoughts withdrew from the Old Pope buried under the stone floor of the nave.

"*Hail Mary full of Grace...*"

The images conjured by the tales told by those who saw his body—

and said that his skin in death was black and blistered—lifted away as peace returned to them.

"The Lord is with thee…"

The Roman fever killed him. That was the official account. The horrific images receded like a lifting fog.

"Blessed art thou among women…"

He had come down with the Roman fever, they said, after a particularly Lucullan feast. It was punishment for his excesses, they hissed.

"and the fruit of thy womb…"

Others whispered that it was punishment for his cowardice, his softness his disgrace. Privately, the Colonna's took the credit for killing him, but so did the Orsini's and, as time wore on, so did all the others. Fingers were pointed at the French. They were in league with the Emperor, some concluded. No, it was most certainly a Venetian plot. They are so very good with poison.

"Oh, Blessed Virgin, pray to God for us always…"

Everyone claimed to know the truth. Some said that they had it first hand from the servant girl who overheard the doctor that the Pope's skin had turned black; that it had shrunk, blistered, split and peeled; and that his body had exploded from its skin like a roasted sausage. Was his grave a portal to Hell? A maiden fainted dead away and swore she saw steam escaping from around the edges of the gravestone.

"that he may pardon us and give us grace, so to live here below that he may reward us with paradise at our death. Hail Mary full of Grace.

The men prayed until they were interrupted again by the clatter of construction and a workman cursing in the street.

"Now let's get down to business," said Ximenez. His knees cracked as he got up. "We received a communication from Seville informing us that a commission has been organized to consider the governance of Spain's new colonies. Some policies are interesting. He waved at sheaves of paper scattered across the floor. " I want to share them with you, because we may find them encouraging to us in guiding our endeavors here in Rome." Anticipating Fra Juan's response, he smiled hideously, the scar pulling up the corner of his mouth. "No, no, my dear brothers, I am not suggesting that we become conquistadors in the heart of Christendom, tempted though we may be at times." All but Fra Juan rose to the humor and shared a polite laugh. "In its supreme effort to perpetuate the Faith it has become the practice of the Holy Spanish Church to eradicate all pagan symbols in her new colonies and to replace them with suitable Christian images. Pagan places of worship are to be destroyed and replaced by cathedrals dedicated to the glory of the one true God. Depictions of pagan gods and the monstrous creatures of superstition are to be defaced and destroyed, eliminated from public view and, therefore, the public consciousness, as efficiently as possible, so that Devotion may be redirected toward appropriate and true Christian images."

The men all nodded approval, relieved to know that the instructions were written and therefore true.

"If I may say so," Ximenez said relaxing, "it seemed to me that we may, ourselves, have had some influence on these policies. Our work here in Rome being of a similar purpose: to bring Christians back to the true faith and away from the diversions that we all recognize and abhor."

Juan mustered his moral tone, "Let us not congratulate ourselves and succumb to the sin of Vanity, brothers."

Ximenez wanted to puke. He just can't get beyond the platitudes, can he? But he said, "Point taken. Yes, point well taken. Thank you, my Brother."

Fray Juan puffed up a little, mistaking Ximenez' remark as encouragement. "But art, design, painting, sculpture. Are we qualified to make choices about these things? We are simple men. We dedicated ourselves to lives of poverty. What do we know of these things. I confess to you. I am lost."

"We must put our Trust in God. He will guide us," said Ximenez sympathetically, but asking himself, How can I make this any more simple. It is simple.

"I fear that involving ourselves in high art puts us beyond our selves," Juan was beginning to whine again.

"But you recognize beauty, my Brother. The grace of your penmanship, your exquisitely rendered manuscripts and documents, inspire us all," pleased to see that Juan's plaintive attitude was diminishing his stature with the others. "Beauty transcends its purpose. Your work is inspired by God. Its beauty redirects our admiration and our love to Him. We seek beauty. And just as we know that beauty can be found everywhere we also know that we can encourage its creation."

The men, nodded, and to his relief, appeared satisfied.

Relieved to have found words Ximenez continued, "So let us not speak of violence and vanity, but only of beauty, beauty whose purpose it is to direct our admiration and gratitude to God," There, he thought, that ought to hold them. Now maybe we can get something done.

"But," said Juan undeterred, "do we not risk attempting to create an earthly imitation of…of…I don't know. I am lost I fear…I always found the Old Basilica a place of great beauty and meaning, but now…Help me."

The others looked at Ximenez imploring him to end the conflict.

"Of course, of course, but then beauty is more than meets the eye. Beauty on the surface, of course, does meet the eye, but at the same time it can represent depths of depravity and corruption. Think of the whores along the Ripetta. The Old Basilica, Rome itself, is more than meets the eye. Do you not feel beslimed by its corruptness?"

"But it always leads me to God. It is consecrated ground."

Ximenez was not ready to drop to his knees again to beg the blessed virgin for help. You've let me down, sweetheart, he thought, glancing upward. He was fumbling and knew it. But he said, "That is because you are a pious man and with Him always. You will find God on a rooftop or on a ship, because, as you are always with Him, He is always with you. For the rest of the sheep, however, the Church has become a sideshow, a vulgar place, cheapened by its association with profane things." His eyes began wobbling in their sockets.

Encouraged, but needing more assurance, Juan said, " Personally I find this new art …problematic. I wouldn't say vulgar because, as you say, there is beauty in everything, but nudity, acrobatics; saints and angels swirling through the air like circus clowns, dressed as if in a seraglio. I am finding it hard to find words. I am drawn to this new art and am at the same time ashamed by its allure." He blushed. "It encourages…these are things best reserved for the confessional, perhaps. It arouses worldly desires." He brought his hands to his face, trembling.

The others stared coldly at Ximenez.

"Perhaps you must view it as a test," said Ximenez, his mouth a thin unmoving line.

"But it is a test devised by men."

"By God, through men."

"No, no. I cannot accept that. It's just as before with Borgia," Juan cried out, panicking. "We are harnessing base instincts, the sins of envy and lust, to direct us to God! I cannot accept that. We are creating a false path to Grace."

His patience worn thin, Ximenez said quietly, "Perhaps you're right. These musings of yours would best be reserved for the confessional, brother Juan. I suggest you retire to pray and contemplate the thoughts you have expressed."

Juan was stunned by Ximenez' abrupt dismissal and felt the rebuke as sharply as if he had been struck a blow. He got up slowly. He felt dizzy. He nodded to his colleagues and struggled to compose a dignified exit.

One down, thought Ximenez as he waited for the door to close behind the old monk.

"Now, let's get back to business. We were discussing the communication from Seville. But first, at the risk of sounding dismissive of the talents of the great Artists we support, it must be made clear that the content, even the skill of their work is immaterial. Our work here is to create an image for the new church that is distinct and separate from the old. It is our mission to erase the old and corrupt and replace it with a new and shining vision. The nature of the new does not matter. It need only be new. The purpose of art and design, the task of these artists and architects is to help us recast history, or shall I better say, erase history, so that it may be presented as we would have it. They may not be aware of it but that is their job."

The four soldiers still on their knees, nodded in agreement. Overcoming his timidity the youngest of them said, "You make it sound as if anything new would serve the purpose."

"Yes, my boy, that is correct, fresh images for a refreshed Faith."

The rhythmic chink-chink-chinking of stone being chipped for Riario's palace next door filled the room again, offending Ximenez. Half Bramante's work force was there. Construction had slowed to a crawl on the new Saint Peter's. The chipping went on and on, chink-chink-chink, making fun of him. Chigi would be at his doorstep demanding money. He couldn't avoid him indefinitely. The leather courier's pouch slumped on the floor, its flap hanging open as if brazenly laughing at him, or worse yawning indifferently. Ximenez' black eyes swam in his head like loose stones in a jar. He prayed for money.

14

La Taverna nel Teatro di Pompeo

"Try to remember it," The Professor said, as he picked dead leaves out of his garland.

Piero closed his eyes and imaged himself once again in the subterranean chamber. He smelled the dust. He pictured the ceiling and the border of twisting vines and animals, that seemed to grow and come to life in the flickering lamplight.

"The words," insisted the Professor.

Around them Pompey's Tavern bustled with activity. Professor Laetus was to give a reading of Sallust's *Catiline Conspiracy*. And race day was a week away . All the local riding clubs were gathered, planning their events. Tables were spread with tack and colors, torn banners were being mended, leather was being oiled, armor was being shined. Gossip about odds on favorites and betting strategies filled the great hall. Antonio looked toward the cooking fire and inhaled noisily. "Anyone going to have something to eat?" he asked. When no one responded he attempted, unsuccessfully, to mimic the rumble of a hungry stomach.

The Professor shot him a disgusted look and repeated, "Piero, the words." His eyes closed, Piero shook his dark curly head in frustration, "Antonio, you translated it. Can't you remember?" Antonio fingered the ends of his stiff sandy hair and stared as if mesmereized at the savory joint roasting on the spit. His blank look offered no hope of retrieving the inscription.

"You are hopeless. Try, for God's sake." The Professor rapped the table sharply. "Think."

Piero's eyes fluttered and then, as if in a trance, he began to recite, "*The arrangement of the names of Christ is manifold . . .*" The Professor listened carefully as Piero haltingly reconstructed the entire passage they had seen on the ceiling that ended with, "*. . . Because he has revealed what is to come.*" verbatim.

"Well done," said Professor Laetus, "You have just recited the Decree of Damasus. Piero's expression was as blank as Antonio's. "You should know something of Saint Damasus," said the Professor. "He was the subject of some controversy recently, controversy that relates directly to you and your work." He placed the garland on his high brow and waited for the young men to appear suitably attentive before proceeding, " There was a dispute over where his old bones were laid to rest. Some said he was buried on the site where Riario is building his palace. Others refuted that and maintained that he was buried out at St. Agatha's. Still others say he was moved to a tomb somewhere out along the Ardeatina where you were shown the inscription.

"But who was he?"

"Ah," said the Professor rubbing his hands together, relishing the prospect of offering a lesson. Damasus was born in Rome in 307. The Emperor Constantine was still alive, mind you. They knew each other. A priest, he was elected Pope in 366, and was ordained in his own parish church of St. Laurence. St Laurence in Damaso is the church now being engorged in Bramante's palace for Riario."

Piero nodded, making the connection. The church that succeeded the original St Laurence, was well known to him. When he wasn't in the studio, or at the new St. Peter's, he was on Riario's construction site.

"In his lifetime, remember, Constantine established the Church as the

Roman Empire's true religion, and ordered the construction of St. Peter's Basilica. Damasus was about your age, Piero, when the Old Basilica that you are so gingerly tearing down, was begun."

Piero blushed. He tried to connect a real man named Damasus to the words he had seen written in the catacomb and to the heap of disregarded stones strewn about Riario's construction site.

"It was Pope Damasus who instructed his secretary, St Jerome . . . ," The professor's raised eyebrows that dared them not to know that name, " . . . to translate the Bible from its original Greek, Hebrew and a other more obscure languages into Latin" Piero's expression became expectant. "The significance of that eludes you, I see. Pay attention. If Damasus had not ordered the translation that produced the Bible, as we know it, written in the language people could understand, the people of his day would have had to trust the priests who were able to read the original languages to translate their true meaning."

"Like now," Piero said.

The Professor swallowed hard. "Like now," he agreed. "Some of the old families were in an uproar that Riario, and your Maestro Bramante, would dare to even consider building a palace on the site of Damaso's church, on consecrated ground, but all that seems to have calmed down. The Romans have been quiet lately. The Pope's Roman Peace seems to be keeping them from wreaking havoc." He risked a glance up at the Hornet's Nest, where Ottavio Colonna and a few companions were huddled.

"Was Damasus buried there?" asked Piero.

"All anyone will say for certain is that it was the site of his parish church. It's so long ago even I can barely remember," he laughed.

"But his body wasn't there."

"Well, who really knows? Riario's opponents, unable to find proof that he was, retreated to the position that the site was sacred to Damasus' life and great works and therefore, should not be disturbed, That was the argument that prevented Bramante's work from proceeding until now."

"If you look at it that way, since something has always happened before, every particle of dust could be said to have meaning." Antonio said dismissively and rolled his eyes.

"Ah yes, of course, but just because something, at some time in the past, took place on a patch of ground does not qualify it to be consecrated. Your every particle of dust is not necessarily significant."

"What if…" Piero blushed.

"What if what?" said the Professor.

"What if something extraordinary and wonderful happened in a place but everybody had forgotten?" Piero asked, his eyes wide, his question not merely idle banter. "Or what if something amazing had happened and no one knew? Say, time had erased all memory of it, and then someone dug the place up and built over it. Would they be guilty of defiling the place?"

"You are occupying your mind with imponderable nonsense," said the Professor. "You would be better off devoting your energy to this," and he waved the text he would soon be reciting. "If I were to follow your logic, which I do not wish to do, nor do I even recognize it as logic—you really ought to read Aristotle—no one would build anything anywhere for fear of defiling something that may or may not have once occurred there. Do you see how preposterous your line of thinking is?"

Piero's blush deepened, "Except in the Wilderness."

"No," said the Professor rapping the table, "No, not even there. Follow your own logic." Piero shrank, feeling like an ignorant bumpkin. "You said, what if something happened in a place, but no one knew. That's what you said."

Piero nodded, tentatively agreeing, knowing he was being led, embarrassed in advance by his impending shame. "How would you know that nothing ever happened in the wilderness? The wilderness isn't nothing. We know that. It is filled with strange beasts and savages. And, and, I stress, it is part of Creation. If you were correct then the wilderness would have to be considered apart from Creation, Nothing in other words. If you claim the Wilderness is Nothing then you deny it to God. In some quarters, my curly headed young friend, that would be heresy."

"Heretical is letting that roasting leg there get overcooked," said Antonio.

Confused, Piero looked at his hands and shuddered at the very mention of the word heresy being applied to him.

Part III

Race Day

15

Rome's Birthday

April

Midnight. Ottavio Colonna stopped and looked up into the clear sky as heaven's black dome rotated like a great clockwork, and clicked one notch forward to mark Rome's 2,261st birthday. He stroked Tempest's cool neck and felt him shiver at the touch. Testarossa, draped in a plain black cloak that covered her from head to hindquarters, was tethered behind like an ordinary pack animal. The sky's progress marked his last day with the beautiful red-maned horse. He had fulfilled his end of the deal with Chigi. He had trained her to be a champion. Each day without fail he had ridden out to the Moor's, so that Testarossa, his Testarossa, could become Agostino Chigi's trophy. Looking up he wanted to leap from Tempest and fling himself onto Testarossa, tear away her shroud-like vestment and ride her into the sky. He wanted to feel her flaming red mane blowing in his face. He wanted to race upward and seize the machinery of heaven's clock and jam it and make it stop. He wanted to ride her back in time to his world and stay there with her. Not a cloud, neither a branch of leaves, nor even a swooping bat obscured his sight of the night's relentless passage.

Ottavio urged Tempest gently forward. He approached Rome hesitantly. What had his uncle said that night by the campfire in Bracciano? Something about losing being the same as winning. It made no sense. They picked their way slowly along the deserted trace that led from the Moor's settlement, deliberately avoiding the Via Appia and the Porta San Sebastiano. Even at this late hour there would be a chance of being seen. Further along the trace followed a canal that entered the city at the less frequented Porta Metrodio. He was not eager to reach it.

Proceeding slowly, he recalled the other time he and Testarossa had traveled this route. It was at night, and then, as now, she was concealed in her black vestment. The deal to buy her from Djem had not yet been made. He told the Moor he was bringing the horse to Rome to show his uncle, Count Colonna. He needed the old man's approval, he said. In truth, she had been taken to seduce Chigi. And seduce him she had. Ottavio had known she would. The fat assed banker gasped when her cloak was removed and Testarossa tossed her fiery mane. The Count said she ran like the wind. Chigi seemed pleased, but he really didn't care. It was her beauty that mattered, and he agreed to pay the 40,000 ducats without quibbling.

Ottavio saw Chigi's lust shine like fool's gold through water, watched him swell to the notion of joining the ranks of the cavaliers, of having his own magnificent steed to enter in the races, one worthy of his own magnificence. He would no longer be merely a wealthy patron sitting on the sidelines, known for contributing generously to his local riding club. Ottavio saw how the banker loved making a manly deal with his uncle. Count Colonna was a soldier, a *condottiere*. His name, his stature, his respect, his history, his nobility by contagion seemed to inflate Chigi. When they closed the deal and Count Colonna suggested they keep it secret Chigi frowned and shook his head no, absolutely not. He wanted to show Testarossa off. He wanted her right then and there. He had snapped his sausage like fingers for his fat son to run to the vault for the money. But when Ottavio's sly old uncle suggested that he would make a bigger impression on race day by surprising everyone, Chigi's eyes lit up. He liked that. Count Colonna then offered, as part of the deal, to board and train the horse on their estate, so that when race day came they would have the advantage of surprise. His uncle had nudged the banker and said, "We'll both make a killing." They laughed and laughed, Colonna making Chigi feel like a member of the club.

As far as Djem knew Ottavio had been training Testarossa for himself.

Angered by the recollection of Chigi beaming and clasping his fat hands to his chest, Ottavio slipped through the Porta Metrodio and followed the Via Navicella across the Oppian Hill. He skirted the Amphitheater of Flavius and crossed the cattle field behind the Capitoline Hill to the Villa Colonna; there to await Chigi and his rider who would take Testarossa away from him.

At dawn a delirium of clanging church bells and the thunder of repeating cannon fire startled Rome out of dreamy sleep. Their hearts pounding, men, women and children leaped from their beds to throw open their shutters. Doves, swallows and pigeons flapped, chittering, from their roosts and swirled into the air. Cocks squawked. Bats, murmuring, chirping and keening, flapped from their dark hollows to pepper the sky. Rats scurried for cover. Cats arched and stared. Dogs bayed. But the world was not coming to an end: it was Rome's 2,261st birthday. Children ran from their houses to fetch water from splashing fountains.

Suddenly, wide awake, everyone was ready to celebrate their long history and to having survived another plague winter. Preparations had been underway in every quarter of the city for weeks. Colorful banners, stitched during the long winter, were unfolded by mothers and daughters and sisters to be carried in processions by sons and brothers and fathers. Polished metal bits and freshly oiled saddles and bridles were laid out. Horses were made parade ready. Tails were braided and manes brushed and tied with ribbons. Boots were polished, armor buffed to gleaming. Fresh linen, spanking white, was pulled from wash lines. Faces were scrubbed and hair combed.

The blood and heat of Etruscans, Sabines and Latins still coursed through the beating hearts of these men and women. Their beasts were descended from the dogs and cats and birds which fed on the scraps from Alba Longa's table, which scratched the walls of Nero's golden house, and which peed on the wheels of Caligula's chariot.

Light illuminated the hilltops. Cypresses and forests of umbrella pines cast long dark shadows. A misty veil clung to the Tiber. It was a scene from the beginning of time when the plain was farmed and fertile; when the forests were thick with game; when laughing girls frolicked in Demeter's pools, rubbing cool water on their pregnant bellies; when life in all its fearsome and joyous frenzy erupted from every stone, tree and cloud; when Rome was new. The booming went on and on. The bells rang. Tufts of gunsmoke smudged the brightening sky.

Piero bolted out of bed at the cannon's first boom and dressed quickly. He ran up the morning side of the Janiculum Hill, along a path behind St. Spirito to catch the day's first light. The morning sky was crystal clear. He watched the mist below him wind its way through the city, like a ghostly serpent, hovering above the Tiber. He reached his special place and sat back against a gnarled oak. The sun's hot arc appeared above the distant Apennines melting the line between sky and snow covered ridge. He closed his eyes and let it warm his face. Behind and above him buttery light edged the pines. He took out a notebook and with a few rapid strokes captured the scene, annotating the color, the light and the mood. He jotted down some things he wished to say in a letter to his parents. There was so much to tell. He stayed there for no more than a few minutes, savoring the light and the view. He then quickly descended, not giving the harsh light of day the opportunity to blanch and expose the bitter present and spoil his inspiration. He wanted to paint the background for a Madonna before he had to meet Bramante and Antonio. The morning's scene of mist, mountains and golden edged trees would be just right.

Antonio was not to be the first one on the street. He had started celebrating Rome's birthday the night before at Pompey's, which led to a heated debate with a group of German pilgrims over the virtues of beer versus wine. The argument erupted when he, under the influence of the latter, announced that the former looked and smelled like horse piss. Making matters worse, he then went on to compare the drink to the drinkers. Not amused, the Germans bellowed their indignation, which led to the brawl. Not quite recovered, but proud of himself for having defended the grape, he emerged into the light of day dressed in a fancy new outfit: a feather in his cap, a new black tunic over his bunched white blouse. Red tights showed off his legs. He was an eligible young man with a record of accomplishments and a serious hangover, looking forward to a day of fun. His plan was to do everything: round up Piero, go to mass, make a round of visits, go to the races, the processions, and finally, attend the Shadow Play at the Villa Colonna.

The Hornets spent the early hours riding conspicuously through their neighborhoods, their traditional fiefdoms, distributing money to their local riding clubs, throwing coins to the musicians and jesters and passing pouches of money to the leaders of their militias. This was not a day for any member of the nobility to look stingy.

Pope Julius II awakened in a bad mood, annoyed by the silence. Work had stopped on the new Saint Peter's, the crowning jewel of his papacy. The holiday was not the reason. His architects and engineers had abandoned him because they had not been paid. Where was his banker? Wasn't that what bankers were for? Wasn't that what Ferdinand and Isabella were for? He lamented, whined inwardly, pouted behind his fluffy white beard. He looked out the window into a large hole in the ground with a gray puddle at the bottom of it. No noise, not a sound, nothing moving. A steady stream of pilgrims filed through the old Basilica. If a hunk of the old heap fell and crushed a few of them maybe the bankers would be a little more generous with their line of credit, he thought. He quickly crossed himself and kissed his own ring.

Donato Bramante padded around his bedroom as the bells clanged raucously, and the cannon boomed. As far as he was concerned he hadn't been left much choice. When had it become his burden to foot the bill for the new church? He had a work force of two thousand men to support. They had families of their own to feed. Pope Julius had a lot of nerve expecting him to keep a full crew on the job sixteen hours a day without pay. If the old goat had worked a little harder selling the design in the first place they wouldn't be in this bind. He flipped through his wardrobe deciding what to wear. The sky was clear, and in spite of the Pope's unreasonable demands and harsh words Bramante smiled to himself, determined to enjoy the day. He had promised to take Piero and Antonio up to the Janiculum and show them the little temple he had designed at San Pietro in Montorio. Besides, much to his amazement, Riario had come through. Work had resumed on his grand palace at full speed. He never thought he would see the day. Well, who could predict God's grand design. He made a barely perceptible sign of the cross as he selected a cloak, and pressing his calloused thumb to his lips whispered, "*Grazie.*"

Young Chigi crashed through the office door like a wounded hog. His father, still in nightclothes, stood at his desk waving a letter and bellowing. "Where is Ximenez!" he boomed. "Have you found him yet?"

"He has retreated to San Pietro in Montorio for the holiday. So said Fra Juan."

"He's hiding from me, that bastard. Get dressed we're going up there." Chigi, the elder, shook the note at his son. "The Pope insults me, mocks me, calls me a piker, says it's my fault that work has stopped on the new church. Read it, yourself." His face was livid. "The Vicar of Christ spends money like a drunken sailor and the world is supposed to stand still for it. Wakes me up for this!" He grabbed the note from his son, tore it into tiny pieces and rolled it into a ball. He then threw it across the room. It bounced off the wall and rolled across the floor. Chigi flung himself after it and jumped up and down on it screaming, "Ximenez made a deal! We had a deal! Spain made a deal! We were not to be at risk!" He fell against the wall, winded. "We're going up there and shake the money out of him. He heaved himself away from the wall, threw open the door and stormed into the courtyard just as Testarossa was being led through. Her dark vestment had been removed. She tossed her head at the sound of the door being slammed. Chigi looked at her but rushed on in no mood to admire her. Seeing her reminded him of the fragility of his status and that she cost 40,000 ducats that he didn't at present have.

❧

"Levi," the kid whispered from under the table.

"Tell me." Levi was setting up market stalls at the eastern end of the Circus Maximus. He had been there since before sun up. "What do you hear?"

"Not much. It's early. What you would expect. Ottavio Colonna is riding Tempest. Then there's the horse from the Spanish Guard . . . "

"Name?"

"El Indio, the same one as last year. They say he's stronger this year and looks good."

"Anything new?"

"No, at least not yet."

"Keep your eyes and ears open."

The kid scooted off. Levi went back to arranging an assortment of fake relics, Veronica's shawls, splinters from the true cross, painted chicken bones, nettle crowns, cooking pots and anything else that would sell. He hurried to get things ready. Betting always started early.

The riding clubs already started making book. Each club took 15 percent of the pot. To compete Levi, charged only 10 percent and kept his business quiet. Those who placed their bets with him kept their mouths shut, liking the five point advantage he paid out when they won. Unlike the clubs, Levi deployed a gang of urchins to circulate through the crowd and gather information for him, so he could follow the trends and refine the odds.

Another kid peered around the stall. "Anything new?"

The kid shook his head, "Too early."

"No fresh faces?"

The kid shook his head no and darted away.

Why was Colonna riding Tempest? Where was that Redhead, that Testarossa, Djem told him about? Nearby enormous war horses, fully caparisoned, were being led onto the track. People were starting to mill around. The day's favorites were The Spanish Guard's El Indio, and Ottavio Colonna's Tempest. A few contenders from the Parione and Regola clubs were being talked about, but with little enthusiasm.

A runner whispered from underneath a stack of Veronica's folded veils, "One of those military type guys running out of the Monti Club is racing today, but nobody knows on what."

16

San Pietro in Montorio

Ximenez sniffed, offended by Chigi's tone of voice, not to mention his presence. "Just because I don't have the money doesn't mean we don't have a deal, Chigi," the gaunt priest said, attempting a conciliatory smile with the functioning half of his face. "A momentary interruption in our liquidity. Be patient."

Chigi and his son, florid and overdressed, stared at him, finding his response unacceptable. They had cornered Ximenez at St. Pietro in Montorio, a church recently built by Spain on the Janiculum Hill. They stood in the cloister, the centerpiece of which was a monument, designed by Donato Bramante, to commemorate the exact place where Saint Peter was crucified 1400 years before. It was called the Tempietto, little temple. The cloister was still unfinished. Two sides were open. Below them on one side Rome was celebrating her birthday. Braying horns, drums rat-tat-tapping, the muted sounds of marching and singing men rumbled up the slopes. The other side opened onto a dry meadow.

Chigi was angry. "I entered into this agreement with the understanding that I would not be at risk. That is what you said." His son nodded vigorously in support.

Ximenez turned and strode away from them. He did not invite them to sit, but chose instead to walk around the cloister, forcing the two stout bankers to keep up. A cannon boomed in the distance. "I understand your disappointment." He stopped and turned to face them. Chigi was lumbering close behind and almost fell against him. "You can imagine mine," he said looking at them soulfully, "Not to mention our disappointment. Work on the new Saint Peter's has slowed to a crawl."

"I sympathize, but you don't have the Pope climbing all over you," protested Chigi.

Ximenez made a clucking sound that was sympathetic, but also dismissive, "You have the Pope. We have the Spanish Crown, the houses of Aragon and Castile who are . . . " he smiled his half grimace, "how shall we say—*very* disappointed? It was assumed, when we selected you for this delicate arrangement, that you had the substance to withstand an occasional interruption such as this. You are the Pope's, the Church's, banker after all."

Chigi was speechless, aghast and horrified by the thought that he was being discussed in such terms at the highest levels. "But we had a deal," he whined.

"I am sorry to say there is nothing else I can do right now. Our most recent dispatch from Seville just said that there was a delay. The fleet is late in returning. It said no more than that. It gave no reason." Ximenez shrugged helplessly, showing empty hands, imagining wind tossed seas and ragged sails. There really was nothing he could do other than, at least, appear sympathetic. Chigi was the key to his mission. He had made a commitment to him on behalf of the Spanish Court to honor the Church's debts.

The elder Chigi struggled to mask his annoyance, and if the truth were told, his panic, "This puts us in a very tight bind." He looked out into the glaring white haze. We committed ourselves to meeting the Church's payroll based on your guarantees. Months have gone by and we have seen not one copper *solido*. We are strapped. We had no choice but to stop paying out hard cash," he huffed. "Scrip is not useful to workmen. Did you think that Bramante was going to take paper to pay his artisans forever? He needs hard cash and our cash is already committed. Let me explain, in order for us to get the best prices and the best quality materials, not to mention the finest craftsmen that the Vatican *demands*, we have to pay for it in advance, and we have to pay in cash. We are out of pocket to the quarries in Carrara, to the mines in Germany for minerals and pigments, to the fabric merchants in Genoa and Venice. Let me not bore you with my problems, but the Venetians now refuse to buy alum from my mines, which is costing me dearly. I was counting on that cash. From the standpoint of cash on hand we are tapped out. We were counting on that constant influx that you assured us would be there. My suppliers will not accept any more paper. They have been spoiled with all your Spanish silver." Chigi was measured and polite in his comments, but his tone was firm.

Ximenez looked off into the bright haze and sighed. A cannon boomed. A distant cheer arose. His temples began to throb. Cry, why don't you, he wanted to shriek into the bankers fat face, whine a little. The priest knew full well that the merchant bankers' transactions were paper and that hard cash was used only for direct payroll expenses, to buy goods at the retail level and to finance shipments of goods that were loaded and sent to the Spanish colonies in the new world. He didn't need a lesson. The ships' holds that were late in arriving held not only the Spanish Crown's money but also the immense profits that merchants like Chigi would make.

Turning back to Chigi Ximenez said, "The fleet could arrive any day. For all I know it may already be there. The silver may be on its way to the Port of Ostia as we speak." He also knew it might be strewn across the floor of the Atlantic Ocean. "For the time being you will have to accept a note from the Spanish Crown and advance the Church for the amount required to pay for the work."

Chigi was about to explode in a tirade when the door from the chapel opened.

The three men turned to see Donato Bramante stepping backward into the cloister. "Be careful," the architect said, "there is a small step."

Piero and Antonio, like two blind men, followed him from the church. "Don't open your eyes until I say so—no cheating," Bramante barked. The sounds of Rome's celebration grew louder in the background. A cannon boomed. "NOW!" Bramante shouted and spun around with his arms outspread to present his two apprentices with their first sight of his gleaming Tempietto. His arms fell when he found himself face to face with Ximenez and the two bankers. Piero genuflected. Antonio squinted into the glare. "How foolish I must appear," Bramante laughed.

Chigi forced a smile, neither warm nor cool. Ximenez scrutinized him as he would something not quite right.

"I hope I'm not intruding," Bramante hurried to say, "We can return another time."

"No. Stay. The Chigi's are just leaving," said Ximenez glad for an excuse to be rid of them.

Not to be rushed Chigi said, "We were discussing your most noteworthy project, Bramante."

"Favorably, I hope," said Bramante.

"Chigi, here, was just saying how disappointed he was at the slow progress of the work," Ximenez lied.

"I hope no one is blaming me for that," the architect snapped back. Chigi is disappointed, is he? Well, he was not about to share his own disappointment. He would not stoop to burden them with his tales of humiliation at the hands of the Pope, the tongue lashings and the insults, of being expected to work endlessly and not be paid. He wasn't about to look like an old crybaby.

"No. No certainly not. No one blames you," said Ximenez, "Not for a minute, but you have spoiled us, Bramante. You teased us with your magnificent design, and now we are all impatient to see it in the flesh, so to speak."

Bramante, not wishing to pursue the matter, Changed the subject. "I brought my two assistants here to show them the Tempietto. Its design is relevant to our work. I thought having them see it would provide a better lesson than studying the drawings would. Drawings can be so cold." He turned to Piero and Antonio, "Spain, incidentally, commissioned this little work before Father Ximenez came to Rome." He began steering them away, but turned back. "Is Fra Juan here?" he asked. I know he would enjoy hearing my lesson."

"I am sorry to say Fra Juan is indisposed. He was running a fever and we thought it best that he stay behind," Ximenez replied.

"Pity," said Bramante, "Let us leave you to your business."

Chigi turned to his son, "It's time to go. We have a lot to do today." To Bramante and his assistants "The Magnificent" offered, "If you have time we would be honored to have you stop by and see us. Although, I hesitate asking the great Bramante to my humble abode." The Palazzo Chigi was far from humble. "Guests will be arriving soon, and there remain a number of errands we promised to do," Chigi continued. "With a vivacious young daughter, determined to make an impression we will have Hell to pay, forgive me Father, if we neglect our duties."

Piero and Antonio exchanged looks at the mention of the daughter.

"Rules," Bramante announced while Father Ximenez escorted the Chigis out. "Rules are the basis of perfection in architecture, as they are in everything else. Follow them faithfully and they will prove to be a dependable guide. Ignore them and you will be lost." Piero accepted the pronouncement as gospel. Antonio had heard it before.

"This place affords us a splendid opportunity to illustrate that maxim." Bramante spun around to face them and, beaming, said, "Observe this little treasure. Study its perfect balance. Its proportions adhere to the rules set forth by Vitruvius during the time of Caesar Augustus. Note the spacing of the columns, the height of the little railing above the circular peristyle. Note the height of the drum and the jaunty spring of the little dome. All the elements are in perfect harmony. And, incidentally, you should note that the structure was built to mark the exact spot of St. Peter's crucifixion."

Piero turned to the view. The rich, evocative scene he had enjoyed at dawn was now faded. The sun burned faintly white through the haze. In the foreground bright new buildings of the New Rome, like sharp white cubes, stood out against the soft worn brown ones of the old. Piero's scalp tingled. The ground throbbed beneath his feet. He felt warm droplets sprinkle across his face and looked up. He blinked. A long hank of filthy, blood clotted hair hung out of the sky over his head. He looked at Bramante, who was pointing to something. The architect's lips were moving, but he heard no sound. Piero strained to hear what he was saying, but to no avail. He turned to Antonio, who was nodding in serious agreement, obviously hearing Bramante's words. Piero blinked and looked up again. The hanging hair whipped back. A man's face appeared, lead gray and upside down, with smashed teeth. Blood streamed upward from his mouth into his nose and eyes and hair. Then his whole body appeared, suspended, gray and still. Suddenly, like an acrobat, the figure made a quick upward flip. The cracked and calloused soles of his two bare feet vanished with a rush up into the swirling white air.

"Never doubt the numbers," Bramante's words broke through, sounding suddenly too loud. "They will always be true." He cleared his throat warming to his subject. He turned his back on his little creation and looked across Rome, languishing in the haze below them, and as if to embrace it, flung his arms wide. "A commanding view!" announced the Architect, and with a flourish pointed, "There, right there, you can see Riario's palace!" Bright white, its one finished corner sparkled through the glare. "See it?"

Ximenez watched and listened. He tensed his jaws. His eyes yawned. A commanding view: a crucifixion with a view. The door from the chapel clicked open. The priest glanced over without turning his head. Dreading the return of the Chigis, he was relieved to see Professor Laetus slip in. The Professor had seized Rome's birthday celebration as another excuse to go about in toga and oak leaf garland. Ximenez groaned inwardly at the sight. The old Pagan put a finger to his lips not wanting to interrupt Bramante's discourse.

"Over there," Bramante wiggled a scolding finger at the Pantheon, ghostly visible, across the Tiber. "See the Pantheon? Look at that dome?" He made a chopping gesture with his hand, "It's a little flat," he announced.

The Professor cringed. He loved the Pantheon. It was one of ancient Rome's few remaining intact structures

"Doesn't it look a little flat to you?" The architect asked grandly and reached out toward the Pantheon as if to grab it. He slowly brought his hands together making as if to squeeze the building, thereby puffing its dome up to a more satisfactory height. He even grunted with the effort. He then turned to the high drum and tall dome of the Tempietto as if presenting a waiting dignitary. "When I make a dome it really leaps into the sky," he said, relieved that he didn't have to squeeze air into it, too. With a wink he then said, " I always tell my boys that half the job of the architect is to take chaos and turn it into rectangles!" Professor Laetus had heard this countless times before, and visibly sagged. "And then I went and fooled them with this!" Bramante strode forth and opened his arms, as if to embrace his little round temple. "Fooled you!" he said throwing his head back and barking a laugh of thorough satisfaction." Piero's eyes burned and he felt bewildered. He had not heard the bit about chaos and rectangles before. Antonio nodded sagely. Bramante bowed involuntary and announced," Now that's a dome!" A cannon boomed, and another cheer arose from the city below. "See that," said Bramante, "Everyone agrees."

Professor Laetus whispered, "Sublime."

Ximenez appeared to rinse his teeth of something foul.

"And there, of course," Bramante said pointing dramatically out into the haze, "you can see the little temple of Vesta, or whatever her name is; Vesta, Fortuna, one or the other, right down there along the Tiber, near the Tiber Island. Can you see it? For my part I always thought Vesta was too tall, gangly, like a woman with long skinny legs."

With surprising energy the architect rushed back to his little Temple and ran up its few steps in one bound. Standing between two columns he pronounced, "The proportions of this structure are perfect. The columns are not too tall. They're not too short. They're not too thick. They're not too skinny. The columns are perfect. Can you see the spaces between the columns? The spaces between the columns are not too narrow. They're not too wide. They're perfect. Everything is perfect. Perfect. Perfect." His voice was a breathless squawk by the time he reached the final repetition of the word, "Perfect. Perfect. Why are they perfect, you ask? I'll tell you why they are perfect," he gasped for air, "And let me stress, again. Perfection in architecture is essential. They are perfect because I followed the rules. In his great work the "Ten Books on Architecture"

The Roman Master, Vitruvius set down all the rules to achieve perfect proportions. I follow those rules. You will, too." He wagged a finger at them and spun around to scold the Pantheon and the little temple of Vesta. "Whoever designed those buildings did not follow the rules. They screwed up. They built temples that were too tall or too short, and domes that were too flat. They just didn't know what they were doing. We're going to do it right this time."

The audience was numb. Ximenez clenched his feet. Professor Laetus looked away. Piero rubbed his face. Antonio had heard these proclamations before and was looking forward to the rest of the day, which promised lots of food and maybe even real sex.

Bramante stepped back into the Tempietto's shaded colonnade with his hands clasped to his breast and slipped out of sight behind the little structure. When he reappeared, he stopped short and spread his arms to announce, "One day you will see the vast dome of the new St Peters rise above the ridge of the Janiculum!"

Ximenez wanted to gag, but said, "It will be a splendid sight, indeed." If enough people believe it splendid, that would be enough.

"If you learn nothing else from me . . " Bramante was about to go on but saw Ximenez' cool indifference and faltered. The architect, proud of being able to hold an audience, deflated a little. He also noticed Professor Laetus standing off to the side looking mischievous. The two had not reconciled since their disagreement at Pompey's Tavern over the new church. He sought a graceful way to change the subject, when a loud cheer rose from outside the cloister.

The noise came from the field below. All heads turned, grateful for the distraction, to a gathering of people watching a game. The men wore the uniform of the Spanish Guard. The women were dressed for the holiday. They and their children sat in a circle on the grass watching two boys at play. The boys were perhaps ten years old, and dressed in colorful holiday clothes. One of them held two branches tied together to resemble a rack of horns at his forehead and ran around with his head down charging at the other boy. The branches were sharpened. The second boy carried a long sharp stick and a piece of rude black cloth.

Professor Laetus walked to the edge of the cloister to get a better view. "What is the game?" he asked looking to Father Ximenez.

Ximenez, glad to be free of Bramante's discourse, joined him, "A child's game. That's all. A simple country game we play in Spain."

Piero watched. The boys circled each other slowly. The one with the horns lunged. The crowd cheered. "Father, tell us about it. Everyone is having so much fun." Antonio looked restlessly beyond the gathering. Down below the city's streets were filling up with celebrants getting ready for the procession to the Circus Maximus. The boy with the long stick stepped aside and the spectators cheered again. Piero looked to Ximenez.

Ximenez collected his thoughts before proceeding, "It is just a country game, a game for rustics, really. It's odd to see it played here within the walls of Rome. I must confess that as a little boy I used to play it myself." Professor Laetus raised an eyebrow at the image of the austere, humorless cleric playing at anything. "Yes, yes I did," said the priest seeing the professor's surprise. "Even I was a child once." It seemed impossible. "Spain, we were taught, was once, this is many, many centuries ago, overrun with wild bulls. The bulls were truly wild and fearsome. The people were afraid of them, but in their pagan way they revered and worshipped them, too, because they needed them. They could not live without them. Their flesh was a source of food, their hides provided material for clothing and shelter. Every part of the beast was used in some way. To survive, men hunted them and killed them. The game those two little boys are playing is an enactment of the ancient hunt. One boy is playing the hunter and the other the bull."

"Oh yes, oh yes, I have read of it," remarked Professor Laetus, " but I have never witnessed it. This game between men and beasts has its roots in antiquity."

Piero whispered to Antonio, "the cloth looks like one of Veronica's shawls," meaning those their guide Levi had for sale by the dozens out beyond the city gate.

The "bull" charged. The crowd cheered. The "hunter" leaped back and waved the cloth at the bull to distract him. The "bull" swerved, lowered his head and thrust his horns upward. The cloth snagged. They heard it rip. The hunter leaped back sweeping the cloth over the bull's head. Blinded, the bull swerved, and lunged again. His horns caught the black cloth. He twisted and shook his head to get free. Whipping the cloth away, the hunter ran backward facing the bull. The bull raised his head and blinked, confused, into the light. The boy's face was red. His hair matted down. He was tiring. Everyone saw his fear.

Ximenez watched intently and said, "The boy playing the bull really is the bull."

The Professor whispered, "It's very compelling. I can't take my eyes from it." The hunter relaxed his stick and cloth and loosened his shoulders. He tilted his head toward the bull, relaxed and calm, as if to say, what are you waiting for, bull? "Father, you said that you played the game yourself as a boy. What was it like? When you played the bull were you really the bull, as you say?"

Ximenez' black eyes were riveted to the game, "I can tell you that as a boy, when I played the bull I was the bull. I felt that I was the animal. I thought the way the beast would think. Yes, I was the bull." The crowd was silent. The bull was tiring. His head was bowed. He wiped his nose on his shoulder and stood still, thinking, pressing the rude horns into his forehead, making them firm. Thinking what?

The Professor asked, "Did you then behave as one? I mean in the sense that when you played the bull and believed you were a bull did you not act cleverly the way a man would, but rather stupidly the way a beast would?"

The little bull lowered his head slightly, but remained otherwise still.

"When I was the hunter I thought like the hunter. I was the hunter. When I was the bull I thought and acted as the bull ."

"What is the bull thinking now?" asked Piero.

Ximenez made light of the question, "Children are always play acting. They are impressionable. They can be made to believe anything. In that sense yes, one does think stupidly, as a beast. But one is not a beast. But what are these boys doing? Watch."

The hunter became restless, impatient with the bull's inaction. The bull did not move. From down the hill, the dull beat of a parade penetrated the haze. The hunter stood up straighter, showy and arrogant, and draped his cloth across his lance in a parody of extreme confidence. He extended it ever so slowly, toward the tiring beast. A few spectators applauded his aplomb. He shook the cloth. The bull suddenly dropped to one knee. A woman in the audience moaned in pity.

The Professor whispered, "This is excruciating. The bull is pursued, but the hunter is also pursued by the bull. Then there is that cloth, that shawl or cape, whatever it is. The hunter tricks the bull into thinking that he must pursue the cape in order to survive. The beast's survival depends, he thinks, on killing the cape. The hunter knows that the cape is only a diversion. The bull is enthralled, diverted by the cape. It is the object of his lust, fear and, I dare say, he may think it holds his salvation. When you played the bull, when you were the bull, as you said, did you see the cape as your salvation?"

Irritated, Ximenez said curtly, "It was so long ago. Who can remember? I am sure I did not. Bull's do not conceive of salvation." There was no movement on the field.

"Killing the cape is the bull's salvation, he thinks," whispered the Professor. "The cape is the hunter's salvation, too. The hunter knows without it he would be nothing. His physical strength alone is no match for such a great beast." The hunter moved slightly closer to the beast, and stamped his foot. The bull remained on one knee, his head bowed. The hunter slowly waved the shawl.

"Look," exclaimed Laetus, "see how the cloth diverts the bull?" With renewed strength the bull leaped to its feet. The hunter flinched, but stood his ground. The entire crowd shouted "Toro! Toro!"

"They're cheering the bull," Piero shouted.

The bull, his body taut, moved slowly toward the hunter in a wide arc. The hunter stood, teasing the beast, slowly waving the shawl.

"The shawl makes the hunter's victory possible," said the Professor. "Without the shawl the hunter is vulnerable. In itself the cloth has no strength. The cape intrigues me. The cloth hides the sword. "Do the children, the boys, understand what the game means?"

"They don't need to understand. They just need to know what to do." Ximenez dismissed the remark, "I think you are reading too much into this. It's just a game after all, a pastime. The art of the game lies in diversion, in sleight of hand. I'm sure the bull could be distracted by anything. It could be a stick, or a pebble, or a hide or a branch sweeping the ground and making noise, any distraction would do. The hunter is simply trying to focus the attention of the beast away from his own true motive. Of course doing it with elegance and grace plays to the crowd."

Bramante quietly watched the game, listening to the whispered conversation, the Professor's eager questions, Ximenez reluctant responses. He looked out into the torpid white day, down into Rome, at his Rome, his city. He glimpsed the Palazzo Riario, its grace, the grace and elegance he gave it, apparent even from here. Grace and elegance, aren't they what Ximenez' little hunter is expected to provide? For the crowd? For them all? He turned to his Tempietto, his own little temple, and in that instant it was no longer his. His eyes burned. They felt tired and dry. He slumped. Gravity dragged his flesh earthward, and a bitter taste filled his mouth. These treasures were no longer his. A door opened. He stood fast before it. It moved a little as if to hasten him through. He refused to pass. Am I just a shawl maker? If so then, who is the hunter and who the beast?

The bull and the hunter stopped again, fixed in space at the center of the ring. Then the bull turned. With his head down he sprang forward and raced toward the exposed flank of the hunter, away from the moving shawl.

The crowd roared "Toro! Toro!"

"He's not fooled,' Piero said, turning excitedly to Bramante, who stood agape as if in a trance. Ximenez was gripped by the maneuver. Fear flashed across the young hunter's face. He faced the bull holding his lance and the shawl in a relaxed position behind him. The bull charged. "Jesus Christ," called Piero.

The bull ran headlong toward the hunter, toward his empty left arm. The hunter faced the onrushing bull without flinching. At the last possible moment he spun, and jumped back, but too late. The bull swerved to meet him.

"Fool, run forward to meet the bull!" hissed Ximenez.

The hunter ran backward no longer in control. The bull charged and stumbled onto one knee. The hunter jumped sideways. The bull recovered and charged. Whipping his lance and shawl from behind, the hunter ran to meet the bull. The two boys crashed into each other. The hunter fell over his lance. The shawl fell over the bull's head and became tangled in his horns.

"Shit," called out one of the fathers. The boys scrambled to their feet and looked around as if awakened from sleep. Sweaty and tired, they hugged each other. Everyone applauded. The parents ran over to congratulate their sons and clean them up for the feast that was to follow.

"Do the children, the boys, understand," asked Bramante, his voice grave and low, "that the hunter uses the energy and the belief of the bull to conquer him?"

Having forgotten that the architect was even there, Ximenez coolly replied, "They don't need to understand." He looked Bramante in the eye, "They just need to know what to do." Bramante looked into the black void of the priest's eyes and felt emptied, robbed, hollowed.

Piero asked, "Does a bull ever learn that it's only a cape and that the hunter is the real enemy?"

Ximenez smiled, "They are not so smart these bulls."

"But what would happen if he did?" persisted Piero. The fire behind the priest's eyes caused him to regret the question. He looked to Bramante for an answer, but found in his face a faint quiver of fear and grief. He looked to Ximenez and blinked. The black spreading form of a raven beat the air.

Ximenez smiled thinly, "The hunter would find something else to wave. May I offer you some refreshment?"

Bramante, his voice small, "We must leave. We thank you for your hospitality and for the opportunity to learn something of the Spanish tradition." He turned to Piero and Antonio, and with a valiant effort at *bonhomie* said, "I am sure you are eager to meet the vivacious Chigi daughter.

The thumping, the bleating, the painful squeezing sound of sheep stomach bagpipes came up from the city and assaulted them as they all left St. Pietro in Montorio. The procession had begun. The Professor, seeing the young men's eagerness to join the celebrations, waved them on ahead. He would catch up with them either at the races or at the Colonna fete. Piero and Antonio did not protest, but bolted down the hill. The Professor turned to Bramante, anticipating his company and a leisurely walk back down to the City. He wanted to talk about the little spectacle they had just witnessed, and to patch up their tiff. But Bramante, preoccupied, had already begun walking slowly uphill toward the St. Pancrazio Gate away from him.

17

The Palazzo Chigi

Mounted guards stood at either side of the entrance to Palazzo Chigi, closely watching the faces of the people streaming along the Via dei Banchi Nuovi. Above the street the open windows of the main floor salon revealed a glittering assembly, talking and gorging themselves at tables laden with elaborately presented delicacies. The sound of horns resonated through the narrow street. The guards were particularly vigilant today, on the lookout for crashers, pranksters and troublemakers. Rome's birthday was a day for hospitality. Revelers, slightly inebriated even at this early hour, were making their rounds of holiday visits. Guests were welcome, but intruders, and strangers most certainly, were not.

The guards spotted their boss and his son turning the corner. The two fat men shoved their way through the crowd. By the time they arrived, the great oak doors had been swung open and the two rushed into the central courtyard where servants were ushering guests up stairs. Chigi the Magnificent was in no mood for guests. Ignoring them he hurried through a small door at the corner of the colonnade, his son following.

"That skinny son of a bitch!" Chigi bellowed closing the door to his office. He threw his gloves on a chair. "We have a deal!" His son nodded in vigorous agreement. The elder Chigi rubbed his face. The dull clank of bolts being thrown back announced the arrival of more visitors. Raucous street noises filled the courtyard. The doors to the street banged shut. The voices of friends, colleagues, admirers and enemies greeting each other heartily outside his door, and the sound of footsteps, lots of them, on the wide stone stairs, stopped Chigi's fulminating tirade. He took a breath. "I was looking forward to this, but not now," he waved at the door. "Shit," he said. There was a timid knock, "Who is it!" he shouted.

"The Signora wants you to know that the guests are arriving and everyone is asking for you."

He pounded the table making everything on it jump, but in a calm voice he called, " Tell her I'll be right up." He looked around the office. Signs of his violence were plainly evident. Heavy, leather bound ledger books lay askew on the table. Ink spattered the whitewashed wall. A heavy crystal inkwell lay on the floor where it landed. The ledgers told of the enormous sums Chigi had advanced to Pope Julius for his grandiose construction projects: the new St. Peter's, decorations to the papal apartments, repainting the Sistine Chapel, for the demolition of entire blocks of houses to make way for two new streets, the Via Giulia and the Via della Lungara. Those were loans, not gifts. They were made with the understanding that the Spanish crown would back them up. And, to their credit, they had done so faithfully, but only up to a point. They were now three months in arrears. He had made his own plans and investments based on the assurance that the Vatican loans were risk free, that there would be no interruption in payment. They were hardly to be loans at all. He was simply to be a conduit for the Spanish money in exchange for an exorbitant fee and a piece of Spain's trade with the Indies. He had counted on that uninterrupted flow of easy money, and in hard currency, gold and silver. Spain's cup runneth over. Her ships were bursting at the seams with bullion. At least that was the picture Ximenez painted. Convoys of huge galleons loaded with treasure from the far ends of the earth were arriving without interruption in Spain's ports. That was what Ximenez told him. He hadn't been dreaming. When a discussion was about money Chigi paid attention.

And now look; the next bit of good news, he supposed, would be that the ship he had a share in was the one that got lost.

"Motherfucker" he said. "Ximenez is having a cash flow problem, is he? What about me?" he bellowed. Money was going out faster than it was coming in. He had signed contracts and made deposits for minerals, for lead, for copper, for bronze, for colored marble, for hardwoods, for powdered mineral pigments: all the materials the artists and artisans needed and demanded for the new Rome they were creating. The annual fair was coming up. Balances were due. He didn't have the cash, to settle his accounts. "One ship is late in arriving and my life is on the line."

And then there was the villa, the fancy new place he had begun to build for his mistress on the new Via della Lungara. "Jesus, I'll be the laughing stock of Rome if I have to stop the work. The Roman aristocrats will have a field day seeing me fall flat." He rotated his head to get the knots out of his thick neck. The heavy doors to the street groaned open. The sound of laughter and merrymaking filled the office. Chigi said to his son, "I never thought I'd see the day that my fortunes would be riding on a goddamned horse."

Piero and Antonio were swept into the Palazzo Chigi on a wave of jubilant revelers, eager to meet Chigi the Magnificent's vivacious daughter. Antonio waved and called out to a few familiar faces as they mingled with the crowd pressing up the broad stone stairs to the main floor salon. Piero didn't know anyone and felt self-conscious among the glittering assembly. He recognized the elfin face of Niccolo Machiavelli talking with Cardinal Medici, and a few others from the presentation at St. Peter's.

No sooner were they announced than a young woman emerged from the crowd and came toward them, her hands extended in welcome. She wore an expression of delight like a little girl and seemed to float across the room. Her coppery hair lifted around her face as she approached, as if borne aloft on a fresh sea wind. She alighted before them like an angel. "Antonio, Piero, Bramante's gifted apprentices, I am so pleased you have come." Her voice was sweet.

Transfixed by her beauty, by her softness and radiance, Piero felt bathed in her warmth. Her topaz eyes glinted with gold. Her mouth was like a strawberry. Stammering and hoarse, barely able to say his own name, he bowed. "Your father invited us to meet you. We saw him this morning at the Tempietto."

"No. No," she laughed, "that's Tino's daughter over there." She pointed to a short young girl, encased in a hive of pearl encrusted damask, surrounded by a swarm of well groomed cavaliers. "She is pursued by every young nobleman in Rome. They are drawn to her as bees to honey."

Antonio assayed the girl and her gang of admirers. Flies or hyenas came more readily to mind than bees; and honey was certainly not the first substance he thought of as he smiled in the direction of the hefty young Chigi girl. He excused himself and went to join the swarm.

"I am Imperia, the mistress of the house," she said, her strawberry of a mouth shaped in a tiny, heart-shaped smile.

Piero looked from her eyes to her mouth and then to her chin. Around him everything but Imperia faded into darkness. His eyes followed the roundness of her chin to the soft surface of her neck. The sounds of the party: tinkling glasses, silver clinking on china, women's dresses rustling, became muffled in his enveloping dusk. He felt himself shrinking, sinking, deafened by his pounding heart; willing himself to be lost where the white and rosy skin of her shoulder disappeared into the folds of her dress. She took his hands. Her soft warmth, and the tips of her fingernails tickled his palms. He looked at her delicate wrists, and imagined traveling along them under her lace cuffs into a soft and rolling landscape of golden flax that went on and on into a twilight realm beneath her gown. His balls felt like lead.

"We're building a new place on the Via della Lungara. You must have heard about it," Piero emerged from his reverie. "It's going to be a real showplace. I plan to do some wonderful things with the decorations." She sighed, "I don't know why, but for some reason I've always identified with Galatea." Piero blinked trying to recall who Galatea was, but needn't have bothered. Imperia proceeded at length to regale him with her version of the story: of how Galatea was married to the ugly Cyclops, of how she had to constantly prove that she had no passion for anyone but him, of her strength and purity. "One wall must be devoted to telling that story. I would even be willing to pose for it," she said.

Piero's throat went dry and he felt the blood in his hands draw back and up through his arms to gorge the caverns of his thundering heart. Her mouth, her beautiful strawberry of a mouth, was pursed in a kiss of a smile.

"Can't you see it?" she asked in a whisper, "a roiling sea of maidens being vanquished by hairy, swimming satyrs?"

"Swimming satyrs?" he asked. "Yes, yes, of course I can see it. How marvelous!"

"And," she went on breathlessly, holding a soft small hand to her breast, "Galatea, depicted by me, of course, would be praying to god, naked, to preserve my virtue against all odds, a foamy sea, wind in my hair. And, oh yes, there have to be some Negroes. I adore Negroes."

"Negroes," Piero repeated, "Negroes?" He looked across the room. Two Moors, dressed as Turks, stood as ornaments at either end of the banquet table. "I know," he said excitedly, "You could be riding on a giant scallop shell that's being pulled through the sea; through the middle of all of that danger and temptation by two Negro dolphins!"

Imperia was dumbstruck. "Oh, Piero!" she gasped. "You are a genius!" She pulled him close. Her tiny strawberry of a mouth disappeared between his grinning lips to plant a kiss on his teeth. She took his hand and looked admiringly into his engorged and throbbing face before dragging him into the crowded salon to introduce him to the assembled guests.

Chigi, his son lumbering after, hurried from the office. They slipped out through a service door into the back alley, unseen by their guests. Splay legged, and with thighs scraping, they rushed passed the sentry who manned the service entrance. Huffing and puffing, flapping lame salutes, they swept into the gloomy maze of guards' quarters, workshops, kitchen, scullery, and larder beneath the palazzo, and made for the stalls. They pushed past their rider, dressed in navy blue and white silks, just as a groom was removing Testarossa's black hood and cloak. Their standard, bearing the Chigi mountains and star, was carefully draped over a rail. Testarossa shook her red mane free and snorted.

"She is even more magnificent than I remembered," Chigi said.

"She is even more powerfully built than I recall," the younger replied. "She has been well exercised." Even in the dim light Testarossa was impressive,. strong, yet light and elegant.

"And her flaming red mane!" exclaimed Chigi. Testarossa snorted again and shook her head. Chigi dropped to his knees before her, as if she were an altar, and looked up into her great brown eyes. The groom stepped back. Chigi the Magnificent clasped his hands into a tight ball and pressed his face into them, breathing in their bread and leather smell. He squeezed his eyes shut and gnawed his knuckles, praying that the beautiful Testarossa would restore him to solvency.

18

The Villa Colonna

The high iron gates to the Villa Colonna were pulled open at one o'clock in the afternoon to admit the first wave of visitors. The children's tournament began at 2:00 with a no less eager crowd than the one that had assembled at the Circus Maximus for the races. Old Count Colonna, weighted down in antiquated military garb, but wearing a floppy jester's hat, urged his tired old steed, Pegasus, through a sea of children who were entangled in furious mortal combat. Dressed as kings and queens, princes and princesses, emperors, soldiers and gladiators, Rome's next generation, to the delight of their parents and the radiant glee of the Old Count, were avidly smacking each other senseless with weapons made of wood and paper painted to look like metal.

The tournament, which had begun with a formal greeting by the count exhorting Rome's long history of honor, virtue, fairness and dignity, descended quickly into chaos. A troupe of midgets and dwarfs had been recruited to compete in the games. They were attired in outsized diapers fashioned of old bed linens. Those with beards and abundant body hair

were particularly striking. Their job was to make sure that the genuine
children did not become bored. They ran backward in the races, did back
flips, fell on their lumpy diapers under the weight of make believe javelins,
and almost, but never actually, won an event. Children screamed at them
in indignation and pummeled them with their fists. Seesaws, rigged as
miniature catapults, were set strategically in the shrubbery around the
playing field. When interest in the games flagged, a burst of midgets was
shot aloft, kicking their little legs and flapping their stubby arms. Honking
like geese, clucking like hens and quacking like ducks they landed helter-
skelter on top of battle weary children. They plopped into the laps of
matrons and skidded through platters of sticky sweets. On landing they
rolled head over diaper and bounded to their feet. After wiggling their
bared bottoms they would run off into the crowd making slurping sounds
and crying, "waannh, waannh, waannnnhh!" before slipping under ladies'
dresses and jumping up and down. Expelled after much kicking, gasping
and unladylike writhing, the midgets and dwarves, their fingers placed
innocently to their lips would say, "goo goo," before running off to their
next bit of mischief.

Count Colonna, exhausted, slumping in the saddle, picked his way
carefully through the litter of worn out children. Darkness had fallen.
His evening's guests were arriving. Bejeweled, bewigged, seemingly
enameled, trussed, cinched, propped and buttressed in their imaginatively
constructed costumes, they emerged from the darkness onto the candle
lighted path. *"Brava,"* The old Count clapped sloppily, trying not to slip
from his horse, *"Stupenda! Aaah! Che bellezza!"* he crowed and coughed.
Judging from the turnout the party would be his most successful ever. He
was in heaven as he stationed himself near the gate and waited eagerly for
Ottavio's triumphant arrival. The day's weather had been perfect. There
must have been a huge turnout. The purse must be a fortune. He cackled,
contemplating freedom and independence from the bankers and the Pope.

The crowd turned to the sound of thundering hooves. A phalanx of
young barons, Ottavio Colonna at the head, pounded through the gate.
Their hair was soaked and pasted to their flushed and dirt streaked faces.

Clods of turf were stuck to their sweat-soaked, mud spattered silks. Their horses were lathered in froth.

A groom ran to meet them. Ottavio leaped to the ground and slammed Tempest's reigns into his hands. He tore off his gloves and threw them to the ground. He ran at them, jumped on them and ground them into the dirt. He looked toward his uncle, back at the gate, then turned away and stormed to the stable. The other barons jumped to the ground and hurried after. Ottavio stopped and lowered his head. He slammed the wall, hard, once, the full force of his shoulder behind the blow. After a moment he slammed it again, and then again. He shook his hand in pain. His cohort of Orsinis, Caetanis, Savellis and Frangipanis stood back. To the guests watching from the terrace, their hands and mouths full of food, drink and in more than a few cases, various protuberant portions of one another's anatomy, it was plain that something had not gone well.

Piero and Antonio came running through the gate, and seeing the commotion ran to the stable. Ottavio faced the wall not moving. His friends stood back, giving him space. Puzzled, curious to understand what had gotten into him, they called out, offering help. Ottavio hung his head. Piero and Antonio watched from a distance. More people came running through the gate. They were yelling, pumping their fists in the air. Ottavio shouted and once more slammed his hand against the wall, before doubling over shaking his wrist.

Knowing from experience that it was unwise to go near the "boys," the older guests maintained a respectful distance. Distance, however, did not prevent their becoming involved. Watching the scene unfold, curious about the outburst, eager to know the story behind it; they were still not quite curious enough to abandon the food, the drinks, or the immediate company they had carefully begun to cultivate, to get into the thick of it. Their polite retreat from the sweaty mud-caked young men, however, permitted them, or, more to the point, obligated them, positively demanded, that they rise to the occasion. Educated guesses, and opinions, which were firmly based on other guesses, along with well-founded hearsay and outbursts of speculation surged. Gossip—ignited as if by a volatile accelerant—inflamed their imaginations and animated their tongues. Best guesses began to congeal into truths. Bullshit became gospel. No one really knew the cause of the outburst and, to tell the truth, the truth, under the circumstances, was immaterial. Important, absolutely crucial, was having an opinion and stating it emphatically. They hissed and whispered in amazement and shock, thrilled by the possibilities of their inventions. An authorative voice rose to be heard, "Well, of course but . . . " to be drowned out by a shouted, "It could have been guessed that . . . " to be trumped more loudly, "But then why would they be so pissed?"

"Why? I'll tell you why," doubting the plausibility of the explanation that had not been heard. "Ottavio thought he had the race rigged . . . " someone shouted. "Thought? He always has it rigged."

"There was a ringer . . . "

"They were robbed . . . "

"The riggers were robbed?"

"But who won?" Voices were becoming hoarse. Everyone was yelling, getting closer, shouting in each other's faces, not hearing. "A horse from the Spanish guard!"

"It was not!! A horse showed up that no one had ever seen before."

"Nonsense . . . Couldn't happen. There are no secrets in Rome Everybody knows everything here . . . "

"The rider got sick . . . the jockey threw the race . . . somebody got paid off."

"The one that was supposed to win?"

" NO . . . ! NO . . . ! NO . . . ! Couldn't happen. The rider was what's his name's cousin's brother once removed. He's been a member of that Club since before he was born. Never happen . . . They just lost . . . I was there . . . "

"You were *not* . . . !"

"What club?!

" I was *so* there . . . !"

"Who won?!"

"That's what I want to know!"

"You were *not* there, because *I* wasn't there and you were with *me* . . . "

"Fuck you, too . . . and the horse you rode in on." Some one shoved and, like a tightly packed herd of cows, an entire segment of the elegant assembly flopped to the ground. Their shouting and chattering continued like rattling cicadas in a gale force wind, "Someone fed Chigi's horse something . . . "

"Chigi's horse!? . . . Chigi never runs any horses. What are you talking about? Those fat things he keeps can barely walk. He just parades around on them all dolled up. Last year you couldn't even see the horse for all the ribbons and the banners, and the armor. He could have been riding on an ostrich, or a bear, or a sow . . . "

" Armor, for Christ's sake!!! And the gold bridle and bit . . . Can you see that fat ass mincing off to battle all trussed up like an I don't know what! . . . "

"A goose!!"

"A sofa!"

"Chigi came bouncing onto the field, bouncing and shaking up and down. He looked like a pudding. One of his minions was holding up a banner displaying mountains and a star . . . Mountains and stars and lions . . . "

"Don't make me laugh . . . Is there no truth in heraldry?"

"Better his crest should show head lice or roaches at war on a pile of unsalted bread," stated with a patrician sneer.

"You don't know what you're talking about . . . Today Chigi ran a horse . . . He ran this fabulous looking horse . . ."

"Yeah, well, this horse, this fabulous looking, previously unknown horse stopped in the middle of the final straightaway to have a crap. Swear to God and hope to die. I was there."

"You were *not* there . . . "

"What horse stops to take a shit? My horses keep running . . . My horses can run and shit at the same time..."

"Like owner like horse."

"I said the horse crapped out. I did not say the horse crapped!"

"I was *so* there!" With a shove another section of the assembly hit the grass, still talking, sideways, unfazed.

"The horse the Spanish guard ran looked a little fucked up to me. If you ask me, something was going on . . . ”

“Nobody asked.”

“Shut up!!”

“But why should anyone care if Chigi's horse was fucked up? . . . His horse can't run.”

“Chigi's horse wasn't fucked up. Chigi's horse stopped to take a crap. The Spanish horse was fucked up . . . ”

“ Oh, and a horse stopping to take a crap in the middle of a race isn't fucked up, you're telling me?” Pushing and shoving on their knees, bellowing and extending their fingers obscenely, the guests trampled each other, struggling to get to their feet.

“Piero! Antonio!” Professor Laetus reached out from among the fallen. His toga was plastered with bits of food. His garland had been reduced to silage.

“Professor Laetus!” Piero dodged through the scrambled guests and hauled the Professor to his feet. “Wait til I tell you! You won't believe it!” His eyes were bright and his cheeks flushed.

“Yes. Yes. Tell me.”

“I'm going to design a fresco for Chigi's new villa! Can you believe it?”

“Splendid. Splendid. I want to hear all about it. But first, what's going on over there? What happened at the race? Who won?” Antonio and Piero yanked the Professor to his feet. Stepping carefully they carried him by the elbows to an uncluttered bit of ground. “Did you get to see the race? I can't make any sense at all out of what these people are saying. What happened?”

“We went to Chigi's right after we left you, you know, to meet his daughter. That's where Imperia,” Piero stopped to catch his breath, “Imperia, the mistress of the house, asked me to design a fresco for her. I can already picture it in my mind, all done, a scene from classical mythology. I am so excited!”

“Wonderful, but what happened at the race?” the professor asked, patting the young man on the back.

Antonio, hoarse from shouting, broke in waving his hands in the air, “By the time we left Chigi's it was getting late. We caught up with the guys we know from St. Eustachio at the Corso. All the clubs and militias were already gathered in vacant lots getting ready for the final parade to the Circus Maximus."

"You should have seen it," said Piero.

"It must have been an impressive spectacle," Professor Laetus said, his impatience starting to show. The air behind him fried with speculative accounts and expert opinions that he could not hear.

Antonio raised his voice, "It took us awhile but we finally found our guys. They were near the Palazzo Venezia waiting to join the parade. The order of march was chosen by lots. Since we were toward the back, we got to watch most of the other clubs pass. It's a good thing that you told us to go on ahead. We never would have made it in time." He bent forward, put his hands on his knees and took a big gulp of air, like a runner at the end of a race.

"So, when you got to the track, what then?" The professor asked. He knew they were showing him the wonderful time they would have missed if he had not encouraged them to go on ahead. They were thanking him. He was grateful. It was torment all the same. He took another slow breath and remembered, as through a fog, being a kid once and seeing his first big procession. He clenched his teeth.

Piero shouted to be heard above the trampled mob, "It was a madhouse: flags waving, the colors . . . " He grabbed the Professor and jumped from the path of a stampede heading toward the stable, " . . . fighting lions, stars, lilies, mountains, chevrons, flames. The banners were all hoisted up high; wild colors against the sky, blue and gold, red on green, black and yellow, checks, zigzags and diamonds. Silver and gold fringes fluttering and glistening. All the bands were tuning up, practicing. There were horses decked out to look like dragons . . . " The Professor knew well the brilliant surge of staged violence that streamed down the Corso. He had seen it all a hundred times, but he listened, resigned to hearing Piero tell him all about the low rhythmic drumming, the teams organizing into formation, about the tinny sounds of horns and pipes, about the smells of horses and leather and men, about people leaning out windows. "Way up front a horn signaled that the parade was on the move. I could feel it. The rhythm of the drums stepped up and caught my heartbeat and I just started to march without having to look around to find out why. I just knew that it was time and I knew how to do it. The horses were moving, too. They knew it was time to march, too. Their restless shuffling and snorting stopped and the scrape and clap of the hooves began to beat in time to the drums."

Professor Laetus looked off into the distance, blinking. He tensed his jaws, "The race! What happened!?"

Antonio stepped in shouting above the commotion around them, "You couldn't have imagined it a few minutes earlier. As far as you could see, were the clubs from Trevi, Trastevere, Monti, all led by the rich families who give them money. They were all there: Parione, Regola, Campitelli, Ripa, Ponte. The clatter of hooves echoing off the walls was like thunder."

Piero jumped back in, "When we got to the foot of the Capitoline Hill. I swear I felt like a Roman. My heart was filled with pride. Tears came to my eyes, the music, the colors. I felt part of it."

The Professor nodded. "Then I would guess there were speeches at the foot of the Capitoline," hoping to hasten Piero to the end of the parade and past the all the politicians and clerics who, he most certainly knew, had been assembled there to unfurl their own glutinous interpretations of the City's evolution which, annually and inevitably, arrived at the preposterous conclusion that all those present had been the cause of Rome's glorious past.

"Exactly," said Piero, undeterred, "We were right behind the club from The Borgo that has a strong cavalry of Swiss riders. In front of them were the guys from Pigna. Up ahead I saw the contingent from the Campo Marzio. Their banner, with the trident, flew higher than everybody else's. The Spanish Guard was there. The priests were marching with them."

The Professor appeared numb. He wiggled his toes. He wanted Piero to speed up and get to the race. He cupped his hands and called above the feverish chatter frying the air around them, "Is it true that Chigi rode in the parade!? Someone said he was with the club from Trastevere, that he was on a spectacular horse. Did you see him!?"

Piero took a breath, gearing up for a verbatim recounting of every speech that was made and to tell how he managed to sidestep a pile of horse shit to avoid ruining his new shoes and how the parade then continued past the Theater of Marcellus, and how, yes, Chigi the Magnificent was riding an unbelievable horse with a tossing red mane, and, yes, he was with the club from Trastevere, when a loud voice boomed, "Ottavio!! Ottavio!!"

Everyone in the jumbled mass shut up and turned to see Cardinal Riario pushing his way through the crowd wearing a broad grin. "Ottavio!" he shouted as people cleared a path for him. He approached Ottavio and dropped to one knee. Colonna turned away from him and slammed the wall again.

The Professor's eyebrows leaped and he turned to Piero and Antonio frantic to know what in God's name was going on. The extinguished crowd reignited, singeing the atmosphere with renewed speculation.

Antonio picked up the thread, "That's right, Chigi marched with the club from Trastevere. We didn't see him until the procession reached the circus Maximus. Those guys came across the Tiber Island late and joined the parade behind us."

"And the horse he was riding?"

Piero cut in, "The parade went around the Circus once. Then everyone disbanded. The south side of the race course was set up for honored guests," He went on to describe in excruciating detail where the box for foreign embassies and the Church hierarchy was set up, how they were ornamented, how the sun was to their backs so that the scene before them was played against the backdrop of the vine entangled arches and vaults of the Palatine Hill, how the stacked up remains of the palaces built by Rome's emperors over a period of a millennium glowed orange, " . . . The finish line was at the center of the straightaway on the south side in front of the box. The public could assemble anywhere else. The horses and riders were kept in the shady place at the east end of the track for water and to get ready for the trials . . . "

Antonio noticed the crowd around Ottavio breaking up. If Piero didn't get a move on someone else would tell the story, "Once the parade broke up we could see a lot more. That's when we finally saw what all the oohing and aaahing was about."

The Professor's scalp prickled. He steered the two away from the noise, the better to hear Antonio, "Everyone was craning their necks to

get a look at the horse. Chigi himself was riding it. He never did that
before. He looked very puffed up.

"He didn't race, did he?" asked the Professor, astonished.

"Christ, no. He dismounted and a jock from the club in Trastevere
took over," answered Antonio.

"That was when the Pope arrived in a chariot dressed as an emperor,"
interrupted Piero.

The Professor raised his hands, "Stop! Stop! Stop! Later for the Pope!
What happened with the race?" He looked to Antonio.

Unstoppable Piero started to laugh, "So the Pope shows up. There's
this big commotion. The Germans freak out at the sight of the Pope all
dolled up like a Roman Emperor. There's the Pope, this old man with a
bushy white beard, clattering out of a chariot propped up on a cane that's
disguised as a broad sword. It's all wrapped in silver cloth. It didn't fool
anybody, not for a second."

Antonio spoke loudly over Piero and over the commotion.
"Everybody was looking at Chigi's unbelievable horse. The whole scene
was fantastic." He pointed to the stable. "Ottavio Colonna was there on
Tempest, his great black horse. And then Chigi comes in on the one with
the red mane. No one ever saw her before. No one had heard anything
about it. She's jet black, very tall, with a fiery red mane. I never saw
anything like it. All the horses were kept at a distance, so we couldn't get
up close. But even from a distance you couldn't take your eyes from it."

"What happened? The suspense is killing me," said the Professor.

"It was crazy," Antonio pulled Piero and the Professor away from
the hubbub. "After that the whole place went crazy. People started betting
up a storm. You know, last week everybody pretty much knew who they
were going to put their money on. You know how word gets around.
Everybody knows everything in Rome. Everybody knows all the horses
in the City like everybody knows where the best girls are. Then, out of
the blue, this new horse shows up and it's Chigi's. And, you know, whatever
Chigi does is a big deal. The richest man in the City, maybe the richest man
in the world, so all bets are off. Everybody's confused. Everybody's saying
'if it's Chigi's it must be a great horse.' They all want a piece of Chigi.
Before you know it everybody's running around looking for a bookie."

"What were the odds?" asked the Professor, his mouth dry, a closet gambler who liked a sure thing.

"I don't know. I don't understand any of that stuff. I was going to bet on Tempest, everyone was, or on that Spanish horse, that huge brown one. He was supposed to be really hot. We were talking about it all week at Pompey's," looking at Piero who nodded in agreement. "Then somebody calls out 'Bet Red! Bet Red!' I don't know where it came from, but right away other people started calling out 'Bet Red! Bet Red!' Before I knew it I was chanting "Bet Red" too. I don't know why. You were, too," he elbowed Piero, "And not only did we chant 'Bet Red,' but we joined the mob scrambling to find a betting booth. We spotted the guy we met out past the gate, the Jew's cousin, and I bet all the money I had on Red."

" I did, too. It was wild," said Piero.

Antonio stopped him, "The Jews were giving better odds than anybody so I bet with them.

The commotion died down. The three turned and saw Riario making his way toward them. He was saying something. They tried to hear. The crowd closed around him. They could only hear snatches of what he was saying.

" . . . I heard all that and I looked at the horse and I thought to myself, Chigi buys a horse? It must be a great horse. It looks like a great horse, like a fabulous horse . . . " Antonio, Piero and the Professor strained to hear him. " . . . But I never heard anything about it. I would never bet on a horse I didn't know anything about. I knew Tempest, and so I bet on him to win and on the Spaniard to place second. And guess what?" New guests pushed forward elbowing The Professor, Piero and Antonio out of earshot.

Antonio, unable to hear, yanked Piero and the Professor off to the edge of the crowd again to finish the story, "Everybody was in a frenzy, hot for the race to start. More and more people were yelling 'Bet Red! Bet Red!' At the same time there were these pulling contests going on. Huge horses pulling logs, pulling sledges with rocks, boring as shit. Everyone started hooting 'Start the race! Start the race!'"

The Professor agreed, "Start the race!"

"The Pope stood up and someone said that he said, 'Start the fucking race, already!' I don't know if that's true."

"He said something," said Piero. "I saw his lips move."

"All the horses that were entered in the event made a final parade around the circus—real slow. The redhead one was fantastic. She paraded with a light bounce, like a dancer. After that they lined up in front of the Box, where the Pope was, and everything quieted down. The Pope stood up and waited for everyone's attention. He raised his so-called *sword*. When he dropped it they took off. Everyone there must have been holding their breath. That's how quiet it was. The turf was wet, so there wasn't much noise, no thunder of hooves, just a soft heavy padding sound. At the start the redheaded one was outside, Tempest was inside. The Spaniard was next to Tempest. The Orsini's ran a great dappled gray that pulled out front right way."

Piero said, "The odds on him were long because everyone knows him for a starter but not a finisher. He'll be pulling logs next year." The Professor glared at him.

"They made the first turn and the Redhead hangs in there and starts moving to the inside. Ottavio pulls a little ahead. The Spaniard moves up on Orsini so its Orsini, the Spaniard, Ottavio's Tempest and the Redhead as they come out of the first turn and into the straight-away. People are starting to make noise now, yelling 'Move! Move!' The bets are closed and as soon as they get into the straightaway the Redhead moves out and it's like she's flying. She overtakes Tempest. The Spaniard, it's a heavy horse, powerful, digs in and plows past Orsini who's tiring. You could see him breathing hard. It's a long straightaway. There's no sound on the track. It's soft and they're digging in. The crowd is tensed, taut like a viol string, freaking. Everything's at a high pitch. People are keening. Chanting starts from over at the stalls. 'TES! TA! RO! SA!, TES! TA! RO! SA!, RED! HEAD! RED! HEAD!' Ottavio seemed to hold Tempest back. You could see it. 'He's holding back!' someone shouted. 'RED! HEAD!' the crowd roaring. All of a sudden the Redhead pulls up alongside Ottavio and Tempest digs in. It's almost like Ottavio isn't even there, like he was just baggage.

"Ottavio on Tempest and the Redhead pull up on The Spaniard. It's three of them neck in neck going into the turn. Ottavio on Tempest has the inside. The Spaniard is in the middle, the Redhead on the outside. All of a sudden the Redhead starts to gain in the turn! It was unbelievable! Everybody's yelling, "TES! TA! RO! SA!, TES! TA! RO! SA!,' When they turned onto the final stretch the Redhead is in the lead by half a length with Tempest second and the Spaniard third by a full length and falling back. No one else is even close. The crowd is going crazy. Everyone's shouting for the Redhead when all of a sudden she just runs out of steam and Ottavio's horse, Tempest, flies past her. Ottavio looked shocked. He looked back at the Redhead. He was riding low, but he seemed to be pulling back because Tempest was straining. He must have already figured on losing. He looks back at the Redhead sinking behind him, and the Spaniard pulling past her."

"So?"

"Ottavio won by a nose."

"So what's his problem?" the Professor asked, dumbfounded, as the Old Count, slumped astride Pegasus, made his way carefully to the stable where Ottavio stood like a man awaiting sentence.

Riario's voice boomed, "Thank you! Thank you, my dear friend!" All heads turned. "Your splendid nephew just made me a fortune!" Cardinal Riario stood looking up at the old Count. "Everybody switched their money to Chigi's Redhead at the last minute. In a matter of seconds the odds on favorite, Ottavio's magnificent Tempest, became the long shot!" Riario threw his head back and laughed deliriously. The Professor's was not the only puzzled face in the crowd. Cardinal Riario patted the old Count's thigh affectionately.

"So what's his problem!" someone shouted.

"His problem?" answered Riario overcome with hilarity. "Ottavio had all his money on the Redhead!"

❧

19

The Shadow Play

The stage was set against a high wall at the back of the garden. Count Colonna remained astride Pegasus. His rump drooped to the left. His shoulders sagged to the right. His head rested forward on his chest. Thoroughly exhausted from the day's celebration and despite the setback and public humiliation that he knew would follow in the wake of Ottavio's stupidity, he was determined to enjoy the evening's performance, a reading from Orlando Furioso. His little granddaughter, Alessandra, was playing the role of Angelica. Ludovico Ariosto, the author himself, would narrate and act the part of the hero Ruggiero.

The lanterns were extinguished, plunging the party into darkness. The guests, their fire spent by the truth of the race's outcome, marooned momentarily with nothing to say, stared silently into the dark, like refugees from a ship wreck, waiting for the play to start. A drum began pounding a deep slow rhythm. The strong voice of Ludovico Ariosto filled the darkness as he began to sing the passage:

"The colossal monster now appeared half submerged; like a sleek low and stealthy ship" . . .

The garden wall was suddenly bathed in light.

A long sinuous shadow appeared, undulating slowly. It was the sea monster, the terrible Orc. The shadow thrashed and shook its scaly spine. The midgets, fed and refreshed crouched at the foot of the stage, bearing lanterns. Their job was to aim them so that the actors' shadows were projected, larger than life, onto the garden wall. They moved the lanterns up and down and forward and back to alter the sizes and shapes of the characters. They shook the lights and flashed them to make the shadows quiver. Eight additional midgets were inside the costume of the sea monster.

"Driven before the wind . . ."

Reedy horns and a shivering tambourine announced the north wind. They were coming to the part the old Count loved best. He wanted to applaud, but was afraid of falling. He rested his head forward onto Pegasus's neck. His hands thus freed, he enthusiastically slapped his thighs. Pegasus, awakened, pissed. Guests, dozing, awoke to a deep growl and a piercing shriek.

"So appeared the terrible Orc as it approached the juicy tidbit shown to it."

The Count cackled gleefully. The lamps flashed off and then on to illuminate the shadow of the enormous whale-like, serpent-like, bird-like beast with open jaws and sharp teeth as it leaped from the sea.

"The young girl tied up on the beach was petrified . . ."

The scream was a new touch. Alessandra thought it up herself and persuaded Ariosto to stage the variation that, she knew, would give her grandfather his full measure of pleasure and delight and also give herself, as the fair Angelica, a speaking role. The Orc roared again, a blaring ram's horn.

"The Orc, a beast I can only describe as a great coiling twisting mass with protruding eyes and tusks like a wild pig . . ."

The midgets twisted and coiled, and coiled and twisted. The shadow loomed and arced. Angelica shrieked again, a prolonged bloodcurdling howl that soared upward to the top of her range before plunging through a spine-chilling glissando to a disconcerting glottal finish.

Ruggiero on a flying horse suddenly appeared in a pose of exaggerated surprise and fury. He thrust his mighty sword at the monster's head.

"Ruggiero struck at it between the eyes, but he might as well have been striking iron or stone."

There was another shriek. The silhouette of a maiden about to be burned at the stake appeared, quivering, at the far right side of the wall. "Aaaaah. Nice touch!" called the Count, "Brilliant girl." He slapped his thighs, "That's my grand-daughter." he said into Pegasus' neck. The old horse snorted softly and shook.

"So powerfully did the Orc thrash the water with its tail that the seas surged up into the sky. Ruggiero could not tell if he was swimming or flying, fearful that the spray would sink his winged mount . . . He hit upon a new and better plan. He would dazzle the beast with his glistening shield."

But suddenly the shield, so long awaited, fell into the sea. "Oh shit, now what," said the Count. That was new, too. The maiden screamed. The shadow of the winged horse with Ruggiero mounted on its back leaped back to the shore and landed beside the maiden. Behind them the shadow of the serpent thrashed and coiled, and coiled and thrashed, in the roiling sea.

"Ruggiero dismounted and ran to the maid, plucking her, stake, kindling and all, into his arms in a courtly embrace. He then took up his station. The sea beast was approaching the shore, its belly displacing half the ocean before it. Holding the maid on her stake like a tasty treat on a skewer he waved the tantalizing morsel under the monster's flaring nostrils. Victory is mine thought the great beast and he reclined into a great laugh," sang Ariosto to the rhythmic beating of the drum.

"No! That chicken shit son of a bitch! He's going to feed her to the monster to save his own skinny ass!" moaned the Count.

"But then, as the beast opened its enormous mouth and flashed all its razor sharp teeth, Ruggiero changed his stance. He lifted the stake, the kindling and the morsel herself, as he would a pike and charged into the mouth of the beast. 'Orc,' said the Orc, 'orc orc.' Its great protruding eyes blinked as if to ask, "Where have they gone?" It thrashed, and in that instant Ruggiero righted the stake, with Angelica still tied to it, and wedged

it between the monster's great jaws. With its body writhing furiously the Orc screeched and squawked but could do nothing more. Ruggiero quickly untied Angelica leaving the stake propped between the beast's jaws and with her in his arms ran for the safety of the shore."

"Aaah," the count sobbed. "Beautiful, beautiful." The evening had grown cool. He shifted in his saddle and farted, emitting a small puff of steam.

Giulia Farnese, notrious for being the late Borgia Pope's mistress, shifted her weight when the scene ended. She was reclining in the Roman fashion, dressed in a flowing white dress. Her hair was piled high in a heap of ringlets. Her costume was, while prone, as she was then, or on all fours, as she hoped eventually to become, the she-wolf of Rome. Standing, she was a dead ringer for the many breasted Artemis of Ephesus. Her shoemaker had fashioned a clutch of pigs' bladders into small wine skins, ever so cleverly stitched together, to resemble an array of lovely, if somewhat small, breasts. Her lounging companion, the even more notorious Vannozza de Cataneis, who had borne Borgia his four fearsome children, was dressed as a fresh fig. The two were like sisters, inseparable.

Alessandra, holding a lighted lamp beneath her chin, descended from the dark looking like a ghost. Ludovico Ariosto set her gently on the ground beside Giulia and Vannozza, and then disappeared. Alessandra's feet were still bound in kindling.

"You look absolutely hideous," said Giulia. "How do you expect to kick up your heels in that getup?"

Alessandra sighed a sigh that asked if she really had to explain it all again. Alessandra worked hard to make herself repulsive, and had so far succeeded. She made a habit of powdering her face a ghastly white. She moped about looking sad, and mumbling prayers. It was a strategy that worked to preserve her from being married off, but it was a tricky business and she had to be careful. She was not repulsive. To the contrary, and to her growing consternation, she was blossoming into a very lovely young woman.

"Play your little game with your grandfather all you want, Dearheart. All I can say is, I hope you're getting a kick out of it for its own sake, because it could backfire in your face just like that." Giulia snapped her fingers. "You know the way I feel. Another plague year and we could all be dead. Why not have some fun right now?" She leaned toward Alessandra. "You don't like hearing me say that, I know, but let me tell you, it's not *if*, but *when*, because the unexpected is inevitable. I've lived long enough to know." But Alessandra already knew that she had to be careful to not over play her hand. If she appeared too pious and too repulsive the family could decide to cut their losses and dump her in a convent, or, worse, make her learn to cook and do laundry. "Time is still on your side, Alessandra," said Giulia. "You're still a kid after all. You have time. I don't."

"You. What about me?" asked Vannozza, the fig.

"What if this turns out to be another plague year?" Giulia asked, "I was paying attention the last time around. I remember the way it was. When the plague hits no one wants to know you. No one wants to be near you. And it's not because of anything you did. It's just fear. The plague descends and everyone is afraid of everything. Fear is everywhere: fear of the air, fear of the water, fear of a kiss or a glance. Death rides on a wink, a hickey on your neck. "Look, look, she has it," somebody says. And when that happens you might just as well really have it, because you're already dead, killed by their words and their fear. No one will let you into a shop. You won't be able to get a meal or draw water from a fountain. You might as well dig your own grave and jump in. 'Lovely thing, but, aah, what a shame,' they'll say. People will say anything to draw attention away from themselves. You won't even be able to make confession because those little pricks of priests will be afraid to get into the confessional with you. They see someone coming to the church and they scurry off and hide like rats. So there you are, unconfessed and unconsoled, in a state of sin, Hell waiting. Everyone is in the same boat as you, but does that make them have any pity? Just the opposite. They fan the fire of your damnation, accuse you, "She must be in league with the devil. That's her punishment for having fun. It's her reward for screwing the Pope."

Vannozza piped up, "And if it's not the plague it'll be Roman fever, or the French army, or the Spanish, or God help us those Germans. Ugggh. God help me. Lucrezia always says, 'if you're patient true love will come your way.' Give me a break, I say. Go ahead, wait for love. Know what you'll have to show for it? War will break out somewhere and you'll get an armload of your husband's weapons wrapped in a banner spattered with guts and horseshit." The fig rested her case.

"And now there's that lard-ass from Wittenberg blowing halitosis all over the place, telling us we're already at the gateway to Hell. Well," said Giulia, " I for one am willing to take him at his word, because if Heaven is the reward for a life on earth with someone like him in charge I'll take my chances in Hell. Yes, yes, my dear, I live as though there is no tomorrow. For poor Rodrigo there was no tomorrow. I went to bed and woke up the next morning with a blotched corpse beside me. Not even a whisper in the night. No one wanted me after that, let me tell you. I thought I would be next. For all I know I was next. We may already be dead. Just look at you." She and the Fig clicked their tongues, "Tomorrow? I'm afraid not."

Alessandra listened. The role she defined for herself in this evening's entertainment was meant to show her piety, but also to show that she had too much spirit to be convent material. She wanted to make her grandfather happy so that he would never ever wish to be without her. But the plague? She hadn't thought of that. What if her grandfather fell to the plague? And yes, Roman Fever. Giulia and Vannozza were crazy, but they weren't necessarily wrong. The way things were going with the plague knocking people off, young and old, like flies every winter, well . . . A whole crop of young girls bit the dust this past winter and the pickings were slim for men seeking brides. She shivered. They were looking for matches that would benefit their families and here she was, pasty face, crucifix, kindling, title and all. Maybe she should make it look like she'd already got the plague, she thought. Maybe she could use fear of the plague to make herself virtually unapproachable.

"Listen, Dearheart," Giulia offered, "your grandfather is a noble Roman just like all the others. You can make yourself as revolting as you want. All those second sons of second sons standing over there in their riding colors are looking to buy their way into the action, and you're a potential ticket. Their fathers would marry them off to blind dogs if they thought it was to their benefit. And you know what? If it was to somebody's benefit to have their son marry a blind dog, or a sheep or a fence post, and they were willing to pay enough to make it happen, the Pope would bless the union and that would be that."

Professor Laetus, trailed by Piero and Antonio, stepped from the darkness into the soft glow of Alessandra's lantern. The sight of the three women startled them. "My what a lovely cluster of breasts," The Professor stammered. "Artemis, I presume." Smiling Giulia leaned back and propped herself up on both elbows to give him a better view. Two midgets, their extinguished lamps still smoking, appeared suddenly from the darkness. Each attached himself to a breast and took a swig. The Professor, embarrassed, said, "let me not interrupt," looking from the fig to the martyr. Piero's eyes were wide. He grinned. He knelt beside Giulia, and with a piece of charcoal from his pouch, signed one of her many breasts.

Giulia threw her head back and laughed. Delighted she jumped to her feet, thrust her arms above her head and leapt into a graceful cartwheel. Upright once more she grinned, a true grin, a little girl's grin on the verge of laughter. With her hands on her hips and her head to one side, she looked Piero straight in the eye before flinging herself into the air and like a gigantic cookie cart-wheeled off into the night. Piero, thrilled, leaped into the air and cart-wheeled after her. Antonio sat down beside the less athletic Fig. Alessandra, Giulia's remarks fresh in her mind, hopped to her feet, but impeded by the kindling binding her legs, plopped sideways onto the grass. Antonio and Vannozza rolled away. The sky was plum. Fireworks exploded, flashed and hissed into oblivion.

Levi reached the sepulcher late. Djem was waiting, working the abacus, checking accounts. The Moor seemed pleased, satisfied, but not surprised by the weight of coin Levi heaved onto the altar. "My friend," was all he said. Levi was grateful to be safe and secure in the underground chamber and free of his heavy load. "Have something," Djem offered a plate of sweet cakes. A pot of mint tea was brewing over a small fire. Levi started to say something. He didn't know where to begin. Nothing had gone as it usually did. He wanted to talk about their windfall, about the day's extraordinary events, but remained silent. The food and the warm light of the sepulcher relaxed him. The long, cold roundabout trek, backtracking to avoid being followed had taken all his strength. His shoulders were stiff, his back tense. He stretched. His head ached.

He sat. Without a word Djem opened the sack and began sorting and stacking the coins by denomination, clicking sums on the abacus and entering them in a ledger. Levi found the silence deadening and heavy, the lack of conversation odd. He wanted to talk. The numbers were still spinning in his head. A fortune was sitting on the altar. He had done his best to keep track of the amounts, but the odds changed so suddenly. By some miracle when it was all over the money was there to pay off the few big winners. His percentage was intact. The take was good, because a lot of money was bet. Riario walked away with a fortune.

Levi shook his head. He wanted to ask Djem what he thought of Chigi being carried aloft after his red haired horse lost the race. People seemed pleased in a strange way that they and the Magnificent Chigi all lost money together. It was a communion of sorts between themselves and greatness, a shared defeat. Chigi became one of them. They became one with him. After the race the crowd swarmed around Chigi and carried him aloft as if his horse had won. Levi shook his head, again, thinking about it, trying to fathom it. Chigi loses and is treated like a winner. He wanted to know how Chigi ended up with the red maned horse that Colonna had bought from Djem.

He wanted to tell Djem how when the crowd started chanting his bowels turn to mud, that he had visions of being stampeded and trampled to paste by the herd, who, he well knew, could be turned into a wolf pack for no reason at all. One guy wanted to place a bet on credit. When he refused the man got physical. The bruise on his cheekbone was the proof. He wanted to joke about the group of German pilgrims who foamed at the mouth when they saw the Pope dressed up as Caesar. He also wanted to hear about everything that Djem had seen.

Djem stopped counting and sat back. He was so tired he feared he would collapse if he stopped working. He smiled wearily and said, " To answer all your questions. We didn't "BET RED."

"So you're the one who started it."

Thirty miles south of Rome a band of Moors, escorting a string of horses southward into the Kingdom of Naples, camped in a thicket off the Via Appia. One horse was a magnificent black two year old shorn of her mane. A faint residue of red tint remained on the stubble.

Part IV

Instructions from Seville

20

The Palazzo Riario

Bramante showed up at the Palazzo Riario construction site early. Piero and Antonio were waiting for him in an old hen house that served as an office. They gave him a brief overview of the progress that had been made since his last visit. Then as was their habit, the two apprentices ran through a list of questions. As he provided the answers, Bramante, a stickler for detail, watched carefully making certain that their notes and sketches faithfully recorded his answers.

When the meeting was over the three stepped out into the hazy Roman morning. Dressed simply, the venerated Bramante assumed an aura of dignity and authority as he strode through the clatter, the smoke, the debris and the mud; energized by the deafening sound of stone being crushed and the squeal of iron pulleys straining under their loads, by men shouting, by the smell and sweat of horses pulling sledges, by the pungent forest smell of freshly hewn lumber. The commotion, the sounds, the smells and cursing, every bit of it, groaned and shouted out to him the promise of seeing another of his designs brought to life. After more than

50 years his work continued to exhilarate him. Where others' work had gone stale his had continued to evolve. He still took pleasure in trying new and risky things. His eyes were bright as he took in the work. One crew of workmen sorted piles of stone, another crew poured water — bucketful after bucketful—into a basin to slake lime for mortar. Bricks were being wheeled in barrows to the base of a tall section of scaffolding where they were hoisted, along with buckets of fresh mortar, to the top of a newly built wall. At the upper most tier of scaffolding dust-covered laborers passed the bricks and mortar along the catwalk to masons who buttered, tapped and set them in place.

Looking around him, Bramante was pleased with what he saw. He almost always liked what he saw, but today he felt particularly grateful to Piero and Antonio. They were well organized. The other men respected them. Piero in particular had come a long way since he first came to work in the studio. He had made maximum use of the site, permitting the different crews to do their jobs without getting in each other's way. Bramante was pleased to see very little waste either of manpower or materials. Bramante demanded efficiency. Efficiency increased profits.

Bramante squinted into the haze and took a deep breath, scrutinizing the emerging building. It was his gift to be able to see a finished structure in his mind almost from the very instant he conceptualized it. He knew which rooms would have sparkling daylight in them. He knew at precisely which hours of the day sunlight would dance across a floor. He could hear musicians tuning their instruments in a music room as his hand drew its design on paper. He could hear plainsong reverberating in chapels yet unbuilt. He once thought that everyone could do this, imagine things the way he did. When he realized that his gift was rare he suppressed his impatience and frustration with people who were less adept, and developed his ability to convey in drawings, paintings, models and simple, patient words, what he himself envisioned so naturally. His ability to develop and communicate a full and clear concept, and to then work single-mindedly toward its fulfillment had made him a master of his craft.

Bramante wanted this particular project to go up quickly. He didn't want any more setbacks. He wasn't getting any younger. To that end he had authorized work to proceed on the façade of the complex surrounding the old Church of San Lorenzo in Damasus before the foundations were laid for the rest of the palazzo. It was a strategic decision. The Pope was still blaming him, unrelentingly, for the work stoppage at Saint Peter's. Bramante had a reputation to repair. He would show the Pope that when a client had the will and the means, he had the manpower and the energy to get the work done. To prove it he decided to complete a portion of Riario's palace as quickly as possible. Riario was fickle. It was imperative that people be able to see something tangible and to see it soon. Bramante decided to get him invested in the project by spending a lot of money fast. That way, he wouldn't be so inclined to change his mind, as he had several times before. The project to build this palazzo had been in the works for years. It would start. It would stop. It would start again then stop. Decades were slipping by. Bramante shook his head. But for the fluke of a horse race and the Pope running out of money. He took a deep breath. "Act on the moment," he barked sharply to his two young apprentices. "That is a lesson. Act."

Bramante reached into a trough and squeezed some mortar between his fingers. Riario was a tough patron. He would spend what it took to show himself off, but he had to be assured that every *solido* spent had an appreciable impact. In more conservative quarters of Rome, among the patrician families to be precise, the entire enterprise of building such an immense palace was viewed as vulgar. Bramante knew what people were saying; he knew that, by association, he was being derided as a panderer to the Cardinal's conceits. Cardinal Riario was thought a fool. Bramante knew, also, that you couldn't make everybody happy, and that if you were going to pander it had better be to a patron and not to the wise guys in the street. That fool, Ottavio Colonna, he learned from his two assistants, had in a boozy scene at the tavern, winked a glassy eye and congratulated them with a smirk for getting some the old pig's money. Bramante presumed he meant Riario's. Those same critics, however, didn't mind being paid by the old pig for the stone from their noble family's quarries, or for lumber from their estates in the North, or for the mortar they made by burning the ancient columns, capitals and ornaments that they scavenged from their ancestral estates of legend and grinding it to powder. Bramante brought his hand to his face and smelled the mortar. He squeezed it again, and considered it carefully before nodding to the mason that it was fine.

Bramante clasped his hands behind his back and looked appraisingly at his work. So far as he knew the design was being praised, even by Riario himself. The Cardinal truly was a pig, he thought, but the Riario family was known for that and seemed to take pride in it. Every family had to be known for something, he snorted. They didn't know good from bad, these Riarios. He snorted again. If it played well among their cronies it was good; if it didn't, well, whose fault would that be? Of course, it would be his. It was always the the architect's fault when something went wrong.

Bramante had known and worked for this family for years. Riario's mother was a Sforza. The work he had done for the Sforza family in Milan had made him famous. So long ago. It seemed like a thousand years ago now. And now he was building for Riario, who never tired of reminding him how much he owed his renown to the Sforzas and the Riarios. Bramante never reminded the Cardinal that were it not for the buildings he created for them they would barely exist at all. Flesh needs stone. He never reminded Riario that without him he was merely an ugly man, an animal with ears in need of shaving and nose hairs in need of plucking. A stomach. Meat. Bramante never pressed the obvious: that it was he who gave them form. He shrank. from the conclusion that if he gave them form he gave them life. "What is fame?" he would say to a client, "what is success, what is power, if no one can see it?" But the Riarios were not like the Sforzas. The Sforzas had impeccable timing. They had class. The Riarios, instead, had a knack for making trouble and never finishing anything. When you work for intriguers, he had concluded long ago, you must act fast. Anything can happen, especially nowadays. Now, Bramante knew, was the time to get the job moving and to keep it moving.

Bramante moved through the site with vigor, sidestepping puddles, stepping over clods of earth. Piero and Antonio followed behind, taking notes as he made his remarks, hanging on his every word. Bramante stopped and folded his arms across his chest. He studied the site intently. He then walked briskly to another vantage point. He scrutinized the work in progress, wishing it finished. Construction on the northeast corner of the building was proceeding quickly. He was pleased. The new wall there rose thirty feet in the air surrounding the two street facades of the old church of San Lorenzo. The new wall hid the church like an enormous fence. Bramante stood as far back from it as he could and squinted. His mind edited away the cage of scaffolding, the rigging and pulleys, the bricks and buckets of mortar being hauled up until all he saw was a white, luminous wall, that looked more like a drawing than an actual wall. It appeared to him weightless like a scrim made of pale travertine, at once a building and a mask. The hazy morning light cast soft shadows across the travertine, faint like a delicate shading of graphite on coarse, white paper, articulating pilasters, banding and windows. The mathematical division of wall and window repeated in the subtle, relentless rhythm of its rectangles was intended to subsume everything behind it. Cooking, working, fucking, eating, laughing, celebrating mass, shitting, the torment of a dead saint, all were made equal behind the rigorous, expressionless order of the new white wall.

Bramante had not wasted a minute. When Riario decided to resume the work he jumped at the opportunity. It could not have come at a better time. When work on the new St. Peter's was stopped he was crushed. He was also angry and disgusted that the fortunes of the church could be so capricious. Cash flow problems. The excuse was bullshit. If an asshole like Riario had money to burn, how could the Holy Church not. With no choice and much regret he abandoned St Peter's, and moved his entire work force to Riario's, leaving nothing behind: not a shack, not a tool. For all the years of planning all he had to show was a hole in the ground partially filled with stagnant water and the stump of one pier. That was all. He hoped that St. Peter's would resume, fearing revocation of his plenary absolution he had worked so hard for. He hoped that when the Pope looked out his window and saw Riario's palace rising above the rooftops, white and pure and new, and then saw his own sodden hole in the ground, that his envy and megalomania would force him to find the money. The Pope was not a man to be outdone by Riario, he snorted. We are too much alike. He crossed himself fleetingly, not wanting to be seen doing it.

Bramante pointed. "Those travertine slabs. See them? They are stained."

Piero assured him they had already been identified and were not to be used. The architect was satisfied. He liked Piero and thought he had great potential. He could take over one day. The boy had a good eye. He could trust him. Antonio would be a technician. Bramante needed them both.

The architect stepped back admiring his white wall, satisfied by what he saw. It was everything he hoped it would be. His pulse quickened but he maintained a pensive demeanor. The apprentices and the workman would be permitted to know that he was pleased when he was ready for them to know. It was important for them to be a little afraid, a little unsure of what he thought of their performance. It kept them on their toes. He liked knowing they were a little afraid. To a degree he envied their being able to be afraid. He, by now, was fearless, more annoyed, generally than fearful. He studied the corner. Their fear was a testament to their youth. Perhaps that was what he envied. He recalled Ximenez and the little boy's bull fight. He snorted. He turned away from the wall and walked away with his head down. He stopped short and turned quickly to look back at the wall again as if to take the masonry by surprise, as if to catch it in the act of being less than perfect. To his great relief it was still perfect. It was like a wall of pale ice rising in front of the dark and battered old church.

Contrary to logic he had insisted that the travertine be applied to the façade of the northwest corner. It was illogical because finished stone is always applied last to prevent it from being damaged and discolored. The finished surface would not be seen for another two years if he followed that rule. The roof wasn't even framed yet, but Bramante wanted to see it, he said. He also wanted Riario and everyone else to see it. He wanted the Pope to see it.

Piero and Antonio waited anxiously while Bramante studied the wall, squinting at it, his head tilted to one side. He moved toward it, then stepped back, making them wait for the impending pronouncement that would be the measure of their worth. Bramante finally cleared his throat and after another long silence proclaimed, "It is excellent, just what I hoped for," admiring his wall, not looking at them. When he finally turned to them, he smiled and said, "There is hope for you two yet."

Bramante then brushed past them and strode through the rubble to the other side of the old church. There the site had been leveled. Little remained of the small rustic buildings and garden walls that once formed the church's simple cloister. Piero, right behind him, told him about this place having been the site of the church where the sainted Pope Damasus was born. "Beh!" Bramante muttered aloud. Every square foot of Roman soil had a history and this place was no exception. "You're spending too much time listening to old Laetus. He's living in the past. You are the future. Don't forget it." He jabbed a finger at him.

"There are some who claim that the old Pope's burial place was here, too, right where the courtyard is going," Piero said.

Bramante, not a sentimentalist, brushed the notion aside. Nothing was more important than a building he designed. Clearing his throat he proclaimed, "I know, I know. I have heard that, too. Some say the old boy is buried here. It may be true. For all I know we may have ground his bones into dust to make mortar! Ha! Come on, saints don't stay buried for long, anyway." He made a quick gesture with his thumb suggesting that saints were immediately shot upward, "What are you worried about?"

Piero looked down embarrassed. At his feet the reflected sky, clouds and the ghostly new wall undulated upside down in a puddle. He recalled the Wilderness and the sepulcher. He hoped Antonio would say something. He felt woozy. A grave-sized shaft appeared, a clean stone shaft with steps cut into one side that led down. At the bottom a pale turquoise sea sparkled like diamonds in brilliant sunlight. Two dolphins leapt suddenly into the air, ecstatically.

Piero looked up. Antonio was ahead of him, following Bramante across the littered ground toward the limekiln. The kiln was similar to the one Piero had designed for Saint Peter's. As at the Vatican, excavations for the foundations unearthed broad pavements of marble and travertine, the remains of the ancient Campus Martius. Crushed, cooked in the kiln, pulverized and mixed with water and sand, they became the cement used to build the palace. The kiln was making Bramante a lot of money. It produced enough cement to sell to other construction projects, and quickly paid for itself. The design and its profitability had greatly enhanced young Piero's reputation. Professor Laetus teased him at the Tavern one night, going so far as to say that he had refined the disinternment of Old Pagan Rome and was the *spiritu santu* of its transubstantiation into the New Rome.

The kiln was a long, inclined tubular chamber supported on a row of brick ovens. It looked like a small aqueduct. One soot covered man kept the fires under it stoked, adding wood and regulating the draft, to control the heat in the kiln chamber, while another crew foraged the site, prying up marble, slabs and bits of architectural ornament that lay buried beneath the surface. Piled onto wheeled barrows, the fragments were then carted and dumped in piles, where a work crew smashed them into small bits. The crushed rock was then carted to a raised platform and shoveled into a chute at the higher end of the inclined kiln chamber. The workmen's clothing and hair were powdered white with marble dust. The faces of the men tending the kiln were burned red. The sound was horrendous: rock being crushed, the squeal of iron wheels, cursing, shouting, coughing and spitting, acrid smoke and dust hissing from the kiln. The scene was like a glimpse of Hell. A laborer pumped a large bellows in the side of the chamber. As the intense heat cooked the rocks they slid down the incline. From an opening at the bottom another workman extracted the clinkers, the cooked rocks. When the rocks cooled they were pulverized and mixed with dry powdered clay to make cement.

Efficient, thought Bramante, very efficient. He cleared his throat. His very thoughts were proclamations. One couldn't ask for a better team: orderly.

Suddenly a loud argument interrupted Bramante's satisfaction.

"Are you asleep, Sandro?! Wake the fuck up!" It was Rufo who fed the hopper at the top of the kiln. "We can't get any more in up here!"

"Fuck you! It's all cleared out down here! Push harder, lard ass!"

"Lard ass yourself. Pull from the bottom, faggot!"

"You loaded it too fast, asshole! The fire wasn't hot enough and now the goddamn thing's jammed!"

Piero ran over and jumped up to the platform that fed the hopper.

Bramante raised an eyebrow and turned back to his creation leaving Piero to attend to the jammed kiln. He squinted again at the completed portion of the Palace and, clearing his throat, thought: order and rules. Rules work. Without rules nothing happens. People like rules. People need rules. Rome was looking for rules, begging for them. The Pope begged him to provide order to a city flailing in chaos. His mind drifted to Vitruvius, architect to the Emperor Caesar Augustus. Thank you, sir. You have served me well. Your rules are right here with me, always. Rules are good. Rules can be explained and followed and defended and obeyed. Bramante sniffed, thinking for some reason of that hideous Ximenez and the implicit effrontery of his smirking presence.

Piero stood on the platform and peered into the hopper. "Don't push anymore," he raised a hand to Rufo packing the crushed rock. "Sandro!" he called to the man at the bottom, "Pull! It's jammed at your end!"

Sandro shoved his rake up into the kiln chamber. He looked up at Piero and shrugged. There was nothing there. Piero jumped down and hurried to the lower end of the chute. He grabbed Sandro's rake. Bramante was watching. This was not good. Piero shoved the rake into the opening and poked around. Sandro looked at him as if to say, *What? You didn't believe me? Why would I lie?* Piero kneeled in front of the opening and tried to look in. White smoke poured forth. The bottom of the chute was empty. He couldn't see. He turned away and wiped his face on his sleeve. His eyes burned. He shoved the rake into the opening again as far as he could and groped around, but again found nothing. He resisted the temptation to look back to Bramante. With his arms extended and the rake in one hand he slid into the chamber and wriggled forward. There was scarcely room for his shoulders to clear the walls. The bricks were hot. He pressed forward burying his face under his arm, keeping his eyes tightly closed. Sweat poured from him. Salt ran into his mouth. He called back, "Dowse the last oven and wet down the kiln! I'm baking!" He heard orders screamed and then the hiss of steam as cold water struck the hot brick. He reached foreword with the rake. Still nothing. He wriggled up the incline, groping. He probed carefully afraid of dislodging the blockage and being smothered by an avalanche of cooking limestone. A few rocks came loose and rolled down. He felt a hot stone brand his scalp. Then the rake caught something. It was soft. He pulled it slowly. He heard rocks rumbling loose behind the blockage. He slid back inch by inch, one arm protecting his face, while still pulling with the rake. He felt cool air on his legs and slipped backward out of the kiln onto the ground. He rolled sideways away from the kiln and with his eyes still closed and burning passed the rake to Sandro, "Here, It's loosened up, be careful. A laborer passed him a bucket of cool water and he splashed his face and hair.

"Jesus Christ!" Sandro cried and fell back and dropped the rake. His face was a mask of horror as he stared at the bottom of the chute. He looked first to Piero, then to Bramante and Antonio. He began waving frantically at the ground in front of him, flapping his hands as if trying to shake something off. Men dropped their tools and ran over. Piero dried his stinging eyes. Smoke rose from the ground. Everyone moved in to get a closer look. It became quiet. Workers peered down from the scaffolding, straining to see through the haze, dust and smoke. Piero picked up the rake and, fanning the smoke away, prodded the smoking object. A charred foot and sandal lay on the ground. As he stared, frozen in shock, part of a roasted leg slid slowly down the chute and into view. He jumped back. A shiver ran thorough him. But for the slow exhale of the dying fires there was no sound. Bramante pushed through the men. He took one look and snatched the rake from Piero. Reaching into the kiln, he carefully extracted a blackened corpse.

21

La Taverna nel Teatro di Pompeo

Pompey's was packed that night. Word of the roasted corpse had spread fast. When Piero and Antonio got there they were immediately surrounded. Eager faces called out to them. Hands and arms pulled them to a table in the middle of the vast room. Platters of food were thumped down in front of them. "Talk. Tell us," they called out.

Piero felt sickened. He could not shake off the sight or the smell of the charred remains, the burned clothing. He sank down and pressed the back of his hand to his face. He could still smell the stink of singed hair.

The men pressed closer. Everyone wanted to hear every detail of the gruesome story he did not want to relive.

"So? What happened? Who was it? Tell the story!" The crowd in the tavern, their faces bright, moved in closer.

Piero felt their heat. He smelled their lust—acidic and vegetal. He felt shaky. He shook his head. He hadn't wanted to come, but he didn't want to be alone either.

"Come on, Pierino" coaxed Antonio reaching for the platter of ribs.

"Don't be shy. What would you say? Was he roasted or smoked?" Antonio winked proudly at the crowd.

"*Arrosto o affumato? Gesù Christo!*" Someone groaned, a sound of childlike disgust mixed with delight.

"Move back a little and give the guys some space or they'll be roasted, too," someone yelled. The crowd drew back a little.

A wave of nausea washed over Piero at the sight of the piles of meat on the table. Antonio gulped wine, and wiped his face.

"You start. You were the first one there," Antonio said," Don't be shy."

"What's to tell?" Piero said, resigned to having to relive the scene, "it was just another day on the job."

His flippant remark was answered with jeers, foot stomping and catcalls. Someone shouted, "Don't get cute. Just tell the fucking story!" and flung a piece of bread.

"OK. OK," Piero said ducking. He wanted to get it over with and leave, "We were walking around the site, Antonio and me, showing Bramante around the way we always do when all of a sudden we hear this argument. I didn't think anything of it. The guys are always fighting, especially first thing in the morning. So we ignored it and just kept following the boss around, letting him take his time. You know, the usual. But the yelling didn't let up. It got louder. Rufo, the guy working the hopper, starts swearing up and down, really freaking out. I could see Bramante was getting pissed, so I went over to get the guy to shut up." Piero looked to see if Rufo was in the crowd. He didn't see him, nor did he see Sandro, "The kiln was backed up. It happens all the time when they push too much in. It's my design, so I felt embarrassed in front of the boss, and told Rufo to stop packing it so tight." He was talking fast, "I went down to the bottom end of the chute. Sandro was having a fit. I told him to just shut up and I grabbed his rake." He stopped talking.

The crowd was silent.

"Come on. Get to the good part." Antonio nudged Piero, making him feel like a performing monkey. "Go ahead. Tell them how you climbed into the kiln."

"You climbed into the kiln?" someone called. "You're fucking crazy."

"Shush! Let him finish!"

"What was it like?"

"It was hot, just hot." Piero spoke in a low voice and rapidly described the heat, the steam, the avalanche of hot rock and reaching blindly with the rake and striking the soft body, wanting to get the telling over with, wanting them all to just go away.

Antonio nodded in vigorous agreement, as he spoke, "I couldn't believe my eyes. Little Piero here just dove in. Finally after, it seemed like an hour, he backs out. I see him crawling away from the opening backwards like a crab. Then Sandro who's been standing there the whole time, let's out a shriek. Piero's all hunched over splashing his face with cold water. I thought he'd been blinded. White steam's blowing out of the kiln. Sandro's staring at the ground with his mouth open, waving like crazy. That's when I ran over. There's this thing on the ground. Smoke is coming out of it. I couldn't tell what it was. By now everybody's running over to see."

The whole tavern was as quiet as a tomb. Some of them had heard this, but not from an eyewitness.

"I couldn't see at first," Piero said. He looked up. The crowd pressing closer. He had washed, but his face was red and puffy, his hands were blistered and his hair was singed on top, baring patches of scalp. "I was dizzy from the heat and the smoke, coughing. For a minute I thought I was going to black out." He blinked rapidly, seeing it all over again. "I felt a prickling on top of my head and saw tiny little bubbles swimming before my eyes."

"He was in really bad shape," Antonio cut in. "Everybody was crowding in, trying to see, trying to help. Sandro, I gotta tell ya, he smelled like he'd shit himself, and Piero here is looking like he was going to keel over. What the hell's going on, I thought. That's when I saw it." Antonio pulled the wine over. "I fanned the smoke out of the way, and there on the ground is this . . . foot. I mean a real foot, not a hoof or anything but a foot with a burned sandal on it." He laughed then and said, "I told him, just before, and it's true, that when I was pushing through, before I could even see what was going on I smelled meat roasting." Groans of disgust rose behind him.

"It made me hungry!" said Antonio, ducking his head down into his shoulders. His appetite was legendary. There was uneasy laughter.

"Finish the story! Who was it?"

Piero sighed, " I thought maybe one of the guys had dug into a grave, maybe this foot was mixed up in one of the rock piles. I even thought, maybe this is some ancient Roman's foot, you know, a centurion or something," he looked over at Professor Laetus hearing himself sounding like an idiot. "Just as I was thinking that maybe it was Saint Pope Damasus or somebody, the rest of the leg came sliding slowly down the chute. I couldn't believe my eyes. No one made a sound. Time seemed to stop." Piero fluttered his hands in the air and closed his eyes, seeing it all again. "The leg stopped, half hanging out of the kiln."

"That's about when the boss got there wasn't it?" prodded Antonio.

"Yes."

"What did Bramante do?" someone called.

"He took one look, grabbed for a rake and the two of them, Bramante and Piero, started pulling the leg out," said Antonio.

"Then what."

Piero sat up straight as if to brace himself, "I took Sandro's rake and reached in to see if there was any more and . . . ,"

"And?" trying to coax it out of him.

"There was," Piero looked down and shook his head. His eyes burned.

"Piero, here, starts pulling and tugging and the next thing I see: the rest of the body is coming out the bottom of the chute," said Antonio, "And it wasn't any Roman centurion."

Piero rubbed his hands together as if wasing them, "You could tell from what was left of the clothing that it was a monk or a priest." He placed his hands in his lap. They were shaking.

"Tell them, go on."

"The whole neighborhood was gathered around by now. Word got out fast. We got the body out of the chute. It was still hot, still cooking." He felt a chill. "We did our best to lay it out, lay him out, to try to . . . ," Piero, stricken, turned and looked to Antonio.

"We tried to reassemble the body on the ground in some decent sort of way." Antonio's cocky attitude was gone. "It wasn't easy. He was big and heavy, and the body was twisted and . . ."

Piero mumbled.

"Speak up!" the crowd hooted.

Piero took a breath, "And his hands were tied behind his back," Piero said firmly. There was an audible intake of air followed by total silence. "One of the workmen recognized him, God knows how." Piero pressed his hands between his knees and looked down, "It was Fra Juan from the Spanish church."

Perfunctory prayers for the dead were awkwardly mumbled and hasty signs of the cross were made.

"Everyone in the neighborhood knew him. "He was like one of us. He sat with us right here." Piero didn't look up. His eyes burned. "Everyone liked him."

Piero took a moment to collect himself. His throat was swollen. He swallowed hard, "We needed some air. Everybody moved back out of respect. I was feeling a little light-headed. I don't feel all that steady now," He exhaled slowly before saying, "A little while later, it couldn't have been more than fifteen minutes or so, there was a rumble from the on-lookers. People started moving back. I looked over and there were these five priests coming toward us from the new Spanish church, St. Maria in Monserrato. It's right there, only a stone's throw away. There they were, coming toward us in "V" formation like speeding black geese, plowing through the smoky air. At the head of the pack was that tall one with jet black eyes, Father Ximenez. He looked straight at me and if looks could kill I would have dropped dead right there with a sword through my heart." Piero stopped, frightened anew, seeing again the priest's pent up rage. He didn't want to say any more.

He looked around at the circle of intent expectant faces. He wanted to beg them to leave him alone, but he didn't. He had begun and he would finish, "By then the pieces of the body had stopped smoking. Dust from the lime kiln was settling on them, covering them in a light powder, like sugar. It didn't look so bad. But even so, you could see that Fra Juan's arms were tied behind his back." He sighed raggedly. "About ten feet away the five priests stopped short. Father Ximenez thrust his arms out wide. He looked like a crucifixion. Then he dropped to his knees, buried his chin into his chest and gripped his hands as if to pray. But he didn't say anything, not a word, not a sound. No one did. The other four just stood there behind him in formation, staring at Fra Juan's body. I thought it was weird that no one said, God rest his soul, or anything, but Father Ximenez didn't say one word."

Antonio cut in, "Are you ready for this? Then Ximenez stands up and says, '*Obviously a suicide.*'"

Laughing uneasily someone yelled out, "A suicide?! What did you say to that!?"

Piero turned toward the voice, "Me? What did I say? I didn't say anything."

The voice pressed, "You mean Father Ximenez sees the body, sees the hands bound behind his back and thinks old Fra Juan tied himself up, hopped up the ladder and flung himself into the kiln?"

"I don't know what he thought," Piero said as if in a trance.

"Would it be possible?" someone asked.

"Would what be possible?"

"Possible for someone to tie himself up and jump into the kiln."

Piero did not want to continue. Nothing he heard himself say conveyed the truth. His words cheapened the dead friar and made a shallow fool of himself. Not meaning too, everything he said played to the crowd's morbid need for amusement. He felt the heat and the crunch the rake made when it struck the charred body and then the softness. He didn't want to but he could not stop talking, "There was a burned piece of rope tied to one of the legs. His feet were tied together, too."

Silence. Fear mixed with fascination, enveloped them like a chilling fog.

"Then," said Piero, "Ximenez stabbed me with another look and spat out, 'He was a Catharite,' as if that explained it. I expected him to say more. I must have looked like an idiot, because he just glared at me. His black eyes looked like they were going to shake loose. Then he suddenly turned on his heel. The other four priests jumped into formation behind him and they all hurried back to their church."

"What the Hell's a Catharite?" someone asked.

"Beats me," another answered, "Maybe it's someone who can tie himself up and jump into a kiln. How the fuck would I know?"

"How do you get to be one?" a voice hooted, "I was thinking of a few people I would encourage to convert." Everyone laughed

"Yeah, me, too. Maybe my wife!" someone shouted.

"Yeah," called someone as the gathering broke up. "Maybe your wife!" Laughing.

Piero placed his hands on the table. They were red, and scraped and blistered. His face was red, too, and his eyebrows singed. Antonio called for a plate of butter and began applying it carefully to his friend's burned forehead.

"You are a frightful sight, my young friend," said Professor Laetus after the gawkers left. He took a bit of butter and rubbed it gently on Piero's knuckles. "Did he really say that Fra Juan was a Catharite?"

"I heard it, too," said Antonio. "What does it mean?"

"Well, it would explain why no prayers were said, why there was silence from Ximenez and the other priests. The Catharites were heretics, and as you know unconfessed heretics are damned. Fra Juan, it would seem, if not already there, is on his way to Hell." Piero sank back, recalling the amiable pink faced monk, horrified that such a man would be condemned to Hell. "But, really, to my knowledge there haven't been any Catharites around for centuries. The sect was driven out. They were either burned at the stake, hanged or repented and brought back to the Faith. It sounds preposterous to me. But Ximenez—well I know nothing about the man—why would he, a man of the Church, put something forward if it were not true. Perhaps the cult has risen again."

"Were these Catharites suicidal contortionists?" asked Piero, the image of Fra Juan bound hand and foot still vivid.

"Ha! You are very funny, my young friend. I don't know about contortionists, but suicide was part of—ritual would not be the right word— part of their intellectual construct would perhaps be a better way to describe it. Their name came from the Greek *katharos*, which means pure. They were Puritans."

"I don't understand. How do suicide and Puritanism go together?"

'I'm not a scholar of church history, mind you, and I refuse to vouch

for the reliability of any of what I am about to say, but it is my understanding that the Catharites were in the tradition of Dualists, which is to
say that they believed very simply that there were two fundamental Principals: one Good and the other Evil. I don't fully understand this myself,
being a man whose favorite color is gray; so bear with me. You could say
they conceived of two coexisting and equal Gods: A Good God, the one
who created the invisible, spiritual universe and the Evil God, the one
who created the material world. It's complicated."

Antonio reached for the wine. Piero, salved his burned hands.

"I am thinking aloud now, just rambling," the Professor went on.
"Imagine that God and Satan were equal; that God was in charge of the
kingdom of Heaven and that Satan controlled everything material, all
you could see, feel and smell." He laughed before saying, "Following
their logic we human beings, existing as we do in the material world, are
inherently evil. That was what the Catharites believed. One of their solu-
tions to the inherently evil nature of mankind was celibacy for men and
women. The idea, I presume, was that if you wiped out mankind you
would eliminate the material, the Evil, part of humanness."

Piero just shook his head, not because he didn't understand. He did,
but it bore no relevance to the amiable monk, nor did it explain his gruesome end.

"Well, of course it met with opposition!" said the Professor.

Antonio, his eyes at half mast, asked, "Should we be surprised?"

"But even more bizarre—for the same reason they advocated suicide.
Their thinking was that if you ended your physical, earthly, material existence your spiritual essence would dwell in the realm of the Good for all
eternity.

"Suicide was a virtue," said Piero.

"Exactly," answered the Professor, "You can see, of course, why
Catharism would have, shall we say, limited appeal . . . ,"

Antonio rolled his eyes.

" . . . and how such a philosophy would be unenforceable and would
result in chaos. But it raises all manner of fascinating questions, which I
have not had enough wine to explore," He reached for the flagon, " such
as: how might men rule men if human existence were by its very nature

evil? The rules of governance and the governors themselves would therefore be Evil, wouldn't they? I say this in a whisper." He leaned forward bringing his face close to theirs, "if you follow their logic, the Catharist logic I mean," he paused. His eyes slowly took in the room to make sure that no one was eavesdropping, "You realize, of course, that I pursue this line of reasoning only for the intellectual stimulation. But if you accept their premise that the material world is inherently evil, then the church itself, as the governing entity of the material world, would be at the top of their list of evil things."

Piero lowered his head as if expecting a sword to smite them.

"So where would we all be if these Catharites had prevailed?" asked Antonio.

"Prevailing and being correct are two different things, but if they had prevailed you wouldn't *be* at all—but then it would depend on what it means 'to be.' Is spiritual existence 'being'? '*Are* spirits?' Do spirits reproduce? Would you have to exist physically in the material world before you would qualify to migrate, I could probably find a better word, into the spiritual universe? No one ever did a very good job of explaining original sin to me, my apologies." He drank. "Self immolation was the Catharite's solution. And it's reasonable, isn't it? But going back for a moment. You can see where the established church would frown upon a belief system that would have the faithful killing themselves and refusing to bear offspring. A belief system that might conclude that the world we inhabit is Hell? "

Antonio sounding interested, "Alright, following your line of reasoning, if Fra Juan was a Catharist, suicide would have been part of his make up. If he really did kill himself I wonder what took him so long. He was not young. Why now? Why didn't he bail out a long time ago? Why would he choose to do it now? I don't buy it. Someone killed him."

"Spain doesn't suffer heretics lightly, Antonio. Why did he wait, you ask? Maybe he had only recently adopted Catharism. Perhaps the long fingers of the Spanish Inquisition found out about it and killed him. Killed him in a way that would set an example to other incipient heretics who might be tempted to follow in his path. Did he ever say anything that would lead you to believe he was other than a pious monk?"

"He never said much of anything," said Piero, "He joined us now and then. He listened to our chatter and just seemed to enjoy being among us."

They sat in silence for a few minutes before Antonio said, "The whole mess wasted a lot of time. The boss was not happy about having to stop work for an entire day."

The professor with a mischievous glint, "I can tell you this. If a bunch of Catharites appeared tomorrow you two would be deemed high ranking adherents of the Evil Principle."

"Why?" asked Piero, alarmed.

"Stay with me now. If the material world is the realm of the Evil Principle, then—let me just say it: If the material world is the realm of Satan— it would follow that we are in Hell." He leaned forward and whispered, "Now, what is it that you two talented young men do again?" raising his eyebrows. "I'm speaking from a Catharist point of view, you understand, jumping outside our own frame of reference to view you from theirs." He reached for the flagon, "You design and build buildings. You give solid form to the material world. The work of which you are so proud would be seen by them as designing and decorating Hell." He sat back, pleased at the puzzlement on Piero and Antonio's faces. " The mud wasps of Hell they might even call you!" he exclaimed, so thrilled by his exposition, that he actually stopped talking. The professor smiled privately into space, contemplating how he might torment Bramante with this inside-out line of reasoning.

Antonio lost patience, "Old Fra Juan was murdered. It's that simple."

Jostled from his reverie, Professor Laetus said, "Never mind me. I am just musing. You know me," he patted Piero's arm fondly, "I like nothing better than spinning a logical argument out of nothing, and I enjoy teasing you." He hadn't realized how loudly he was speaking until the background din stopped suddenly.

Loud bellowing, like that of a wounded bull, erupted from deep within the tavern. The three turned to the sound of crockery shattering against a wall and the thud of a heavy table being dragged across the stone floor. A fight was going on way back in the alcove reserved for itinerant pilgrims.

Antonio stood on the bench to get a better view then climbed onto the table. "A large fleshy priest is cursing, bellowing, at the top of his voice, and banging a heavy metal pitcher on the table."

The Professor stood up and leaned across the table trying to hear what was being said.

"It's a fight, but I don't understand what the priest is saying. Can you get any of it? What's he saying?" Antonio asked.

"It's German," said the Professor, cupping his ear. After a moment he said, "Well, how do you like that!" feigning shock, "How appropriate in view of our discussion! He's calling us swine and dogs and telling us that we live in a sewer. He's saying that Rome is the sewer of the world. Wait. No. Let me refine my translation. He's calling our beloved home the asshole of the world."

Antonio pointed up to the hornet's nest, "The boys don't seem to be taking kindly to this guy's remarks. It looks like they're going to come down."

Piero climbed up next to him.

"What language for a man of the Church," gasped Professor Laetus, " I am truly shocked." He translated, relishing every word " 'From what I can see this City is the gateway to Hell!' He is really angry! He's speaking in a heavily accented mixture of Italian and clerical Latin. My God!" They heard the priest shrieking at the top of his voice, "He says Rome is an eruption of Hell itself made of the hot pus of Satan!"

Piero and Antonio watched fascinated by the tirade. "His face is red. His cheeks are shaking. He looks boiled," Piero called down..

"'This place of sin, this place where men cavort with men, where priests dress as women, where the holy church struts and flaunts herself like an overripe street whore!' Good grief," cried the Professor, "another Catharite! What on earth is going on?"

The crowd took the insults to heart and roared back at the foreigner. Plates were flying. Benches were heaved across the room. Piero picked up a plate, and threw it at the German priest. Antonio jumped from the table. He hurled a chair then pitched a heavy platter.

"Brother Martin!" warned one of the German's companions, but too late. A half eaten fish head grazed the German's ear. The florid priest started swinging and throwing things back. He was like an enraged bull.

The crowd went wild throwing food, bottles, anything and everything they could get their hands on. It was then that the hornets rushed fthe Germans. Ottavio Colonna and two of the Orsini brothers grabbed Brother Martin and lifted him up. They passed him from hand to hand over the heads of the crowd and threw him out into the street where he landed like a sack of grain.

"Well, let that be a lesson to him," said the Professor brushing off his hands as if he had done the throwing. Heresy would appear to be rife tonight." He reached for a piece of chicken.

The mob quieted down. Chairs, benches and tables were dragged back into place. The cavernous Tavern returned to normal. The death of Fra Juan as the topic of the evening was replaced by animated condemnations of rude Germans and foreigners in general. Piero jumped from the table and sat back down.

Ottavio and the hornets burst back in. The heavy door slammed behind them. The look on Ottavio's dark face showed his thirst for violence remained unquenched. He moved quickly to Piero. He jabbed a trembling finger in the boy's face. "*Ruinante!*" He shrieked. "*Ruinante!*" and kicked the bench out from under him sending Piero sprawling, backward onto the floor.

⟨ℰ⟩

22

Bramante's Study

Alone in Bramante's study the next day, perched on a stool before a table piled high with books and portfolios, Piero struggled to settle down and work. The neatly stacked folios were stuffed with drawings of Rome's ancient monuments. Beautiful objects, excavated from beneath the City's streets and gardens, were used as paperweights. His mind would not focus. The image of Fra Juan's charred corpse lying in the dust and Ottavio Colonna's pointless assault flooded his mind. His eyes darted everywhere except at the work before him. A Roman matron, her white marble face framed by a diadem of braided hair, appraised him with cool, intelligent eyes from atop a stack of drawings. A dozen easels bearing small, faceless Madonnas rested expectantly against the far wall, waiting to be inhabited by the daughters, wives and mistresses of Rome's fashionable elite. The smell of linseed oil and turpentine hung in the air. Out in the big studio painters were finishing the cartoons for a cycle of frescoes.

"No," Piero said aloud. He got off the stool and walked away from the table. He touched his burned face. It still felt warm. Flustered and touchy, he looked at the pile of papers. The Professor's remarks stuck like a splinter he couldn't remove. The old man's good humored teasing struck him now as ridicule: 'The mud wasps of Hell.' followed by that little laugh of his. And that stupid Ottavio Colonna, what was that all about? Piero wished he could laugh it off—what kind of moron runs a race to win but bets on another horse?—but he couldn't. He returned to the table. Who were they to condemn and make light of his work? They were just jealous, that's all, jealous because they had no vision. They were stuck in the past. They were then. I am now and forever, he thought. He turned away from the table and began pacing. We're the ones, the artists and the architects, putting ourselves on the line to make the New Rome, and look at the thanks we get. Bramante is a hero compared to a worm like Colonna, those rotting snobs. Time will erase them. Time will be the proof. God will make the choices, Piero decreed, his anger making him haughty and courageous now that he was by himself. In the tavern, with Colonna's hot breath in his face, his guts had turned to pudding.

He paced the room, back and forth, back and forth. It was time to get over it, time to get back to work. It was not productive to be thrown off like this. There was work to do. He climbed back onto the stool, rested his elbows firmly on the table and read the notes Bramante had left. They concerned the Palazzo Riario. Bramante was a genius for insisting that a corner of the building be finished for everyone to see. Even Professor Laetus had praised it, even the Professor. Its classicism was, in the language of architecture, exactly what the Roman Academy promoted. Old Laetus fairly sang its praises. He said it was a confirmation of the Academy's unshakeable belief that a new order had to be based on the principals of the ancients. So why did the old Professor play those games with him last night?

"Touchy aren't I?" he addressed the cool marble woman. Taking a deep breath he settled down to work. He was to recalculate the proportions of the Riario facade. It's too bad the boss wasn't there last night, he thought. Bramante would have known what to say. He would have put the Professor in his place, and Ottavio, that prick, wouldn't have dared try anything if Bramante was there.

He spread the Maestro's notes out in front of him. Sketches, drawn on loose sheets of paper, were wedged into a folio. Small handwritten notes were inserted as well, with specific instructions. Rifling through, he read the first one: review Vitruvius' formulas for the proportions of columns in Book IV and convert them to the orders of the pilasters on the face of Riario's palace. The mock up of the corner of the building was useful, but after seeing it, after squinting at it for a couple of weeks, Bramante had decided that it was not yet perfect. Modifications were required.

Piero looked up unable to concentrate. This was as dull as shit. He had done this twice before. He was annoyed and bored, annoyed because he was bored. He flipped to Book IV. His shoulders sagged. Reading, he felt numbed to the point of exhaustion,

> *. . . observing that six and ten were both of them perfect numbers, they combined the two and thus made the most perfect number, sixteen. They found their authority for this in the foot. For if we take two palms from the cubit, their remains the foot of four palms; but the palm contains four fingers. Hence the foot contains sixteen fingers . . .*

Piero crossed his eyes and wanted to gag. Is this punishment? He hadn't slept. His body ached. The burns had him tossing and turning all night. And now he had to wade through this. "Give me a break," he groaned. He looked up. Judging from the light coming through the window time had stopped. He glanced around at the blank faces of the women waiting to be invented. The Roman matron seemed to read his mind. Did she understand or was she just amused, or did she just want to let him know that she had been invented by a better man than anyone he would ever know? 'How many fingers did you have on your feet?' he asked her, reminded that he had heard nothing more from the magnificent Imperia; which meant that he would probably never get to work with her on their fresco of Galatea. Their fresco, sure. He went back to the notes. There was so much to do. He wished all the work to be over and done with, so that he wouldn't have to do anything. He wanted to see it all finished. He wanted everyone to see what he could do. He wanted to shove the new St Peter's in front of Ottavio Colonna's face and Riario's Palace and the fresco of Galatea and all the great and wonderful things he knew he could do, and say. And say *What?* He was agitated. He wanted to work, because his work would prove that he was as good as anyone else. Even better. Validation lay in producing more work, more designs, more buildings, but this morning he couldn't concentrate on anything. His mind wandered, a jumble of boredom, annoyance and insult. He forced his eyes back to the page:

> *Of Socrates it is related that he said with sagacity and great learning that the human breast should have been furnished with open windows, so that men might not keep their feelings concealed, but have them open to the view. Oh that nature should have constructed them thus unfolded and opened to the view!*

"Dear God," he moaned, grateful that there had been no open windows in his breast last night lest anyone peek in and see his doubt and cowardice. His stomach sank. He closed his eyes remembering the blackness and the heat inside the kiln. He felt the rake strike something soft. He saw blackness streaming from the left side of God's throne into Hell where people squirmed, impaled, gouged and half consumed by the demons of their sins: envy, lust, greed, pride. He placed his hands gently against his hot face. He hoped Fra Juan was in Heaven, but if he were, it meant that Catharism was not a heresy. Fra Juan could only be with God if he had been murdered. The choice for Fra Juan's soul—its choice—he heard himself and almost laughed—was between heresy and murder. "How?" he demanded to know can anyone not be guilty of any sin? His mind flailed. He hated feeling like this, confused and hissy, fully aware that he was fueling his own misery, but he knew, too, or at least thought, or maybe just hoped, that anger would drive him to work. He sat up straight. He wanted to slip from his skin and pupate into something else. His world was turning inside out. How could virtue could be heretical? How could the world be Hell? How could his work rather than being virtuous and good be an instrument of Evil. What if without knowing it he was a foot soldier in the service of Satan? "What am I supposed to do?" The Roman matron's cool eyes seemed to understand. She appeared to know more of what he felt, wanted and thought than anyone. But she didn't care.

He raised his fists to bang them on the table, but stopped mid way and brought them down slowly. This was not productive. There was work to do. Where would the stalwart Bramante be if he had given in to such weakness? He pressed his palms to the warm satiny wood and rested his forehead on the cool folio. He sobbed and forced what felt like a hard-skinned bubble of anguish from deep in his chest. He then lifted his head and, recomposed, returned to the folio of Vitruvius:

> *... imprint of a man's foot ... one sixth of a man's height ..*
> *. applied to the principle of the column ... shaft including the*
> *capital, to a height six times its thickness at the base ...*

This is impossible, he thought. His eyelids felt gritty. He pressed his hands to his face, and tried to persevere. Rules. What had he done to deserve this? He blinked and looked away from the page Bramante had marked. He forced himself to look down at it again but his eyes recoiled, darting away for fear of drowning in Vitruvius' mud. He gave up. Taking a deep breath he flipped through the portfolio, through the chapters on weapons, on water screws, on dams, on foundations, on cities, on all kinds of interesting things that he was not supposed to read. He flipped through aimlessly, manically. At the section on war machines he found a blank page marker.

Curious, he read about tension, propulsion and the methods of approaching a wall with a tortoise, or siege tower:

> *The proportions of these engines are computed from the given*
> *length of the arrow which the engine is intended to throw.*

Rules. Numbers, numbers. Was it only about numbers? It was as boring as everything else, and irrelevant to boot. Why was the page marked? Why would Bramante have any interest in this? He inserted his hand to the bottom of the entire sheaf and flipped it over to the last section for the brief satisfaction, for the delusion, of having, at last, put the whole mess of Vitruvius' Ten Books behind him. He placed his elbows on the table and rested his face in his palms. Sighing again, holding his eyes open with his fingers, he read:

> **The freedom of states has been preserved by the cunning of architects.**

He sat back, feeling a spark of interest for the first time that day. "Now," he said to the marble bust and the blank madonnas, "what is this about?" Inserted behind that page was a blank sheet that appeared to be a page marker. He pulled it out and was about to set it aside when he noticed that it was not entirely blank. There was a pale, almost invisibly pale, blue circle three inches in diameter at its center, like the ring left from a glass, but it was centered precisely, not placed at random. Looking closely he saw faint white markings across the pale blue ring. He brought it to the window. The circle was a lovely blue. Holding it at an angle he saw that the page was covered in a sheen of white markings that seemed to have been scribbled across it, like a glaze of hardened egg white. He looked more closely. He tensed. He knew what this was.

He looked at the Roman matron, as if for permission to proceed, but she had lost interest in him entirely. The faceless madonnas-in-waiting, however, shared his curiosity and offered their twittering encouragement. Piero found a pan and filled it with water. He found a jar of washing soda, and a cloth, the few things he would need to make the page tell its story. His father had taught him how to make invisible ink and how to make it reveal its secrets.

He was trespassing now. He felt uneasy like a thief or a voyeur. He feared being discovered, but it was too late. He could not stop. He dissolved a pinch of soda in the water, swirled it around and soaked the cloth. He hesitated, enjoying the tingling arousal his apprehension brought. "I am only reading folios that were set out for me, he convinced himself. Not certain at all that he was supposed to be reading this, but wanting to, needing to now, knowing that once the writing was brought to light he could not turn back. He would not be able to make the ink disappear again. He held the damp cloth over the page. He could, of course destroy the page afterward, or hide it, and not mention it, ever, to anyone. But then, it may say nothing. Maybe it's just nothing, he reasoned, prolonging the delicious agony in his groin, wanting to know but not wanting to cross a forbidden threshold; knowing that no one writes in secret ink if there is nothing to hide. The Duke would send his father notes like this. They were to be destroyed as soon as they were read.

Piero wrung the cloth almost dry and pressed it lightly to a corner of the page then quickly pulled it away. He closed his eyes. There was no turning back now. The words, he knew, were materializing, coming to life, at that very moment under his trembling hand. If I was not meant to read them they would not have been left out for me, he reasoned. Holding his breath he opened his eyes and looked at the dampened page. White script had emerged against a pale blue ground. He pressed the damp cloth to the paper again to reveal more. He held it close and tried to read the words, but it was gibberish. Was it a foreign language? Was it written in code? He felt let down. The Roman matron caught his eye. He thought she winked. He studied the page, and on impulse brought it to a small mirror mounted on the wall. Reflected in the glass the script became immediately legible. It was written in reverse, by either a left-handed person or by someone skilled in writing that way. The first line he read was the same quotation from Vitruvius that first caught his interest:

> *The freedom of states has been preserved by the cunning of architects.*

The next lines read:

> *If the freedom of states can be preserved by the cunning of architects, so can it be altered.*
> *The freedom of states has been altered by the cunning of architects.*

He saw his own face in the mirror above the page as blank as the Roman matron's. Is this for me? He blinked and read on.

> *If the freedom of States can be altered by the cunning of architects, so can it also be denied.*
> *The freedom of states has been denied by the cunning of architects.*

Who wrote this? Are these Bramante's notes? He was suddenly afraid he had stumbled into the Maestro's private writings. More script, white on blue, came to light on the dampness spreading down the page.

> *If the freedom of states can be denied by the cunning of architects, so can its denial be disguised.*
> *The denial of the freedom of states has been disguised by the cunning of architects.*

Piero continued to read:

> *If the denial of the freedom of states has been disguised by the cunning of architects, their subjugation can be disguised as freedom.*
> *The Subjugation of States has been disguised as freedom by the cunning of architects.*

The permutations went on line after line. Their monotony numbed Piero's already feverish brain. His eyes, as if perched above the pale blue page in the mirror, asked: who wrote this? What is it about? Is it from Bramante? Did he want me to see it? Have I seen what I was not supposed to see? It is a message, but is it for me? Was I meant to discover this? If so, what am I to do with it? Should I do what my father does with messages from the Duke, and destroy it? But what if it was for someone else and not for me? He glanced over at the dead black wick of an extinguished candle. Should he burn it? His heart was beating rapidly.

He set the page aside and climbed back on his stool. I am here alone, he said to himself. He glanced at the marble woman and turned back to the chapter he had begun, the one on the proportions of columns and the spaces between columns, the formulas that would tell him how to compose the most perfect of walls, and resumed reading.

The intervals should be made as wide as the thickness of two columns and a quarter but the middle intercolumniations, one in front and the other in the rear should be of the thickness of three columns...

Piero looked up to the ceiling. Could the ancients have had to sit through this shit? Forcing himself to study the text his eyes wandered across the page:

. . . in appearance these temples were clumsy-roofed, low, broad .

'So what?' he muttered and flipped the page. The next page was blank and the next; each of them marked by perfectly centered, pale, blue rings. He stopped breathing. Cold sweat dripped from his armpits. He wanted to leap from the stool, but hunkered down instead and returned to the passage on *"the middle intercolumniations."* ignoring the white pages with the pale blue circles. He listened for a moment to the familiar sounds of hammers and saws coming from the carpenters' shop. He inhaled the comforting pungency of varnish and turpentine. Bramante could walk through the door at any time. He had nothing to show him. He would see the water and the cloth and the washing soda. He hunched over the text. Against his will he pulled another blank page from the folio and reached for the damp cloth. Taking a shallow breath he gently pressed it down. As before, the script emerged, white against blue. He stumbled from the stool and backed away as if the page were alive. His heart thumped five times before he picked it up and brought it to the mirror:

Vitruvius dedicated these guidelines to Caesar so that Caesar could build a new Empire. Make no mistake the same is being asked of you. You are being instructed to build a new empire and to undo enough of what has come before to make

*that possible. Think of your work as being dedicated to God.
Think of your work as His manifestation on earth of his True
Church.*

Who is "You"? Is "You" me? Is You "You"? Piero felt feverish. He
pressed his arms to his sides feeling his cold sweat and read:

*WHEREAS Vitruvius' System of rules and proportions was
the way Rome of the Caesars achieved its empire, and
WHEREAS an enduring Empire is not created by being all
things to all men, but by establishing standards to which all
men must adhere, and
WHEREAS slaughter, such as has been an appropriate and
successful means of subjugation in the Indies, is inappropriate
in Europe, the conquest of Civilized People requires Finesse.
WHEREAS the conquest of Evil is as urgently required in
Europe as it is in the Heathen Realms, and
WHEREAS, at the center of Western Christendom, the
Church and Rome itself have been infected by Evil, and
WHEREAS, God and His Holy Family weep for the corrup-
tion that has beset The Church
The MISSION of your Office in Rome is to purge the Church
and to Purify the Faith.*

Piero hurried to the table for the next page wanting to read it before
Bramante returned. He pressed the cloth down then held it up to the
glass."

*WHEREAS Rome, and the Holy Church itself, must be
purged of heresies and wrong thinking with a degree of fi-
nesse that need not be deployed beyond the wild edges of the
Christian world,
A METHODOLOGY appropriate to the purification of the
Faith in Rome is hereby proscribed.*

IDENTIFY the people who must be subjected to the true faith.
IDENTIFY their heathen, corrupt and heretical ways and DESTROY them.

The Ancients will guide you in your mission. Their method-ology was successful in its day and, because they are revered, indeed Rome's reverence of them is part of her present cor-ruption, you will use their cunning to purify the heart of our Christian realm.

Piero's eyes, above the pale blue page read quickly:

We cite from an old Iberian fable, the legend of King Duplixx, annotated as an example of subtlety, wisdom, cunning and success.
In far Asia King Duplixx desired to possess the land of the Soddisfaxxi, which was a land of great wealth and great so-phistication, but the people there had become lazy and cor-rupt. His motives were base. He envied their wealth and their sophistication. He wanted both. He could easily have con-quered them, slaughtered them, because in truth his armies were stronger than theirs. But to have done so would have been foolish. What would have been the result: The destruc-tion of all that he desired rather than its possession.

King Duplixx was wise and cunning. He sent forth spies to learn the ways of the Soddisfaxxi. He observed that they faith-fully worshipped and sacrificed to their own God, and that they housed their God in a simple but elegant Temple in the main square of their City. The temple was the embodiment of the God and represented all that the God was.
The King weighed his choices.

He could burn their temple, raze it to the ground, eradi-cate it, and topple the effigy leaving no sign of their God. If he were to conquer the people in this way, he thought, he would gain their wealth but neither their loyalty nor the vitality that made them desirable as a subject people in the first place.

He could storm the Temple and turn the images of their God out and replace it with his own God, but he knew that if he did that the people would forever compare him to his predecessor, and resent him because the past is always more perfect in the memories of men than the present. He knew that, as the image of the God will have vanished, the God would not have vanished from the hearts and minds of the people, and he knew that he would never be able to replace the beloved old gods in that way.

In either case, he reasoned, he would be robbing himself of the fullest fruits of his conquest.

King Duplixx decided on another strategy. He requested permission of the people of Soddisfaxxi to make an offering at the feet of their God. The people were cautious but at the same time flattered and granted him permission. After all, how could they refuse a tribute to their own God? Dressed modestly and with his head bared, the King made his sacrifice at the lowest step of the temple. He praised their God and the Soddisfaxxi themselves, their past deeds and their glories. Indeed, he praised all the things about them that he wanted for himself; but he praised them faintly, and with each faint praise he even more faintly praised himself.

He then asked the Soddisfaxxi if he might send his royal architect to measure the Temple so that he might copy it. Flattered by King's Duplixx'appreciation of their cherished Temple they readily agreed. The King then instructed his architect to draw the design for another Temple that would be similar to the old, but newer and slightly larger and slightly, but only slightly, more elaborately appointed than the old. He wished to do this he explained to the people out of respect for them and for the Gods they worshipped.

Deep in his heart he judged their values to be wothless, but he did not let them know that.

His architect did as he was bid. He measured the Old Temple. He measured the base, and the columns and the spaces between the columns. He measured the angles of the roof and the ornaments. He recorded all of the measurements, and then he studied them. He conferred with the King who explained his mission to him, as I am explaining yours to you. And the Architect did as he was bid. In his own heart he knew that he could build a much more wonderful temple than the one he had been asked to replicate. But he did as he was told.

On the public square, facing the old temple he began to build the new one. The base was slightly wider. It was slightly higher above the square requiring that two more steps be climbed to reach the altar. The columns of the new temple were slightly larger, slightly taller. The ornamentation of the columns was slightly larger in proportion to the whole and were slightly more intricately detailed, but only slightly. When it was finished and the people could see both temples together. The old one looked worn and shabby in comparison with the new one. And when the King had an effigy of himself placed in the new temple in the garb of the old God enough people turned their backs on the old temple and the old god who lived there. The old temple fell into disrepair and eventually to ruin. The old gods were blamed for the temple's demise.

Not an arrow was let fly but just the same the High Priest of the Soddisfaxxi and their false old Gods, were slain. King Duplixx knew that the best battle to win was the one that did not have to be fought. And in his wisdom he knew, as well, that a battle faces no resistance and therefore must only be won.

The land of the Soddisfaxxi entered a glorious period in its history and prospered under the leadership of King Duplixx.

When he looked up from the page, Piero encountered his own puzzled face looking back at him from the mirror. Fables, unless they could be incorporated into a painting or drawing, did not interest him. He pressed the damp cloth to the page and read on:

> *Duplixx' Architect constructed the new temple, by reducing the old temple to a system of numbers. In truth his reduction of the Old Temple to a mathematical system foretold the death of the Soddisfaxxi.*

> *Vitruvius understood this. And provided the same service to Caesar that Duplixx' architect had. That was his great service to the Roman Empire. That is the great part you will enable Rome's architects and artists to play for the True Faith. This is the mission God has given you. Your success in this undertaking will be your gift to God. Your reward will be His assurance of the eternal salvation of your soul.*

Piero relaxed, his spirits rising to the task, no less the reward, as he continued to read,

> *As did Vitruvius so shall you:*
>   *IDENTIFY the physical manifestation of those values as they are esteemed in their Arts and their Architecture.*
> *By definition they will have become HERETICAL OBJECTS of veneration.*
> *By the use of science, mathematics and cunning reduce these OBJECTS OF VENERATION to formulas that will enable you to replicate them.*
> *All you have to do is work with numbers. It is dry work that avoids the messy wetness of war. But you are a general nonetheless. Make no mistake. Taking the Church back from the Secularists, from the Academicians, from the Hedonists, from the Godless, from the Pagans, from the Heretics is your*

mission. Use the formulas, the mathematical rules to neutralize them.

The dreaded formulas again. Is that all there is? Piero looked up. What time was it? It must be late. He looked at Bramante's instructions. He had accomplished nothing. Bramante would be back soon. For some reason, or absence of reason, the image of a clumsy roofed building entered Piero's mind. What if the old temple of the Soddisfaxxi was a clumsy-roofed building like the one Vitruvius mentioned? What if it were ugly? Then Duplixx and his architects, whoever they were, would have been making rules based on an ugly building. If that were true then the architect and Duplixx didn't care if the building was beautiful. The thought shocked him. Piero cared about little else. He existed, lived and breathed, to make things that were beautiful, eternally beautiful. He stared at himself in mirror. His thoughts jumbled. Were things inherently beautiful or were they made beautiful only when defined by rules? Might an ugly thing be made beautiful by having rules devised to describe it? He didn't like where this was leading and shut his eyes. He forced himself to retreat from the impending precipice.

But in the fable, the old temple and the new temple were not very different from one another. The story said that the new one was just a little different. The story never described either one as beautiful. King Duplixx' architect didn't reproduce the old temple because it was beautiful. But it must have been beautiful to the people he wanted to conquer otherwise why would they revere it? All the story inferred was that copying it was effective, because, as a strategy to conquer the Soddisfaxxi, it worked. Does that mean that what works is beautiful? Is that all it is? The pages trembled in his hand. Does that mean that beauty is just an invention? He read the next one:

> *It is your privilege and sacred duty to devote yourself to the Purification of the Faith. If the humanistic mood, so called, in Rome calls for the revival of antiquity, then that will be your tool. BUT, for THE STRATEGY to be effective ANTIQUITY will have to be redefined. We cannot have PAGAN IMAGES*

polluting the heart of Christendom. There can be neither Caesars, nor goddesses nor Aristotles nor Platos nor Ciceros diverting us from the True Faith.

You will empty The VESSEL OF ANTIQUITY of its meaning by the sublime and perfect reinterpretation of the classical orders. You will present history scrubbed, sterilized, washed and dried. The task of the SOCIETY FOR THE PURIFICATION OF THE FAITH is to refill the vessel with GOD'S TRUTH.
If you FAIL then the Kingdom of Heaven is LOST FOREVER.

Piero looked up. In the mirror above the page he saw his own eyes filled with doubt. Nausea like warm surf surged in his belly. He lowered the page gently as if it were asleep, something that should not be awakened, and backed away from the mirror. He looked over at his stool, but could not make himself sit. He walked across the room and then began pacing back and forth stealthily, as if he were in the dark and afraid of bumping into something, or as if he were afraid of being discovered, or of casting a shadow, or of making a sound. He felt blinded by what he had read. He felt ill, frightened. Pacing in his private darkness he had forgotten about Colonna's assault, but that was nothing compared to the hollowness he felt now. He returned to the stool. He needed to clear his mind. He shook his head and pressed his palms to his eyes. Terrible images came rushing to him. He saw the ruins of Rome as a stack of bleached bones on a naked beach. He saw them as hollowed out fragments of shell scoured by the wind, their tender morsels sucked out of them by time and driven sand.

Piero stared into an enveloping darkness and saw Rome's ancient landscape draped in a net of iron rods. He saw all the characters he had read about and loved, the entire panoply of the pagan world, Demeter, Minerva, Bacchus, Pan, Hercules, the fair Helen. The philosophers were there, too: Aristotle, Plato; the historians: Herodotus, Livy, Tacitus; the artists and architects, his ancestral brothers: Phideas, Chersiphron, Metagenes. There

was Cicero, even Cicero, a politician. He saw the body of Saint Damasus
flop out of a tumbrel onto the ground, and the sparkling diamond sea
turn gray. He saw Zeus bleeding from his thigh where the knuckle of an
iron link had scraped it. The heavy net began to shake back and forth
across the land. There was no other sound but the clanking iron. No one
was playing the lyre. No one was laughing. No one was reading or lecturing or teaching or explaining or singing. All were scrambling over one
another, beating their way to escape the net. He saw Vitruvius beyond the
net, safe as Judas was safe. He saw trees and flowers, uprooted from the
soft damp earth, dragged over bleating sheep, panicked hares; game of all
kinds: pheasant, woodcock, songbirds, slammed down by falling branches,
as the net dragged and scraped across them shaking the ground. He saw
fires render the flesh from their shattered bones. He smelled the ancient
world being slaughtered, cooked and buried, and he shook with fear. He
heard the chain clanking, the sound of life being scraped away. No one
and no thing was left standing. All that remained were stiff columns, fallen
like white logs, bleached and scoured arches and vaults, statues broken
and dismembered, lying under the net.

All became quiet. The clanking stopped and the crying. The thundering net stopped shaking the ground. Piero looked up and saw angels descending from heaven like butterflies. They filled the sky, clouds of them,
billowing in soft gusts, their wings beating through puffy clouds, floating, smiling swirling through the air, their pale white palms extended,
offering cool love.

Piero got up and went to the mirror. He saw a small, curly headed
soldier, burned and bruised. On the table was the folio of pale blue pages
marked with white writing. He saw the damp cloth sitting in its pan. He
pressed his fists to his sides, afraid that against his will the cloth would fly
to him and wrap itself around his hand, and like a living creature pry open
his fingers and slam them down on another page. He feared that these
pages would not have writing on them. He feared they would be drawings, cartoons, designs: his designs, the ones he had already done and
others he would be expected to make. He imagined he would see revealed
in white on blue the new St. Peter's riding atop a wooden frame, its dome
concealing a battering ram. On another sheet he imagined a paper cutout

of Riario's Palace in the form of a gigantic warship built of Bramante's drawings, rolling on a platform of logs, bellows, perfectly sized, pumping air into its huge square sails as it plowed a swath through old Rome grinding and compressing the earth beneath it as it went. Another sheet would show his design for the limekiln, blue on white cooking and smoking. Another, a finely drafted cartoon, would showed the new St Peter's dwarfing the Pantheon, making it look like a bump in the road, sitting in a gray landscape void of dirt and smells and green and wonder. Turning away he dropped to his knees and pressed his cheek against the edge of the table. He looked up at the Roman matron. Her blank, white eyes like hard-boiled eggs gazed beyond him into a world that someone, he, was being instructed to erase.

He became aware of the smells coming from the workshop. He heard the familiar voices of the artists and artisans preparing to break for lunch. The morning was gone. He had accomplished not one thing. He jumped to his feet and spread out Bramante's sketches and instructions. He stared at the thin ink lines, at the tiny numbers indicating widths and heights. He opened Vitruvius' Book IV, and for the first time felt afraid of the pages, afraid of their bloodlessness, their coldness and whiteness.

He rubbed his eyes, "I have work to do." He stacked the pale blue sheets neatly aside. "Later," he muttered, "out of sight out of mind." On the last blue page he read again,

The freedom of states has been preserved by the cunning of architects.

His stomach tensed. He unwillingly read all the permutations over again. "No," he said aloud and hurriedly squared the pages and turned them face down. On the back of the last page, written up the right hand margin, he noticed for the first time a tiny line of script. He held it up to the mirror:

Translated into Italian from the original correspondence from Seville by Fr Juan. May God rest my soul.

Piero's scalp prickled. Once again he saw the smoke blowing from the limekiln. He spun around. He needed to hide the pages. If only he could reverse the chemistry that had revealed their secrets. He dug his fingernails into the palms of his hands. He was not dreaming. He envied the everyday lunch time sounds coming from the street.

There was a sharp knock at the door. Piero flinched. Bramante would not knock. "God help me," he whispered, beseeching the Roman matron, who if she could, would have thrown her head back and laughed. In a voice that sounded not like his own he called, "*Vengo subito,* I'll be right there." He looked around. He was trapped. He swept up the pale blue pages and shoved them into the Vitruvius folio.

23

Bramante's Study

Piero went to the door, teasing himself with the unlikely possibility that Imperia or Giulia, or even Vannozza, the Fig, might be there. He raked his fingers through his hair and pulled open the door.

Father Ximenez' black silhouette filled the opening. Piero backed away. The priest appeared just as he had yesterday, like a black vulture in the lime dusted air. "How fortunate I am to find you in," he said.

"Maestro Bramante is out."

"Yesterday," said Ximenez, closing the door behind him, muting the familiar sounds and smells of the workshop. "How terrible that must have been for you." He moved toward Piero.

Piero said nothing. He merely shrugged as if to say he had not given it another thought and backed away.

" I came to offer what small comfort I can," Ximenez black eyes bore steadily into Piero's. He spoke softly, sounding concerned.

"Thank you, Father, but . . . I'm not letting it get to me."

The priest seized Piero by the shoulders, "Good for you. You're strong." His grasp was firm. "Buonarotti would have gone into a swoon and moped for days, Bramante, too." He winked at Piero who had tried not to smile. "But it is upsetting, I'm sure." He roughed up Piero's curly hair.

"That was yesterday. I have a lot to do and don't have time to think about it," Piero moved away. The priest smelled faintly of oranges.

"So I see." Ximenez turned away abruptly and folded his arms. His black eyes looked around the room moving from the table piled with notes and folios to the unfinished madonnas. "But still," he said over his shoulder, "people like us are not made for such harsh encounters." He went over to the table, "and then—the audacity. How outrageous. I was told of the incident at the Tavern. Those Germans and then Ottavio Colonna—so rude, so rude." He said it calmly, not in an angry way, but dismissive, as if to say that people like that were beneath people like them. "How can anyone take the remarks of such a fool seriously?" He was, of course referring to Ottavio both winning and losing the race. The story was all over the City. "He is a laughing stock, but I must admit, I am a little bit grateful to him." He spun suddenly to face Piero, the scar hiking up the side of his face in an awful smile. "I won some money for the poor by betting on him."

Piero tried to smile at the priest's joke, "Those things the German was shouting . . . and the suicide . . ."

"The suicide. Terrible. Did you know Fra Juan?" The priest's eyes bore into Piero's.

"Not well," Piero said looking away. "He came to the Tavern a few times."

"Did you two speak?"

"He never said much. He just seemed to enjoy being among us." Piero's eyes welled. He brushed the tears away. ". . . and now Fra Juan is damned in Hell"

"Did he ever give you anything?" Ximenez asked sharply.

". . . and then the Professor said that the world could be Hell."

"Old Laetus said that?" Ximenez cocked his head to one side. He moved closer and loomed over Piero.

"It made me angry and confused, and then that Ottavio Colonna . . . I would be lying if I said it didn't bother me," Piero's bravura crumpled.

"Your burns . . ." Ximenez lifted Piero's chin and ran a finger lightly across his brow.

Piero turned his face away, "They're nothing."

Ximenez dropped his hand and turned to peruse the spines of Bramante's tomes, running a long forefinger across the rolls of drawings. He picked up the bust of the marble matron and scrutinized her for a moment and then carefully put her down. "What are you working on?" The priest was standing over a drawing filled with Bramante's hastily scratched notes and figures. They were incomprehensible to him.

"It's Riario's palace."

"Fascinating. Simply fascinating, I'm sure."

"I was supposed to rework the layout for the façade but I haven't been able to focus. Bramante will be back soon, and I haven't accomplished anything."

"I mustn't keep you from your work then," Ximenez said, making no move to leave.

"Everything that happened yesterday . . . I couldn't sleep. I woke up angry." Piero watched Ximenez long bony hands resting on the drawing. The pale blue pages were in the folio to the right of it. He wanted to pull them out and hand them to the priest and be relieved of the burden of knowing what they said and to be relieved of what they made him think, and to be forgiven for having trespassed. Was it stealing to know something that one was not supposed to? He wanted to open the folio to the chapter on 'the intervals of intercolumniations,' and the dimensions and proportions of ballistae, tortoises and siege towers and say, look, look they are all the same. Buildings are weapons, too. They are weapons when people think they are beautiful, but his words dared not come. Beauty is a weapon, but no one knows. Someone knows. I know. It was Ximenez who killed Fra Juan. He was certain of it, but he was a priest and as a priest he could absolve him and also relieve his anguish, ". . . I started thinking this morning that what I was doing was not worthwhile . . . or even good."

Ximenez feigned surprise, "You mean your work? You doubt your work? How could you doubt your work? You are the most promising of young men in an age of great and gifted men."

Piero reached for the folio containing the designs for the new St Peter's,

"I was very disappointed when the work stopped on the new church, but it may have been for the best." He pulled out a drawing. Ximenez came and stood very close, his face almost resting on Piero's shoulder. His pleasant fragrance of spice and orange everywhere.

The priest placed a bony hand on the edge of the page to stop it curling and made the deep, appreciative sound a connoisseur makes when enjoying something rare and wonderful, like an epicure tasting a fine wine. Their shoulders touched. He turned to Piero, their faces just inches apart. "It is exquisite," he whispered, "How could you possibly have any doubt about your work. Masterpieces such as this mark the dawn of a new Golden Age."

Piero's cheeks burned.

Ximenez leaned forward to study the drawing more closely. His arm brushed Piero's. After a thoughtful moment, "How can you doubt your ability, your skill?" His eyes left the page, searching the spaces between the stacked folios.

"It's not my skill that causes me doubt," Piero caught himself sounding vain and more confident than he meant to, less in need of reassurance. He did not want to discourage the priest's solicitations, nor did he want the priest to feel they were without effect. "What I mean to say is, my doubt is not strictly self-doubt, doubt about my ability. I began to doubt the value of making beautiful things."

Ximenez turned to Piero staring at the drawing but seeing something else. "You are still conflicted by the terrible events and insults of yesterday. They have shaken your confidence." He said it in a way that inferred that he could not believe that Piero, so clever a young man, needed more reassurance, but implied, at the same time that he was there to offer comfort if needed.

Piero turned to him not hearing the priest's words as much as absorbing the sounds and the warm scent of his presence.

"The doubt is there. I see it in your eyes," Ximenez said, their faces almost touching, "Let us hope your doubts are not so profound as to border on heresy." The dreaded word was said in a light, vague way, suggesting that he merely joked. His words hung there requiring a response.

"Heresy," Piero recalled the charred steaming pieces of Fra Juan being pulled from the lime kiln and braced himself against the table. The folio of Vitruvius' Ten Books with the coded sheets inside was to his right, the priest to his left. He felt afraid of Ximenez, but did not want to lose the comfort he offered, nor for some reason did he want to not fear him.

Piero asked, "Is doubt heretical?"

Ximenez, in a way that suggested his words had been carefully considered, "Not necessarily."

"How can I be sure that what I feel is not heretical? How can one be sure that my doubt is not heresy?" He spoke rapidly in a rising pitch.

Ximenez studied the side of the young man's face: his flushed cheek, his black unruly hair pushed back behind his ear, his ear where it met his jaw, his mouth barely moving, his eyes wide open, looking, he knew, at something still unstated. The priest withdrew a fraction. Their shoulders no longer touched. His retreat was almost imperceptible. He wanted to not disturb Piero's mood, but feeling it fleeing, wanted to threaten that he could withdraw. "If I can assure you that your feelings are not heretical, but merely the fleeting self doubt that afflicts all gifted and creative men I will."

Aware of cool space between them Piero said, "The work I had to do today was . . ."

"I'm sure it was important." Ximenez bowed his head, and moved so their shoulders once again touched.

"Bramante would say it was, but I must tell you," with a self deprecating laugh, " that it is also very boring." Piero faced the priest to let him know that having said that was a great breach of trust.

"You have my complete confidence. And trust."

Knowing that with Ximenez' help he could flirt with heresy, but be pulled back from it's maw and rescued before he was smoked like a ham, calmed him. Piero closed his eyes, "These Rules of Proportion—they are endlessly dull. They are profoundly important, I know, but all morning my mind kept straying. I couldn't focus. There was a moment when I began to doubt the rules, doubt their worth, doubt their truth, doubt their validity. They are so cold and indifferent. I was sitting right here. I had to rub my face for fear of falling asleep." He raised his hands to his face. "For some reason the numbers all began to run together and made me think of money. 'What does this have to do with money?' I said it out loud. I heard myself." He felt stupid all over again for saying it; but at the same time he was glad he had, as if saying it, were itself, a kind of currency to be exchanged with the priest. The more he said the more Ximenez would have to give back in exchange. "But then I thought: the rules are like money. They're just like money. They're just a cold means of exchange. All this arithmetic is just a medium of transference, like money is. Vitruvius gave Caesar the means to reproduce any building he wanted to. It let Caesar buy and own them, at least buy and own what they look like, and then manipulate them the way King Duplixx had." He had said too much, but he could not stop.

Ximenez, beside him, listened, barely breathing. His black eyes began to shake.

"What if these formulas were not meant to produce buildings that were beautiful? 'God help me,' I said it out loud. 'What if Vitruvius thought that some of the buildings he was codifying were ugly, but, but what? Did he have other reasons for codifying them? Was it to transform them into objects of desire. Was that all it meant? I couldn't go on." His anxiety returned. He was talking fast in a louder whisper, "I felt crazed. I felt as if I were being lead somewhere I shouldn't go. But I had to go on. I had to be rid of this idea. It just had to be done with. It had to end. Is beauty just a fragile belief, a changeable one? Is being concerned about making beautiful things a stupid concern. Am I really doing something else that I don't know anything about?" He was confused and frightened. He looked up, straight ahead. His eyes wide open now.

Ximenez said, very quietly, not in a whisper, but in a low voice, "God has given you a gift. To not use it is to defy Him and to doubt His wisdom. That is heresy." He let the word sink in, "and ingratitude." He said it in a soft way that was neither an admonition, nor a threat. He said it with understanding and compassion.

Piero froze, not daring to look at the priest, feeling the black eyes inches from his face, his heat and scent.

Ximenez said, "To doubt the value of God's gift to you is to doubt God himself. This is a serious breach. You must confess these heresies and be cleansed. I will confess you." He grabbed Piero roughly by the shoulders and spun him around so that they were face to face. He pushed Piero to his knees.

Piero closed his eyes tight and made the sign of the cross, "Forgive me father for I have sinned . . ."

Ximenez grasped the young man's head.

"Forgive me father for doubting your wisdom," Piero began to sob. "Forgive me, Father, for my ingratitude." He mumbled his confession. He pressed his eyes shut. He saw the earth torn open for Riario's Palace and recalled what Professor Laetus told him about the sainted Pope Damasus, about how he instructed St. Jerome, his secretary, to translate the Holy Bible into Latin, "Forgive me, Father, for believing my gifts to be my own and not gifts bestowed by you to be used for your glory." He saw the body of the old Pope, the sainted Damasus, in a tumbrel, being pushed away like a barrow full of spent charcoal to be dumped in a ditch. "Forgive me, Father, for the sin of Vanity," and he saw Riario laughing at the party and boasting about being able to afford to take the architects and artists away from the Pope's new Church. "Forgive me Father, for my doubt." His body slumped forward, spent.

Ximenez offered nothing, letting the silence hang, his hands firmly grasping Piero's head, letting the silence speak. The priest's eyes rested on the pan. He saw the damp cloth. He rose swiftly.

Piero felt the room fill with silence. He felt its pressure, its charged fullness. He did not move, unsure of what to do, awaiting a response to his confession, needing to know his penance, unsure if he had been redeemed, if he had been brought back or if he still teetered on the brink and would be pushed over the edge into inevitable damnation. Blood coursed through his body like thunder. A hard silence pressed in. He dared not open his eyes. He heard wine being poured and he relaxed. The sound of Holy Communion, Thank you, God. Thank you.

Without a word Ximenez placed a hand, fingers spread, less than an inch from Piero's face.

Piero felt its heat and opened his mouth, reflexively, to receive the host, relieved, redeemed, his eyes brimming with tears of gratitude.

Ximenez offered not a sound, not a word. He took a folded cloth from his cassock, and from it withdrew a small, gray disk, wrinkled and uneven, and placed it on Piero's tongue.

Piero accepted it. It was sour. A bitter communion: how fitting. It was his sin being drawn away by the body of Christ. But communion even if bitter was redemption from his heretical doubt. He felt warm. His face flushed. The heat comforted him. He relaxed. His skin tingled. He took the wine. "Thank you," he said swallowing hard. There was a faint gust of turpentine and an unbearable loudness as the door to the studio opened and then closed again. He tasted fire.

Part V

Gold

24

Offshore

A lamp on the shore flashed twice. Under a starless sky the stout Spanish caravel flashed once in response and dropped anchor. The captain ordered a heavy sea chest bundled in waxed canvas brought from below. As the sea lapped quietly, two guards dressed as farmers, and a tall young friar waited patiently for the skiff to come alongside. When the oarsman tapped the hull three times the guards climbed down into the skiff and the chest was lowered over the side. When they were satisfied that it was stowed securely they tapped the hull twice. On deck the captain flashed his lamp. Once. Two quick blinks flashed from the shore and the skiff pushed off toward the mouth of the Arrone Creek. Upstream a hay wagon awaited them. The men and their concealed cargo would join the many other carts traveling the Via Aurelia, bringing produce and merchandise into Rome.

An hour later another lamp flashed twice from the beach near the mouth of the Focene Canal. There another wagon waited to take a second sea chest over land to the Via Portuense and into Rome.

Just before dawn a third skiff was hauled onto the beach near the ruins of Laurentium. In the darkness a small crew loaded its cargo onto a cart and buried it under a load of beets. It would travel into Rome along the Via Ostiense.

At first light the caravel raised her pennant. Her white foresail swelled the distinctive blood-red cross of the Spanish crown like the breast of a rooster, as she passed the faro and proceeded up the Tiber's northern fork to Ostia, Rome's port, to wait patiently in the channel for a berth.

25

Santa Maria in Monserrato

Ximenez stood behind his desk and watched as the guards carried in the long awaited cargo. Leather mail pouches lay in a heap against the wall. His new secretary, Brother Nicholas, the lamented Fra Juan's replacement, hovered over the delivery. As each item was unpacked the young cleric carefully checked it against the manifest. The cargo had not been out of the young friar's sight since the ship left Cadiz. There was a lot of mail: Directives, Royal Orders, Instructions, answers to previous requests, personal letters, not to mention the clarifications and modifications to previous Directives, Royal Orders and Instructions. Brother Nicholas carefully sorted the mail into categories and arranged it dutifully in neat piles on Father Ximenez' desk.

But the most important part of the shipment was the gold. Ximenez spread his arms wide and threw his head back. He wanted to crow, but dared not. He dropped his arms and folded them tightly. The sea chests sat open in the nave outside his door. The hay and vegetables used to conceal them were strewn across the floor. Like a bucket brigade, the guards were passing heavy gold ingots from hand to hand into the small office and stacking them like bricks against the wall. Bumpy, crude bricks. The money that Spain had pledged to finance the new St Peter's, the money that had been guaranteed to Chigi the Magnificent to finance the Pope; the money, the hard currency, the gold that was not there when it was supposed to be, whose absence had caused work on the new church to stop, whose absence had forced Ximenez to apologize to the banker, Chigi, and had caused Spain's preeminence to be doubted, had finally arrived. The small room, lined with gold from floor to ceiling, reminded Ximenez of King Midas' counting house.

Silver and gold, weak of themselves, provided very strong links indeed, mused Ximenez. He sat, relaxed for the first time in months, savoring the moment. He shuffled through the papers before him without reading them: the orders, the directives, the copies of letters and journals from the Indies; and marveled at the wisdom and perfection of God's divine justice. How exquisite that God's invisible hand should tear the spoils from heathens, pagans and savages, cannibals, too, according to the letters that came from Seville. How perfect that their hideous idols should be toppled and their vain adornments ripped from their bodies and melted into the bricks that would rebuild Rome. He thought of the brave young brothers, priests just like him, smart boys from poor country towns, just like him, a world away with the conquistadors. They are soldiers, he knew, just as he still was. He closed his eyes imagining the kingdoms they described, empires ruled by Satan, inhabited by people who were virtually animals, barely clothed, painted with paste made from fruit and mud, with feathers sticking out of their heads, creatures who pounded the beating hearts out of each others' chests with sharpened stones. The thought thrilled and disgusted him. How perfect is God's plan. By turning them away from Satan, by depriving them of their wickedness, by saving their souls and bringing them home to the true faith, God was also delivering to him, Ximenez, a simple priest, the means to crush sin and heresy here in the very heart of Christendom. The oneness, as he saw it, showed the unquestionable purity of his mission. The circle of gold wedded all things, ultimately, to God.

The guards finished stacking the ingots and left. Brother Nicolas stood silently awaiting instructions.

Ximenez looked at him, "I will devote tomorrow to making deposits with the bankers. It's time to get this show on the road again. Call on Chigi. Tell him to come tomorrow first thing." His words were drowned out by a thunder of rock and gravel clattering down a metal chute at Riario's construction site nearby. He raised his voice, vaguely gesturing in the direction of the racket, "Our Lord is in agreement it would seem. It will be music to my ears to hear the sound of work resuming at the new St. Peter's. Our instructions, I am pleased to report, are to . . . ," he stopped in mid sentence and reached for a pile of neatly stacked mail. He thumped it once to show that it could be even more perfectly, more squarely, shaped than his new young secretary had already made it. Arching his back Ximenez raised his eyebrows and carefully aimed his black eyes to read the page. It wasn't really necessary for him to read the Directives again. He knew what they would say. He knew them by heart, but stating them without at least the appearance of the words coming from the page, not merely from his lips, would not have carried the authority he felt was necessary. He remarked brusquely, as if it were to have been expected and had no more importance beyond corroborating what they already knew, "We are to proceed with our mission." He sat back, " It would seem that the Holy Office is pleased with our work." And well they should be, he thought. The barons were licking their wounds. Most of them were up to their necks in debt and, because of that, unable to resist the inevitable demise of their power and influence. The brief interruption in cash flow had also served to put the Pope in his place, humble him, let him know where the real power lay. Ximenez' eyes lingered on the wall of gold bricks. Yes, the shortfall put them all in their places. I must remind them that it can happen again. It is important that they not forget.

Nicolas waited patiently for Ximenez to say something more. Finally, he asked, "What specific action shall we take?" The question was a logical one, said in a way that was respectful but also showed an eagerness for action.

Ximenez turned to him. He felt that he had already said enough. It had been a full day and a full night. He was tired. He wanted to finish the day by savoring the arrival of the money and the prospect of getting his mission back on course. He looked forward to holding his head high once again among the princes of the church, of not having to hide from Chigi, of never again having to even entertain the distasteful thought of going to the Jews to borrow money. This discussion could wait. But then . . . Ximenez curbed his predisposition to rebuff the young man's question. After all the young friar had been working hard, too. Nicholas had been by his side for the past twenty four hours, never complaining, never flagging, responding to his every need without having to be told what to do. The young man had potential. He didn't want to discourage him.

Ximenez made as if to scan the instructions from Seville, and again thought of the New World. "Rome is our theater of battle," he said, finally, seeing himself on the front line, imagining the Americas, Los Indios. "We will have to use our imaginations, of course. We can't let our guard down just because we are back in control. All those doubters, we can buy them back, now," he said almost as if to himself. "We can promise them anything. We can promise anyone anything." The chests of money, the ingots of gold lining the office soothed his irritability. The money is back, which means we are back in the game and can and will lure them back to the Truth by any means necessary.

"For starters," he said, sighing a little, "I was thinking that we might round up a few artists, perhaps encourage some young architects. You know, encourage their talent. Give them the means to develop their God given gifts. Bramante is so, I don't know, what would you say, so yesterday. There's a promising boy in Bramante's studio, Piero something or other. We can invite him here." He stifled a yawn.

Making every appearance of having considered Ximenez' remarks, Nicolas said, "Would it make any sense . . . just a thought . . . to . . . in addition to what you just said . . . which is brilliant . . . to . . . to back a new Pope? You know, one that comes with his own money, this time . . . . Just as a fall back." Brother Nicholas blushed as if he felt that he might have spoken inappropriately.

Ximenez looked up from the page that he had not been reading and stared directly into the young man's face, seeing him for the first time as a being truly worthy of his attention, not merely his sufferance, "A commendable thought." He wanted to address him by name, but had forgotten it. "Did you have any candidates in mind?"

Nicolas, not blushing this time, "Might it be time for a banker to rise to the task?"

Ximenez returned quickly to the page and thanked God, first, for the arrival of the money and then for this. He felt a rush of pride, the kind he was sure fathers feel, when they see their sons demonstrate the potential to finally become men. "My son, he said, you are wise beyond your years." To test him he asked, " have you no reservations about unleashing the corrupting force of money?"

Nicholas shot Ximenez a hard look, "As we all know corruption sanctioned by God, ordered by God to defeat corruption, to uproot, rip out, drive out, and expel heresy and corruption is not corrupt."

Ximenez' throat caught. He lowered his head and swallowed hard. Nicolas' words and the passion with which he said them filled him with emotion. His eyes brimmed with tears of joy.

26

Palazzo Chigi

Looking surprised, as if he'd never seen them before, Agostino Chigi fanned his cards onto the table. "I think I'm getting the hang of this game." He was extremely pleased. The pot was large. Wide-eyed he looked around the table, as if to ask from where on earth might such a perfect hand have come. His lavish hospitality shone on the rosy faces of his friends, nestled in layers and folds of cloth finely interwoven with gold and silver thread. He was teaching them the latest variation of Primero, a game whose object was to accumulate particular suites and sets of cards. "You know, the French are mad for this game," Chigi gushed reminding his guests that they could always count on him to be up on the very latest trend, and that it would always be he and no one else who would introduce them to novel pleasures like this. He basked in his colleagues grudging admiration of his uncanny ability to always be a step ahead of them. They all knew, as only the most successful businessmen and bankers know, that without a crystal ball to truly see into the future, the future had to be invented— invented so that it could be claimed, bought and then sold. At this Chigi was preeminent.

The evening had been a great success. The deep, sweet chords of a string trio drifted from the *salotto* where the wives and ladies—fragile beauties, ethereal beauties—dressed gorgeously, had withdrawn to gossip. Chigi smiled when he heard Imperia's laughter rise above the music. In the dining hall the servants whispered as they cleared the platters, crystal and china from the table. Chigi had spared no expense. He no longer had to. Course after fabulous course: lobster, fish, game birds, meats, all perfumed with spices and herbs; wines and sweets, were presented in novel and delightful ways. The bankers were sated, glazed, stretched and stuffed to exhaustion. Rosy circles rouged their cheeks. The world as it was, in its entirety, as they owned it, filled the room. The fireplaces glowed and hissed, scenting the air with oak and apple.

He had invited them to celebrate and to give thanks. The panic was over, a momentary inconvenience, nothing more. The year of uncertainty had passed. Gold and silver were back, replacing the paper that had accumulated in their vaults. The brief interruption in trade from the Indies had dampened things, surely, caused them concern and even doubt, but they had persevered. Hardship strengthened their trust. Overhead the massive fluted arms of a new Venetian chandelier refracted soft candlelight across their contented faces. It had not been easy, but it had not been the end of the world. Deadlines had come and gone, but in the end they had honored every contract. They were honorable men. Even the Jews had been repaid their piddling sums. Their power had grown. Chigi and his associates no longer pretended to be competitors. Necessity had made them One.

Chigi reflected on how twenty year's trading with Eldorado had extended their commercial networks around the globe. They had grown used to a market gorged with hard cash, and had come to count on it. They had become complaisant. When last year's treasure fleet was lost, for whatever reason—piracy or weather, it made no difference—and their profits, indeed, their capital, lay scattered across the ocean floor, they realized how gossamer was their web of trade. All available gold and silver had been hoarded. Businesses, that for awhile were willing to trust their associates, became reluctant to accept promissory notes in lieu of cash. There was too much paper in circulation and too little cash on reserve in the banking centers of Florence, Paris, Amsterdam and London. Word had gotten out that Chigi had been reduced to making short-term loans from the Jews to keep his affairs, and the Pope's, afloat. But all that was behind them. Chigi had seen the last of that Goddamned Jew, as he called him, who came banging at his door every Sunday morning—Sunday no less—begging him for their money.

The bankers knew better now. In future they would hedge their bets. They would never let it happen again. Chance would not take them by surprise. That's what they said, but touching the newly minted gold pouring into their counting rooms made their caution and anxiety fade to relief, which in turn—with breathtaking speed—became cocksuredness.

Chigi belched softly and leaned forward, "Can I take the money now?" With his fat hands folded in front of him and the hint of a smile on his face, he looked like an inflated version of a delighted little boy asking his mother if he might have another cookie.

Guido Spannochi, seated to his right, found the question uproariously funny and in the tones of a proud mother said, "Yes, Tino, now that you have eaten everything in sight you may have your cookie."

Maximillian Fugger, of the German banking house, slapped his hands on the table and threw his head back. His face turned red, his eyes teared, his mouth opened, but in a pantomime of hilarity no sound emerged.

Chigi, with great delicacy, scooped the pile of coins from the table into a mysterious fold in his robe and pursed his red lips.

Cardinal Medici pushed himself a few inches away from the game and said, "Now that things are back to normal we all expect to be able to proceed apace with the construction of the new Church." His tone was neutral.

Chigi ignored the subtle reproach. It had all been dredged up again the day before by Ximenez. The Church expected its line of credit to be in place immediately, implying, again, that he had let the Church down, informing him that Spain was offended that he, Chigi the Magnificent, had allowed the Church's financing to be interrupted.

Chigi bigger, certainly broader, than life, flicked the barb aside, "Let me tell you, no one was sorrier than I to see the work stop. I know, I know I am the Pope's banker." He put his hands to his breast, the true anatomy of which must have surely existed in actual flesh deep beneath the layered folds of velvet and damask, behind the serving dish sized medallion that proclaimed in embossed gold, his 'Magnificence. "*Mea Culpa*, but . . . ," making light of it, not wanting to acknowledge even a hint of failure or to accept even a breath of blame, not wanting to spoil the evening's honeyed mood, ". . . no one was more disappointed than I that the work had to stop. It just proves that in hard times we all have to make sacrifices." He looked sharply at Medici, "We bankers as well as the Mother Church. You have no idea of the depths to which I stooped to keep the construction going for as long as I could. I could regale you with the bills I honored from Bramante, from all the purveyors to the Holy See, for which I must remind you, I have not been repaid. But this is neither the time nor the place to complain. Work will resume shortly. The Pope was pleased when I told him that a sizable advance has already been made on Maestro Bramante's account." In his warmest baritone he then said, "This is an evening to celebrate a new beginning," and spread his ponderous arms as if to embrace them all.

Spannocchi raised his glass. "Too bad Spain didn't make one of us an offer like the one they made me years ago to keep old Borgia afloat."

The toast dropped like a turd.

"Well maybe 'afloat' was a poor choice of words," he fumbled. The late Pope's son, the Duke of Gandia, found floating in the Tiber, his innards streaming in the current, was a distasteful image on a full stomach.

Cardinal Medici, a banker himself, stood and said, "Yes, all of that is behind us, now. I meant no offense, Chigi." and he unfurled a long flowery toast in a classical vein dedicated to endless prosperity, the New Church and the new Rome, bringing them neatly back to the celebration.

Chigi cleared his throat, retrieved his reins as host and crooned, "To celebrate the beginning of a glorious and prosperous future I would like to share another novel treat with you." He reached for a mahogany box that contained six tightly rolled brown cylinders that looked like the spoor of a medium sized animal, possibly human. "Tobacco, they call it," and displayed them proudly for all to see, "Take one." He passed the box around the table. The merchants studied them, sniffed them and held them up to the light. They had all heard of it, but none of them had ever seen it. The things stank. They were impressed.

Amused, the younger Chigi watched his father labor to make it appear that there was a protocol to the use of tobacco. If there was, and indeed perhaps there was, it was not known to anyone there, Chigi included. Devising a ritual as he went, Chigi reached for a taper and lighted one end of his *rollatino di tobacco* and puffed, carefully, at the other end, suppressing the urge to cough. Coughing would have been a *brutta figura*, bad form, revealing that he didn't know anything about what he was doing. Taking a shallow breath he slowly exhaled a cloud of acrid blue smoke and watched it rise. Then he smiled, a smile of thorough satisfaction, a smile that said at once both aah and mmm. The others watched and one by one followed suit, passing the taper from one to the other. Each inhaled. No one coughed. Chigi tilted his head back and smiled, satisfied. "Isn't it marvelous?" he asked, at last, as if he had a basis of comparison, which to some extent he did: it was the best tobacco he had ever smoked. He never lied. Management of the truth was his more accurate description of the way he shared information. "I have just secured a shipment through a Spanish associate. I mention it only to let you know that it will be available in limited quantities for a select few, through us."

The men grew accustomed to breathing in the smoke. They experimented with ways of comfortably holding their *rollatini* without looking like novices, and watched each other through the smoke. The stink soon became a smell, which finally became a fragrance; and they took comfort knowing that they were the first people in Italy to enjoy its pleasure.

Cardinal Medici inhaled slowly and deeply, admitting the rare and precious vapor into his lungs. He squinted at the smoke swirling around his hand. He savored its physical effect and experienced it as a sacrifice that was passing through him, a sacrifice more profound than that which merely whooshed by with a priest's careless wave of a censer. Relieved and unburdened, relaxed by the tobacco, his eyes followed the smoke curling and roiling heavenward. Pure incense. He tasted the earth of the Indies. He smelled the hands and fists of the heathen savages who picked the leaves and hung them to dry. He smelled the sun and the air of the new world. He felt it enter him and was thrilled by it, thrilled knowing that those creatures of Satan were being purified through him. He breathed deeply.

"It was a gift from Ximenez . . . ,"

Chigi stopped himself but not before old Spannocchi, squinting through the haze finished his sentence, "for borrowing from all of us, so that you could have your financing guaranteed by Spain." He then looked at the rolled tobacco in his hand as though it were a piece of shit, "Nice work, Tino."

Inhaling, Chigi nodded majestically to Spannocchi and Medici feeling their power fuse and expand, filling the room. It pushed into every corner. It pressed inward and upward against the legs of chairs and tables, against paintings and tapestries and outward against the room's very walls and ceiling, making a solid block of the void around them, encasing even the flickering candles in its invisible amber, forming the cornerstone of the new Rome.

ॐ

27

The Sepulcher

Djem entered the rock cut chamber and was surprised to see that Levi had arrived first, "You beat me for once." The oil lamp cast a warm glow across the soft stone. The pot hissed in its niche. A cloth piled with sweet little cakes was spread on the altar. "What is the occasion?"

Levi showily spilled the contents of a leather pouch onto the stone altar.

Djem, delighted by the sight, sat down and ran the large gold coins through his fingers. "Chigi," he said simply.

"Yes, Chigi. He was as good as his word. His paper wasn't just nothing."

"I am relieved. After all that time without a word, I never thought we would see it." Djem began stacking the money in neat piles, and quickly ran a tally on his abacus. " The interest is here, too—all of it. I am truly astonished." It was a small fortune.

"He sent a note," said Levi sliding it across to Djem, who slipped it delicately from its envelope. He ran his fingers across the red wax seal bearing the Chigi insignia of mountains and stars. It was addressed to Levi's father.

My esteemed Friend,
 Kindly accept payment in full for the modest amount you so graciously extended. You will see that the sum includes principal plus the accrued interest as well as a little extra for your patient understanding.
       Your most humble servant,
       Agostino "il Magnifico" Chigi

Djem looked up, tapped the note back into its envelope and passed it to Levi.

"He sounds quite sincere. My father was moved by his kindness." Levi said.

Djem changed the subject, "Business is picking up."

"Yes," said Levi slipping the note into his pouch, "work has resumed on the new church, which means the pilgrims will be returning in droves. Everyone in Rome has a paying job. We will be in good shape."

"That explains the increased demand for dyed cotton and silk we have been seeing." He reached into his robe for the week's list of new loan requests. A tinker needed a short term advance to purchase silver for plating. A tinter needed a loan to buy a quantity of murex to make purple dye, "Royal purple has become a vogue even among the less than royal, it seems." The requests were modest and reasonable. The applicants were known. All were approved. Indicating Chigi's carefully stacked coins Djem said, "We can put this to work right away."

"Chigi's son is getting married," said Levi as he made entries in the ledger.

Djem was working the abacus and dictating sums. "I pity the poor woman, whomever she may be," said the Moor. She'd better be as strong as an ox to have that behemoth bouncing on her belly.

Levi raised a finger as if to say, now now.

"I know, I know. He pays his debts, at least his father does; I shouldn't make fun, but he's still a big slob."

Without looking up Levi said, "My father says Chigi's looking to give his son a horse, not just any horse, but something special and fast. When Chigi's minion asked my father if he knew of one my father shrugged his shoulders and said, you're asking me about a horse? Jews don't know about horses. We walk."

When they stopped laughing Djem shook his head, "A horse and a wife. Isn't he a lucky boy. I'll keep my eye out for him. I am expecting a string from Naples soon. There's bound to be a winner among them." Suddenly he stopped and laid the abacus aside. He put a finger to his lips, cupped a hand to his ear and pointed. Without another word he blew out the lamp.

28

La Taverna nel Teatro di Pompeo

Professor Laetus hurried into the Tavern and fanned through the smoke, the way a swimmer would under water. The noise was deafening. Loud voices reverberated through the brick caverns. The air was thick with good food smells. He squeezed carefully between a bench full of high-spirited revelers and the hot cooking trough that ran down the middle of the main hall. Drippings from roasting sides of meat hissed and flared on the coals. The fat was on the fire. The fat was back. The upbeat mood bordered on hilarity. Everyone was beaming, talking loudly, singing, tossing bright new coins at the serving girls. Cash sat in piles on the tables. No one bothered to count it out. Construction of the new St. Peter's had resumed. Everybody was back at work. Everybody was happy. There was nothing like cash to raise the spirits. The professor imagined the Pope as Caesar sprinkling silver into the streets. Boisterous, rambunctious good fun; eating, drinking and joking, resounded under the vast, ruined belly of Pompey's theater. It had been a long time since the Tavern had seen a Saturday night like this.

Professor Laetus darted from one chamber to another squinting through the steam and smoke, looking for Piero and Antonio. Skirting the alcove where fellows of The Roman Society were having an argument, he waved, but moved past quickly. Club meetings were in full swing. The local militia preened in their dress uniforms. His eyes burned. The band from the Campo Marzio, was rehearsing under a fallen arch. A trumpet shat a wet bleat. He raised his chin, offended, and glided by, raking the air, searching. He looked up at the Crow's Nest. It was empty. Dark. Good. Above it, framed by an arch edged in silver, the night sky was clear.

Frustrated, old Laetus stopped and looked around. He was just about to abandon the search for his young friends when he spotted Piero and Antonio sitting in a dim recess. He elbowed his way over to them. They were sitting by themselves, not speaking, and seemed immune to the upbeat mood. "Why the long faces?" The Professor asked and made room for himself next to Piero, "I'm not sure I want to join such depressing company." Trying to lighten them up, "I thought you would be celebrating!" and he banged the table, *rattatatat*, as if it were a drum to awaken them to the jollity all around them. "Your project is starting up again. I should think that you two, more than anyone would be overjoyed! Your hearts and souls are in that project, and now it's going forward!"

Piero's hands were in his lap. He looked downward. Antonio smiled weakly. "What's the matter?" Laetus asked, "You look as though you've lost your best friend." Piero's rueful smile made the professor look more closely at each of them, and he abandoned his playful cajoling. Antonio shot the professor a furtive look that said, be kind.

"You are looking much improved. Your burns have healed nicely." Laetus roughed up Piero's hair and looked imploringly to Antonio for an explanation.

Piero placed an envelop on the table and folded his hands over it.

"News from home?" asked the Professor.

Piero, did not look at him, but said simply, "I'm leaving Rome tomorrow. For good."

Stunned, the Professor made a small noise that expressed disappointment, regret, sadness and curiosity all at once. "Is something wrong back home?" he asked, delicately, "Is someone sick?"

Antonio looked to Piero. He knew what had happened, but it was not his story to tell.

"Everything at home is fine." Piero's hands moved slightly on the envelope. "I received a letter, two letters: one from my father and another from the Duke." He stopped himself, before finally saying, "It's an order from home. I have to leave Rome and work on a project for the Duke." He looked up for the first time. Saying it now was easier than it had been when he told Antonio. This time it was just words. He looked at the Professor, "That's all."

"But . . ." Professor Laetus was appalled, ". . . why?"

He was about to ask what other project could be more important than his work here in Rome when a loud cheer erupted. They turned to it. Around them men were jumping to their feet. There was another cheer. It swelled like a wave, and filled every corner of the grotto-like tavern, " Bra-MAN-te! Bra-MAN-te!"

Antonio climbed up onto the bench to get a better look. "It's the boss. He just came in." A wave of applause thundered over them.

"The wrecking ball has landed," muttered the Professor.

Antonio jumped onto the table, "He's walking around shaking hands." He waved his arms trying to catch Bramante's attention. "Bra-MAN-te!, Bra-MAN-te," he shouted, adding his voice to the roaring chant, pumping his fist in the air. "I think he saw me," he called down.

Bramante, the master builder, was going from table to table. He employed most of the men there on one or another of his projects. Grateful for their jobs, overjoyed that the big job at St. Peter's was going again, they pressed in close to grasp his hands.

Antonio looked down at Piero and Professor Laetus, "He's coming this way," he said, jumping and waving.

Piero slid his envelope back onto his lap.

"It must be an important project to take you away from us," the Professor said. "Does Bramante know?"

Piero turned and reddened.

"He's coming. He's coming." Antonio called down.

Bramante backed through the smoke and the commotion, clearly moved and elated by the reception. Antonio jumped down. Smiling with the corners of his mouth turned down, Bramante turned and sat heavily across from Piero. He thumped a heavy, elaborately wrapped package onto the table. "I heard all about it," he growled, and looked at Piero. He was clearly annoyed. "I am not happy about your leaving, not happy at all. I have a lot invested in you. I had high hopes." The chanting died down. A few men called his name. Bramante turned to the room and waved, smiling. When he turned back to the table his smile was gone, "but there is nothing I can do about it." He said it fast to get it over with. "It's between the Duke and the Pope. It was their deal to begin with— you coming here. The Pope told me that he needs the Duke's support and if the Duke wants you back he won't fight it."

"It's the Pope's loss," said Antonio, the only one among them who knew the true depth of Piero's anguish

"It's my loss," proclaimed Bramante.

Piero dropped his head. He felt like crap, discarded. Maybe he wasn't as good as he thought he was. Maybe, after all, he was just a moderately clever boy from the sticks who got lucky. He didn't say what was on his mind, that a month from now no one will even remember my name. He saw himself at work in his father's workshop. A draft like a cool blade grazed the nape of his neck, and he lifted his collar.

"Pull yourself together," said Professor Laetus to cheer the boy, "It sounds to me as if you have the Pope and the Duke squabbling for your talent!"

Piero looked at him, but didn't say, 'bullshit.' He looked away. Above Bramante's head, through the arch in the Hornet's Nest a thin crescent moon came partly into view.

"The Professor's right," said Antonio. "If the Duke didn't know how good you are he wouldn't be calling you home." Piero shook his head, regretting his boastful letters home.

"I was counting on you," Bramante barked. "Now? Who knows," He turned to wave at a well wisher. "I know how you feel, but your leaving is going to be hard on us, too." He heard himself sounding maudlin and cleared his throat.

Piero looked down. He felt like a mule. He heard himself on the brink of whining like a child and changed the subject. Sitting up straight he looked directly at Bramante, "According to my father the Duke likes hearing about what we are working on, but he wrote to me that my letter about the horse race and everything made him angry and that he didn't like my working on Riario's palace. Later on when I wrote that work was going to start up again on St. Peter's, my father said the Duke was extremely annoyed. It was after reading that letter, according to my father, that the Duke said he wanted me to come home. He didn't see any advantage in my staying in Rome, either for me or for himself."

Antonio looked surprised. Piero hadn't said anything about that before. Bramante shook his head in disgust.

"So? What's the deal?" Professor Laetus asked trying to sound up beat. He wanted a drink. "What does the Duke want you to do? He's not calling you back north to milk sheep is he?" He laughed. "Or is he?" He asked again, wide eyed, and gestured for a serving girl to bring them a flagon.

Piero, placed the letters on the table making sure that the Duke's seal was showing. He wanted his new assignment to appear more important than he knew it was. "I'll skip all the homey stuff from my father," he said and put that letter aside. He smoothed the elaborate sheet from the Duke and said, "I guess I ought to be honored." He looked at each of them. Professor Laetus caught a glint of cynicism he had not seen in Piero before. "Duke Orsini requires me to make a survey of his waterworks, the flow of all the water into and out of Lake Braccciano. His Lordship states that it is important that the waters of the Papal State be more carefully managed. He is concerned that the level of the lake is falling." He looked up from the page, shrugged and said, "And that's it."

Professor Laetus sounding too impressed exclaimed, "Why, how extraordinary! That is a brilliant assignment!" He looked to Bramante and then to Antonio for reinforcement. The wine arrived. "There is so much wonderful work that needs doing in this wonderful new world of ours." Antonio nodded in full agreement. The Professor poured. Raising his cup he said, "Here's to your part, Piero, and yours, too, of course, Antonio, and yours," he clicked beakers with Bramante without looking at him, "in this most wonderful new age."

Piero in an effort to show gratitude offered a weak smile and drank.

Over his shoulder Bramante smiled and waved to another well-wisher who called out to him. When he turned back he rested his forearms on the table and said, "You know, da Vinci got his start in plumbing, or hydraulics, or whatever it's called. You'll be fine." He slid the beautifully wrapped package across to Piero, "This is something you will find useful. Open it."

Piero was surprised. "I don't know what to say," he said in the formal way that well brought up boys are taught to when receiving a gift from a respected elder. Piero carefully untied the gold ribbon and peeled back the wrappings. With great care he pulled a heavy, tooled leather folio from its sleeve. It was Vitruvius' Ten Books, the text he had been studying the day after Fra Juan's—misfortune—as it had come to be called. Piero blushed. "You pay me too much honor," he whispered staring at the extravagant gift.

"It's full of all kinds of information on building, water wheels, weapons, irrigation, boring but useful stuff," Bramante immediately regretted his words. They implied that Piero would be engaged in boring work and he rushed on to say, "I mean that it's written in a very boring, academic way, as you well know." He raised an eyebrow at the Professor, imploring him to help absorb and deflect his unintended insult.

"Oh, yes," Professor Laetus said, "blame the academicians for all the boring things in life."

"By the way, Piero," said Bramante. "You never mentioned that Father Ximenez stopped by."

"I told him you were out."

Bramante tilted his head and waited for a more detailed explanation. When none was forthcoming he patted the Vitruvius folio and said, "You have heard me say it again and again. I can't stress it strongly enough. Follow the rules. You will never be sorry. At first Vitruvius bored me to death, too," he breathed in loudly, "but you will see that it's very interesting and useful. You'll be amazed." Bramante then leaned across the table. He said to the Professor, "Laetus, you will be interested to know that I have successfully persuaded young Raphael Sanzio to come down from Florence and work here in Rome." Piero took a small sip of wine when Bramante, laughing, said, "he'll give that prig Buonarotti a run for his money!" Antonio laughed, too. "You'll get along well with him, Tonio. He's a good team player. He knows the game."

Piero inched away when Professor Laetus brightened and exclaimed that he'd heard of Raphael's work. He ran his fingers lightly along the edges of the folio trying to feel if the pale blue pages were still where he had wedged them. He glanced at his three companions talking, but could not hear them. Silence enveloped him. He watched Bramante laugh suddenly, and Antonio respond enthusiastically. He watched Professor Laetus open his mouth and call for more wine and noiselessly snap his fingers. Piero folded his arms across the Vitruvius folio. He watched the thin crescent moon make its slow passage through the high arch, up and beyond Bramante's head, and waited for the evening to end. The moon reminded him of a silly smile, amused by something that was happening elsewhere.

29

La Porta Maggiore

Orsini, the Duke of Bracciano, sat rigidly erect astride his dappled charger. He was dressed completely in gray. Beside him Count Colonna, in black, slumped sideways on Pegasus. They had not shared each other's company since that meeting in Bracciano. Scarred and ropy, like oaken roots, the two old men did not look at each other. Neither wanted to witness the other's failure nor to have the other as witness to his own. Behind them, sheltering them from the wind, the ancient Aniene aqueduct ended its long loping run across the plain of Latium by slamming through Rome's wall. Half moons of blue sky, framed by the vast structure's arches, stretched eastward to the foothills. The encounter had thus far been wordless. Neither moved to dismount.

Colonna squinted into the sunlight and closed his eyes. With his eyes open he felt exposed, laid out flat like a page, readable and predictable. "At least we kept them on their toes," he said at last. He was seething. He was sinking under a growing mountain of debt while the bankers were growing richer. His church was being smashed to the ground while someone else's was going up in its place. Their strategy should have worked. But for his nephew's indefensible stupidity, it would have. They were given an opportunity and lost it. He should have known better than to entrust Ottavio with anything more complicated than waking up. And everyone knew that he should have known better. Orsini knew it and his coolness enraged him. Behind his eyelids his pulse beat red. "Let's call a meeting of the alliance."

Orsini felt the sun on his dry cheeks and on the lids of his tearless eyes. He watched the sky, filled with evenly spaced white clouds, scudding southward over fields of golden grain and quivering olive trees. "Who would join us now?"

Colonna bristled. "We could throw our weight behind the Emperor. And there is always Naples. We can ally ourselves with them. It's our land. It's ours to offer in exchange for their support. All of us together can pledge the wealth of our estates. That's what we said. None of that has changed." He heard himself sounding like a fool and shifted in the saddle.

Orsini made a dry sound that was a laugh, but bitter and utterly mirthless. "Why don't we just kill each other now?" The racing clouds reminded him of a fleet of white ships. Their shadows slipped silently down the aqueduct, down his face, across his hands and up his stallion's neck, moving south, alternately darkening and brightening the landscape, making the ground appear to rise and fall as if breathing. He did not bother to say, we left the field, our own lands, open to our enemies, because we were pigs. You. Me. Our fathers and their fathers. We forfeited the game. It's not ours any more. We thought it was all or nothing, and after all, it has turned out to be nothing. And now you offer me the endlessly failed opportunity to form yet another self-defeating alliance and join, or should I say, invite another army to come in and do what? Conquer? Who? Us? Again? Instead he said, "So that's our salvation?"

Colonna contained his rage and said, "But this time we would be together." He swallowed hard. He resented Orsini more as an ally than he ever had as an opponent. Their blood feud came with rules: rules of engagement, formal rules, a code of conduct that was legible. There were prescribed responses, which would be responded to in turn with other ordered responses, and so on and on and on, the way it had always been, down through the ages. Those who had to know knew how it worked. Those who had to know knew the signals and the responses, round after round. Those who had to, understood their opponent's options. Victory was a matter of analyzing, and anticipating, which option would be deployed, which move would be made. Under those rules he knew Orsini. He knew *that* Orsini, the one who was his enemy, just as his father knew Orsini's father. But the man sitting silently beside him he did not know at all. This Orsini was not *that* one. Excommunication had turned Orsini into someone unknowable, a man almost translucent, a diaphanous ghost. Colonna sensed that excommunication had liberated Orsini from the rules they were born to observe, and had been taught to manipulate; and he envied him that. He envied his freedom and serenity. He sat there, sentenced to eternal damnation, as cool as snow. He, Colonna, did not seek damnation. His rage boiled. He opened his eyes fiercely, suddenly afraid of being lost, alone, in the beating, red pulse behind his eyes. If not Hell itself, this was close enough. He resented Orsini's aloofness, was infuriated at not being able to know him, to grasp him, place him in any familiar context that would permit them to engage. There was no shared context for them any longer. Where before he felt enmity, now he felt hatred and they were different. Their Roman Peace was worse than war.

Orsini made that sound that was not a laugh. This time it implied indifference, and an awareness that the animosity between them was, and had been, pointless; that their conflict, scarred by now into their bone and sinew, was the very weapon that had defeated them. He did not tell Colonna that in the gray dawn he had ridden through the Borgo, and entered the atrium in front of St Peter's. It looked as it always had. The mosaic above the portico shone dull gold. He did not tell Colonna that he rode his charger softly around the fountain and up the steps where he braced himself and reared up, or that he then rode into the church. He had not dismounted and had not bared his head. The nave was as he knew it, and he promenaded slowly down its length, past the chapels and the ancient frescoes, liking the unfamiliar ringing of hoof beats on the worn old floor. At the foot of the nave, where the apse had been, where the pavement ended, he emerged into daylight and stopped. Where the roof was bashed in raw daylight blanched the heart of ancient mystery. The tomb of the saint was now merely a hole in the floor with a fence around it. Overlooking the excavation he watched the workmen arrive. He listened to the squeal of iron barrows and heard the roar as timbers ignited under the limekiln. He understood, but could not explain, how his pride and vanity, his very way of life—what he understood to be civilization— everything he was and all he was—had been forged into a single weapon that had found its way into the hands of others and betrayed him. "We are drowned," Orsini said, simply, squinting into the light, in a way that implied he knew what that meant.

Colonna shook his head angrily, "I refuse to accept defeat. If we cannot beat them then we dispense the hardships we planned when we met in Council." Mustering his steel, "If our options are reduced we will make maximum use of those that remain. At least no one knows we've been defeated."

Orsini looked across the rolling plain, cloudshadows passing over him, knowing that what they were about to do was stupid. He didn't care one way or the other. He understood Colonna's desperation and was embarrassed to find himself amused by it. He didn't care about Colonna's rage. He just didn't care about any of it, neither the why nor the how of it. "Who cares if no one knows we've been defeated," he said, and made that sound again that was not a laugh.

"If that young Piero what's-his-name of yours, is as smart as you say, the Pope's cook will be serving him broth made from his leftover bathwater by this time next year," Colonna growled, retreating again to the red warmth behind his closed eyes, "I'll have Ottavio escort him back to Bracciano for you."

◦∢

30

The Villa Colonna

Alessandra Colonna stood silently outside her grandfather's study. She had considered making a dramatic entrance. She had thought of binding her feet and tying herself to a stake the way she had in the shadow play, and hopping in, but finally decided not to.

Her heart fluttered. Time had stopped. She was aware of every sound, every small mark on every surface around her. She had never before noticed the uneven, patched plaster on the ceiling. There were cobwebs spanning the rung of a chair. She jumped when a pan clanked in the courtyard and waited to hear the water splash onto the cobbles. Circles of window glass cast pearly light across her dress. She listened to the low familiar bark of the orange dog and heard pigeons flapping outside in the dovecote. The hall smelled of lemon oil and beeswax. It was the last day of her life. Why would someone polish the floor on the last day of the world?

She didn't want to embarrass her grandfather. Instead of tying herself to the stake she stuffed her bed with sticks and leaves. She had slept fitfully since it was announced. She hoped the dark circles under her eyes would cause him to take pity. She had eaten nothing but cake since her grandfather told her he had important news. Sharp red pimples poked through her white face powder. Small scabs in her hairline showed where she had scratched and picked at them. Behind her caked and scratched face she looked like a frightened little girl. The game was over. She was exhausted.

She heard a racket downstairs. A pigeon had gotten loose in the house and was being chased. It was screeching and flapping, hitting the walls. Her eyes felt gritty.

She rapped the door lightly and closed her eyes. When she heard her grandfather's familiar grunt she entered.

Young Chigi was sitting beside the old Count—to his left—fat and beaming, festooned in every possible roll, twist, drape and balloon of every imaginable fabric of every type, sheen, color and pattern that could be obtained from any corner of the world. Alessandra watched him smiling down at his fat hands. When he looked up at her it was not in adoration or with pleasure, but in a way that said he was satisfied.

The Count saw the door open to his waif of a granddaughter, his tiny angel, his little princess, stricken and denied, resigned and lost.

end